STALKED

At first Barbara heard only the slamming of her own heart, but soon she was able to discern another sound approaching along the fence across the driveway from her, the sound of stealthy footsteps, not hurrying, pausing every now and then, advancing again. Only when the crouching figure was parallel with her did Barbara move, aiming the flashlight and snapping the switch all in one motion. The beam of light seemed to leap across the driveway and land on the dark-clad figure opposite, like a live thing, like a pouncing cat. The circle of light framed and froze the figure, which twitched upright and made a low whimpering sound, not even a human sound, but a noise that a frightened animal might make. Barbara was already registering the sound when the face seemed to leap into focus, white and round above the dark shirt, dilated eyes staring blind into the sudden light. Then she saw the face crumble into abject terror, a horrible trans-formation, just before the whole form lurched and then burst into motion, whirling past her to the street before she could move the light. In three more seconds, the fog had swallowed up the running figure. Then there was the sound of a slamming car door and the sudden screech of tires.

BLOCKBUSTER FICTION FROM PINNACLE BOOKS!

THE FINAL VOYAGE OF THE S.S.N. SKATE   (17-157, $3.95)
by Stephen Cassell
The "leper" of the U.S. Pacific Fleet, SSN 578 nuclear attack sub SKATE, has one final mission to perform — an impossible act of piracy that will pit the underwater deathtrap and its inexperienced crew against the combined might of the Soviet Navy's finest!

QUEENS GATE RECKONING   (17-164, $3.95)
by Lewis Purdue
Only a wounded CIA operative and a defecting Soviet ballerina stand in the way of a vast consortium of treason that speeds toward the hour of mankind's ultimate reckoning! From the bestselling author of THE LINZ TESTAMENT.

FAREWELL TO RUSSIA   (17-165, $4.50)
by Richard Hugo
A KGB agent must race against time to infiltrate the confines of U.S. nuclear technology after a terrifying accident threatens to unleash unmitigated devastation!

THE NICODEMUS CODE   (17-133, $3.95)
by Graham N. Smith and Donna Smith
A two-thousand-year-old parchment has been unearthed, unleashing a terrifying conspiracy unlike any the world has previously known, one that threatens the life of the Pope himself, and the ultimate destruction of Christianity!

Available wherever paperbacks are sold, or order direct from the Publisher. Send cover price plus 50¢ per copy for mailing and handling to Pinnacle Books, Dept.17-386, 475 Park Avenue South, New York, N.Y. 10016. Residents of New York, New Jersey and Pennsylvania must include sales tax. DO NOT SEND CASH.

FAMILY CLOSETS

MARJORIE DORNER

PINNACLE BOOKS
WINDSOR PUBLISHING CORP.

For my dear parents,
Michael William Dorner and
Leone Burkart Dorner—*sine qua non*

Acknowledgments

For invaluable help with the manuscript of this book, I am grateful to Judith Weber. For technical advice about farm machines past and present, I thank Michael Dorner, Leone Dorner, and Barry Dorner.

1

When Barbara Mullens drove up over the hill on County Trunk H, she thought for a second that she'd made a mistake, had taken a wrong turn off the highway. The horizon looked decidedly unfamiliar, and it gave her the odd sensation that she was dreaming, one of those dreams where the scene shifts suddenly without warning, without logic. Of course, she told herself, it was because the house and the trees were gone. Even the barn and silos looked foreign without their expected foreground.

She had made a resolution three days ago never to travel this road again, not as long as she lived, because she knew how much it would hurt her to see the beloved landscape so changed. But now, without any time to prepare her imagination for the shock, she was being dragged back here to see this savaging of her childhood home.

The call had come just after lunch when she was helping her mother to decide which carton to unpack next. The dining room of the apartment was still so littered with packing from the good china that Barbara could scarcely make her way to the phone. It was Duane Pankratz, the man who had bought the farm from her mother.

"I think you'd better come out to the old place," he said after Barbara had explained that, no, she was not Mrs. Hoffman but Mrs. Mullens, Mrs. Hoffman's daughter.

"Why?" she asked, annoyed by his conspiratorial tone.

"Well, the bulldozer uncovered something you maybe oughta see. Don't bring your mother, though. You maybe wanna decide afterwards about what to tell her."

She could get nothing else out of him, but was finally convinced that she'd better go.

"I don't know what's going on," she had said to her mother, who was at first determined to go along. "But whatever it is, I don't think you want to see the place after two days' worth of bulldozing, do you? I'll give you a full report, and if it's gold they've turned up, I promise I'll split it with you, okay? Now see if you can decide before I get back where you want to hang Aunt Polly's landscapes."

As Barbara's car approached the driveway, she saw the huge hole which had been dug in the pasture west of the barn. It was there that the bulldozer had simply shoved the house, two box elder trees, and four flowering crab apple trees. The house had been built in 1883 by Barbara's great-grandparents; some of the logs that had made up its outer walls still jutted up out of the burial hole. The bulldozer was silent, parked over the scraped ground where Barbara's swing set had once stood. Two men straightened up from where they'd been leaning against the big machine's mud-covered wheels.

As Barbara climbed out of the car, she saw that one of the men was Duane Pankratz, a squat, solemn-faced man whom she had disliked on sight when she'd met him the week before. Of course, she had to admit to herself that her mother's account had prepared her in advance to think ill of him. He was not a local man, but an outsider who was buying up farms all over the county, hovering like a vulture, waiting for debt, bad weather, or death to drive farm families out. He wasn't interested in the local tradition of dairy farming, but wanted only to plant and harvest cash crops. When Barbara had asked him what he would do with the house, he had first shrugged elaborately and then glanced sideways at her mother.

"Didn't your mother tell you?" he asked at last. "I need the room to turn and park the big reapers. The house will have to go. I'll just gravel this whole space," and he made a sweeping gesture at the house. "Of course, I'll keep the outbuildings for storage." And now Barbara told herself that she ought to have known that he would be a tree hater, too, like those nasty vandals who'd come in the night to snap off the newly planted red maple trees in front of her Chicago apartment building. What atavistic horror of wilderness, of mystery, drove such people?

"What is this all about, Mr. Pankratz?" Barbara said, trying not to look at the place where the house had been.

"Ron here called me over about an hour ago," he said, tipping his head toward the other man, whose grime-circled eyes looked out from under a stained cap; he was obviously the operator of the bulldozer. "When he pushed over the north wall over there, one of the logs punched a hole in the flooring. What he found is in the basement, in the southwest corner. There looks to be some kind of an old cistern under there, dried up."

"Yes," Barbara said, remembering the cistern wall

she had seen every time she went into the fruit cellar to bring up tomato sauce or canned cherries or corn relish. "It hasn't been used since way before I was born."

"Well, it's in there," Pankratz said, glancing at Ron, who had that alert but closed look that simple men get when they're in the presence of something that puzzles or scares them.

"Could we stop being so mysterious?" Barbara said, her voice edgy and a little angry. "Just show me what you found."

"I just wanna make sure you're prepared," Pankratz said, his heavy features pulled into an expression of concern that Barbara thought looked a little forced.

"Oh, for God's sake!" she snapped. "You make it sound as if there's a body in there or something."

The two men exchanged a look, and Pankratz rolled his eyes up at the cloudless June sky.

"You're crazy," Barbara said and strode away from them toward the platform where her home had once stood. Her heart squeezed in pain as she recognized through the rubble the familiar white linoleum of the kitchen floor. A gaping hole about three feet across and seven feet long had been torn through the boards. Barbara stepped carefully over the chunks of plaster and lath and peered down into the hole, which the midday sun seemed almost to be spotlighting.

The skeleton was just enough to the right of the hole that very little of the debris from the floor had fallen on it. The skull was unmistakable, gleaming white, face down, and the moldered remains of clothing had sunk down around shoulder blades and a rib cage so distinct that Barbara could have counted the ribs. The light showed the outline of one arm, the right arm, lying

12

stretched out next to the skull, but the legs were hidden in shadow. A hovering dust seemed to fill the space between the skeleton and Barbara's eyes.

"We didn't touch nothing," Pankratz said, next to Barbara's left ear. She whirled toward him, her hand lifted in terror as if he were an apparition in a nightmare.

"You got any ideas about this?" Pankratz asked, gesturing at the hole in the floor.

"Ideas?" Barbara gasped. "Ideas?" It was as if he had spoken in a foreign language and she were trying to get him to rephrase the question in English.

"No, I didn't think so," Pankratz said. "I bet that stiff has been there longer than you been alive." He took one more long look into the cistern before taking Barbara's shaking arm to lead her away. Ron had stayed with his bulldozer, his curiosity apparently satisfied with the first look.

"The sheriff is on his way," Pankratz said. "I called him from the next place up the road, same time I called you. But he's gotta come from Oshawanee, and that's further away than New Augsburg. I expect he'll get here in twenty minutes or so."

He let go of Barbara's arm when they reached the shade made by the bulldozer's shadow. Both men seemed to crave the proximity of the big machine as if they depended on it for some kind of protection. Ron stooped a little to look into Barbara's face, and then he climbed up into the cab of the bulldozer. When he came back down, he was carrying a metal flask in one grimy hand and a jacket in the other. He dropped the jacket onto the ground.

"You sit down right here and drink some of this," he said, thrusting the flask clumsily at her hand. "You had a bad shock, and this'll do you some good."

Barbara looked up at him, her brain too numb to take in what he was saying. But she recognized the kindness in his pale eyes, the simple desire to help her.

"It's whiskey," he said sheepishly. "I take a little belt now and then, not much. It'll steady you down."

Barbara took the flask and sank down onto the denim jacket. The whiskey felt cool in her mouth, scalding in her stomach. She sat for a long time without looking up, hugging her knees and swinging the flask back and forth in her fingers.

The police car arrived just about the time Pankratz had said it would, no sirens, no haste even, just pulling slowly up next to Barbara's Volkswagen beetle. The man who stepped out was tall, hatless, his brown uniform hanging loosely on a lanky frame. He lifted his hand to shade his eyes while he scanned the scene. Then he walked toward the group in the shade, his stride long but unhurried. Barbara struggled to stand up, and Ron looked away from the sheriff long enough to help her, his big hand so strong that she found herself almost sailing upright, the speed of her ascent and the whiskey combining to make her feel dizzy.

She found herself looking up at a lean, rather pale face, light-hazel eyes, and a thatch of sandy hair. It was a boyish face with a light sprinkling of freckles over the bridge of the nose, a nose that had once been broken, by the look of the sharp little bump on its left side. He looked, Barbara thought, like the legions of Midwestern college boys she had seen lounging across campuses for most of her adult life. Yet the fan of wrinkles around his eyes showed that he must be in his thirties, about her own age or even older.

"Over here," Pankratz said and walked ahead of the

sheriff toward the kitchen floor. The sheriff squatted next to the hole for a long time while Pankratz hovered near him, glancing over his shoulder from time to time.

When they came back to the bulldozer, the sheriff spoke directly to Barbara, though he had hardly seemed to notice her when he arrived.

"I'm Sheriff Paul Gillis," he said. "Who are you?"

"Barbara Mullens," she answered. "I grew up in this house. Mr. Pankratz called me to come out here."

"I didn't think her mother should see this," Pankratz said. "But I figured you'd wanna talk to somebody in the family."

"My father died last year," Barbara explained, drawing a shuddering breath and feeling the taste of whiskey in her mouth. "And my mother just moved into town. She sold the farm to Mr. Pankratz here."

"Has the farm always been in your family?" the sheriff asked, taking a small notebook and pencil stub out of his shirt pocket.

"Yes, always," she said, looking out past the barn toward the curve in the cow lane that was as familiar to her as the veins in her own hand.

"Mullens family," he said, beginning to write.

"No, Hoffman," she said, looking back at him. "My name used to be Hoffman. The family homesteaded the place back in the 1880s. Nobody else has ever lived here."

"Barbara Hoffman," he said, stooping a little to look sharply into her face, but she didn't notice the change in his eyes.

"My father was Joseph Hoffman, and his parents were John and Anna Hoffman," she went on, as if this were vital information.

15

The sheriff had straightened up and was writing again.

"How long did your mother live in the house?" he asked.

"Since 1949," Barbara said, her gaze pulled involuntarily back toward the ruined foundation. "She came here from England with my father in that year. They'd been married in London, after the war, you know."

"Other relatives?"

"None." It had always been one of her secret regrets. "Oh, some cousins, but they've lived out West for two generations now. We don't really know them." She wondered if she should tell him that her father had once had a brother, but it seemed silly to her as soon as she thought of it; why should she tell about someone who hadn't been in contact with his family for over forty years?

"Has the house always been occupied?" Sheriff Gillis said, after a brief pause while he scribbled.

"Yes, I think so," Barbara said. "Except for the war. During the Second World War. My father was in the army in Europe and then for another hitch after the war. But I don't know about before that." It passed through Barbara's mind that she actually knew very little about her family's history before 1949. Though her mother had often spoken of her childhood in England, her father had almost never talked about his own growing-up years. It was almost as if, for him, his life had begun after World War II.

The sheriff had stopped writing and was looking intently at Barbara's dazed face.

"Your mother might know more about that, I suppose," he said softly.

"Yes," Barbara said distractedly. "Yes, she might."

"Then I'll ask her some questions about it," he said. "Maybe tomorrow morning. Do you think that would

16

give her time to get used to the idea of this?" He gestured at the platform where the hole was.

Barbara's attention came back to the sheriff. She saw his slightly worried frown and realized that he must be imagining her mother as some frail, aged woman who needed to be "prepared" for nasty shocks. The idea almost made her smile.

"Tomorrow will be fine," she said firmly. "How long do you think it's been there?" resolutely thinking of the skeleton as an "it" in an effort to achieve some distance. But she shivered anyway, despite the warmth of the sun.

"Well, I don't know," he said, tucking the notebook and pencil back into his pocket. "But my guess is that the corpse has been there quite a while. It takes a lot of years to uncover all the bones like that." When he saw her face pull into a grimace of distaste, he added, "Sorry. Did your family ever use that part of the house after your dad got back from England?"

"No," Barbara said. "It was sealed up as long as I can remember, and there was no way into it from the rest of the basement."

"There was once a trapdoor, I suppose, for drawing water up into the kitchen?"

"Yes, I suppose. But I don't know much about that. You'll have to ask my mother." She was thinking how, even as a child, she had wondered, "Does he tell *her*? Does he talk to her about when he was a little boy?" whenever her father would gently turn away one of her questions by speaking about the past in general terms. His parents, his only brother—all lumped together as "my family" and spoken of almost as one might speak of half-forgotten acquaintances.

"Well, I'll tell you what," Sheriff Gillis said. "You don't need to hang around. I'm going to get a photographer out here. And an ambulance. We'll have to take the bones into Green Bay where the medical examiners can do their poking around.''

''What can they find out?'' Barbara asked, looking up at him. ''You can't even tell if it's a man or a woman.''

''I know,'' he said, taking her elbow and piloting her toward her car. ''But the medical examiners will be able to tell.''

''Under the house,'' she said. ''All these years.''

''Do you think your mother will take this hard?'' The sheriff slowed his long stride to keep pace with her.

''Well, it's not going to cheer her up,'' Barbara said. ''She's just moved out of her home—thirty-eight years she lived here. She's still grieving for my father, and now this. But you mustn't imagine that my mother is frail. You'll see when you meet her. She's a tough cookie.''

The sheriff paused to grin down at her. ''A tough cookie?''

''It's what she always says about herself,'' Barbara said with a weak smile. They had reached her car. The sheriff gave the white Volkswagen an affectionate pat.

''How's your bug been behaving?'' he asked, and she saw how nice his eyes looked when he smiled.

''Oh, it's holding up,'' she said, a part of her mind aghast that she should be having such a normal conversation. ''But it's getting harder to find parts when something goes wrong.''

''I used to have one of these,'' he said, opening the door for her. A breeze had begun to move the dried dirt in the yard around in little swirls. ''Got me through college and a few years more. I'm sorry I ever traded it away.''

Remembering at the last moment a recent kindness,

Barbara looked past the sheriff's shoulder and called, "Thanks for the drink, Ron." Ron straightened up and lifted his hand to the brim of his cap.

As Barbara pointed the car back toward New Augsburg, she lifted her eyes to the rearview mirror. Sheriff Gillis's tall frame was bent over next to the squad car; he was using the radio to call for the ambulance, probably. Duane Pankratz had returned to the hole in the kitchen floor for another look. A cloud of brown dust, stirred by the wind, whirled up around the yard. In the bright afternoon sunlight, it seemed to hover like some evil spirit over what had once been Barbara's home.

2

"I remember so well when we covered that trapdoor," Barbara's mother was saying as they sat together at the counter in the small kitchen. The clock in the tiny, apartment-sized stove showed 3 P.M. They were drinking the sweet, milky tea which was one of Eileen Thompson Hoffman's more noticeable British contributions to Hoffman family tastes. She made the tea whenever there was anything that might pass for a crisis, and Barbara had carried the tradition into her own adult life-style. "It never occurred to us to open it up one last time. I don't know now if I'm sorry or relieved that we didn't."

"Didn't Dad think he should check to see if it was dry under there?" Barbara asked. She and her mother seemed to have made a tacit agreement to talk about the cistern, not about the body, the bones, inside it.

"Well, he explained about that. The cistern had been pumped dry and sealed up years before the war. The outside of the house looked pretty tattered when we got here, but the foundation and the roof were still sound enough to convince Dad to salvage the rest. No leaks anywhere, he said. You know what he always says about those old tin roofs; they'll last for donkeys' years." She paused to shake her head at her own habit of referring to her husband in the present tense, and to give Barbara a rueful smile because she knew it bothered her daughter. It was when she used expressions like "donkeys' years," expressions not common among Wisconsin dairy farmers, that her slight British accent was more noticeable.

She stood up now and walked the three steps to the counter where the teapot was waiting under a hand-knitted tea cosy.

"It's hard to think about all those years of walking up and down over a dead person," she said quietly with her back to Barbara. "Who could it be? What was he doing under my house?"

"We don't even know that it's a 'he,' " Barbara said, accepting this sharp veering back to the subject that was really preoccupying both of them. "But it's awful, I know."

"It must have been there from the beginning," the mother said, a shudder passing from her shoulders to her voice. "Already there when we came from England. We just put a new floor down over it. Horrible, horrible."

Barbara stood up and joined her mother at the counter, but she didn't touch her. Instead, she stood next to her and poured herself another cup of tea.

If some stranger had come upon them from behind, standing next to each other like this, he would never have taken them for mother and daughter. Eileen Hoffman was a small, spare woman with fine bones, small hands and feet. At sixty-three, she still stood perfectly straight, carrying her head high on a graceful neck which did not yet display the ropy folds of aging flesh. Her once-dark hair was now liberally streaked with gray. Only on her hands had the years of hard work left their marks, calluses and the thickened knuckles which showed that arthritis had begun to be a problem. Barbara was cut on a larger scale, her father's German heritage having passed to her the prominent bones, the wider hips, the more generous bosom, all of which seemed to dwarf her mother by comparison, though Barbara was in fact a slim, athletic woman with what Americans call a "good figure." Even Barbara's honey-colored hair, cropped close to her head and lightly curled, seemed to owe nothing to Eileen's side of the family.

When they turned from the counter, lifting their tea-cups in almost perfect sync, the casual observer would at last have seen a resemblance. Mother and daughter had round, deep-blue eyes, widely spaced under high, arching brows. Barbara's nose was narrower than her mother's and her jaw was slightly more prominent, but her small, cupid's bow mouth was identical to the older woman's mouth as both of them blew steam away from the surface of the hot tea.

"You and Daddy couldn't have known," Barbara said finally in a soothing tone. "It must have happened while Daddy was away in the war."

"This is so appalling," Eileen said with a trace of anger in her voice. "Why couldn't the machine just have buried the foundation without breaking it open? Then we wouldn't ever have found out about it."

Barbara didn't answer, but just blew at her tea again. No use arguing, no use opening another skirmish in the long-running battle she and her mother had waged over whether "some things are better left alone" (Eileen's position) or "the truth is better" (Barbara's position). This was not the time for old wars.

"I know what you're thinking," Eileen said, an edge having come into her voice during her daughter's silence.

22

"You're thinking that we might never have had to find it out if I hadn't sold the farm."

"Please don't tell me what I'm thinking, Mother," Barbara sighed, moving back toward the table. "Remember what I *told* you on the phone in January. I know you couldn't go on living out there by yourself now that Dick Schneider can't lease the land anymore. I said it was time for you to make the move now while you're still healthy and vigorous, not wait until some crisis would make the decision for you." She didn't look at her mother while she spoke.

"But you were so upset last week about the house being torn down," Eileen said, following Barbara to the table, standing while Barbara sat down.

"Yes, Mother, it was a surprise," Barbara admitted. "The house was over a hundred years old, a sort of landmark. You know how I feel about preserving old buildings." But now there was an edge in her voice, too, despite her effort to sound reasonable, detached.

"You don't have to imagine that I believe you're so objective as you try to make yourself sound, either," Eileen said after taking a sip of her tea. "I know how you feel about the farm, about the house. But you're not the only one to have such feelings. I hated having to give it up. I know it seems like a betrayal of Daddy."

"Don't be silly," Barbara said, but bitter tears had sprung to her eyes. She turned quickly in her chair to keep her mother from seeing her face. "Daddy would understand why it had to be done. There's just nobody in the family to take over the farm. It's nobody's fault."

"I would have liked so much to sell it to some nice young family," Eileen said. "But the farm economy is so bad now that there was no chance of that. Mr. Pankratz made the only decent offer I got in five months and I didn't know he meant to tear down the house until after we'd closed the deal. Really I didn't.''

"I know, Mum, I know," Barbara whispered, looking up at her now. Eileen's eyes filled with tears, too, the second she saw her daughter's tears.

"Oh, Barbie," she said. "It was my home, too, you know. I know every square inch of those eighty acres. Dad and I took such pride in making it all go."

Barbara knew it was all true. Only someone who didn't know her mother could ever believe that this slight woman was frail. She had come from a city background, was well-educated—she had trained as a schoolteacher in England—but she'd learned everything there was to know about dairy farming. She drove the tractor, ran the combine, pitched hay down from the loft, helped to deliver calves. Barbara had helped every summer with her mother's big garden, but was fast asleep during the long evenings while Eileen canned beans and stirred pickling spices into the brine that covered the freshly picked cucumbers. And the next morning, she would be up at dawn to help her husband with the milking. Yet she'd always seemed to thrive on the hard work. Except for her illness following Barbara's birth, she'd been a marvel of vigor and cheerful industry all of her life.

"Mummy, my mummy," Barbara said, using the phrase she had learned almost as soon as she first began to speak. She stood up and folded her mother in a hug, stooping a little to bring her own cheek against the smaller woman's face. "It'll be all right. We'll get over this, too. You're going to get to love it here, once we get all this moving mess out of the way. You and Mary Wenner will be running yourselves ragged in no time, going to card parties. She might even get you to take up golf.''

24

"Golf," Eileen snorted. "Well, I suppose it beats a rocking chair and reruns on television." She dabbed at her eyes, looking a little embarrassed about the tears; she had never been a "weepy" woman. "I don't mean to fuss at you, Barbara. But it seems it's just one bloody thing after another lately. This skeleton business is a nasty shock. It makes me miss your father even more because, of course, my first thought is that I want to talk it over with him, hear what he thinks."

"So do I," Barbara laughed, passing the palms of her hands under her eyes. "He'd probably make some joke about it to cheer us up and then do his fretting in private."

"Yes, you're right, of course," Eileen said, "but sooner or later, he'd tell me what he was really feeling about it, and then I'd have to cheer him up. We pretty much always took turns that way."

They sipped their tea in silence for a while.

"Do you want to help me pound picture hangers?" Eileen said at last. "It's better to keep active when—at times like this."

"If you don't mind, I'm going to change and go for my run now," Barbara said. "I'll help you hang everything after dinner, I promise."

"Do you have to run every day?" Eileen asked, her fine brows knitting into a little frown of disapproval.

"I just got back up to ten miles a day after a lazy winter," Barbara said, setting down her cup, "and I don't want to get flabby again."

"Ten miles a day!" Eileen said, shaking her head. "It's too much. I'm afraid you've always had an obsessive streak, Barbara."

"Remember what you say about speeches with 'you always' and 'you never' in them," Barbara said a little grimly. "Bound to start fights."

"I know, and I'm sorry. But I worry about you. I'm allowed, aren't I?"

"Yes, you're allowed, Mother. But there's no need to worry in this case. Running is for me what sewing is for you. It clears my head."

Eileen was silent, her small mouth pursed.

"Would you rather I stayed?" Barbara asked, more gently. "Do you want to talk some more, or just have your obsessive daughter around?"

"Nonsense," Eileen said briskly. "Unpacking books will keep my mind off of skeletons in the basement. Don't you fret about me."

Barbara did her limbering-up exercises in the parking lot behind the apartment building. As she pulled her right heel up toward the small of her back, she looked up at the windows of what was now going to be her mother's home. There were three buildings set next to each other at the edge of the village on what had once been Michael Jonnet's farm. Eileen's apartment was on the right of the middle building. Each building had four identical apartments with four identical doors facing the parking lot across four tiny back porches. Living room, dining room, and kitchen were downstairs. And upstairs, one bedroom faced the street, while the other, smaller bedroom and the bathroom faced the parking lot. Eileen had sold most of her furniture at an auction in May so that what was left could be fitted into these narrow white plaster rooms.

It was the sort of development that Barbara loathed even as she recognized the need for it—ticky-tacky boxes stuck onto the fringes of gracious old country villages like New Augsburg, where the spacious brick and frame houses of the turn of the century sat comfortably side by side with small businesses and public buildings. The developers seemed not to care that the new buildings simply didn't blend in with their more traditional surroundings. But, Barbara realized with a sigh as she began jogging in place, aging people whose children had moved away couldn't go on living through thirty-degrees-below-zero winter days in farmhouses buried in snow at the end of graveled lanes five miles from help if something went wrong.

Barbara ran out to the street now and worked her way up to her "cruising" stride by the time she'd completed the four-block run to Main Street. There she turned left and ran past the IGA store and the post office, McMartin's furniture store and McMartin's funeral parlor. Across the street was the house where the town's dentist had had his office in his front room for thirty years. As she started up a shallow hill, Barbara ran past the appliance store and Treml's Sundries Store, which faced each other across the side street down which she'd driven so often. Her best friend in high school, Cheryl Blahnik, lived then in the pale-green frame house whose corner she could glimpse as she ran by. At the crest of the hill, she crossed the railroad tracks and went by the Farmers Trading Company and the grain mill, built next to each other to save farmers time on their trips to the mill.

By the time yesterday's stiffness was leaving the long muscles of her legs, she had descended the hill on the other side and was running past St. Mary's School where she'd spent six years of her childhood, and the church with its black-topped parking lot, so handy for roller skating at recess on the brisk fall days she could

27

remember with such immediacy, such clarity. At the south edge of the village, she ran past the sign that said "Pop. 1627." She had raced happily away from this town to "go east" to college, but now it was almost painfully dear to her. At thirty-four she'd made such a mess of her personal life, had lost so much that she could hardly turn her mind toward the pain without weeping. So this town, this countryside, almost unchanged since her earliest experience of it, as if preserved in amber, seemed like the only solid reality she could still hang on to, believe in.

When the phone call came about her father's death, she had been working on a seminar paper at the kitchen table of her tiny apartment. The whole scene in front of her eyes had seemed to float up and away into the Chicago skyline, and she saw instead a vision of the farm on an August afternoon with the box elder leaves first approaching her face and then receding from it, over and over, as her father pushed her on the board swing he had first rigged for her when she was three, long before the new swing set from Wards had taken its place in the yard. In her agony, the vision was the only comfort she found.

Eileen Hoffman had had a difficult pregnancy with Barbara, and the delivery had almost killed her. For two years after Barbara's birth, her mother was ill, weak, and too drained most of the time to get out of bed, the aftereffects of toxemia, the doctors said. There were no female relatives to help out. Joseph Hoffman's parents were dead, and he had no sisters. His only brother, the one he never talked about, had gone away "before you were even thought of," as Eileen would later say to her. Eileen's mother and sister Polly lived in England, and

28

there was no money—on either side of the Atlantic—to bring one of them over to help. So Joe had done everything himself with only occasional help from Mary and Jim Wenner, across-the-road neighbors who had four kids of their own to occupy their attention.

Thus Barbara had formed her first major attachment in life, not to her mother, but to her father, to the large quiet man whose big farmer's hands could be surprisingly gentle. She had grown up a "daddy's girl," riding around on farm machinery, bundled into the front seat of the pickup when her father went to the mill, the only child in the fourth grade to have *both* parents at the Christmas play. Joe Hoffman had been everybody's rock, the steady, patient, kindly man who was never sick a day in his life until he fell over in the barn a year ago in January and died. "He went down like a stone," Eileen had told Barbara. "Not a cry, not a gesture of pain. Just like himself to the very end. He never was one to complain." Massive cerebral hemorrhage, the doctor had said.

Her relationship with her mother had always been a rather prickly one, at least as long as Barbara could remember. Eileen was demanding, a teacher rather more than a nurturer, a mother who expected her child to earn approval. Once Barbara had started school, she'd begun to blame her mother for her own sense of "differentness." She had been the only child in the first grade at St. Mary's School who said "cutlery" instead of "silverware," "tea towels" instead of "dish towels." And she was the only child she knew who had no relatives her own age, no built-in allies in the school environment. Irrationally, she also blamed her mother for this lack of cousins, though she knew her father had been more of a "solitary" at their marriage than Eileen had been, and it was he who had taken Eileen away from her family in England to a strange country. She also felt obscurely that her mother was to blame for there being no brothers or sisters. Barbara was incapable of blaming her father for anything by the time she was six years old.

Since Joe Hoffman's death, Barbara had made frequent visits to her mother, finding home dearer than ever because of his loss, always shaken by the feeling that the back door would open any minute and he would appear, stomping snow off his boots or pulling off a sweat-stained cap, calling toward them, "How're my girls?" the same question every time, the same smile. It had been an effort made at great emotional cost for Barbara to encourage her mother when Eileen had first mentioned on the phone that she might sell the farm. Dick Schneider had been leasing the fields, but he'd been ill lately and couldn't keep up his former pace. At last her mother called to say that the sale had been made.

"Wait till June when my semester is over," Barbara had said calmly, while scalding tears poured down her face and dripped onto her sweater. "I can come for a few weeks and help you move, before my summer job starts."

So here she was, absorbing the additional news that the house would be razed, that the rooms and surfaces she had memorized in her hands and feet, as well as in her mind's eye, would be no more. And now this additional blow, an ugly secret buried under the sunny normality of her childhood. A skeleton in the basement! As she pounded along the roadside, she found herself half-agreeing with her mother's wish that the bulldozer had simply buried the secret a little deeper in the ground.

When she reached the highway, not even having worked up a good sweat yet, she turned east, away from the road that would have brought her, three miles to the west, past the ruined foundation with the grave-sized hole in the kitchen floor.

3

The next morning, Barbara was finishing the breakfast dishes when the front doorbell rang. Because her mother was in the basement utility room moving laundry from the washer to the dryer, Barbara dried her hands and went to answer the door. Sheriff Gillis was leaning against the wrought iron railing. When he saw Barbara, he came to attention and smiled.

"I've come to ask your mother some questions," he said. "Is she in?"

"Come on in, Sheriff," Barbara said, leading the way. "My mother is in the basement. She'll only be a few more minutes."

In the kitchen, Barbara turned back to him to find the sheriff looking at her with a wry, quizzical expression on his face.

"What?" she said, recognizing at once that he seemed to expect something from her.

"You don't remember me, do you?" he said, the smile widening. "I thought maybe you were sort of in shock on Tuesday, or didn't catch the name."

"Should I remember you?" Barbara asked, peering more closely at him now.

"Probably not," he said. "It was a long time ago. But I remember you, all right."

"How?"

"I played basketball for Oshawanee High, varsity in my junior and senior years. When I was a senior, you were a sophomore cheerleader for Gale High."

"Oh, God! Cheerleader. That's part of my past I'm trying to live down."

"Well, I saw you at the first conference game at Oshawanee and started to bug everybody I knew for an introduction, but nobody knew any of your friends. By the time we traveled over to Gale for the second conference game, I'd worked up my courage. You don't recall a tall, skinny guy with a bad complexion coming over to you just before the start of that game?"

"That was you?" Barbara asked, remembering now.

"That was me," he said, grinning without embarrassment, the lines around his eyes crinkling. "I asked you to go for a hamburger after the game."

"And I said I couldn't because I was going steady."

"That's when I just turned and ran. Were you? Going steady, I mean? I wondered about it for a long time."

"Sort of. My parents wouldn't let me call it that, but Jerry Paulson and I were definitely an item that year."

"Why are you trying to live down being a cheerleader?"

"My, you are a cop, aren't you?" Barbara chuckled. "Would you like some coffee?"

"Sure," he said, "if you've got some made." He stood next to the table while she poured the coffee. "Is the question about cheerleading controversial or something?"

33

"No," she sighed. "It's just that some people don't understand why I'm a little ticked about it."

"Try me." He looked genuinely interested.

"Well, I'm a pretty good athlete," she said, pouring herself some coffee, too. "But I didn't find it out until I was almost thirty. I could have been a varsity athlete in high school and college instead of just cheering for other athletes, if I'd been encouraged in that direction. Guys I went to high school with got athletic scholarships to go to college."

"I see what you mean," he said. "But athletic scholarships can be more grief than they're worth, too. I had one my freshman year, and I slaved so hard at basketball, trying to make the varsity, that I almost flunked out of school. After that, I gave up being a jock."

"Where'd you go to college?" Barbara asked.

"UW Madison," he said. "Class of '72."

"Oh, *those* years," Barbara said, raising her eyebrows.

"Yes, yes," he said. "And I was out on the picket line with everybody else. I'm one of the guys who used to call cops 'pigs.' Ironic, isn't it?"

Barbara smiled up at him, and they both sipped coffee for a moment.

"What are you doing with yourself these days?" he asked.

"Oh, I'm a student again. Working on a master's degree in history at Northwestern. I'd like to work for a good historical society someday. I'm helping my mother settle in right now, of course. I've got a summer research job coming up at the end of July when my major professor gets back from Europe."

"You and your husband live in Chicago, do you?"

Barbara took another long swallow of coffee.

"Ex-husband," she said tonelessly, not looking up. "I've been divorced for three years. But I live in Chicago, yes."

Before the sheriff could speak, Eileen came through the back door into the kitchen. She had tied her hair up in the back and looked girlish in her jeans and work shirt.

"Mother, this is Sheriff Gillis," Barbara said.

"I know it is. Hello," Eileen said, sticking her hand out in front of her in her frank way. Barbara had grown up hearing about this from classmates. "Your mother shakes hands," Edmund Herkens had said to her in the third grade. "Men shake hands, not ladies."

"I remember your campaign," Eileen was saying. "After Sheriff Spitzer retired, we all began to say that it was time for some nice young man to take the job." To Barbara she added, "There was really no competition once the ladies had seen this chap's picture on the posters."

Barbara noticed that Sheriff Gillis was actually blushing.

"I know you have some questions for me," Eileen said, "so come on into the living room and sit down. Don't mind the mess. I'm not completely settled in yet."

When they were all seated in a rather formal arrangement, the sheriff set his coffee cup down and took out his notebook.

"I'm eager to help, but I don't know what I can tell you," Eileen said. "I was awake a long time last night trying to account for this—this horror, but I haven't a clue."

"Well, Mrs. Hoffman," the sheriff said softly, "you may be able to help in ways you don't even know about yet."

35

"Perhaps," she said, and then squaring her shoulders and lifting her jaw, she added, "Fire when ready."

"You moved into the farmhouse in 1949?" he asked, glancing down at his notes.

"Yes, that's right. My husband and I came by ship from England. I suppose Barbara told you we'd been married there. But we didn't move into the house right away."

"And why was that?"

"The house had run to seed in my husband's absence—windows smashed, doors warped, that sort of thing. We moved in with the Schneiders for a bit—old friends of Joe's, my husband's—while we worked to set the house right. The Schneiders had used the land while Joe was away and had maintained the outbuildings, but didn't pay much mind to the house."

"How long was the house abandoned?"

"Almost six years. From September of 1943 until May of 1949."

"There was no other family to live there?"

"No. Joe's parents died before the war, and his only brother left New Augsburg about the same time Joe enlisted."

The sheriff paused to scribble for a moment.

"And while you were fixing up the house," he went on finally, "did you ever look into that old cistern?"

"No, we didn't," Eileen said, exchanging a glance with her daughter. "It had been sealed up for years before the war, after a pump was put into the kitchen. When Joe found there were no cracks in the foundation, he said that meant the cistern would still be dry."

There was another pause while Sheriff Gillis took notes.

"Do you think," Eileen began and then hesitated until he looked up at her. "Do you think it—the body, I mean—might have been there already at that time?"

"I don't have any report from the medical examiner yet, ma'am," he said. "He says it'll be Friday before he can tell me much."

"It's just so hard to think of its having been there all along," she said, "while we washed the floor over it, put canned carrots next to it."

"I understand, Mrs. Hoffman," he said with a sympathetic smile. "Did you and your family ever leave the house for a prolonged period of time after 1949?"

"Just the odd weekend," she answered.

"I don't mean weekends. It would have to be a matter of months."

"Why?" Barbara said. She had been sitting next to her mother sipping coffee, listening intently.

"Otherwise somebody would have noticed the smell," he said, turning his hazel eyes onto Barbara's face.

"Oh," Eileen breathed, her face going even more pale. Then she recovered and sat up straight. "No, sheriff. We were never gone away for months. Farming demands year-round attention, you know. We couldn't just go larking off somewhere."

"Then we have to assume that the body was already in an advanced state of decay when you began working on the house in 1949."

"But how could it get there?" Eileen said, a flash of impatience coming into her voice. "And who is it? Who could be dead under our house?"

"I'm checking missing persons reports," he said. "But it takes a long time to work back that far. It's possible we'll *never* know who it is."

"That would be awful," Barbara interjected.

"Why?" he asked, turning his nice eyes towards her again, his face genuinely curious.

"I don't know," Barbara said. "I just feel it's important to find out who and why. It would be worse somehow to always wonder."

"Well, don't count on it," the sheriff said firmly. "It looks like the body got there sometime during the years the house was deserted. Anybody could have broken in. Bums coming through on the railroad, anybody. There could have been an accident. Or a fight. Other drifters just pushing the body through the trapdoor before moving on. They might do that if one of them died from sickness or old age even."

"That's so sad," Eileen said softly. "To think of someone so alone in the world that no one would miss him, not in so many years."

"The medical examiner can make certain tests," the sheriff was saying. "He can tell us the sex, age at time of death, maybe even cause of death. He can check for dental work, and we can look for some match in missing persons records, but this is all pretty iffy. A positive identification might be impossible."

When Eileen came back into the living room from walking the sheriff outside, she was carrying the mail.

"Letter from your Aunt Polly," she said, waving the familiar blue airmail letter. "And about time, too."

"You've been complaining about Aunt Polly's bad letter-writing habits for twenty years," Barbara said with a wry smile.

"Longer than that," Eileen said. "There's a letter for you, too. From Tom."

Barbara sat back in the chair and set her coffee cup down carefully.

"You might as well just throw it away," she said.

"Why should I do that?"

"I already know what it says. No matter what the words are, it boils down to 'Please reconsider our divorce.' I told you what he's been saying for months now."

"But what would it hurt to read his letter?" Eileen had sat down and was leaning earnestly toward her daughter.

"I didn't say it would hurt anything," Barbara said, her jaw setting. "It's just that it can't do any good, either."

"Why not?" Eileen was beginning to sound exasperated.

"You seem to have a short memory, Mother," Barbara said, standing up. "Mr. Thomas Mullens made his bed, and just because little Debbie Sanders isn't sharing it anymore, it doesn't mean he doesn't have to lie in it."

"Oh, I don't think he ever meant to live with her in the first place," Eileen said. "But he felt rather forced to do it when you insisted on getting a divorce."

"He was having an affair with her long before the thought of divorce ever crossed my mind. I didn't 'force' him into that, did I?"

"All right, Barbara. He hurt you and we all know it. But can't you accept that there might have been just a wee bit of fault on your side. You know you were so changed after the baby—." She broke off because Barbara had shot her a fierce warning look.

"That's what he said right from the beginning, when he first told me about Debbie," Barbara said, and she was almost shouting. "Like all of it was my fault. Well, forgive me for grieving because my baby died. What an awful woman I must have been!''

''Nobody is saying that. Don't put words in people's mouths.'' Eileen stood up and made a step toward Barbara.

''No, Mother,'' Barbara said, spreading her hands in front of her to warn her back. Her voice had returned to an icy calm. ''I needed Tom most of all in that year after Andrew died, and the son of a bitch betrayed me. There's nothing more to be said on the subject.''

''Barbara,'' Eileen said, ''if it were really all over between you and Tom, you wouldn't still be so angry. That's all I will say on the subject for the moment. But I'm not throwing away any letters. I'll put it here on the buffet, and if you want it thrown away, you can do it yourself.''

''I'm not mad at *you*,'' Barbara sighed.

''I know,'' Eileen said more softly. ''But I think I'm a little irritated with you for not being happier than you are. It breaks my heart to see you hurt, but sometimes I think you hurt yourself.''

''Read Aunt Polly's letter to me,'' Barbara said, deciding that it was best to change the subject.

''All right,'' Eileen said. ''After that I have to do some shopping.''

While her mother was at the IGA, Barbara sat down in the living room and opened Tom's letter. It was a single sheet of paper written in his cramped handwriting.

Dear Barbara,
    I will keep my promise and not follow you to Wisconsin, but I never promised not to write to

40

you. Maybe I can say what I mean better on paper because we won't be getting so emotional the way we do when we're together.

I think you should give me another chance. We both went a little crazy after Andy died, but just in different ways. I needed comfort so much but I didn't know how to comfort you. It was like there was some kind of force field keeping us apart. I could almost feel it crackling in the air. You didn't talk for days at a time, and every time I talked, the words were wrong. I don't just mean that you took them wrong. They were really the wrong things to say—all that 'snap out of it' stuff was insensitive, and I know it now. But it never meant that I felt his death less than you did. I was in pain, too.

So I made the wrong choice. I went elsewhere for comfort. But it was a mistake. Debbie never meant to me what you did, not one-tenth as much. I think now that I only told you about her to force some sort of crisis, so that we could get out of that impasse we were in. I'm going to remind you again that I'm the one who broke it off with Debbie right after your father's death, when you wouldn't even let me see you. I knew then more than ever that the only woman I want to spend my life with is you.

We had seven good years of marriage before everything went smash, and I think we can have a good marriage again. I'm not going to give up on you, Barbara, because I love you too much to quit trying.

Tom

Barbara slowly crumpled the letter in her left hand. Clichés, she thought, just a bunch of clichés. "She never meant anything to me. You're the only woman I ever loved.'' How many times in the history of the world had women had to listen to those lines? But another thought crossed her mind, unbidden and a little surprising. Had those lines become clichés because they were so often based on truth? Could it be that the feeble-sounding excuses were actually sincere? She opened a drawer in the coffee table and pitched the crushed letter inside, wondering at the same time why she didn't just cross the small apartment to the wastebasket.

She had met Tom Mullens in 1974 when he'd flopped down next to her in a chemistry class she was taking for the second time. She was a junior at Ohio State, and he was a senior, a dark-haired, intense young man from Duluth, Minnesota. What began as chemistry tutoring quickly became chemistry. Tom was serious, hard-working, ambitious, but he had his lighthearted and playful side. He was the eldest of four children and his repeated references to relatives soon made Barbara know that he was the product of a large, closely knit clan of Mullenses and Olsons. Part of his charm for her had always been that he absolutely took for granted the primacy of family. He'd won over Barbara's parents on his first visit to Wisconsin. They were married as soon as Tom got his bachelor's degree.

Tom plunged into his graduate studies, and Barbara "made a home" of their dreary graduate-housing apartment, papering walls, lining kitchen shelves with bright paper, coupon-shopping all over Columbus to make his stipend go further. She made a little extra money typing student research papers. They agreed to postpone children until Tom's career was set. It was in many ways a fairytale marriage. Tom was not exactly Prince Charming, but he was close enough to Barbara's need for a hero—good-looking, kind, loyal, going places.

Tom's degree and his publications while he was still a graduate student got him an assistant professorship at the University of Chicago, and both of them were thrilled to be moving closer to their respective families. Now they decided it was time to start a family of their own. Barbara had suffered some anxiety about this step because her own mother had had such a hard time conceiving and then had suffered through two miscarriages. But her fears were apparently groundless. She was pregnant three months after quitting the pill and had a "textbook pregnancy," as her OB-Gyn had put it. Andrew Joseph Mullens was born on October 24, 1982, a perfect little boy with tufts of dark hair and midnight blue eyes. On February 6, 1983, only two weeks after he'd begun to sleep through the night, he died in his sleep. Sudden Infant Death Syndrome, the doctors declared. Crib Death. Cause unknown.

Barbara's heart had simply frozen in her breast, turned to stone. She went through the funeral like a zombie, cleared out the baby's room, and hauled all of his things to Goodwill in three trips. Then she began to run, just jogging at first, pounding through the slushy streets as winter turned into spring, but then longer and longer every day, faster and faster. Only when she was running could she keep her mind from saying, "It's my fault. If I had checked on him, if I had got up in the night to look at him, he wouldn't be dead." If she ran far enough and fast enough, she didn't have to think about anything at all.

When she thought about those months now, that whole first year after Andy died, she knew that she had been almost indifferent to Tom. At first she was terrified that he blamed her for the baby's death, had even asked him about it. But gradually she came to believe instead that he just didn't care the same way she did. He went back to teaching, picked up his research project. He seemed to want to cling to her only in bed, in sex, not to talk about their loss the way she wanted to talk. Barbara had felt disgusted by the sex, angry with Tom for wanting it so much, so she pulled away from him, found excuses, manufactured ailments. Eventually he became less importunate.

So why, she wondered now, *had* she been so surprised, so outraged when he'd told her about Debbie, the graduate assistant who graded papers for him? She could scarcely let herself think about that weekend in Minnesota when he had confessed everything. Her rage seemed to be part of somebody she didn't know and it had scared Tom into cowed silence.

She had filed for divorce the moment they got back to Chicago, over Tom's protests that he didn't want a divorce. She slept in what had been the baby's room for three nights while she looked for an apartment. Only when she'd settled into the three rooms where she still lived did she take a quick trip to the farm to tell her parents about the separation. Her mother had counseled caution, urged her to reconsider divorce or at least wait before "taking such a drastic step." Her father's reaction had been quite different. She could still see his normally gentle face setting into stony outrage.

"Get rid of him," he'd said. "Don't you even consider taking the lying bastard back again."

Barbara had been touched by this unusual display of anger from her father, certain that it resulted from his deep feelings for her, but she was also a bit surprised.

44

Her father had always seemed so fond of Tom, had accepted him almost as a son.

"Don't be like that, Joe," Eileen had protested. "Tom's been so unhappy himself lately. He'll straighten out, I'm sure."

"No, Mother," Joseph Hoffman had said, his voice colder than Barbara had ever heard it when he was speaking to his wife. "The man is not the person we believed him to be, and that's all there is to it."

It was so close to what Barbara herself believed that it made it easier for her to ignore her mother's pleas for patience.

Since Christmas of this year, though, Tom had been calling her, dropping by. How was graduate school going? Didn't she sometimes get lonely? Would she agree to just date him, as if they were meeting for the first time? She had turned a deaf ear, trying to strike a casual tone with him. "Couldn't we just agree to be distant acquaintances?" she had said, taking some pleasure in seeing that this hurt him. Why *was* she still so angry, she wondered now. Could her mother be right that it wasn't really settled? She shook her head sharply and reached out to push the drawer of the coffee table shut with her toe, watching as the crushed letter rolled a little to one side and then disappeared.

4

For two days Barbara tried not to think about Tom's letter, not to think about the bones in the basement, not to think. She drove herself harder on her daily runs. On Friday morning, she ran almost twelve miles, from the edge of the village to the county line and back again. In the past four years, she'd become almost addicted to running. She didn't run to "keep in shape" the way some of her friends did, or to enjoy the great outdoors. As she ran, she scarcely noticed the familiar landscape or the red-winged blackbirds wheeling up out of the ditches at the sound of her approach; she hardly glanced at the tender new leaves, yellow-green, on the white birch trees. She ran because of what the running did for her mind, the way it seemed, after a few miles, to wash her brain clean, to put her outside of herself where her personal unhappiness, or anxieties, or terrors, no longer seemed to exist.

Back at the apartment, her hair still damp from her shower, Barbara stood up from the sofa at the sound of the doorbell.

"I'll get it, Mum," she called up the stairs to Eileen, who was arranging books on the shelves in her bedroom.

46

Paul Gillis was standing on the shallow porch, and at the sight of him, Barbara felt a flash of alarm. What could he want? What news could there be since Wednesday?

"Come in," she said a little breathlessly, pushing her wet hair behind her ears.

"Hi," he said, smiling and walking past her into the living room. "The M.E. has made some preliminary findings about the body, and I thought you'd like to know."

"Yes, of course," Barbara said, and then called, "Mother! Sheriff Gillis is here." But Eileen was already on the stairs, having heard the bell and the voices.

"Hullo again, Sheriff," Eileen said. "Is there some news?" She, too, looked a little alarmed, and Barbara wondered how often Paul Gillis had to see that expression, whether he had ever adjusted to the half-guilty reaction that even innocent people felt in the presence of a cop.

"I was telling Barbara that the medical examiner in Green Bay has been discovering some things about the skeleton in the basement of your old house," Sheriff Gillis said, smiling in a disarming way, obviously conscious of a need to put these women at ease.

"Can I get you some tea, or coffee?" Eileen asked.

"No, no. I can't stay long. Can we just sit down for a few minutes?"

"Of course," Barbara said, gesturing at the sofa.

"It's not very cheerful news," he began, folding his long body carefully to avoid knocking the coffee table with his knees as he sat down. He did this smoothly, the long habit of a tall man in spaces meant for shorter people.

"It was an adult male, mid-twenties," he said at last. "And it looks pretty much like he was murdered."

47

"Murdered?" Eileen breathed the word softly and glanced at Barbara.

"I'm afraid so," Sheriff Gillis went on. "The back of his head was smashed in just here," and he put the edge of his hand across the base of his own skull just above the neck. "It was done with a narrow, heavy instrument, something like a poker or a pipe."

"Couldn't he have been injured by falling?" Barbara asked.

"Not likely. Certainly not by falling where he was found. Not enough distance for that forceful a blow, and he was lying face down. No, somebody hid him there after the blow that killed him. The location of the body is the strongest argument for murder."

"Can the medical examiner tell how long he's been dead?" Eileen asked.

"Not with any precision. But when I told him the house was empty during a lot of the Second World War, he said that would be about right for the time of death. He can make a guess based on the degree of decomposition."

"Poor soul," Eileen said, shaking her head. "Who could have done such a ghastly thing? Nobody around here is like that."

"There's not much to go on. From the fragments of the clothes, we can tell that he was casually dressed. That means nothing very fancy about the shoes or belt. Seems to fit our theory that he was a drifter."

"There was no sign of identification papers, no wallet or anything?" Barbara asked.

"Nothing. And we went over that cistern pretty thoroughly. He didn't have much in the way of dental work, so that doesn't look like it will help us much in making an identification. One strange thing, though. The last two fingers of his left hand were missing, and the M.E. says it happened long before he died because the bones were all healed and shrunken back a bit.''

Barbara and Eileen sat forward with one motion, and both faces registered the identical expression: blue eyes wide, mouths agape.

''Uncle Tony!'' Barbara gasped.

''What?'' Sheriff Gillis said.

''Tony,'' Eileen breathed, looking first at Barbara and then back at the sheriff. ''Anton Hoffman. My husband's brother.''

''How do you know?''

''The fingers,'' Barbara said. ''His hand. It would be too much of a coincidence.'' But her mind was crying, ''Not Tony! Not Uncle Tony!''

''What happened to his hand?'' the sheriff asked.

It was Eileen who spoke now; it was as if she and Barbara were so breathless that they had to take turns answering.

''When my husband was ten and Tony was about twelve, their father was killed in a farm accident. He fell into a feed cutter while they were putting corn into the silo. Those were very dangerous machines, you know, not like the modern combines that do everything on the field. A feed cutter had no safety devices to speak of, and men had to put the corn bundles into it by hand. One slip and they were on a conveyor belt just two feet from rolling steel teeth. Tony saw it happen, heard his father scream. Apparently, he tried to pull him out, but he couldn't. He lost the fingers trying, the little finger and the ring finger on his left hand.''

''Mrs. Hoffman,'' the sheriff said slowly. ''When you

mentioned your husband's brother leaving New Augsburg about the time he enlisted in the army, I just assumed you were in contact with this brother. Barbara told me about some cousins on the West Coast.''

''No, those are second cousins,'' Eileen said vaguely. ''Joe's second cousins. We never knew where Tony was.''

''But how did that come about?'' the sheriff said. ''How could it be possible that you and your husband wouldn't have known the whereabouts of his brother all these years?''

''I know it seems strange,'' Eileen said. Barbara had moved closer to her mother on the sofa and had taken her hand. ''But it was the war again, those strange years during the war. When my husband enlisted, Tony was still at home, running the farm. Men could get deferments if they were involved in a 'vital industry,' and farming was considered vital, to feed the troops, you know. But when Joe finally wrote to some neighbors back here, we found out that Tony had left very soon after Joe did. Everybody hereabouts just assumed that Tony had joined up, too, without telling anybody. Later, everybody thought he had been killed or lost in the war and that nobody here was informed because there was no next of kin for the authorities to tell. They were the only children, and their parents were both dead.''

''But the army would have told your husband, no matter where he was stationed, Mrs. Hoffman,'' Sheriff Gillis said.

''Well, Joe always wondered about that,'' Eileen said, brushing her bangs to one side of her forehead in a distracted way. ''It's what made him think the neighbors were wrong, about Tony enlisting, I mean. Joe just thought he'd chucked everything and run off somewhere looking for adventure and then never came back. He was rather a wild boy, Joe said, with big notions about what he could do in the world. Maybe farming for the war effort wasn't what he wanted to do, especially after Joe joined up.''

"Didn't your husband think it was odd that his brother never answered his letters or tried to get in touch with him?''

"Well, " Eileen said, and then she seemed reluctant to continue. Barbara looked at her sharply, squeezed her hand. Finally she went on, ''Joe never wrote to Tony while he was in the army.''

"Not once?'' Sheriff Gillis had raised his eyebrows.

"It sounds dreadful, I know,'' Eileen hurried on. ''But after their mother died in 1940, the boys seemed to drift apart. Even though they lived in the same house, they had different lives. When Joe left New Augsburg to join the army, he meant to cut all ties, to start a whole new life. We would have stayed in England after the war if the economy hadn't been so bad there. Then Joe wrote to Dick Schneider and found out that Tony was long gone and that Dick had been paying the taxes on the farm in exchange for using the fields. So we decided to come back. The farm was Joe's now, it seemed, and it was a way to make a living, a place to have a family of our own.''

Barbara had let go of her mother's hand and was staring at the surface of the coffee table. She had long known that her father must have had some falling out with his brother. Though he'd always refused to discuss Tony, she had been able to read his face whenever she'd asked about her mysterious uncle. But it was news to her that Joe Hoffman had once considered never returning to New Augsburg. What could it have been to make him want

51

to cut himself off so definitely? And what could it mean that her mother, usually so confidential, had never told her this before?

"I take it then that you never met your husband's brother," the sheriff was saying.

"Oh, no," Eileen said. "And Joe never talked much about him, even to me. He never had much to say about his life before the war."

"How can we be certain it's Uncle Tony?" Barbara asked, wanting now very much for the skeleton to be someone else.

"He has a few dental fillings," Gillis said, "and some molars had been extracted. Would there be local dental records?"

"I suppose so," Eileen said. "Doctor DeWane, on Main Street, took over the practice from his own father. There might be records going back that far."

"I'll just go over there today," the sheriff said, making a note of the name. "And I wonder if you can give me the names of people who would have known Tony Hoffman pretty well."

"You're going to try to find out who did it, aren't you?" Eileen said, and she didn't sound pleased.

"Well, Mrs. Hoffman," he said. "There's no statute of limitations on first-degree murder, so I'm obliged to investigate."

"But if I give you names, will those people be suspects?" Eileen asked.

He smiled, a slow smile that was partly amused, partly sympathetic.

"For all we know, whoever did this could be dead by now," he said. "But I've got to gather as much information as I can. That's all I want the names for, to help me get a little information from that time."

So she gave him the names: Richard and Rosa Schneider, Charles and Geraldine Novak, Mary Wenner, the Heim brothers, and several others.

"I'm not sure how well they knew Tony," she finished, "because I've never heard any of them talk about him, but they were all neighbors in those days, were at school together, that sort of thing."

"It's a place to start," the sheriff said, standing. "I'll keep you posted."

He began to move toward the front door, and both women rose to follow him. At the door, Eileen said, "How much longer will those doctors need to look at the bones?"

"I don't know," he shrugged. "Maybe another few days or so. Why?"

"Well, he's family," she said simply. "We'll have to bury him."

"I'll let you know," he said.

Barbara followed him to his car.

"How seriously are you going to pursue this, Sheriff Gillis?" she asked, her arms folded tightly to keep herself from shaking.

"God, I hate to be called 'Sheriff,' " he said with a rueful shake of his head. "For the sake of the past we almost had, couldn't you call me Paul?"

"Yes, I could," she said with a tense little smile. "Now, about my question."

"Well, I have a whole county to cover," he said, "and only four part-time deputies. It's my duty to do what I can on this case, but frankly, I think this one's impossible. We're talking about a very cold trail here. How do you feel about my pursuing it?"

"Oh, I want to know what happened," she said firmly. "I hate things to be unresolved."

"But you know what this might mean, don't you?" Paul asked. "Your mother seems to know."

"What?" Barbara asked, genuinely puzzled.

"Well," he shrugged, "all law enforcement experience shows that crimes like this are seldom committed by strangers. More than eighty percent of the time, the murderer is well-known to the victim. How will you feel if it turns out that the killer is someone you've known all your life?"

Barbara mused for a moment.

"That can't be helped, I guess," she said at last. "I want to know the truth. And, as my mother said, Uncle Tony was family—even if I never knew him." It would be impossible to make Paul Gillis understand what Tony Hoffman meant to her, though she'd never met him, never even heard much about him.

Back in the apartment, Barbara found her mother rinsing the teapot, the first step in making the consoling brew Barbara knew she was craving.

"Mum," she said, trying to look into the older woman's face, "why didn't I know that Dad was never going to come back here? What was wrong between him and Uncle Tony anyway?"

"Don't be upset by that," Eileen said, patting her daughter's arm. "It's not such a mystery. By the time you were old enough to talk to, we had both come to love the farm, had put so much of ourselves into it that it hardly seemed possible even to us that there was ever a time when we didn't want to be there. And as for the way he felt about Tony, well, he never wanted to spoil your imaginings. You know that you'd already thought up your stories about Tony by the time you were eight, and Dad wanted to let you keep your ideas about him."

Yes, Barbara thought, that was how her mother had always regarded her elaborate childhood fantasies, so filled with romantic people and places—just "your stories."

"What was wrong between them?" Barbara demanded.

"It's hard to explain," Eileen said, setting the kettle on a burner as she spoke. "He just never talked much about his brother, even to me. That's the truth, Barbara. They were very different from each other, he said, not much to say to each other. That happens in families sometimes. Dad said that Tony was very changed by their father's death, that he just didn't seem to get over it."

"But Daddy was always so kind," Barbara protested. "It's hard to believe that he would just have dropped his own brother like that. I never *could* figure out why he wouldn't talk about Tony. You remember how I used to pester him for information."

"I'm telling you that it was the war that changed everything," Eileen said, pausing now to look straight up into her daughter's eyes. "When you're in the middle of it, you can't think very much about anything else. Just about whether or not you're going to die, or whether your friend next to you is going to die or be maimed horribly before your eyes. When the bombs were falling all around me in London, I didn't think much about writing letters either, and my parents and Polly were just up in Edinburgh then, so Polly could be safe."

Barbara remembered her father saying to her when she was a child, "You must know that your mother is a very brave woman. She stayed in London to help in the hospitals even though she was in a lot of danger, and she was only a teenager then. So she was on the front lines, too.''

"Okay, Mum," Barbara said. "I think I understand. But he must have wondered, after the war I mean, where Tony was. But I remember asking him—when I had the pictures, you know—asking all about Tony, and Daddy would say only vague things about him. Didn't Dad *try* to find him?''

"I know it's hard for you to accept," Eileen said. "But not all siblings are as fond of each other as Aunt Polly and I are. Not all of them *want* to stay in touch. Must we go on about this? It's been such a shock.''

For the first time, Barbara noticed that her mother's hands were shaking.

"I'm sorry, Mum," she murmured. "For me, too. I can't absorb it, can't realize it. 'Murder' seems like a word you hear, or read in the papers, not something that actually happens. At least not to anybody connected to you. The only uncle I ever had and somebody killed him, on purpose, and then just pushed him down there. I saw him, I—" and she found she couldn't go on.

Without looking at her daughter, Eileen turned and slipped her arms around Barbara's waist. Barbara closed her own arms around the thin shoulders, which were shaking with suppressed sobs. The crown of Eileen's head came just to Barbara's chin. The tea kettle began to whistle, sputtering and wheezing at first, and then rising to a thin, piercing shriek. Neither of the women moved to stop it, the noise seeming to express somehow the feelings both were holding inside.

* * *

56

After lunch, Eileen said she must talk to Father Hodeck about burying Tony, and besides, she needed to get out, to walk, to think by herself for a while. Barbara understood, and volunteered to haul boxes down into the basement storage room while her mother was out. There were some things from the farm that just couldn't find a place for themselves in this small apartment, and Eileen had repacked them.

The last of the boxes was in the back bedroom where Barbara was sleeping these days. It was a cardboard carton labeled "Photographs." Eileen had said that the box couldn't go into the basement for storage until Barbara had decided what pictures she wanted for herself. So now Barbara sat down at the small desk which had once filled one corner of her bedroom at the farm and opened the box. She began at once to hunt for the pictures of her Uncle Tony. She knew there were only three because she had pawed through this box several times during her growing-up years, looking for the fuel she needed to generate her fantasies.

The first photo she picked up was not of Tony, but of her father and her. It was a five-by-seven blow-up of a picture taken at Bay Beach Amusement Park. Her father was squatting in the sunlight next to the wading pool, grinning directly at the camera while he tried to hold onto his squalling three-year-old daughter who clearly didn't think the water was fun. Tears stung Barbara's eyes, and she turned the picture face down on the desk. This was exactly why she had resisted the picture-sorting job; it was still too soon after her father's death to wade around in the memories.

Very quickly now, without closely examining anything, she put photos onto the bed until she had found the pictures of her uncle. Then she lined up all three pictures on the desk directly under the light from the lamp. One was a grainy class picture labeled "1928." Tony was the third kid from the right in the back row, a towhead squinting so hard into the sun that his eyes had seemed to disappear. His squared shoulders and jutting jaw made him look like any other posturing ten-year-old; in fact, several other boys in the picture had struck the same somber pose. In the second picture, a snapshot taken during some long-ago hay harvest, Tony leaned to his right with his hand braced against the rump of a huge black horse, one half of the team hitched to the loaded hay wagon. He had a straw hat perched jauntily on the back of his head and was smiling broadly. It was a teenager's face, not yet wholly formed, but already handsome and cocky-looking, as if he knew he should be photographed.

The third picture was a semiformal photograph—a portrait of head and shoulders—of the sort men of that era had taken so they could give it to a girlfriend, the kind of picture for which a young man got a haircut and put on his Sunday suit. Here was the mature face, perhaps twenty-two years old, of a very handsome man: pale hair waving backward from a wide, prominent forehead; dark, bright eyes; a straight nose and a long, closely shaven jaw; sensuous lips parted in a lopsided smile over bright, regular teeth. The whole expression suggested careless confidence, a flair for mischief.

It was this photograph which Barbara had confiscated and kept in her room from the time she was seven until she went away to college. When she first found the photos, she hadn't known who he was, had asked her mother about the handsome young man. It was Eileen who had given the bare outline of Tony's life, his accident, his going off mysteriously before "you were even thought of," Eileen had joked. The very vagueness of the details had fed Barbara's childish imagination. In an environment where almost all of her classmates had four or five siblings, eight pairs of uncles and aunts, and twenty-five or thirty cousins, she had felt starved for relatives. This dashing uncle whose whereabouts were a mystery even to her father more than filled the bill. He appealed to all her girlish need for romance and adventure.

She'd always refused to believe that he could be dead, as some of her schoolmates suggested when she spoke of him, but imagined that he'd run off to South America or even Africa, where he had dangerous adventures and was making himself fabulously wealthy. She had pictured him cutting his way through jungles, his maimed hand hidden in a black glove so no one would pity him; saw him mucking about (a phrase of her mother's that she had rather liked at that age) in diamond mines. "My only uncle," she would intone to the kids at school, asserting his singularity in the face of the dull hordes of ordinary uncles they all enjoyed, "is making his way in the world." Of course, she believed that he would one day appear in New Augsburg and dazzle all her friends into dumbfounded silence. That his picture made him look reckless and even a little wicked increased his appeal for her immensely. She could never imagine him becoming middle-aged or old.

Whenever she asked her father for more information about Tony, Joe Hoffman spoke in gray-toned generalities, the way he did about everything in his own past. Tony had gone to school like everybody else, though he left high school without graduating; he had run the farm; he had gone away. Once, when Barbara was thirteen, brooding and rebellious, more conscious than ever of her separateness from New Augsburg ways, she had spoken crossly to her father when he wouldn't answer questions about Uncle Tony.

"Why can't you remember? Why can't you tell me what he was like—really, really like?"

And Joe had turned his clear eyes toward her, saying a little tensely, "Maybe you wouldn't think so much of him then."

"Why? Why wouldn't I?" she had demanded, starting to cry a little. At thirteen, she had a low frustration threshhold.

"Nothing, nothing," he had said, clumsily patting her arm. "Never mind, honey. Never mind."

But she had clung to her "only uncle," her idea of him, persuading a high school boyfriend who was taking shop to make a frame for this portrait.

Now Barbara turned up the photograph of her father and held it next to the picture of Tony. How odd it was, she thought, that the same set of parents could produce such different-looking sons. Her father's dear face was, she recognized, rather ordinary, his slate-colored hair lank and straight, his nose and cheeks punctuated by dark moles. His gray eyes were lovely, of course, kind and direct, but she knew that people would pass him on the street and never look at him twice. The picture spoke of steadiness, absolute reliability, gentleness—how his hands held her without hurting her—all the qualities Barbara prized but had considered pretty ho-hum when she was a starry-eyed girl.

Her gaze went back to Tony's handsome head. This was the skull in the cistern, she thought. Someone had smashed in this head when it was not much older than it had been in the picture. Right there, across the back of

60

his neck, a small part of which could be seen, for his head was turned slightly to the right. She put her finger down onto the spot, feeling a surge of blinding anger. She had been robbed. There were no diamond mines, no adventures of any kind. Only a sordid death, a hidden corpse, bones. Life had robbed her of so much—her baby, her marriage, her father—but through all of that she'd felt powerless to retaliate; there was simply nothing she could do. But now there was a specific place to direct her anger. Whoever had killed Tony Hoffman would have to be found out, exposed, punished. She heard the front door open then and stood up quickly.

"What were you doing?" Eileen said, pulling off her sweater as Barbara came down the stairs.

"Sorting the pictures," Barbara said, trying to sound casual.

"You mean looking for the pictures of Tony," Eileen said with a concerned frown. "I know you pretty well, you know."

"Don't show off, Mother," Barbara said, giving her a little hug. "What took you so long?"

"I was at the cemetery for a while," Eileen said simply. Barbara looked away. She had avoided the cemetery ever since her father's funeral. His grave was in the new section that had been recently opened across the road from the old part; its lonely expanse, covered in snow, was firmly fixed in her memory.

"Telling Daddy the news, I suppose."

"Yes, yes I was," Eileen said, and then added, more briskly, "Father Hodeck says there's enough room to the left of our plot to bury Tony. If we use a narrow box, that is."

"Well, I saw him, Mother," Barbara said acidly, her recent anger about Tony's death still fresh in her feelings,

61

"and I don't think he'll need a regular-sized coffin, if that's what you and Father Hodeck are worried about."

"Don't be flip, Barbara. The plot on the right is already sold, so unless we bury him next to the hedge, we'd have to put him somewhere further away. There's no room at all in the old cemetery where Grandpa and Grandma Hoffman are buried. And I think he should be with his family, don't you? With us, I mean?"

"Yes, Mum," Barbara whispered because she found she was in danger of sobbing. "You're right. He should be with his family."

5

It was already mid-morning of the next day when Eileen told Barbara that Mary Wenner was coming to the apartment for lunch.

"I called her last night to tell her about Tony," Eileen said, as if that were sufficient explanation.

"If she waited a few more days, she could read about it in the newspaper," Barbara said. New Augsburg had only a small weekly paper, but most residents had the *Green Bay Press Gazette* delivered to their homes daily. Wednesday's paper had a page-two headline reading "Skeleton Found in New Augsburg Farmhouse." Barbara felt sure the grapevine had by this time spread the news to every corner of the township, even to those isolated farms which received no newspaper at all.

"I know," Eileen said, "but Mary deserves to hear about it from me. She's my oldest friend."

Mary was, as usual, a little late. She came bustling into the dining room, gave Barbara a hug, and then demanded, looking back and forth between them as she slowly intoned each word. "What do you make of this business about Tony?"

She was a large, garrulous woman, gossipy and a little obtuse, but so fundamentally good-natured that everyone forgave her excesses gladly. She and her husband Jim had lived on the farm across the road from the Hoffman farm for all of their married life, but Jim had died of a heart attack in 1983 and Mary had moved into the village to live in an apartment attached to her oldest son's house. She had been the first woman in New Augsburg to befriend Eileen, who was, as Mary had once told Barbara, "like a Martian to these folks—not local, not American, not Catholic. Three strikes against her." But Mary's sponsorship of the small Englishwoman had worked a change over the years, and eventually everyone came around. Eileen had never forgotten, though, who had been big-hearted enough to take her on faith from the first day.

"Why don't we have something to eat while we talk," Eileen said, gesturing at the table. Barbara and Mary sat down to a cold salad of tuna and macaroni, a meal Barbara had grown up with as a once-a-week lunch through every summer she could remember. Today's slices of cantaloupe and kiwi fruit had been added to the menu at her suggestion, something too exotic to be a normal part of New Augsburg cuisine.

"We were stunned when we heard," Barbara said. "I don't think it can be anybody else."

"Well, no," Mary said, shaking out her napkin. "Your mother told me about the fingers. It hardly seems likely it could just be some *other* three-fingered person passing through."

"We think it must have happened when Daddy was away in the war," Barbara explained. "That's why nobody discovered the body, because nobody was using the house."

"Mercy," Mary exclaimed. "To think of the times I looked across the road at that house, thinking what a pity it was to let it go to pieces. Dick was using the fields, and Jim would sometimes help him out over there at harvest time, but nobody went into the house except for kids interested in a real quiet place, if you know what I mean."

"Well, at least the buildings and fields were kept up," Eileen said from the kitchen. "It was decent of Dick to work so hard on a place that wasn't his own."

"Well it was only right," Mary said. "My Jim always said that Dick felt real strong about that, used to say we all owed it to Joe. So Jim was glad to help, too."

"Owed it to him?" Barbara said, offering the plate of fruit to Mary. "Why?"

"Well, because he was off fighting in the war, I suppose," Mary said. "We were doing what we could here, to raise food, you know, but Joe was actually putting his life on the line."

"Didn't you all think Tony was doing the same thing?" Barbara asked.

"Hmp!" Mary snorted. "We didn't give much thought to that, I suppose. It was his job to take care of that farm, and he ran out on it."

She paused, looking stricken.

"At least that's what we thought he did," she said. "We were sure wrong about that, weren't we? He was there all the time."

"I don't know much about my uncle," Barbara said as Eileen approached the table with a plate of warm dinner rolls. "Nobody ever talked much about him."

"Well, I don't think most folks could say they knew

him very well," Mary said, glancing up at Eileen. "He was not an easy person to get close to."

"Why was that, Mary?" Barbara asked. "Was he quiet, withdrawn, a dreamer, maybe?" It fit her childhood fantasy about him.

"Oh, no," Mary said with an exaggerated shake of her head. "He could charm the birds out of the trees when he wanted to, and, of course, he was so good-looking that people most always liked him when they first met him. But, I don't know, it's hard to explain. There always seemed to be something *behind* the niceness, something kinda dangerous, like maybe he wasn't really *sincere* when he grinned that beautiful grin of his. And some people said he had a mean streak." Again she stole a little glance at Eileen which Barbara could not help noticing.

"Well, surely it couldn't have been so awful as to make anyone want to kill him," Eileen said, settling herself into her own chair.

"I've been pawing around in my memory since you called me last night," Mary said. "I thought and thought about that last summer before the time we figured Tony went away. The summer of 1943 that was. Well, like I say, I searched through my mind, and I got a theory." She paused, looking back and forth between them, waiting for a prompt.

"And what is your theory?" Eileen said, so used to Mary's way of getting to a point that she spoke almost automatically.

"It was one of them motorcycle toughs," Mary said. "Or maybe even a whole bunch of them." Again she made a dramatic pause.

"What motorcycle toughs?" Barbara prompted.

"Tony bought a motorcycle that spring," Mary said.

"He was roaring all over the country with it, even got stopped for speeding over in Gale once. He was sure sore about that ticket. Then he started hanging around with some guys from Green Bay. They all had motorcycles, some so big they looked like trucks. All of them crashed Henry and Alice Wagner's wedding dance at the Rendezvous. It looked like things might get pretty ugly for a while, but then your Joe got them to leave. Tony would sometimes listen to Joe. And sometimes not, too."

"What makes you think the Green Bay guys might have killed Tony?" Barbara asked.

"Well, it seems they were hanging out a lot at your farm," Mary said, after swallowing some tuna salad. "Not that I know this first hand, mind you, because Jim and me weren't living there then. We didn't get married until Christmas time of that year, so Jim hadn't even bought our farm yet. But talk gets around. People said Joe didn't like those guys being there, but Tony wouldn't pay any attention to him. Said he could have his friends in his house if he wanted to. You know, he always thought the farm was his, not Joe's, because he was older."

"But Mary," Eileen said patiently, "you still haven't said why you think the motorcycle boys would hurt Tony."

Mary had taken a big bite of a roll and waved her hands to indicate her inability to speak. Barbara and Eileen picked at their salads while they waited.

"I don't know how you can even ask," Mary said at last. "They were drunken thugs. They could probably turn on a person for no good reason at all. Just smack him in the head, and when they realized they'd killed him, just dump him in the basement and roar off on them damn bikes."

"But Daddy would have known that Tony was missing," Barbara said.

"Well, sometimes Tony would just disappear for days and days," Mary said. "People said he had girlfriends in the city, if you know what I mean. But what if those hoodlums killed Tony right after your pa joined the army? Then he couldn't know what happened."

"When did Dad leave for the service?" Barbara said, turning to Eileen.

"Early September of 1943," Eileen said.

"Well, Mary? When was the last time you can remember seeing Tony?" Barbara asked.

Mary puckered her brow and rolled her eyes at the ceiling.

"I'm trying to go through the weddings and coin showers from that summer," she said. "Those're pretty much the only times I got out in those days. Jim and I were engaged, of course, so we went everywhere together. And all our friends were in the process of getting married, too, so somebody was always having a shower or a wedding."

Coin showers, as Barbara knew, were an old New Augsburg tradition. The groom's family simply rented a hall, hired a band, and set up a few barrels of beer. Then postcards summoned everyone of both sexes in the acquaintance of both families to dance, eat homemade sandwiches with their beer, and leave an envelope with several dollars inside in a big, paper-trimmed box. Traditionally, the engaged couple used the money to buy their bedroom set, so it was always an occasion for ribald humor, as well as more conventional merriment. Many local families still gave coin showers for engaged couples, though the college-educated young people were trying to discourage it.

"Let me see," Mary was saying. "I remember my cousin Angeline's shower was in October that year because they got married just before we did, but everybody was already talking about Tony being gone, saying he had probably joined the navy or something. Just like him to do it without telling anybody, folks said. I remember that shower because Jim took sick and we had to leave early. He had a touchy stomach all that fall. My mother said it was cold feet about getting married himself."

At any other time, Barbara would have been amused by Mary's wandering off the subject, a comfortable reminder of all the years she'd listened to this woman's habits of speech, but now she was feeling impatient.

"The last time you saw Tony, though," she hinted firmly.

"Well, I'm trying to think," Mary sighed, "but it's hard. I'm pretty sure it was in the late summer, toward the end of August sometime, that we went to the Hemmel wedding. That can be checked, of course. Laura and Barnie Hemmel. Tony was there, and everybody was talking about him and Caroline Heim. I don't mean that Caroline Heim was there, because she wasn't, but everybody was talking about her."

Barbara had noticed her mother's eyes widen and then drop toward her napkin at the first mention of Caroline Heim.

"Who was Caroline to Tony?" Barbara asked.

Mary and Eileen looked at each other across the table, and Barbara could see a question and a reassurance pass between their eyes, the kind of dialogue that only old friends are capable of conducting.

"It had come out," Mary said, her face still a bit guarded, "because her brothers were so het up about it. Their pa was dead a long time by then so they felt sort of responsible for her. Seems Tony had been driving Caroline around on the back of that motorcycle and not to public places, if you know what I mean. It'd been going on most of the summer, but the Heim boys had just found it out. Of course, they thought along with everybody else that she was still going with Joe.''

Barbara looked quickly at her mother, but Eileen was inspecting her salad pretty carefully.

"She had been dating my father?" Barbara said.

"Well, yes," Mary said. "For almost a year. Of course, they were young. He was maybe twenty-two and she was only about eighteen, so we didn't think it was serious yet. Then it turned out she was sneaking around with Tony while she was still going to dances with your pa. Shameless little thing." Mary's face was filled with the disapproval of the virtuous woman for the Jezebel.

Barbara felt a dryness in her mouth, a slight wave of nausea. It was something that happened to her lately whenever she heard about sexual infidelity of any kind.

"What became of her?" she asked, still looking at her mother's lowered face.

"Her brothers put a stop to her seeing Tony, I can tell you," Mary said with a certain amount of relish. "She got married that November to a forty-year-old farmer from up near Medford. Her pa had known the family a long time. Her first baby was born the following March." She paused to allow this to sink in.

"Was it Tony's baby?" Barbara asked.

"Nobody was saying for sure," Mary said. "She was living up in Medford then, of course, so we didn't get to see the baby. It was a boy, we heard from George Heim."

"So," Barbara said, eyeing her mother, "I might have a first cousin after all. Too bad I never knew about it."

Eileen looked up at her briefly and then turned to Mary.

"Has that nice young sheriff chap called you yet?" she asked. "You should tell him what you told us, about the motorcycle people, I mean."

"I haven't heard a peep from him yet," Mary said. "But I'm sure he'll think what I do about it, and that will be the end of it."

"Yes," Eileen said. "You're probably right. These things are usually not very complicated at all. They probably had a fight, maybe didn't even mean to kill him, and then just panicked afterwards."

Mary was silent for a moment, looking uncharacteristically serious and uncertain.

"Do you think I should tell the sheriff that I once went out with Tony?" she said at last.

"Did you really?" Eileen said, really surprised this time.

"Just a few times, early in 1942, before I got serious about Jim," Mary said. "But I put a stop to it."

"Why?" Barbara asked.

"Oh, he was too fast for me, Barbie," Mary said, blushing a little. "So good-looking and so—well, he couldn't keep his hands where they belonged, if you know what I mean. He kept saying there was a war on, and he would probably join up pretty soon, so I should give him something to remember."

"Oh, no," Barbara groaned. Surely her Uncle Tony couldn't have used so hackneyed a ploy!

71

"Oh, I was young," Mary smiled, "but I knew a line when I heard one. I just started saying no when he asked me out again. He didn't take it very well."

"In what way?" Eileen said.

"Well, he kept coming around," Mary answered. "At dances, he would always cut in, try to get me to go outside with him. Even after I was going with Jim. At the Easter dance at the Rendezvous that year, Jim punched him."

"They had a fight?" Barbara was amazed, having known Jim Wenner as a quiet, inoffensive man.

"Well, it wasn't really a fight," Mary said. "Tony kept trying to get me to dance with him, asking me right in front of Jim. Jim told him to go away, but he kept it up. Finally, Tony leaned over and said something to him, real quiet so nobody else heard. Then Jim just hit him, punched him in the stomach. He never would tell me what Tony said to him."

"What did Tony do?" Eileen asked. Coffee was getting cold in their cups, and the lunch was largely untouched.

"That was the funny part," Mary said. "He didn't do anything. He straightened up and just sort of smiled at Jim, one of those big, toothy grins of his. Then he left the dance. He'd been drinking quite a bit, I think." She put her fork down and pulled her napkin up into her hands. "You don't think the sheriff might get the wrong idea from that, do you?" she said at last.

"Oh, Mary," Eileen said at once, "don't be such a silly. Nothing else happened at the time, did it? Well, no, of course not. And you and Jim went on to get engaged. Tony disappeared more than a year later, didn't he? So of course the sheriff isn't going to suspect that Jim would have hurt him. That's just too ridiculous."

"I'm glad you see it," Mary said, breaking into her smile. "Because I've been worried since you told me about it last night and about the sheriff asking questions. Somebody might tell him that Tony and Jim once had a fight, and he would get the wrong idea."

"Just put it out of your mind," Eileen said firmly. "Now I'm going to freshen up our coffee, and we're actually going to eat the rest of our lunch."

When Barbara and Eileen had returned to the living room after seeing Mary to her car, Barbara blocked her mother's retreat to the kitchen.

"Shouldn't we talk, Mother?" she asked, trying to get Eileen to look at her. "I'd like to find out what else has been a deep, dark secret in my family."

"You're being melodramatic, Barbara," Eileen said. "We can talk about this while we do the washing up."

"The dishes can wait," Barbara said firmly. "I want you to sit down right here on the sofa and look me in the face. You knew all about Caroline Heim, didn't you?"

"Not all about her," Eileen sighed, sinking onto the sofa and looking up at her daughter. "I didn't know about the child, about that first baby."

"Why wouldn't Dad have told you that, do you think?" Barbara said, sitting on the edge of a sofa cushion so that she could face toward Eileen.

"I'm sure he didn't know about it," Eileen said.

"Oh, come along!" Barbara said impatiently, using one of her mother's expressions.

"But how would he have known? He would scarcely have gone back to ask her after he learned that she'd been seeing Tony behind his back. And her family

73

was hardly going to advertise the fact. Think what a scandal unwed pregnancy was in those days. Then your father left so soon after. And by the time he came back to New Augsburg, the scandal was so old and so much else had happened that no one ever mentioned it to him."

Barbara's face was looking so skeptical, so on the edge of another cynical outburst, that Eileen hurried on.

"It might have been different if she'd been living around here. But she married that man—his name was Bower, I think—and moved way up to Medford. They had five children in all, I've been told."

"Is she still there, in Medford?"

"No. Her husband died back in the mid-seventies somewhere. He was so much older than she was. George, her brother George, told us she lived with one of her daughters for a while. But since 1980 she's been living with her brother Peter, the one who bought a farm up along the Bay, near Red Banks. He never married, you know. She's been keeping house for him, I guess."

"But Dad told you about her?" Barbara said, looking intently at her mother's face, feeling again the old resentment that her parents' intimacy had seemed to shut her out.

"Yes, of course he did. We didn't have many secrets, you know."

"Except from me," Barbara said. "You never saw fit to tell me, and when I asked you yesterday what was wrong between Dad and Tony, you didn't tell me then, either."

"You're making it sound as if it were some big, terrible secret," Eileen said, exasperated, "and it wasn't like that a bit. By the time Dad told me, when we were engaged, it was so far in his past and so much of a really

74

staggering nature had happened to him since, that it hardly seemed important to him anymore. He had been through the D-Day invasion. He had gone with the infantry across Europe in one of the most bloody mop-up operations any army has ever had to do. He saw his buddies die and his best friend so badly wounded that the medics had to take pieces of him back in separate bags. Now you know he never talked much about those things at all, and almost never to you, because he wanted to spare you the worst about the world. But things like that, what he went through in the war, they change a person's perspective. The old life seems so far away that you seem to yourself to have been a different person then. I'm sorry to make you such a long speech, Barbara, but I want you to see that Dad wasn't keeping secrets from you. It's just that the old past didn't seem important enough to him to bring up in the present."

"Okay, Mother, okay," Barbara sighed. "What did Dad say about her, about Caroline Heim, when he told you about her?"

"He said that she had been the only girl he'd ever been interested in besides me," Eileen answered. "I'd asked him, you see, once he was my 'bloke,' as we used to say. He said she was pretty, blonde, that he'd taken her out for about a year."

"And what did he say about how it ended?"

"He said he found out she'd been going out with Tony all that last summer before he enlisted and that ended it, of course."

"That's all?" Barbara was incredulous. "What did he say about Tony?"

"He said he knew Tony wasn't really interested in her. He said, 'Tony only took her because he knew I wanted her.' "

"My God!" Barbara cried. "Wasn't he angry? *How* did he say that? Did he sound bitter?"

"I'm not prepared to give the line a 'reading,' Barbara. He said it simply and quietly. Like it was all over and done with."

"Well, no wonder he didn't write to his brother in six years, and no wonder he wasn't going to come back home," Barbara said, standing and beginning to pace. "Why didn't you tell me this yesterday?"

"You seemed so cut up about Tony being dead," Eileen said simply. "And I remembered how you used to keep his picture in your room and make up romantic stories about him. It just didn't seem necessary to add to your grief with those old stories."

"Well, I seem to have been pretty wrong about Tony. What a wonderful judge of men I've turned out to be," Barbara said with her back to Eileen, a salty taste of bitterness in her mouth.

"You know," Eileen said thoughtfully, "it's true that your father seldom mentioned his brother even to me, but when he did, it was with a kind of pity. He said that Tony's life had been spoilt by your grandpa's death, that he was changed after that, cocky and wild, as if he were daring death to come near him again. Those were your father's words. Whatever he felt about Tony in 1943, I believe he got over it. He forgave him."

"You know what I'm wondering right now?" Barbara said. "I'm wondering how the Heim boys stopped Tony from seeing Caroline. You heard Mary say that Tony kept after her when she said she wouldn't see him again, so maybe Tony tried to see Caroline again, too. And when the brothers found out she was pregnant, why didn't they just grab Tony and insist that he marry her? It would have been the best way to avoid scandal."

"But Tony had disappeared," Eileen said, standing now, too.

"Why didn't they look for him, try to track him down, instead of marrying their sister to an old man from out of town?"

"Well, we don't know that they didn't look for him," Eileen said. "It's not the sort of thing you ask somebody."

"Maybe that's something the sheriff *should* ask George and Peter Heim," Barbara said, turning to look significantly at Eileen.

"What do you mean?" Eileen looked stunned, her blue eyes wide.

"Well, think about it, Mother," Barbara said. "What Mary says about a motorcycle gang is all very well, but those Heim brothers actually had a motive for killing Uncle Tony."

It was only when she had finished speaking that another sentence flashed across her mind, completed and intact as if someone else had spoken it: "And so did my father." She turned sharply away so that Eileen wouldn't see her face.

"Rubbish!" Eileen said, almost as if she'd heard Barbara's thought. "The Heims are good people, people like us. Goodness, if brothers committed murder every time they found out their sisters were pregnant, the population would be greatly reduced."

"Yes, yes you're right," Barbara said numbly. "People like us don't go around smashing in other people's heads, do we? No matter how mad we are at them. Forget I said it. Let's get these lunch dishes cleaned up." And she fled from her mother into the dining room.

6

By Monday afternoon, Barbara was feeling anxious and impatient. She had spent two restless nights trying to absorb emotionally what she had learned about her family, trying not to let the errant thought back into her head. It was nonsense anyway, she told herself; Joe Hoffman was not the sort of man who could kill anyone, least of all his own brother. But she was restless. She wanted answers, something definitive. She'd half-expected Sheriff Gillis to check in with them, to report on the rest of the medical examiner's findings, to let them know what, if anything, he'd learned from the people whose names Eileen had given him. She was planning to return to Chicago in a week, and she expected to take away with her some reassurance that the case was moving speedily toward a conclusion.

"I think I'm going to call the sheriff," she said to Eileen, "to see if he's learned anything else."

"You never did win any prizes for patience, Barbara," Eileen said. "The number is right on the inside cover of the phone book."

Barbara was surprised when Sheriff Gillis answered

the phone, identifying himself in a deep, formal, "telephone" voice.

"This is Barbara Mullens," she said. "Don't you have somebody to answer the phone for you?"

"Oh, hello, Barbara," he said warmly, sounding much more like himself. "Sara, our office dispatcher, takes a break every day about this time, so anybody who's here has to answer the phone. What can I do for you?"

"Well, I was wondering how far along the medical examiner's report has come. I mean in making a positive identification of the—the body." She could no longer call it "our skeleton."

"Well, no further at all," he said after a brief pause. "I saw your dentist on Friday after I talked to you, and he said his father kept all his old records in the basement, the ones on 'inactive' patients. He said he would take some time over the weekend to look around down there to see if there were any records for Anton Hoffman. I was going to check in with him after Sara comes back from her break. To see if he found anything, that is."

"And have you started interviewing people?" Barbara asked. "I mean those people Mother told you about, the ones who knew Tony back then."

"No, I haven't. Don't see much point in it until we can say for sure that the body is your uncle. Dental records of some kind will help, along with what you and your mother told me about the injury to his hand."

"Oh. I see," Barbara said, but her exasperation was clear in her voice.

"What's the matter?" he asked.

"Nothing," she said coldly. "It's just that I imagined that a murder investigation would move a bit more quickly."

"Well, Barbara," he said, and she could hear the

79

chuckle just behind the words, "I don't think speed is a top priority here. What did you have in mind, road blocks and a house-to-house search?"

"No, I guess not." She found herself smiling. "It's just that I'll be leaving New Augsburg in about a week and I was hoping there would be *some* answers by then."

"Oh, I'm sorry to hear that," he said. "About your leaving, I mean. Well, for sure I'll check in with you about the dental records this week and I'll get the M.E. to release the body, so you and your mother can have it buried before you go back to Chicago."

"Right, right," she murmured absently, thinking for the first time that it might not be such a good idea to have Tony resting next to her father. "Thank you, Sheriff."

"Hey, I thought we had a deal about that 'Sheriff' stuff," he complained good-naturedly.

"Sorry," she said. "Thank you, Paul."

"I'll call you," he said. "That's a promise."

"He seems like a sensible young chap," Eileen commented when Barbara had explained her conversation with the sheriff.

"I'm sure you're right," Barbara replied. "But one thing seems certain. I'm not going to find out much more about the family murder before I leave for Chicago, not unless I do some asking around myself."

"Now, Barbara," Eileen said, eyeing her daughter narrowly, "don't go mucking about in this business. If you would do what I want you to do and stay longer, that nice sheriff will have found out everything there is to know—which probably isn't very much—and then he can tell us all about it."

"Well, you know I've been meaning to look in on the Schneiders anyway," Barbara said. "And they've always

80

been neighbors, so they can probably add something to what Mary told us.''

''Remember that Dick hasn't been very well lately.''

''All the more reason for me to make a courtesy call.''

''A courtesy call is fine, my girl, but don't you go putting a strain on him by pumping him for information about things he hardly remembers. That obsessive strain of yours makes you sometimes forget yourself in dealing with other people.''

''You can come along if you want to, Mother, to make sure I behave like a well-bred daughter should,'' Barbara flared.

''No, no,'' Eileen said. ''You go ahead. I'm not ready to go back out there just yet. I think I'll walk up to the hardware store and see if they have a bicycle I might like, not one with all those confounded gears.''

''A bicycle?'' Barbara was surprised and amused.

''Yes, a bicycle,'' Eileen said, bristling a little. ''Now that I'm living here in town, I don't see the sense in going everywhere by car. I never was one for driving the car anyway. That was always Dad's department. Winter is another matter, of course, but now that I don't have my garden anymore, I can use the exercise.''

''Well, more power to you, Mum,'' Barbara laughed. ''I'll be back about five, I should think.''

As Barbara climbed into her car, she glanced at her watch. It was 2:15. It occurred to her that she had time to make two visits before her mother would begin to expect her back.

The original homestead of the Heim family was two miles east and one mile south of the Hoffman farm. Barbara had grown up traveling country roads with her

81

father, and there was not a house for five miles in any direction where she couldn't have named the residents. For twelve years, she'd gone to school with children who grew up in these houses. Most of the Heim children, however, were just enough older than she was that she hadn't been a visitor at this particular farm. When she pulled her little car up to the back porch of the T-shaped house, Barbara saw a large brown-and-white dog rise up from the shade of the porch and launch itself into the sunlight that surrounded her car.

The dog was some mix of Labrador and mastiff, heavy-jowled, droopy-eared, aging by the look of his grizzled muzzle. But he knew his job. He came to a stop three feet from the driver's side door of Barbara's car and barked ferociously, a deep, dangerous-sounding roar of a bark. When Barbara rolled down her window, intending to speak soothingly to the animal, he bared his teeth and snarled convincingly before returning to his louder sounds of warning and menace.

"Cut it out, Buster!" A woman's voice drew Barbara's attention to the back porch. "You pipe down now, dog, and come here." The dog gave one last half-hearted roar and then shambled toward the porch. The woman in the doorway was short and round, wearing a floral print housedress and a bibbed apron; her thin hair was white and frizzed all around her moon-shaped face. The face itself was wearing an expression Barbara recognized; it was not hostile, but closed, watchful, a look she'd seen on her own mother's face at times over the years. It said, "Stranger in the yard."

"Hello, Mrs. Heim," Barbara called. "Is it all right for me to get out of the car?"

"Sure," the old woman said. "He ain't gonna hurt you if I tell him not to." But her face remained suspicious. "If you're selling makeup or something, you're wasting your time. I don't need any a that stuff."

"No, I'm not selling anything," Barbara said. "I'm Barbara Mullens."

The old face remained impassive.

"If you came to see Raymond, he's out cutting hay," she said.

It took Barbara a second to understand this reference. Raymond was the Heims' youngest son, a forty-year-old bachelor who had taken over the management of the farm. Clearly, Mrs. Heim thought Barbara might be a "lady friend" of Raymond's, a possibility so unlikely that it made Barbara smile.

"No, Mrs. Heim," she said, approaching the porch with one eye cocked nervously at Buster, "I came to talk to you and your husband."

"Oh? What about?" As yet, Mrs. Heim had made no move to reopen the door or to suggest that her visitor might be asked to enter her house.

"About Tony Hoffman," Barbara said.

Now the old woman's face simply slammed shut. She looked Barbara over from head to toe through squinted eyes, waiting a long time to speak again.

"And who might you be to be asking questions about him?" she said.

"I'm his niece," Barbara answered. "I'm Joe Hoffman's daughter."

All of Mrs. Heim's pudgy body relaxed.

"Well, for heaven's sake, girl!" she cried. "Why don't you tell people who you are first thing?" And she came to the edge of the porch. "Now that you say it, I do see some resemblance to your mother. You been away quite a few years now. Where you living these days?"

"Chicago," Barbara replied and then forged ahead to forestall any chatty questions about her marriage. "Is Mr. Heim at home? I'd like to talk to both of you."

"He's out to the milk house," Mrs. Heim said, gesturing with her head. "Trying to fix the backup generator. Too stubborn to hire somebody who knows what he's doing."

Barbara looked across the yard toward the barn and several other smaller outbuildings.

"Maybe we could just walk down and have a little visit while he works," Mrs. Heim said. "He hates to quit in the middle of a job."

They walked together across the tidy yard, Barbara slowing her steps to keep pace with the old woman's rolling walk, having to pause while Mrs. Heim pointed at and described her vegetable garden. Inside the milk house, a low cinder block building, they found a figure crouching over the generator. Behind him loomed a gleaming 1500-gallon milk cooler. All the familiar smells of a dairy came into Barbara's nostrils.

"This here's Joe Hoffman's girl," Mrs. Heim called to the man without any preliminaries and without even waiting for him to look up.

George Heim stood up slowly and turned around. He was a huge man, tall and barrel-chested with big hands, one of which was holding a pliers. His face was deeply lined, permanently suntanned, but his eyes were still sharp under the shaggy eyebrows. His thick hair was a wonderful silvery white. He was perhaps seventy-seven or seventy-eight years old.

"Is it now?" he said, looking hard at her. "Your name is Barbara, isn't it?"

"Yes," Barbara said, oddly pleased that he would remember.

84

"What's this I read in the paper about bones in your folks' house?" he asked, his voice calm, even bantering.

"Yes, a skeleton," she said. "I saw it for myself last Tuesday. We believe it was my father's brother Anton, Tony." She watched his face intently, waiting for the reaction.

George Heim and his wife exchanged a slow glance, guarded, giving nothing away.

"You don't say now," George said, looking back at Barbara. "What makes you think that?"

"Fingers missing on the left hand," Barbara said. "You must remember his accident, when he was a boy?"

"Oh yes." George raised his shaggy eyebrows and gave a little nod. "I remember. But what was he doing in the basement all these years?"

"The sheriff said he may have been murdered," Barbara answered, again looking hard at the sharp old eyes.

"Really? Really now?" he said evenly. He didn't sound surprised, and his face remained impassive.

"The sheriff says someone hit him hard on the back of his head. Fractured his skull."

The old couple exchanged glances again.

"That's a real shame," Mrs. Heim said at last. "A shame for your family. What a thing to find out, so soon after your pa passed on."

"Yes, we're very disturbed about it," Barbara said, at a loss as to what to make of this imperturbable calm. George had actually bent over the generator again while his wife was speaking. "Mary Wenner was telling us yesterday some of the things that went on in the summer of 1943, just before my father enlisted. She said Uncle Tony was hanging around with some pretty tough characters on motorcycles, and she thought maybe one or more of them might have killed Tony. You know, after my dad went into the army."

"Oh, I don't see how that could be," Mrs. Heim started to say and then stopped abruptly, looking at her husband. Barbara glanced back at him just in time to see him looking away. It was obvious that he had sent his wife some kind of warning look.

"What do you mean?" Barbara said. "Why are you so sure that it couldn't have been those people?"

"I didn't say I was sure," Mrs. Heim said, fiddling with the pocket of her apron.

"You sounded sure," Barbara insisted.

"Well, I'm pretty sure," the old woman said, giving in. "Your pa made them guys stop coming around, and we never seen a one of them again after that. And that was before your pa went in the army."

"My father made Tony's friends go away?" Barbara asked. "When was that?"

"Early in August," Mrs. Heim said after a moment of wrinkled concentration.

"How can you be so sure of that?" Barbara said, her own high forehead lowering into a slight frown. "After all these years?"

"Well, we was there when it happened," she said emphatically, as if it offended her to have her memory called into question.

"You were where when what happened?" Barbara asked, looking back and forth between them.

"Well, maybe we should start at the beginning," the old woman said, turning now to her husband's averted face.

"Ya, I suppose we should," he sighed, facing around toward Barbara and straightening up to his full height again. "That whole summer, them damned cycles"—he pronounced it "sickles"—"would go roaring by here, cuz this road is the shortest way from the highway to your place. We had kids, some of 'em little, and those fools would go tearing past sixty, seventy miles an hour, not looking what they might run over, and the kids was curious, would go to the road to watch. It was a worry to us all the time." He still sounded angry about it.

"He tried to talk to Tony about it," Mrs. Heim said, with that curious country habit of avoiding her husband's name. Women of her generation didn't say "George" or even "my husband," but always "he" or "him," with the assurance that people would always know what "him" was meant. "But it didn't do no good. I think they tried harder to make a ruckus after that."

"Me and Mae here was driving home from a card party one night," George said. "We had that 1940 Ford then."

"That's why I remember when it was," Mae said. "Church card party for summer was always in early August, before everybody got busy making second-crop hay. Now, of course, that's earlier."

"Well, all of a sudden them cycles was all around us," George went on as if his wife hadn't spoken, "roaring their motors, and them fools screaming. This road was just gravel then and we nearly choked on the dust. They wouldn't pass nor drop back, just stayed in front and on both sides of us for a mile. There must have been six or eight a them. I couldn't even see if I was still on the road. I seen that one of them was Tony, though."

"What happened?" Barbara asked.

87

"They finally roared off," Mae said. "They had women riding with them, too, you know, on the backs of the bikes. Risking their lives like the fools they was."

"Well, that was just enough for me," George said, waving the pliers in front of him. "I just drove straight on over there after them. I was gonna have it out right then and there."

"He told me to stay in the car," Mae chimed in. "But I was not gonna let him go in there alone. By the time we got to the door, though, it was real quiet inside. It was just the screen door, being hot outside that time of year, so we could hear what was going on inside."

"And what was going on?" Barbara said, picturing the big kitchen just inside the back door where the Heims must have been standing.

"Your pa was talking," Mae said.

"Ya, we could see him, too," George went on, "leaning on the table with his fists and talking to Tony right in front of all those tough-looking fellas. 'You don't ever bring these people here again,' he says. 'This is our mother's house and you're bringing women like this into it.' He was white as a sheet and shaking, he was so mad, but he was dead calm while he was talking."

"He had quite a temper in those days," Mae said. "Of course, when he come home after the war, he was so changed, he never again raised his voice that anybody ever heard. We used to wonder what happened to him to make such a change."

"A temper?" Barbara said, stunned. "*My* father?"

"Well, now," George said, looking significantly at his wife, "most young men have tempers, don't they? Your pa's was no worse than any other, and he outgrew it real nice, didn't he?"

"Yes," Barbara responded automatically, still unable to absorb this revelation.

"Anyway," George went on, "whatever it was, and maybe it was the mention of their mother, a dear sweet lady she was, pity you never knew her, Tony made those toughs take their liquor and their women and clear out."

"We didn't see a one again, like I said," Mae finished. "It was real peaceful for a while, cuz even Tony's bike wasn't roaring around. We figured he just went into the city to carouse with those folks there."

After a pause, Barbara looked up at George and asked, "Did you know at the time that Tony had been seeing your sister?"

The old man's face stiffened; his eyes became flinty.

"Mary Wenner talks too much," he said, turning away from her.

"I'm sorry," Barbara said feebly. "This is all new to me right now. But I'm trying to find out what was going on that summer."

"Ain't no point in dredging it all up," he said shortly, reaching down into the machinery with the pliers.

"I wouldn't," Barbara said, "if there weren't a good reason. Somebody killed my uncle, Mr. Heim, and sooner or later, the sheriff is going to be asking you these same questions."

"Look," George said, turning to Barbara again and pointing at her with the pliers, "I always had a lot of respect for your pa. He was a good man. But Tony was a no-good, and that's all there is to say about it." And he went back to his work.

"How was he a no-good?" Barbara said, determined to keep the dialogue going, but also feeling a flash of anger at this criticism.

"From the time he was a kid," George said, his face still averted, "he was wild. He was hard drinking by the time he was sixteen. He got kicked out of school for setting a fire in a cloakroom. Burned up the winter coats of half the kids in the district. Just wild."

"Dad said he got that way after my grandpa's accident," Barbara said, feeling a strong need to defend and explain her uncle. "It must have been terrible for him to watch his father die that way when he couldn't save him, losing part of his hand trying to save him."

"Oh, right, right," George said, shaking his silver mane from side to side. "That's the version he wanted people to believe."

"Version?" Barbara repeated. "Are you saying my father lied?"

"Oh, not your pa," George said, exasperated. "Tony. Making himself sound like some sorta hero. He probably convinced Joe of it over the years. But I was there, working on the field crew."

"What are you trying to say?" Barbara said, stiff and flinty-eyed in her own right now.

"None a this is easy," George said, looking at Barbara with real sympathy in his eyes. "But, like you said, the sheriff is gonna be asking questions, so it'll all come out anyway. Your grandpa didn't die right off in that feed cutter. His arms jammed up the rollers and the belt popped off the pulley. He musta screamed, but the tractor was roaring real loud by then without the drag of the pulley on it, so nobody could hear him up at the house, and the rest of us was in the back twenty. When Tony seen his own hand, he ran away and hid. Do you hear what I'm saying to you? He didn't try to tell nobody, nor to get help for his pa, nor nothing. He hid."

"Try not to take it too hard," Mae said, catching sight of Barbara's face.

"When we come in with the next load," George went on, relentless now, "we found John, still alive, but just barely. He bled to death before we could get him out. I found Tony in the straw barn, crouching in a corner with his pocket handkerchief wrapped around his hand, looking like some chop-tailed cat you'd run over with the binder sometimes. He didn't say nothing, but I figured it out. He didn't lose his fingers trying to get his pa outta there. The rollers jammed when John's arms went in. No little fingers was gonna get nipped off after that. Tony fell into that feed cutter first and John went in after him, snatched him back after Tony's hand got caught and threw him free. By that time, it was too late for John to save himself—it was slippery in there. Corn is slippery you know. John saved that boy, and then Tony just ran away from him and let him die."

"How awful!" Barbara gasped. "Think how terrified he must have been. He just panicked. He was only twelve years old, and he was wounded himself in such an awful way."

"He was a coward," George Heim said flatly.

Barbara stared at him open-mouthed as if he'd struck her.

"I see," she said at last, her jaw setting. "He was suffering terrible guilt over his father's death, and then he had to face *that* from all of you. No wonder he went off the deep end."

"Hmp," George snorted and went back to his tinkering.

"Where was my father?" Barbara asked, looking at his broad back.

"Joe was laid up that time," he said without turning around. "He was getting over the rheumatic fever. Left him with his heart enlarged a little, I guess. That's why the army wouldn't take him the first time he tried to enlist. By the second time, they weren't so fussy no more, I guess. We didn't tell him about Tony. His ma knew, but I don't suppose that's a thing she would want to tell a kid. Maybe nobody ever told him."

"My father tried to enlist more than once?" Barbara was learning yet another new fact about the man she'd thought she knew so well.

"Ya, when he was about nineteen," George said. "Right after your grandma died."

There was a long pause now. Barbara struggled to regain her train of thought.

"You didn't answer me about Tony and your sister," she said finally, feeling relentless herself and a little angry with George Heim.

He turned his big head slowly to look at her.

"Caroline was only seven when our ma died," he said. "Pa was already gone three years by then, heart trouble on that side. Peter and me raised her by ourselves like she was our own kid. She was only eighteen when your pa started courting her. Peter didn't want her going out with nobody. He was always real protective of her, even overprotective, some would say. But I was older, married with kids of my own by then, so I stepped in and said she could go with Joe. I told Peter that Joe was a good boy and could be trusted. But Tony was a different story. He sneaked around after her, he oozed all that phony charm on her, and he—he—debauched her." It was clearly a word he had taken home from some Sunday sermon.

"Yes, I know," Barbara said quietly. "But I'm trying

to find out when you first knew that. Mary Wenner said there was lots of talk about it at some wedding in late August.''

''Oh, the gossips had a field day, I'm sure,'' Mae clucked.

''She told us on August 21st, a Saturday night,'' George said, as if he were reciting some date from a history lesson. ''Peter caught Tony sneaking her into the back of the house when we thought she was at the movies in Oshawanee with Joe.''

''Did she tell you she was pregnant then?'' Barbara asked.

Mae gasped and lifted her hand to her mouth, and George swung his head from side to side with his eyes shut.

''George,'' Mae said.

''Never mind,'' he growled. ''We never really thought it was a secret, did we? Small town, people are gonna talk.'' Then he looked straight at Barbara. ''She didn't know for sure, but she thought she was. Said we'd have to let her marry him.''

''Poor Peter,'' Mae said. ''He was just wild. I didn't know what we was gonna do with him.''

George gave her a long, dangerous look, and she fell silent.

''Why *didn't* you promote a marriage between them?'' Barbara asked. ''It's what's usually done, isn't it?''

''He would never a married her,'' George said emphatically. ''She just wouldn't believe that. But, more important, we would never a let that happen. Even if she'd a had the baby without no husband at all, we couldn't let her marry Tony Hoffman. Out of the question.''

"Why not?" Barbara asked, defiant again. "He might have settled down."

George Heim stared at her for a long moment.

"No chance," he said at last. "He didn't care nothing about Caroline. The only reason he kept after her was to get back at us because we knew what he was. It was like, I don't know, if he couldn't get respect from people, he would just take things from them, whatever he could grab."

Barbara remembered suddenly what her father had said about Caroline: "Tony only took her because he knew I wanted her." If Tony couldn't have his brother's respect. . . . She shook her head sharply.

"So you arranged a marriage with Mr. Bower," she said.

"He was a good man," George said. "Caroline was willing by that time, too. It's not like we forced her. Tony'd disappeared, and she naturally thought he'd run out on her."

"Naturally," Barbara said, pausing significantly. "I'd like to know the last time either of you can remember seeing Tony alive."

"It was that night," George said at once. "I never wanted to set eyes on him again. We didn't go out much for a while after that, either."

"I saw his motorcycle go past a few days later," Mae said. "I didn't tell him"—a nod at her husband—"or Peter about it."

"And you *never* saw him again?" Barbara asked, looking hard at the old man.

"Never," he said, carefully pronouncing both syllables and returning her look without a waver in his gaze.

"Did my father know about the pregnancy?" she said at last. "I mean before he went away."

Again the old couple exchanged a glance.

"We don't know what Joe knew or when he knew it," George said. He closed his mouth in a rigid line.

"You didn't see him before he left for the army?" Barbara asked.

"Listen here, young lady," George said firmly. "I'm tired of all your questions. Don't think I can't see what you're up to."

"George!" Mae said, shocked at this departure from decorum.

"Never you mind, Mae," he said. "I respected your father all his life, Barbara, like I said before. I couldn't be his friend after what passed between his family and mine, but I respected him, and I don't want to be rude to his girl. So this talk is at an end. Good day to you." And he turned back to the generator.

Mae Heim walked in silence next to Barbara as they recrossed the yard to the Volkswagen.

"Can *you* answer some of my questions, Mrs. Heim?" Barbara asked as she reached for the car door.

"No, no," Mrs. Heim said firmly, shaking her round head. "He wouldn't like it." And she tipped her head in the direction of the milk house.

"You must have felt very sorry for Caroline," Barbara said, trying a new tack. "Woman to woman, I mean."

"Well, yes," Mae said, looking nevertheless a little dubious. "But I agreed with the men." Then she put a pudgy hand on Barbara's arm. "You should give up on asking around about your uncle. There's things about him, other things, that you don't want to know."

"What things?" Barbara asked, leaning forward toward the old face.

"I said too much already," Mae Heim said. "Too much already." Then she marched up onto the porch and into the house.

Barbara sat down into her car and stared for a moment at the back of the house. As she turned the key in the ignition, the old dog struggled to his feet and began his roaring bark. Barbara could still hear it as the car rounded the house and turned out onto the road.

7

On her way to the Schneiders' farm, Barbara drove two extra miles to avoid passing in front of her old home. As she turned into the familiar driveway, it struck her that on most farmhouses, the front door was just for show. It faced the road and was often decoratively framed, but no path or walkway led up to it. The driveway almost always curved around to the back of the house so that people arriving by car—as most visitors did—would naturally use the more humble back door. It had been that way at Heims' and here was the pattern again. Of course, she reminded herself, her own childhood home had been arranged in exactly the same way. And now, as she thought about it, she remembered that even when country people walked to each other's houses, as they sometimes did if the two houses were within a half mile of each other, they would walk around to the back door before knocking or ringing the bell. Many farmhouses had no lights over their front doors, while the backyard was usually flooded with the brilliance of the yard lights that came on automatically at dusk.

She parked her car, wondering why or how this tradition had evolved. Was it that farmers wanted to turn a forbidding face to the outside world, while saving the homey back-door welcome for friends, neighbors, insiders? Or was it something more simple, a habit formed over many years because the principal pedestrian traffic on a farm was always between the house and the barns and sheds which were behind it. She smiled as she remembered her father using the back door to walk out along the driveway to the mailbox, when the trip would have been less than half as long if he had used the front door.

Rosa Schneider came to the screen door when Barbara knocked. She was a sweet-faced woman whose weak eyes looked perpetually surprised behind large, thick glasses. She wore her gray hair in the old-fashioned way, pulled back into a knot at the base of her neck, except for Mamie Eisenhower bangs. Like most of the women of her generation, she never wore anything but dresses—"good" dresses for the store and church, simple cotton dresses, like the one she was wearing now, for housework. In the days when she had worked outside, shocking up grain or driving a tractor, she had simply pulled a pair of her husband's overalls up over the dress, stuffing the skirt inside.

Now she squinted once at Barbara and then cried, "Barbie! Barbie Hoffman, you come right here." And she spread her arms for a hug. Barbara laughed as she folded Rosa in a warm embrace, thinking how easily she accepted her childhood name here in New Augsburg, when she would never allow any of her Chicago friends to call her "Barbie." Her father, she remembered, had sometimes even called her "Barbie doll," to tease her.

"Come in the kitchen and have some coffee," Rosa

said. German farmers always seemed to have pots of strong, hot coffee at the ready, no matter what the season. Barbara was so used to this tradition that she accepted a cup without thinking whether she might rather have a cold drink on such a warm June day.

"I'll tell Dick you're here," Rosa went on, after seating Barbara at the wide oak table. "You haven't seen him since Christmas, so you'll notice a change. But he's on the mend now. The doctor says no more of those awful treatments."

"Don't get him up if he's resting," Barbara said.

"Well, he's resting most of the time," Rosa said with a wan smile. "But he'd be real mad at me if I let him miss seeing you."

When Rosa came back into the kitchen a few minutes later, she said, "He'll be along in a minute. He's just as pleased as he can be that you came to see us." Then she sat down with her own cup of coffee and focused her earnest gaze on Barbara. "How is your mother taking to her move? Must be pretty hard on her."

"Well, you know my mother," Barbara answered. "She takes things in her stride, stays cheerful and busy, no matter what she may be feeling inside. She's thinking of buying a bicycle so she can go tooling around now that she's a 'townie.' "

"Yes, that's just like her," Rosa said, taking a sip of her coffee. "Still—and now this terrible business about those bones in her basement. I can't imagine having to think that something like that was under my house."

"I'm afraid it's even worse than you read in the paper," Barbara said. "Those bones were once my Uncle Tony, and the sheriff says he was murdered."

"Tony!" Rosa gasped, her eyes opening even wider.

99

"And murdered! That can't be right. How could anybody tell who it was? The paper said it was a skeleton."

"Well he had those fingers missing on his left hand," Barbara explained. "The back of the skull was struck with some heavy, narrow object."

"I can't believe it," Rosa said. "Did you hear?" directing her gaze past Barbara to the doorway behind her.

"Yes, I heard, I heard," a familiar voice said.

Barbara turned around in her chair to look. No amount of warning could have prepared her for the change in Dick Schneider's appearance. He had once been a robust, well-muscled man, spry for seventy, with a florid complexion and pale-blue eyes. The man who stood now in the doorway, huddled inside a maroon-colored bathrobe, was someone Barbara would not have recognized if she'd met him on the street. "Wasted" was the word that came into her mind. His skin, so pale it had almost a bluish cast to it, hung loosely on the big frame whose bones were clearly visible at the open collar and at the wrists. His head was completely without hair, not even eyebrows, and his face was so sunken that Barbara could see the outline of his teeth through his skin. The eyes above the hollowed cheeks glittered with that brightness so often evident in people who have borne pain for a long time. In his gaunt face, they looked immense and much darker than Barbara had remembered them.

"Dick," she said, standing up. All her growing-up years, Barbara had thought of this man as "Uncle Dick," but such titles were not easily accepted among people who reserved familiarity for blood kin. "How nice to see you."

"Now don't be scared by what you see," he laughed, for he had taken a good look at her face. "We've got this cancer thing on hold now and I'll be getting back to my old self in no time. Chemotherapy isn't good for the hair or for the appetite, but now Rosa is gonna fatten me up again." And he smiled at his wife, a sweet, tired smile. She had gone forward to hold a chair for him, and he sat down carefully, lowering himself by bracing his thin hands against the tabletop.

"Should I get you some juice?" Rosa said.

"No, no," he said quietly. "You sit down to your coffee." Then he turned his bright eyes onto Barbara. "So you're saying Tony Hoffman has been dead all these years when we all thought he was in the Foreign Legion."

"That's what it looks like," Barbara answered.

"Folks always said he must have gone off and died in the war," Rosa said. "But Dick never thought so."

"Didn't you?" Barbara asked him. "Dad never did either."

"I didn't think he was the army type, that's all," Dick shrugged.

"I knew so little about him," Barbara said. "Dad never had much to say about his life before the war. Ever since we first thought it might be Tony's body in the cistern, I've been trying to find out about him. You lived so near him all his life, you must have known him pretty well."

Again, Barbara saw two long-married people exchange a look which seemed to speak volumes, a look that asked, "How much should we tell her?" Then Dick Schneider looked down at his emaciated hands.

"Well, Barbie," Rosa began. "We always knew your dad better of the two boys. Joe was such an easy person to like. Of course, you know that." She fell silent and looked at her husband.

"Look," Barbara sighed. "I already know that Uncle

101

Tony wasn't very popular, that he was wild and sometimes drank too much. And I know that he got Caroline Heim pregnant while she was supposed to be going with my father.''

"Well, well," Dick said. "You *have* been busy finding things out."

"What I'm trying to focus on is that last summer before Tony disappeared, the summer of 1943. Maybe if we can piece together the events of that summer, we can figure out how he died, who killed him."

Again, the old people looked at each other, as if trying to decide which one of them should speak.

"That was so long ago, Barbie," Dick said softly. "Whoever did it might be a long-time dead."

"I know that," Barbara said. "I'm just trying to understand, that's all. I don't have a lot of family, you know, that I can just shrug off my uncle's murder."

"What do you want to know?" Rosa asked, putting her hand onto Barbara's arm.

"Well, Mary Wenner thinks he was killed by those tough guys from Green Bay, the ones on the motorcycles, but Mrs. George Heim tells me that Dad made Tony get rid of them in early August. The Heims also told me they found out about Caroline's pregnancy in late August, and Mrs. Heim let it slip that the younger brother, Peter, was crazy with rage at Tony."

"I can believe it," Rosa interrupted. "That man was fierce about Caroline. He spoiled her when she was a child and then hovered over her like a guard dog when she was a teenager. I'm not surprised she kicked over the traces. If you ask me, there was something abnormal in the attachment Peter had to that girl."

"Do you mean incest?" Barbara asked.

Rosa's eyes became even more enormous behind the thick lenses.

"Lord, no!" she cried. "What a thing to say! Do you get those ideas in college? I just mean that he was too preoccupied with her, with keeping boys away from her, that's all. Gracious!" She huffed a little and fell silent. Barbara thought it was best not to talk about the symptoms of latent incestuous feelings in front of Rosa.

"Did you know about her seeing Tony, about the pregnancy?" Barbara asked.

"Not at the time," Rosa said. "I mean, we heard she'd been sneaking around with Tony, but we didn't know she was going to have a baby until after she'd had it. Quite a while after. Mary Wenner told us it was a boy, and 'very early, if you know what I mean.' " Rosa did a perfect imitation of Mary's confidential whisper.

"Do you think Peter Heim could have been angry enough to kill Tony after he found out?" Barbara said, looking hard at Dick.

"No, no, of course not," Dick said. Suddenly a look passed over his face that made both women sit forward on their chairs. If possible, he looked even more pale.

"Is it pain, Dick?" Rosa said, her face almost as stricken as his.

"No," he whispered. "Just a bit of the nausea. But you know the doctor said we could expect that for a while yet. It gets less every day."

Then he looked back at Barbara, folding his thin hands on the table in front of him.

"If Peter Heim was going to bash in Tony's head, he would have done it as soon as he found out his sister was going to have a baby. Well, you said that was in late

August, but we saw Tony after that. He showed up at the Rendezvous kermiss, and that's always the first weekend in September.''

"But just suppose," Barbara said, leaning toward him, "that Caroline tried to sneak out to see Tony after that night when her brothers learned she was pregnant, just bided her time until they stopped being so watchful. She thought Tony would marry her, George Heim said. This would have been after my father enlisted. Peter might have noticed her gone and followed her over there. If he actually caught them together, he might have gone a little crazy and killed Tony. Because George insisted they would never have let Tony marry her.''

"You got a rich imagination," Dick chuckled.

"Well, I don't know about that," Barbara said, a little miffed that he should take this attitude toward the theory she had been working out on her drive over. "Mrs. Heim let it slip that Peter was 'just wild' when he found out about Caroline's baby. Those were her exact words, and George just looked daggers at her to make her keep quiet. What if George *knows* that Peter killed Tony and doesn't want anybody to put the pieces together?''

"Now look, Barbie," Dick said. "I've known the Heim family as long as I've known your family and I don't think for a minute that either of those boys would do any such a thing. They might beat a man up with their fists if they thought he deserved it, but they would own up to it, maybe even brag about it. They wouldn't kill somebody and hide the body.''

"Well, maybe Peter didn't mean to kill him," Barbara said. "Maybe he just grabbed a poker and started swinging.''

"Poker?" Dick said, looking up at her with his glittering eyes.

"Well, the sheriff said the murder weapon might have been a poker," Barbara explained. "There was a wood-burning range in the kitchen then, so there must have been pokers."

"Well," Dick snorted, "pokers or no pokers, don't go around making up wild stories about good people like the Heims."

Barbara took a long swallow of the tar-black coffee. This was what the sheriff was going to be up against, she realized, this stonewalling from people who had lived next to each other for three generations and whose unspoken code was "protect your own." Only it would be even worse for Paul Gillis, because everyone would regard him as an outsider—a nice boy, but not "one of us."

"When do you remember seeing Tony last?" she said finally.

Again Dick and Rosa exchanged a glance, this time a simple and open quizzical look.

"I believe it was at that Rendezvous kermiss," Rosa said. "I don't remember seeing him after that. And pretty soon, people were saying he'd joined up, too, like your dad."

"Why do you remember that kermiss so clearly?" Barbara asked, looking back at Dick. "And why did you say Tony 'showed up' there?"

Dick was silent for a moment, tugging at the sleeves of his robe.

"Well, Tony always showed up where there was drink to be had," he said. "But I had another reason to remember. There was sort of a scene."

"A scene?" Barbara asked.

"Yes. There were already some rumors about Caroline and Tony. About his having been hanging around her, I

105

mean, not about any baby. Well, Tony came strutting in big as you please, like he wanted to have people whisper about him and point. Your dad came in later, went straight up to Tony, and started talking to him. Well, yelling at him, really. Telling him to come outside because he wanted to say something to him. But Tony wouldn't budge. 'Just say what you want to say right here,' Tony says. 'In front of all our friends.' Your dad finally just ran out.''

"Was it about Caroline?" Barbara asked, feeling again the cold fear she had first experienced on Saturday.

Again Rosa and Dick looked across the expanse of oak table at each other.

"Sure it was," Dick said. "When we got home, we found Joe waiting for us here." And he gestured at the other side of the table. Barbara could easily believe that the Schneiders would have left their doors unlocked and that her father would have felt it was all right just to walk in and wait for them to come home.

"He said he'd been trying to see Caroline for two weeks," Rosa chimed in. "But George and Peter just kept running him off the place, no explanations. He'd heard some of the rumors but wouldn't listen to them. You know, he always hated gossip, even as a boy.''

"But that night, Peter just told him straight out about Caroline sneaking around with Tony all summer," Dick said. "Not about the baby, though. They were determined to keep that a secret, I guess. So he came to the kermiss to ask Tony about stealing the girl away from him.''

"Did Tony confirm it?" Barbara said.

"No, but Joe knew by the way Tony was acting," Rosa said. "He was cut up something terrible about it, just crying and mad all at the same time. He really cared about her, I think. I know it's hard to believe when you look at those big, clutzy Heim boys, but Caroline was a beauty in those days, all blonde and pink and slim like a colt. It wasn't hard to believe that young men would lose their heads over her.''

"What did he say he was going to do?'' Barbara said, her lips feeling a little numb.

"He said he was going to try to see Caroline herself,'' Rosa went on. "To hear her tell him herself that she didn't want him anymore. And if she didn't want him, he was gonna enlist, just *make* the army take him.''

"And did he see her?''

"We don't know,'' Dick said. "But I guess so, because he enlisted. He was gone the next week.''

"Yes,'' Barbara said. "Gone for six years. And you're sure you didn't see Tony again after that?''

"I don't believe we did,'' Rosa said distractedly. She was looking at her husband's face, obviously attuned to every nuance in that ravaged countenance. "You're feeling sick at your stomach again, aren't you?'' she said. "Maybe you'd better lay down for a while.''

"Sure,'' he said, and his breath sounded strained. "Maybe I should.''

Rosa helped him from the room after he and Barbara had exchanged farewells. When Rosa came back, Barbara had rinsed the coffee mugs in the sink and was waiting with her purse in her hand. Rosa walked with her onto the back porch.

"We got no fields planted this year,'' Rosa said, looking out over the farm. "The boys came from the city last year to help, but this year, it's just too much for Dick. I think pretty soon we'll be selling out the way your mother did. Time was, a man's sons took over the farm, but nowadays—well, I don't know."

"Rosa," Barbara said from the second porch step, "when Dad went into the army and Tony disappeared, you began to use the fields for extra crops."

"Sure," Rosa said. "Dick said it would be a sin to let the fields run to seed just because Tony ran off and left them."

"Did anybody go into the house that you know of?" Barbara was thinking of the smell the sheriff had mentioned.

"Oh, no," Rosa Schneider said. "Houses are different. Private. After a few years, when kids started hanging around there, breaking windows, I told Dick we should do something, take care of the house. I was willing to keep it clean inside even, but Dick said I had a house of my own to take care of and he wouldn't let me overdo."

Barbara was silent for a moment. Then she looked back at Mrs. Schneider's kind face.

"Mrs. Heim told me it was a mistake for me to ask questions about Uncle Tony. What do you think about that?"

"Well, Barbie," Rosa sighed. "Some things are better left in the past. Only heartaches in digging them up."

"Mae Heim said there were 'other things' about Tony that I wouldn't want to know. What could she have meant?"

Rosa squinted into the late afternoon sun, her surprised eyes gone vague and a little distant for a moment.

"Oh, who knows?" she shrugged finally. "Folks said Tony had women in the city. You know, prostitutes. Mae Heim would probably think that was too shocking for any family to find out about one of its own."

"Well, thank you for the coffee," Barbara said, stepping down onto the graveled driveway.

"Don't you be a stranger now, Barbie," Rosa said. "When Dick is better, he'll be good company again. Bring your mother out."

8

On the drive back to the village, Barbara couldn't stop thinking about the confrontation between her father and his brother at that long-ago dance, the younger brother, sober and plain, bringing his painful questions to that good-looking older brother whose drunken posturing was obvious to everyone who looked at him—who already had a reputation for drinking while he was still in his teens.

Barbara was seeing for the first time the background behind one of Joe Hoffman's lifelong habits. In her memory, her father never drank, not even beer. He didn't make a large issue of it, didn't complain when Eileen bought wine for Christmas or Thanksgiving, was willing to serve beer to friends who came over to play cards. But he always poured soda for himself, or asked for ice water if he were a guest in someone else's home. Among the good Germans of New Augsburg, such abstinence was unusual, even peculiar, and it was only the respect that neighbors had for Joseph Hoffman that made them refrain from comment.

As the Volkswagen chugged along, Barbara found herself remembering Smeltzer's tavern and an incident that had happened there when she was about eight years old. She'd gone with her father into the village to find Arnie Rueckl, a neighbor whose hay baler they needed to borrow. Mrs. Rueckl had said they would be most likely to find him at the tavern, and sure enough, there was Arnie's Ford pickup among the other local cars in the parking lot.

While her father talked to Arnie, refusing the offer of a beer, Barbara wandered over to a corner table where three men were playing cards.

"Well, Barbie," one of them said, looking up as she approached. "Look at you. Does your pa put you into those overalls so you can help around the barn?" It was Earl Mueller, the father of one of her classmates.

"I help a lot," Barbara said shyly.

"Well, I'm sure you do," Mr. Mueller said. "And now you come in here to wet your whistle, right?"

"Daddy's talking to Arnie Rueckl," she said, gesturing lamely behind herself because she was uncertain what was meant by "wet your whistle."

"Well, he ain't had time to buy you a drink then," Mr. Mueller said, winking at the other men. "Here, you can have some of mine." And he held up the half-empty glass toward her.

Barbara had never tasted beer and had a real curiosity about it. A newly poured glass of beer always reminded her of lemon meringue pie—that white foam atop the clear yellow liquid. What did it taste like? Was it sweet and sour all at once like the pie? Mr. Mueller was offering her the beer, holding it out toward her. She lifted her hand toward the glass.

"Barbara!" The voice was right behind her, and its uncharacteristic tone made her jump and cringe all at the

111

same time. She turned to see her father looking down at Earl Mueller with an expression she'd never seen before—hard lines around his mouth, his gray eyes steely. He pulled her against his side, but he didn't speak, didn't look at her, just kept staring at Earl Mueller.

"It's only a little beer, Joe," Mr. Mueller said, but he looked sheepish, even a little scared.

"It starts with a little, Earl," her father answered, hardly moving his lips to speak. "Don't give beer to my girl."

"Whatever you say, Joe," Mr. Mueller said, and he looked away from the fierce eyes.

All the way home in the truck, her father said nothing, just stared over the steering wheel, and Barbara had felt obscurely frightened, as if she'd done something bad and had lost some of her father's love. But he didn't ever talk about it to her. And she hadn't tasted beer until she was in college.

Now as Barbara pulled into the parking lot behind her mother's apartment building, she realized for the first time that her father had feared drink, had determined to keep it from scarring his family any more than it already had. Drunkenness was Tony, and Tony was irresponsible, sneering, disloyal.

That night in her room, Barbara took out the picture of her uncle and leaned it up against the wall at the back of the desk. Did those eyes look mean, not just mischievous as she used to think? Was that smile really a sneer? Well, she thought, shades of the *Picture of Dorian Gray*! But it wasn't the picture that had changed, she knew; it was the eyes looking at the picture. But surely an eighteen-year-old girl, overprotected by ferocious brothers, would have found that face irresistible if she had been intent on breaking out. Joe Hoffman didn't look like adventure, but Tony Hoffman certainly did. Barbara tipped the photograph face down and got into bed. Sleep eluded her for a long time, though.

She kept revolving in her mind all the stories she'd now heard about the uncle who had been so strangely mysterious to her for most of her life. Those horrible details of how her grandfather had died! And Tony having to live with the shame of his own behavior, being reminded of it every time he lifted his hand into his own line of vision. Had he been reminded of it every time he saw the Heims? Had he seen or imagined contempt in their eyes? That might have been half the reason he set out to "debauch" their sister. Drinking and whoring and running around with outsiders—all futile attempts to blot out the picture of his father's agony and his own panic. And all of it making him more and more an outsider among his own kind, making him more defiant, more disposed to shock and outrage the people whose respect he had so irrevocably lost when he was only twelve years old.

Barbara put side by side in her mind the bits of information she had learned about the Heim brothers. Mary Wenner had said that George and Peter "put a stop" to Caroline seeing Tony. And George didn't want Mae to discredit Mary's theory of the motorcycle gang as the killers. Was that because it would have been more convenient if everyone believed so simple a version of what had happened? Mrs. Heim had particularly remembered Peter's outrage over Caroline's suspected pregnancy. And poor Rosa, even in her innocence, had seen "something abnormal" in Peter's attachment to his sister. George Heim was hiding something, Barbara felt sure,

113

holding back some important information and warning his wife with his eyes not to let it out. Was August 21st really their last contact with Tony?

Even while she focused hard on the Heims, Barbara found other details creeping irresistibly into her mind: Mae Heim saying that her father "had quite a temper in those days," and George trying to play down her remark; Rosa Schneider remarking that her father was "cut up something terrible" about Caroline's infidelity, that he had "really cared about" a girl so beautiful that Rosa could understand why "young men would lose their heads over her"; Dick Schneider reporting that her father had yelled at Tony in a public place; Mae Heim wondering "what happened to him to make such a change" when her father next appeared in New Augsburg; her own mother recalling the words "Tony only took her because he knew I wanted her" in a tone suggesting that "it was all over and done with."

Barbara had often wondered where her own quick temper came from. Her mother was spirited but not volatile, and her father, she had always believed, was the very model of patience. Violence was not something she could connect with him in any way. And yet—yet. In 1943, he had been a man of twenty-two, in love with "a beauty," bedeviled by a reckless brother whose taste for loose women he knew well—he had driven some of them out of his mother's house. How would he feel when he learned that this brother had deliberately and cynically seduced the young girl he loved?

Though she tried to fight it away from her consciousness, Barbara found herself remembering the weekend in Minnesota when Tom had told her about Debbie Sanders. By July of that year, she had begun to wonder if her marriage could be salvaged, if she should make a concerted effort to get dialogue started again. The initial agony over Andrew's death had abated a little, and she had begun to think that there would be a day, not yet but someday, when she might like to have another child. So she was both mildly surprised and rather pleased when Tom suggested a getaway weekend at his uncle's cabin in Minnesota, a rustic retreat, as Tom called it, on an isolated lake. He had spent a bit of each summer there when he was a boy. "It will be just the two of us," he had said, and Barbara began to hope that his recent aloofness was only in her imagination. They could talk at last, she thought, and it would be the start of a return to intimacy.

The cabin had been another pleasant surprise, built of red cedar with a big fieldstone fireplace. Barbara had spent the Friday evening of their arrival stashing the food they'd brought and making up the bedroom. Tom built a fire and unpacked the luggage. When they at last settled down over a bottle of pinot noir, she was sure that the time had come to speak. And so it had. Haltingly at first, and then in a rush of words, he told her that he had been sleeping with his graduate assistant for more than six months.

"I don't know what to do about it," he had said, many times. "I hate the sneaking around, but I just don't know what to do."

At first, Barbara had just sat there with her wine glass tipped slightly forward in her hand, thinking dully, "This is not possible. This cannot be happening." Then suddenly she felt as if her head were on fire, as if the liquid in her eyes were not tears, but blood. She stood up, spilling the wine onto the Navajo rug in front of the fireplace.

"You son of a bitch," she said to him through her

115

teeth. "You miserable—lying—cheating—fucker!" She found that she was scarcely able to breathe.

Tom stood up and tried to touch her. She sprang away from him and ran, out the door and past the car to the dirt road that curved away from the lake. Tom followed, tried to catch her, but he was no match for her conditioning. Eventually she could hear only the sounds of her own feet on the road. She ran until she couldn't anymore, and then she walked, for a long time, through the trees, along winding trails, oblivious to where she was going or whether she would be able to find her way back. Finally she came out at the shore again and realized that she had almost circled the lake.

She dropped down exhausted into the sand. She didn't cry. When she stopped shaking, she found herself unable to keep her mind away from graphic images of Tom making love to Debbie—she remembered having met the girl at the department Christmas party, so she could easily imagine how that pale, somewhat overripe body would look without clothes. All of the things she herself had enjoyed in lovemaking—Tom's mouth on her breasts, the way he stroked the insides of her thighs, the sighing sound he made just before he came—all of these things she now saw in her mind as happening with Debbie. The pain in her chest was so searing that she was half afraid that she might be having a heart attack.

She began to talk out loud and she found that what she was saying didn't even shock her. She pulled herself up and paced while she talked.

"I'm going to kill him. That son of a bitch is not going to do this to me and live. He will never see little Debbie Whore again. Those lights over there are the cabin. If I walk in the sand, he'll never hear me coming up. He'll be watching the road anyway. Or I could just wait until he falls asleep. He's probably asleep already. A lot he cares about me! I could hit him with a log. Or a knife, a knife would be better. The kitchen has that whole set of knives.''

She paused in her pacing and thought for a minute.

"I could say I drove into the village for beer. We passed that bar on the main street. I could even go there afterwards because no one would really be able to tell which happened first. And then I could just say I came back and found my husband dead, some crazy, probably, prowling around these isolated cabins looking for rich tourists.''

She fell silent and began to work out details in her mind, all the while feeling the burning in her chest, the fire in her head. Eventually, somewhere near the middle of the night, she began to walk. It took her almost half an hour to reach the cabin, where she crept to a side window and peered inside. The lights were on and the fire had burned down to nothing, but Tom was not there. She circled the cabin stealthily and then stopped short. The car was gone. Tom was gone.

She waited inside, holding a steak knife in her hand, but he didn't come back. Finally, she just dropped the knife on the floor and sat down at the edge of the sofa. When she heard the car, it was almost dawn.

Tom had stood in the doorway shouting, ''Where the hell have you been? I was sick with worry. The police are looking for you.''

She had not spoken at first, but finally stood up and said, ''I'm going to pack. When we get back to Chicago, I'm going to get a lawyer. Will lawyers take new clients on a Saturday, do you think?''

The memory of that night could still make her shake, lying here in her old bed in New Augsburg. She was not certain even now what she would have done if she'd found Tom in the cabin when she sneaked up to it in the middle of the night. So what about her father? Had he left the Schneiders that night in early September of 1943 and allowed himself to imagine Tony and Caroline together?

She shook her head back and forth on the pillow and discovered that she was shaking tears out of her eyes. No, no, she told herself fiercely, just as she'd been doing ever since she had first thought of her father as a suspect. It couldn't be possible. Joseph Hoffman was a wonderful, gentle, good-hearted man. He couldn't have murdered his own brother. Hadn't he said that he pitied Tony, that he knew Tony's life had been spoiled by their father's death? No, what he'd done was what he'd told the Schneiders he was going to do. He had seen Caroline and heard from her own mouth that it was Tony she wanted, and then he had enlisted in the army, determined to put his life in New Augsburg behind him.

Barbara nodded firmly and turned over onto her side, but another thought came unbidden into her mind. No one had seen Tony Hoffman alive after Joe Hoffman left New Augsburg in early September—not the Wenners, not the Heims, not the Schneiders. Nobody.

9

When Sheriff Paul Gillis called the next morning at 10:15, Barbara answered the phone because Eileen was cleaning some strawberries that a neighbor had dropped off before breakfast.

"Looks like the bones are definitely your uncle," he said.

"Oh? Why?" Barbara asked, not particularly surprised, so sure had she become that the skeleton could not possibly be anyone else.

"Your Dr. DeWane found Anton Hoffman's dental records, and I picked them up yesterday afternoon. The medical examiner tells me that the four fillings match, and there were three wisdom teeth pulled; the fourth one never developed. So it's your uncle, all right, about 99 percent certain."

"Thank you for letting us know," Barbara said.

"You can tell your mother that it'll be all right to pick him up anytime," he said.

"Pick him up?" Barbara asked.

"Your mother talked about burying him. The M.E. is finished with the tests, so there's no reason to delay that."

"Oh, yes," Barbara said. "I suppose we'll send someone. As soon as possible. Thank you."

When she hung up, she found Eileen looking up at her over the strawberries with a little frown between her blue eyes.

"How soon can Father Hodeck make room for Tony's bones?" Barbara said, and even she could hear the cynical edge in her voice.

"Any time we say," Eileen said, pushing a stray wisp of gray hair aside with the back of her hand. "Is something wrong with you, Barbara?"

"Nothing," Barbara said. "I didn't have my run yesterday and I'm feeling antsy, that's all."

That afternoon, Eileen climbed aboard her new bicycle and rode alongside as Barbara ran north out of the village toward the old stone quarry where she had often gone swimming as a teenager. After two miles, Eileen turned back toward town with a wave and a smile, and Barbara kept on at her accustomed pace. She wanted very much to get to the stage where her mind felt washed clean, where she wouldn't have to think about how betrayal and rage can lead to violence.

But this was different from her long runs in Chicago. There, the city sounds and smells seemed neutral to her, just so much background that could be "whited out" because it held no strong associations for her, had no power to evoke memories and disturbing emotions. Here in the countryside around New Augsburg, though, almost everything seemed to conspire to distract her, to postpone her "runner's click." Most of the area farmers were in the process of taking in first-crop hay, and the sweet, heavy smell of new-mown hay was everywhere, reminding her of the harvests of her childhood, driving the tractor while her father stacked hay bales into neat rows on the wagons. In the quiet of a warm afternoon, it was impossible not to hear the high, trilling song of the meadowlarks, a sound that had brought tears streaming down her face the first time she'd heard it last summer, the first summer visit to New Augsburg after her father's death. There were no meadowlarks in Chicago. Their song was the grace note which said "home."

She had put a baby meadowlark in a cage on the back porch the summer she was ten, but her father had warned her that the bird would die if it remained caged. "Listen," he had said to her when the fields echoed with the sweet song. "They're calling to him. You'd better let him go to his mama." He had walked with her to the field where she'd first found the bird, and then he carried the empty cage back home again. At what price, she wondered now as her feet pounded against the wild grasses along the side of the road, at what price had he bought that unusual sensitivity to life, to even the smallest life?

That night, Barbara decided to do what she could to keep the speculations of the night before out of her head. She watched television until well after Eileen had gone to bed, and then she carried a small plate of cheese and crackers and a new novel up to the back bedroom. Propping the pillows up against the familiar old headboard, she settled down to read herself to sleep. Outside, clouds were gathering for what the evening news had predicted would be a "soaking rain" by early morning. A moderate breeze was making the curtains drift in and out with an almost hypnotic rhythm. Barbara fell asleep about 1:30 with the book against her breast and the reading lamp shedding its halo of light onto her pillows.

The sound that woke her was a muffled thudding noise,

121

rhythmic, but slow, enough to send a tremor through the headboard and pillows and into her shoulders, which were still propped in a near-sitting position. When she opened her eyes, she found that she already felt afraid, and it was more than the momentary feeling of strangeness that comes from waking in an unfamiliar room. She held her breath, listening. Again the soft thudding sound sent a shiver into her back. Something was knocking softly against the side of the house, not at ground level, but nearer to her body, on the wall with the headboard against it.

Barbara slid her legs slowly out from beneath the covers; she was not yet fully awake but was moving with an almost instinctive caution. As she sat up straight and looked toward the window next to her head, she saw the top of a ladder sticking up past the outside windowsill. And through the screen she could see clearly the slight rocking motion which produced the soft thud. Someone was on the ladder, climbing. She sprang up in one convulsive motion, her brain suddenly very awake, and her cry was as corny, as idiotic, as every grade B movie heroine in distress she had ever seen.

"Who's there?" she called out, at the same time realizing how absurd the question was. What intruder on a ladder would answer such a cry?

The motion of the ladder stopped and for a frozen moment nothing happened. Then the ladder began to shake with a rapid, jerky motion, and Barbara could actually hear movement outside, too, a body flailing around now that caution had been suddenly abandoned. Whoever it was had begun to climb back down. She could hear the desperate movement receding below her, and it gave her instant confidence. She stepped to the window and, with her forehead pressed against the screen, looked down. The ladder had only a very shallow pitch, so Barbara found herself looking almost straight down at the top of a white cap, and beneath it, a shadowy bulk which swayed dangerously in its haste to be gone. At the last few rungs, the climber jumped free of the ladder. Barbara heard the sound of sharply exhaled breath as feet and knees absorbed the shock of impact with the ground. Then the shadowy figure straightened and moved up against the outside wall so Barbara could no longer see it.

Even as she turned to leave the room, Barbara thought how resourceful this would-be intruder must be to overcome panic enough to prevent himself from running in the open where she might get a good look at him. A sprint across the parking lot would have given her some idea of general size and shape, despite the cloudy night. She had expected it, had waited at the window to get a better chance at a description. Her rush of adrenaline had produced, not a flight response, but anger, an urge to identify anyone who would dare to violate her room.

In the hallway, Barbara thought suddenly that the intruder might have a car somewhere at the front of the building—how would he have carried a ladder otherwise?—and she realized that she might see him from her mother's bedroom window. The door to Eileen's room was open, and Barbara ran through it without further hesitation. Before she could cross the room, however, she saw that the big double bed was empty. Her mother was not there. Barbara stopped short, unable for a few seconds to absorb this fact.

"Mother?" she whispered. "Mother?"

Now panic replaced aggression. She could feel her scalp beginning to tingle, a little wave of dizziness passing over her brain. After turning around in the middle of the bedroom, almost as if she expected to see Eileen materialize in some corner, she ran back into the short hallway and said softly, "Mother?" in the direction of the open bathroom door. At the head of the stairs, she called downward, "Mum? Are you down there?" Only silence, the profound silence of small country towns in the middle of the night, was her answer.

She could tell she was starting to hyperventilate, had to fight to keep herself from gulping air. She tiptoed down the stairs, her thin summer nightgown brushing against the calves of her legs. In the darkened dining room, she paused to call, "Mum? Are you here?" but she couldn't seem to make her voice rise to anything like a normal tone.

The apartment was so small that it took only a few more steps to confirm that Eileen was not in the house. Barbara's imagination began immediately to manufacture images of her mother's small body crumpled in the yard outside, the victim of some horrible, bloody crime. She wanted to reach for the telephone, to summon help, but the feeling that her mother might need her, might require immediate attention, drove Barbara across the kitchen to the back door. She had never heard running footsteps, she now realized. The climber might be waiting outside the door. But her mother was missing, might be a hostage. She *had* to act. She pulled the door open and stepped out onto the tiny porch all in one motion.

The white gravel of the parking lot seemed almost to glow with a dull light in contrast to the darkened lawn and cloudy sky beyond it. The cars sat in a neat row, any one of them a potential hiding place, for no one in New Augsburg ever locked a car. Two short steps brought Barbara to the edge of the porch so that she could peek along the back wall of the building. There was the ladder, stretching up to her window, its lower legs planted just outside the flower bed. In the other direction, the outside wall ran away past the three other darkened apartments. The only light was from the reading lamp in Barbara's bedroom, and the only sound was her own labored breathing.

When Barbara turned her head back toward the direction of the ladder, she saw a white shape float free of the outside corner of the building, exactly as if a cartoon ghost had suddenly appeared and begun to move toward her. When she made a muffled screaming sound, Barbara heard an almost simultaneous scream from the direction of the apparition.

"Barbara?" a voice whispered.

"Mother?" Barbara said, and then ran down the two steps to embrace Eileen's shivering body. Both of them began to talk at once: "What is going on? Where were you? Did you see who it was?" Finally Eileen called a halt. "Inside," she said. "Let's talk in the house."

Inside the kitchen, Eileen slid the chain onto the door and then switched on the light. In her billowing nightgown, with her little hand over her heart, she looked like someone out of a storybook, the startled queen.

"Let's sit down," she said. "I'm feeling just a little faint."

"Me, too," Barbara said, and they sat down at the counter next to each other, hanging on for a moment to each other's hands.

"I was just going into the bathroom," Eileen began, "when I heard a thump of some sort, as if someone had chucked something against the back of the building. I tried to look out the bathroom window, but it's so high, I couldn't see much. But when I looked sideways, I could see the ladder."

"Where did you go?" Barbara said, her voice still having the slightly aggrieved tone of a frightened child.

"Well, I peeked into your room and saw you asleep," Eileen went on. "So I crept downstairs with the intention of getting a look at who it might be. When I got to the back door here, I heard a commotion outside and then someone running. I raced through the house to the front door to see if I could spot him, but there was no one out there, so I thought he might be hiding out back somewhere."

"So you came around the building on the outside?" Barbara gasped. "Are you crazy? What if someone *had* been hiding? You could have been hurt—or worse."

"Well, it's over now, Barbara," Eileen said dismissively. "Did you get a good look at him?"

"No," Barbara sighed. "Just a shape. And a cap. White. Something like a painter's cap."

"Well," Eileen said briskly. "We have to call Ed Granger."

Ed Granger was New Augsburg's only policeman, a sixty-year-old retired farmer who got a kick out of running around in a police car, and whose chief duty was to see that the taverns closed on time. If anything serious came up, such as the time when Alvin Dart threatened his family with a loaded rifle, he called in the county sheriff. It was rumored that he had never taken his gun out of its holster, and some locals doubted that the gun was loaded anyway. When Ed arrived, looking sleepy and a little disgruntled at being hauled out of bed at 3 A.M., Barbara and Eileen had donned robes and were drinking some strong tea. He made a circuit of the building, pointed a flashlight into all of the cars and the utility shed, and took down the ladder.

"I think the ladder belongs here," he said after he had joined the women in the kitchen.

"Belongs here?" Barbara said.

"Yeah. I think your intruder got it out of the utility shed back there. There's a set of hooks in the wall that look pretty much like they should have a ladder hanging on 'em. I gotta talk to Matt Krieger about keeping that shed locked." Matthew Krieger owned the apartment buildings, the grain mill, and the local bowling alleys.

"What are you going to do?" Barbara asked. "About the intruder?"

"Nothing much I can do," Ed shrugged. "No damage to the building. Nothing else out of place. You just lock your doors. You'll be all right."

Barbara was appalled by this casual attitude, but Eileen was more sanguine, offering the man some tea before he left, walking him to the front door when he refused.

"I don't think it helps to get so upset," Eileen said after Barbara had fulminated for a few minutes about the laxity of small-town law enforcement. "Let's try to get some sleep. You can come in with me, if you'd like."

Barbara accepted the offer gratefully. She hadn't often invaded her parents' bed in her childhood. Even in thunderstorms, she had remained bravely in her own room until a loud crack would sometimes send her sprinting down the hallway. Now she settled down in the big bed and lay awake, staring at the ceiling for a long time after Eileen's regular breathing indicated that she was fast asleep. When the promised rain began pattering against the house at 4:30, Barbara was still thinking.

Her uncle's body had been found after more than forty years, and four days had passed since that information had been given to Mary Wenner, plenty of time for the news to spread through a big part of the township. Yesterday she had begun her own investigation into Tony's death. Both the Heims and the Schneiders knew that she was trying to learn who might have murdered her uncle. There was no telling how many people they might have since mentioned it to. And tonight someone had tried to break into her room. Could that be just a coincidence? Or was someone trying to frighten her, to discourage her from further questions about the summer of 1943. Or maybe even to stop her, permanently, from asking more questions?

Oddly, the thought that someone might be trying to kill her didn't fill Barbara with horror; it made her almost smile with relief. If someone wanted her to stop investigating, that must mean that Tony's killer was still alive, that Tony Hoffman's killer could not possibly be Joe Hoffman. Last night, she had almost decided to do what she could to deflect Paul Gillis from beginning an investigation. Now she thought she would call him in the morning, tell him what she knew about the Heims' grudge against Tony, and what she believed about the intruder. Surely someone as obviously bright as Paul would see the connection and wouldn't simply shrug it off the way Ed Granger had done. As the rain made its gentle, drumming sounds, Barbara smiled with renewed purpose, yawned twice, and fell into a deep sleep.

10

Paul Gillis came by in the early afternoon, hatless as always, and looking a bit more rumpled than usual. It had stopped raining but was still overcast, hot and humid, not the kind of weather to keep a man looking neat if he had to spend much time riding around in a car. The concern he'd voiced on the phone in the morning still showed in his nice, boyish face as he sat down in the dining room with the glass of iced tea that Eileen had given him. He had already made a circuit of the building, looking into the flower beds and the utility shed. Now he took a long swallow of the tea and looked up at the two expectant faces across the table from him.

"Well, I don't think there's too much mystery about your intruder," he said. "I know who it is."

"You do? How?" Barbara was stunned. She had been preparing to give the sheriff her own idea about their late-night visitor, her conviction that someone was trying to scare her off from investigating Tony's murder.

"I've seen this pattern several times before," Paul answered. "Not in town, but on some of the county farms. He's getting a little bolder."

"What 'he' do you mean?" Eileen said.

"Oshawanee County's own Peeping Tom," he said. "This has been going on for more than a year. Less in the winter, of course, much more in the summer."

"A Peeping Tom!?" Barbara was scornful.

"I'm afraid so. His habits are always the same. He 'cases' a house for a few days, mostly by peeking into lower windows while people are still up. When he knows which bedrooms belong to which family members, he comes back and concentrates on one window. If he needs one, he uses a ladder, but it's mostly a ladder that belongs to the home owner. I guess that's one of the things he looks for when he's snooping around. You know that people around here almost never lock anything up."

"I've heard some of the stories about this," Eileen said thoughtfully. "But it was mostly over toward Gale, I thought."

"Yes," the sheriff said. "I know. But he's been getting around a bit more lately. The Kollross farm, out where you used to live, had a 'visitation' last week. They have those teenage girls."

"My, my," Eileen said softly.

Barbara had been quiet for a while, her disappointment showing on her face.

"I want to know how you can be so sure that this is the same man," she said at last, her voice challenging.

"I can show you, if you'd like," he answered, smiling a little.

"Please do," Barbara said, standing up.

They filed outside through the back door, and Paul led the women to the back flower bed just below the kitchen window. The annual flowers hadn't yet reached that fullness of growth they would later achieve, so there were patches of open ground among the petunias and marigolds. Paul pointed down at a circular indentation in the earth. The overhang of the roof had protected the spot from the rain, so the imprint was still very clear.

"When a ground-floor window is too high for him to look into," Paul said, "he turns over a bucket and stands on it. One of the pails in the utility shed had dirt all around the edge. There are some marks in the side beds, too, under your dining room and living room windows. A little washed out by the rain, but still there. He might have been spying for a few nights in a row."

"Why us?" Eileen said, wrapping her arms tightly despite the warmth of the morning.

"My guess would be that he's seen Barbara somewhere," Paul said, blushing a little under his new tan and not looking at Barbara. "Maybe at the store or the post office. He would ask about her, I suppose, find out where you lived."

"This is just absurd," Barbara said, not sure why she felt so angry. "If your peeper has never tried in the villages before, why would he start now?"

"I think he's getting bolder, like I said," Paul answered. "He's been getting away with it for so long. He's had so much practice."

Barbara remembered how the intruder had immediately sought the protection of the wall after jumping off the ladder and how she had thought even at the time that it seemed planned. Practice.

"You mentioned the white hat," Paul went on after a little pause to see if Barbara would speak. "One of the Kollross girls got a glimpse of him, too. She mentioned a white cap. She thought it looked like a painter's cap."

"Well, that's what I saw," Barbara said, her shoulders slumping in defeat. "Why hasn't anyone ever seen his face?"

131

"At least three people *have*," he said quietly.

The women exchanged a glance.

"He's been identified?" Barbara asked.

"Not to me," Paul said. "At least not officially."

"And what does that mean?" Barbara said.

"I know who it is, and apparently, lots of other people know who it is, too, but no one will make a positive identification or file a charge."

"Why the hell not?" Barbara's anger had broken through.

"Barbara," Eileen murmured softly. "Language."

"You grew up here, too," Paul said, looking directly into Barbara's eyes. "You know these people, so you must know that they won't go to law easily when something is wrong, especially if the trouble is coming from somebody they know."

"So this is a local man that people are protecting?" Barbara asked.

"Well, hardly a man," Paul shrugged. "He's seventeen. But his parents are good people, well known. The father of one of the victims who saw his face told me they just couldn't do that to 'neighbor folks.' He said he would put good shades on the windows and see to it that his daughter used them."

"But *you* know who it is, too," Barbara said indignantly. "Why can't you set a trap for him and arrest him?"

Paul Gillis sighed and squinted up at the sky for a moment.

"This is a big county," he said finally. "Setting traps is something that happens in the movies, not around here. I can't predict where he's going to go next, and I don't have the time or manpower to stake out farmhouses with pretty girls living in them. Too many pretty farm girls in Oshawanee County." He grinned at his own joke, but got serious again when he saw Barbara's face.

"So the good people of this county are willing to just let this go on," she said. "Couldn't he be dangerous?"

"I talked this over with a psychiatrist," Paul said, looking at her earnestly now. "She tells me that voyeurs, especially young ones like this, are almost never dangerous. Looking is what they do, nothing else. Sometimes they just outgrow it."

"I think we should go back inside," Eileen said. "The neighbors are finding it very interesting that the sheriff is here." And sure enough, several people had drifted out onto their little back porches.

"Yes, maybe you should, Mrs. Hoffman," he said. "But I'd like you to walk me to my car, Barbara. I need to talk to you a bit more."

Eileen frowned slightly, looking from her daughter to the sheriff and back again, but she went inside while Paul Gillis took Barbara's elbow to pilot her around the corner of the building, away from the view of the curious neighbors.

"Doesn't anyone intend to *do* anything about this invasion of privacy?" Barbara demanded as they walked.

"I suppose someday, some father or brother will catch him in the act," Paul said. "And he'll probably get himself pretty soundly beat up."

"Oh, wonderful!" Barbara snorted. "And that, I suppose, will fix everything. They think that's preferable to having him arrested? Better for his family?"

"Well, being arrested and put on trial is just another way of getting beat up," Paul said quietly. "It's just more official and less physical. I don't know which would be harder on his family."

Barbara paused to look up at him. He seemed to be

always full of surprises, of surprising ideas and attitudes, at least.

"But at least if he were arrested," she protested, "he could be compelled to get counseling. Somebody could be trying to help him."

"Look," he sighed, "I've seen the results of court-ordered counseling, and I'm not very impressed. If you go just to please the judge, or to get the law off your back, how much good can it do you?"

"So you're content to do nothing at all?"

"I've talked to the boy's parents, urged them to persuade their son that he needs help."

"And?"

"They won't believe it, of course. They've raised him right, and it's only jealous neighbors starting such sick rumors."

"Well, what did you expect?"

"Nothing," he said, smiling down at her. "When I was at the university studying political science, my professors used to say that politics was the art of the possible. Well, I've found out that law enforcement is like that, too. You don't usually find the ideal, so you've just got to settle for the possible. And accept it when some things are impossible."

"That's either realism or cynicism," Barbara said, smiling back in spite of herself. "I'm not sure which."

"Oh, I'm too young to be cynical," he said.

They had reached his patrol car by this time.

"What did you want to talk to me about alone?" Barbara asked.

"Well," he said, narrowing his clear hazel eyes, "it's come to my attention that you've been getting into law enforcement a bit yourself lately."

"What do you mean?" Barbara said, but she could feel herself blushing.

"Conducting an investigation into the murder of your uncle," he said, lowering his head to look at her more intently.

"Who told you that?" She looked away from his eyes.

"Never mind. You couldn't keep secrets in this county if you worked for the CIA, and you know it. I realize you're feeling impatient about this case, but you've got to leave this to me. You're just going to put everybody on guard by poking around, and then I won't be able to pry three words in a row out of these old people."

"They would clam up on you in any case," Barbara said. "I just thought they'd talk to me because they knew my father and they'd trust me more."

"And you didn't think I was moving fast enough," he said, tipping his head to one side.

"Yes, that, too," she admitted with a little smile.

"Well, you can cut it out now," he said. "Sheriff Gillis is on the case."

"I'm glad to hear that," she said, hoping she didn't sound as dubious as she felt. "You'll let me know what you learn, I hope."

"I promise," he said. "Scout's honor."

As he was starting to open the door of his car, Barbara thought of something.

"Do you think," she said slowly, "that somebody who had heard about the Peeping Tom at Kollross's last week might have deliberately imitated his M.O. last night?"

"Where do you pick up jargon like 'M.O.'?" he asked. "From watching too much television?"

"Come on, now," Barbara insisted, warming to her new idea. "You said yourself that gossip about the peeper is all over the county. And last week he was seen in a white cap less than four miles from where my parents used to live. The Kollross family must have talked about it to lots of people. Anyone could have known about the upside-down pails and the ladders. Somebody could have been imitating his methods so you would afterwards think it was the peeper."

"Afterwards?" he asked, frowning. "After what?"

"After scaring me," she said. "Or hurting me."

"And do you have a suspect in mind?" he said, raising his sandy eyebrows. "Do you think that was a seventy-eight-year-old man on a ladder outside your window last night?"

She stared at him for a full ten seconds. He had apparently gathered a lot of information since yesterday morning.

"I'm not saying it was George Heim," she said, looking him straight in the eye. "But you mustn't think of the Heim brothers as feeble just because they're old. They've always been pretty tough customers."

"All right, then," he said. "If not George Heim, who else could it have been?"

"Somebody he sent, maybe," Barbara said. "His son Ray, for instance. He might be pressed into service to guard a family secret."

"Look, Barbara," Paul said firmly. "You've been the most recent victim of a petty crime committed by a frustrated and overly introverted boy. It's only a coincidence that a skeleton was found in the basement of your old house last week. It's probably exactly the thing that brought you to the attention of this kid. Your name was in the paper, after all. The rest is just a matter of your being a 'newcomer' to him, and a very pretty one at that.''

"All right, all right," Barbara said. "Forget the peeper. Just find out who killed Uncle Tony, and then I won't have to feel paranoid."

"And if it's impossible?" he asked. "Can you accept that it might be impossible to find out after all these years?"

"I've had a lot of recent practice at accepting hard realities," Barbara said. "I can get used to this, too, I suppose."

When Paul had executed a swift, and illegal, U-turn in front of the apartment building, he waved at Barbara through the open window of his car, the warm breeze lifting his sandy hair away from his face as he drove off.

The next morning, Thursday, Barbara and Eileen presided over the burial of Anton Hoffman's bones. The gray hearse from McMartin's Funeral Parlour had been dispatched to Green Bay to recover the skeleton from the medical examiner's lab. The driver and Father Hodeck had placed the narrow box on braces over the hole that Mr. Shauer, the cemetery groundskeeper, had dug in the grass next to Joseph Hoffman's headstone. Only when the hearse had departed did Father Hodeck telephone Eileen to come uptown for the brief service. Barbara had swallowed her reluctance and come along, donning a dress and good shoes for the occasion, less out of respect for the dead than out of a desire to please her mother, who regarded all ceremonies as formal.

A narrow graveled path separated the new part of the

cemetery from the old. The road was lined on the new side by a high hedge, a legacy from the days when Elizabeth Merens, who had willed her property for the addition, had wanted to keep her view screened from her own eventual resting place, the double plot in the old cemetery where her husband was already buried. Barbara could see that many new graves had appeared in the addition since her father's funeral. Under leaden skies and humid air, the grass and the leftover flowers from Memorial Day looked drab, even a bit tacky. It was the first time Barbara was seeing the headstone over her father's grave, for, of course, it hadn't been there on the day of his funeral. It was a simple slab of polished red granite which said "Hoffman" in straight, sharply edged letters. In the lower left corner was chiseled "Joseph 1921–1986," and in the lower right corner "Eileen 1925–   ." Only the date of death needed to be added. It gave Barbara a bad shock to see her mother's name on the stone.

The stone was just inside the hedge, in the first row of the addition, and the hole for Tony's bones was a narrow trench dug almost at the base of the hedge; the south wall of the vault holding Joseph Hoffman's coffin had been exposed by the digging. As Eileen talked softly to Father Hodeck, Barbara found herself staring at the box suspended over the trench. It was a wooden crate, perhaps three feet long and two feet wide, no deeper than twelve inches. The size of the box made Barbara realize the full impact of the word "remains." After forty years, even a big man could be so diminished that his remains could fit inside a doll bed. She shifted her eyes to the wall of her father's vault. He was sealed inside a coffin, and the coffin was inside these cement walls, but he, too, would come to this. The exposed vault didn't look very

138

different from the cistern wall Barbara could remember seeing in the fruit cellar at home.

Father Hodeck kissed the stole before draping it around his neck. As he opened his black, leather-covered missal, a distant sound of thunder rolled toward them from the west across the flat farmlands. He read slowly in his rich, stentorian voice, pausing every now and then to sprinkle holy water onto the box from the silver wand in his right hand. The drops made round stains on the pale wood. The words were intended for the "bereaved," a firm exhortation to set grieving aside and a bald reminder that "all now living must surely follow" the deceased. Eileen stood with her fine head bowed, looking, not at Tony's poor coffin, but at the earth over her husband's body. Barbara stared past her at the western sky, which was growing darker every minute. Father Hodeck finished the prayers, removed the stole, and stood silent for a moment before turning away from the approaching storm toward the cemetery gate. Eileen followed him at once, but Barbara hung back, looking down again at the headstone, the narrow trench, and the wooden crate.

Suddenly, very near, perhaps in the cemetery itself, a meadowlark sent up its sweet, piercing song. Tears sprang unbidden to Barbara's eyes. She found herself in danger of sobbing aloud. All the safety and security of New Augsburg was embodied in that song, and now it seemed like a mockery. Her father was dead; these boxed bones had been lying under her childhood home all the time she'd been growing up there in such oblivious contentment; somebody, maybe somebody she knew, had murdered this man, her uncle, and a part of her was willing to say that he may have deserved killing; corruption, betrayal, violence—they were the real truth under the deceptive tranquility and beauty. And a pervert was wandering the countryside satisfying his sick sexuality by peering through windows at half-dressed women. In "normal" little Oshawanee County, in the heart of America's Dairyland! It was as if she had touched some treasured, beloved possession, and found it crawling with worms.

Thunder sounded, nearer this time, and Barbara wiped her eyes as she turned to go. Then she heard another sound, closer, right on the other side of the hedge, the sound of feet moving in grass. She stopped, rigid, listening. There was no other sound. She stared at the hedge, but it was so high, so thickly leaved, that it was impenetrable. Barbara turned slowly back to her father's grave and knelt down, as if she meant to pray for a moment. Then she bent her face down towards the grass and peered sideways at the base of the hedge, her gaze going straight under the rough box which held Tony's bones. At ground level, the hedge had fewer leaves, only crowded stems. The shoes on the other side were no further than six feet from Barbara's head, heavy work shoes, worn and covered with dirt. The trouser legs above them were dark, some deep shade of green. It was almost the uniform of local farmers.

Barbara stood up carefully, reasoning that a fast move on her part might scare off the watcher—or rather listener, for she doubted that the person on the other side of the hedge could see her, either. She walked briskly, giving the appearance of trying to catch up with her mother and Father Hodeck, who had already reached the cemetery gate. All the way, the hedge towered to her right. When she came up behind her mother, clear of the hedge at last, Barbara looked around the hedge into the road that divided the two halves of the cemetery. No one was in sight. She swept the western horizon with her gaze; the trees and bushes along the back of the cemetery could easily hide someone who had walked in the opposite direction from her when she left the Hoffman gravesite.

"Did you notice anyone else in the cemetery just now?" Barbara asked.

"Visiting a grave?" Father Hodeck asked.

"Or just walking," Barbara said. "I thought I heard someone toward the back of the old cemetery. Perhaps Mr. Shauer is waiting around to finish my uncle's grave."

"No, I didn't see anyone," Father Hodeck said. "And Mr. Shauer has gone back home for the day. He'll finish tomorrow."

A sudden clap of thunder interrupted him.

"We'd better hurry, or we'll get wet," he said. "I'll say a requiem mass for Anton tomorrow at eight. Come if you can."

Barbara and Eileen had just got into Barbara's car when the skies opened. For a while, it rained so hard that Barbara decided that it would be best just to wait in the church parking lot; the wipers needed replacing and wouldn't be able to keep up with this downpour. Both women were quiet, each with her own thoughts. Barbara stared back toward the cemetery, which was only vaguely visible through the curtain of rain. Who could have been listening to Tony Hoffman's little burial ceremony? And why? Who would even know about it? The identity of the skeleton had been given in yesterday's city newspaper, but no announcement of services had been made. What sinister grapevine was carrying their family business to what ears?

As the rain battered her little car, Barbara thought what a muddy hole the wet must be making of the narrow trench next to her father's vault. And by now, it had surely obliterated the marks the holy water had made on the cover of the wooden box.

11

When the rain let up somewhat, Barbara started the Volkswagen and drove out of the churchyard to the stop sign at the highway. A simple right turn would put them onto Main Street. At the stop sign opposite her car, signaling left, was a gray pickup truck, its windshield wipers sweeping away in a steady rhythm at the rain. Barbara came back from her own reverie as she caught sight of the driver of the pickup.

"Isn't that Charlie Novak?" she asked, squinting past the busy wipers on her own windshield.

"Yes, I think so," Eileen said. "He has a truck like that, at least."

"He was one of the people on your list," Barbara said thoughtfully, looking back at the cemetery which was across Main Street from the church parking lot. Someone parked at the back of the cemetery could be arriving at the stop sign just about now.

"Yes, dear," Eileen said, "and he's waiting for you to turn. You have the right of way."

Barbara let out the clutch and turned slowly toward

the village. In her rearview mirror, she watched the truck turn out behind her, following slowly at a safe distance.

"Why did you mention Charlie to the sheriff?" Barbara asked.

"Charlie *and* Geraldine," Eileen said, careful as always to keep accurate accounts. "Well, they're neighbors, of course. The Novaks have owned that farm forever. And Charlie is two years older than Dad, so I imagine he and Tony were at school together. Geraldine, too. She and Charlie have known each other since they were children, and they married so young; their golden anniversary is coming up next year."

"Yes, of course," Barbara said, glancing into the mirror again. "They would have known Tony very well."

"Exactly so," Eileen said, producing one of the habitual phrases that marked her country of origin.

As her car descended the hill into the heart of the village, Barbara saw the truck behind her signaling for a left turn. She slowed down and watched the truck pull off Main Street into the narrow parking lot of the Farmers Trading Company.

"Mind if I just drop you at the apartment, Mum?" Barbara said, speeding up again. "I've got a little shopping to do."

"Sure," Eileen said. "You'll be back for lunch?"

"Yes," Barbara said absently, watching the street behind her in the mirror. "For lunch."

The rain had stopped when Eileen got out of the car. Barbara made a tight U-turn and raced the car up to second gear and then third. She was determined to get a look at Charlie Novak's shoes, at his trousers. The Novaks had lived on the farm just to the west of the Hoffman farm all the years Barbara was growing up, but circumstances had worked to keep the two families more distant

144

from each other than proximity would have suggested. The county line lay between the two pieces of property, so the Novaks belonged both to a different parish and to a different school district. The Novaks' first four children had all been girls born close together, the youngest of whom was almost eight years older than Barbara, so the usual route of children making playmates had not worked to draw the families closer. The youngest Novak child, Billy, was only two years Barbara's senior, but he had been, after all, a boy, and had developed into one of those teenagers whose swaggering efforts at a "tough guy" pose had been a turnoff for her. And, finally, Charlie Novak had always been "standoffish" with her father; Eileen had sometimes remarked about it, and even Barbara had had occasion to notice it. Joseph Hoffman himself never complained about it or offered any explanation beyond a shrug about why it should be so.

When Barbara arrived at the Farmers Trading Company, she turned right and then came to an abrupt stop. The truck was gone. She calculated that it could have taken no more than five minutes to drop her mother and get back here. What could Charlie have had to do in the store that would take such a short time? Had he pulled in here just to avoid her, waited until her car was out of sight, and then driven away? If he *had* been the listener at the cemetery, he could have been caught off guard by the sight of her car; he wouldn't have expected them to be still at the church parking lot. Perhaps he had waited for them to be gone and was thwarted by the fact that she had waited for the rain to stop. But why would he have been there in the first place? What interest would he have in Tony Hoffman's burial?

A horn sounded behind her, and Barbara quickly shifted into first gear. She had been blocking the entrance to the parking lot. As she drove back along the wet streets, looking into side streets for a glimpse of the gray truck, Barbara began to feel foolish. Probably Charlie Novak was just driving to town to run a few errands; that road past the cemetery was one of two ways he would normally use to get into New Augsburg. Whoever was listening in the cemetery was probably some oblivious passerby, attracted by the sound of prayer, who had simply fled when he sensed that his harmless snooping had been discovered. Paul Gillis was probably right when he warned her against playing at investigator in a case where her emotions were so directly involved. Still—there had always been that aloofness in Charlie Novak. What was that about? How far back did it go? Could *everything* be a coincidence, Peeping Tom and all? Or was there some connection to this series of events, so bizarre in a tame place like New Augsburg?

The morning's rain had apparently signaled the passing of a weather front, because it was much cooler by afternoon when Barbara drove again past the cemetery on her way to the Novak farm. She'd told Eileen that she was going into Oshawanee to look for some shorts and a pair of sandals, and got another troubled look for her pains. That morning, when she'd arrived back at the apartment after looking around for Charlie Novak's truck, Eileen had asked what shopping she had needed to do that she'd come back with nothing. Barbara had forgotten all about the excuse. In fact, she was out of the habit of accounting to anyone for her whereabouts.

Barbara was not altogether sure why she felt a need to shield her activities from her mother. She could easily have argued an interest in finding out who had killed her only uncle; she might even have enlisted Eileen's help in gaining the confidence of people who, after all, knew her mother better than they knew her. Eileen might have enjoyed participating, though she would certainly have been more polite in her questions than Barbara was willing to be. But at some deep level, the daughter sought secrecy in this matter *especially* where her mother was concerned. Perhaps it was that she feared Eileen's intuitive powers, recognized that if her mother knew the details of the investigation so far, she would know that her daughter suspected Joseph Hoffman of murder. And Barbara was so ashamed of that suspicion, so appalled by it, that she couldn't bear to think of her mother finding out.

As she turned into the Novaks' long driveway, Barbara reflected gratefully on the country tradition of dropping in without an invitation or even a warning phone call in advance. She would never have dreamed of taking such liberties with friends and acquaintances in Chicago, but it was an old and even expected way of doing things in New Augsburg, and it was a great convenience for Barbara's purpose, because she didn't want these people "preparing" themselves for her questions ahead of time; she wanted to be looking into their faces when she said, "I'd like to talk to you about Tony Hoffman."

The Novaks had a small but prosperous farm: a modern, wholly mechanized dairy barn, four silos, a big machine shed, and a large Holstein herd. After Joe Hoffman's death, they'd bought his best farm machinery at auction. In 1972, the Novaks had torn down their old house and put into its place a sprawling, one-story brick house. Eileen reported that Charlie now employed two hired men full time, up one from the years Barbara could remember. As she parked her car in front of the big garage doors, Barbara noticed that the well-trimmed lawn sported two plastic fawns, caught in attitudes of alert wariness, as if the scent of wolf had just that moment drifted into their sensitive nostrils.

Geraldine Novak let Barbara into the small entrance hall lined with hooks for "barn clothes" that Geraldine wanted removed before men were allowed into her kitchen, for it was obvious from looking at her that she was a scrupulously fastidious woman. She was wearing a matched slacks and blouse set and white sandals; her jet-black hair (surely dyed, for she was sixty-eight) was teased and sprayed into a mid-seventies "do"; her fingernails and toenails were polished to a high gloss, deep rose in color. The kitchen, Barbara noted at once, was spotless.

"What brings you here?" Geraldine asked, but she didn't look surprised to see Barbara, and the question sounded faintly insincere.

"I was hoping to talk to you and your husband about my uncle, Tony Hoffman," Barbara said. "You must have read about it in the papers."

"Oh, yes," Geraldine said. "And Mr. Pankratz called the sheriff from here when the body was found. Called you, too, didn't he?"

"Yes, that's right," Barbara said, remembering. "Is Mr. Novak at home? I'd like to talk to both of you. It's been such a shock for me, because I didn't know my uncle, of course, and I'm trying to make sense of it all, just for my own peace of mind." It was starting to become a practiced opening gambit, but Barbara noticed in the arching of Geraldine Novak's penciled eyebrows a decidedly skeptical look.

"Charlie's out in the shop, working on a tractor," she said. "All this rain the last two days has kept him off the fields, and we have cut hay out there. It worries him, and when Charlie's worried, he just goes to puttering on the machines. Would you like some coffee?"

Barbara glanced quickly around the kitchen, saw no coffeepot, and guessed that Geraldine would make a fresh pot if a guest said "yes" to such a question, even a drop-in guest.

"No, thank you," Barbara said. "I've had about enough caffeine for one day."

"I've got some pop in the fridge, 7-Up I think. Would you like a glass?"

"Thank you. That would be nice."

When the soda had been poured, Mrs. Novak said, "I'll just go out and call Charlie. Would you like to wait out on the deck?"

"Fine," Barbara said, uncertain if this was a thoughtful gesture for her comfort or a wish to keep potentially messy intruders out of the house.

Mrs. Novak led Barbara to sliding glass doors and then turned back toward the other side of the house.

"It's shorter if I go this way," she explained. "Make yourself comfortable out there. It'll be just a few minutes."

Barbara stepped out onto the redwood deck which ran along the short side of the house to a beautifully mitered corner piece and then swept around to the back side to face the yard. She closed the door to the house and then strolled toward the corner. Just before she got there, she heard a man's voice, a deep but controlled snarl of a voice.

"Get out of my way or I'll break your back!"

Barbara came to an abrupt stop. She heard a little whine, and then a black dog, looking forlorn and guilty as only a scolded dog can, came around the corner, shied

149

at the sight of her, and jumped off the deck to the ground. Next, Barbara heard, and even felt in her feet, a rumbling sound, as if something heavy were being rolled across the wooden boards. She stepped around the corner of the house and found herself about to be run down by a man in a wheelchair. He stopped the chair on a dime, his hands expertly and powerfully halting the big wheels. For a second he looked stunned, staring up at Barbara's face as if she were an apparition; then his face lowered into a heavy scowl.

He was a man in his mid-thirties with long, shaggy brown hair and a reddish beard and mustache. He was wearing jeans and a sleeveless T-shirt, revealing narrow legs and an impressively well-developed torso, bulging biceps, the exaggerated neck and shoulder muscles that come from a regular regimen of weight lifting. Behind him, Barbara could see a narrow ramp with low railings sloping away into the yard.

She knew at once that this was Billy, the Novaks' youngest child and only son, but she found herself staring anyway. She hadn't seen him at all since high school days, but, of course, she'd heard all about him from her parents. Drafted three days after he graduated from high school in 1968, Billy Novak had gone off to Vietnam with the cocky certainty that he would come home a hero. But one of his buddies on a patrol had tripped a mine, blowing himself to pieces. A metal fragment from the mine had pierced Billy's lower back and severed his spine. He'd come home to New Augsburg a casualty. No hope. A paraplegic for the rest of his life, and he was not yet twenty years old. Barbara stared down at him, unable to see in this scowling, bearded man anything of the Billy Novak she remembered.

"What the hell you staring at?" he said. "And what do you think you're doing here?"

"I'm sorry," Barbara said, looking out across the lawn. "I'm Barbara Mullens. Barbara Hoffman. I came to talk to your parents."

"I know who you are," he said. "You don't look so different from when you were twitching your behind as a cheerleader."

Barbara felt a rush of anger and looked straight back at him.

"Well, you've changed quite a bit," she said and saw the barb strike home. She regretted it instantly, for the sour face darkened even more.

"Somebody should teach you better manners," he said, and his voice sounded dangerous. "You go sneaking up on people like this, you're gonna get unpleasant surprises."

"Your mother asked me to wait out here," Barbara said, her voice more subdued. "She went to call your father from one of the outbuildings."

"Outbuildings?" he said, mocking her voice. "What is that, some college word? He's in the shop."

"Why are you being so unpleasant?" she asked.

"Yes, 'unpleasant,' " he said, and a sneering smile turned up his full mouth. "Not heroic, not long-suffering. That's it, isn't it? You think I don't know that people can hardly stand to look at a cripple? It just makes them wanna puke. The only way they'll forgive a person for looking like me is if he's all sweet and noble about his condition. If they catch him acting like normal people, yelling at a dog like you just heard me doing, they just purely hate him."

"I don't know what you're talking about," Barbara

151

said, looking away, but she felt the truth of what he was saying, remembered how her own discomfort in the face of a physical handicap was very nearly akin to dislike for the person who had made her feel this discomfort. Now she began to walk past Billy Novak to the redwood picnic table beyond him. Instantly, he swung the chair to block her, expertly lifting the front wheels into the air and then planting them insolently in front of her shoes. He reached his bulging left arm past her body to the railing.

"Don't think we're fooled either," he said. "We know what you're up to."

"I don't know what that means either," Barbara said, holding her ground and taking a sip of the drink, but her hand was shaking slightly.

"Oh, come on," Billy said, leaning forward so far that his beard almost touched her forearm; she pulled back sharply. "You've been running around from farm to farm playing Sherlock Holmes. You're trying to hang the rap on somebody for snuffing your dirtball of an uncle."

"Who told you that?" Barbara asked, really curious now.

"Don't matter who told me," he answered, spinning the chair away from her. "Your Little Miss Innocent act isn't gonna work here. We're on to you."

"Why do you say that my Uncle Tony was a dirtball?" Barbara said to his broad back. "He died before you were born, so how can you have an opinion about his character?"

"I got a opinion about Hitler's character," he said without turning around, "and he died before I was born, too."

"But why compare Tony Hoffman to Hitler?" she asked. "What have people been telling you about him?"

He wheeled the chair slowly toward the picnic table and then turned back toward her.

"He was a sleaze," Billy Novak said, his eyes fixed in a cold stare. "You're trying to get somebody jailed for what was done to that bastard, and you ought to be organizing a party for the one who done it. You got no idea what that louse done in his short life. He——."

"Billy!" a sharp voice interrupted from behind Barbara's back.

She turned toward the corner of the deck to see Charlie Novak with his wife coming up behind him. Charlie was a short, blocky man, almost bald, with wire-rimmed glasses perched on a squashed-looking nose. The wisps of gray hair which stuck up in the back of his shiny head had once been red. In her childhood, Barbara had thought that Charlie Novak looked like Jiggs in "Bringing Up Father." He even smoked big cigars occasionally to complete the illusion. Now Barbara dropped her gaze to his feet; he was wearing soiled tennis shoes and navy blue trousers. Of course, he'd had plenty of time to change his clothes since he got home from New Augsburg if he thought his feet might have been seen in the cemetery. She glanced back at Billy, who had lowered his head and was gripping the wheel rims of his chair, rocking slightly back and forth. An awkward silence had fallen.

"Hello, Mr. Novak," Barbara said at last. "I saw you in town earlier today."

"Did you?" he said, without emotion. "I didn't see you." The sun had finally come out and the light glinted off Charlie's glasses so that Barbara couldn't see his eyes.

"I hope you can give me a few minutes to tell me

153

about my Uncle Tony," she said calmly. "Billy tells me that you've been informed about my curiosity, and *he* seems a little angry about it for some reason that I don't understand. But I calculate that you were a classmate of my uncle's. You, too, Mrs. Novak. Before the consolidation separated Gale district and Casson district, of course. So I hoped you could help me understand what he was like back then, to get at why someone would kill him and then hide his body that way."

"Well, we only went to school with him two years," Geraldine said. "At the high school. He went to grade school at St. Mary's and we went to Holy Martyrs. Tony got kicked out of high school, you know."

"That's what George Heim told me," Barbara said, watching Charlie's face for some reaction, to see if George had been the one to report on her activities. "For setting some coats on fire, he said."

Charlie took two quick steps to get around Barbara, and then he joined his son at the picnic table. She had seen no perceptible change in his face. She followed him to sit down at the table, determined to turn this into a real interview; sitting had the look of a "visit," not just a chat. Charlie sat down, too, but his body language projected reluctance.

"You wanna get me a pop, Gerry?" he said to his wife, who went into the house. Billy just stared at Barbara from under his thick eyebrows, an unblinking stare that had so much hostility in it that she felt inclined to slide further away from him; she sat still, though, determined to maintain some normal decorum in this odd situation.

"What do you remember about my uncle?" Barbara said, looking back at Charlie and assuming a casual tone.

"Not much," Charlie said with a shrug, and again Barbara was struck by his careful calm, as if he had rehearsed how he would behave in this situation, either with her or with the sheriff. "We was neighbors while we grew up, of course, but we didn't see much of each other—different grade schools, like Gerry said. I knew he was kinda wild, a girl chaser. That's about it." Now that he had put his back to the sun, Barbara could see his eyes; he was focusing on a spot just to the right of her face, as if he were talking, not to her, but to the gas grill.

"You must have known about his Green Bay friends," Barbara said. "The ones with the motorcycles. Living just a mile from our place, I mean. And you surely heard about Tony's affair with Caroline Heim."

"That's all old gossip," Charlie said, blinking slowly. "I never had no trouble with Tony's friends, and Caroline Heim was no business of mine."

"What a sassy little thing *she* was," Mrs. Novak said as she approached the table with Charlie's soda. Again, she had prepared nothing for herself.

"Now, Gerry," Charlie said, and his voice had left its monotone to become sharp again.

"Well, it's true," Geraldine said. "I don't know why everybody wants to pretend she wasn't. Imagine defying her family that way and pretending to be such a goodie-goodie while she was going with your father. But I could see what a sly puss she was. If you ask me, I don't think Tony had to work too hard to seduce that one."

"Nobody's asking you, Gerry," Charlie said in a sour voice.

"Well, I'm talking to Barbara," she said, flaring a little, though she seemed not to take her husband's tone very seriously. "Though I think she got pretty stuck on Tony after a while. He was a handsome devil; nobody can say any different about that. I imagine she was pretty

155

worked up when Tony wouldn't marry her, her being pregnant by that time, I mean. Though we none of us knew about that until much later. She might even have killed Tony herself, you know. I wouldn't put it past her."

"Yeah," Billy said, pulling himself upright in the wheelchair. "I'm surprised you didn't think of that yourself, Barbie. A woman scorned, and all that. That's something you should know all about." And he smiled at Barbara, a mean, suggestive leer. She could feel her face beginning to burn, rage boiling up in her brain.

"That's enough a that, Billy," Charlie said, and again Billy looked down at his lap.

"Now, look here, Barbara," Charlie went on. "There's nothing more we can tell you."

Barbara struggled to control her voice.

"Mr. Novak," she said, "forgive me, but I don't believe that. You've been stonewalling me in a very obvious way, and your son here has been almost unbelievably rude to me since I arrived. You're concealing something, trying to protect somebody probably, but it won't do any good. What you call old gossip is exactly what communities like this operate on. None of it is ever forgotten, and there's always somebody who will tell. Whatever you're trying to keep me from knowing is going to come out sooner or later. The sheriff says there's no statute of limitations on first-degree murder, so he'll be doing a lot of digging for as long as it takes."

Charlie had gone pale, his gray eyes steely with anger.

"You don't know what you're doing," he said, his lips curling around the words. "You're hitting out in all directions, and you're gonna hurt somebody who doesn't deserve to be hurt. I got friends all over this township, and George Heim is one of them. I'm not gonna help you or any young smart aleck of a sheriff to accuse him or his brother or anybody else.''

"Nobody's accusing anybody," Barbara sighed. "I'm just trying to get at the truth."

"Are you really?" Charlie said, looking at her directly and searchingly for the first time. "Or are you just trying to keep yourself from looking a little closer to home?"

Barbara pulled in her breath sharply, could feel herself coloring.

"When you're passing along old gossip to the sheriff," Charlie went on, "do you tell him that your own father was crazy about the girl Tony was messing with? Do you tell him how Joe found out and ran away into the army? And that nobody around here ever seen his brother again after that?"

Barbara sprang to her feet, banging the front of her thigh against the hard edge of the picnic table.

"How dare you!" she shouted. "You're only saying that to be spiteful and because you never liked my father."

Now Charlie looked genuinely surprised.

"What do you mean, 'never liked' him?" he said.

"You were always cold and distant to him," Barbara said, her voice shaking now, close to tears. "Did you think we didn't notice? He never said anything about it, but I know it hurt him because everybody else always liked and respected him so much. No one else would ever dream of saying what you did about my father." And now she could feel the tears on her cheeks.

Charlie's face crumpled into a look of remorse and something like defeat.

"No, no," he said softly. "I didn't dislike your father.

Forget what I said. It was only that you made me so mad by saying I was lying to you. By trying to stir up trouble for everybody.''

Barbara found she couldn't speak without sobbing. She snatched up her purse and rushed past Geraldine Novak, who made one small gesture toward her and then dropped her arm to her side. On the short side of the deck, Barbara found a little flight of stairs and, hurrying down them, rounded the house to her car. She sat inside for a while, gripping the steering wheel and trying to steady her breathing. What could Charlie have meant by ''nobody around here ever seen his brother again after that''? Did he mean that people had speculated as long ago as the 1940s about what had *really* happened to Tony Hoffman? Had men in taverns or on harvest crews wondered aloud if Joe Hoffman had done in his own brother before ''running away into the army''? Maybe Charlie had taken the rumors more seriously than the others had, and had held himself apart from Joe Hoffman all those years because of it.

Barbara wiped under her eyes with a tissue from the dashboard holder, then checked her mascara in the rearview mirror. She started to fish her keys out of her purse and then stopped again. She would ask him. She would just march back around that house and ask Charlie Novak what he meant. And what he was doing in New Augsburg that morning. She drew a long breath and got back out of the car.

The big fancy deck was empty. Geraldine had apparently gone back into her tidy house. But at the bottom of the lawn with their backs to her, Barbara saw Charlie and Billy. They were looking out over the fields, the foot-high rows of corn, and beyond those, the paler green of the new oats. Charlie was standing to the left of the

158

wheelchair with his right hand on the back of the frame. The black dog was resting his head on the right arm of the chair, and Billy was scratching absently from time to time behind the shaggy ears. He didn't look at the dog, and the men didn't appear to be talking to each other.

Something in the scene, in the wordless closeness of father and son, made Barbara stop and step back to the edge of the house to shield herself from view should either of the men turn around. She, too, looked out over the farm and began to understand the feeling of the tableau. All of this pretty farm had been lovingly built up, with real sacrifice probably, for the long-awaited son, the last-born, the Benjamin of his father's hopes. And now the son couldn't take up his birthright. Nothing could ransom him out of the Egypt of that wheelchair. Barbara turned around and walked quietly back to her car.

12

The next morning when Barbara went out into the parking lot to do warming-up exercises before her run, she saw that the trunk of her car was standing open. For a second, she paused, thinking, "Did I open it yesterday and forget about it?" the way people do when confronted with something out of place among their most familiar possessions. Then she ran over to the car, knowing with a sick certainty what she would find.

The Volkswagen's engine, always something of an enigma to Barbara, now looked badly awry. Wires and cables jutted up into the air. Some small pieces, black with grease, were lying on the gravel under the back bumper. Barbara trotted along the short row of cars in the lot and back again on the other side. No other car had been disturbed or tampered with.

"Goddamn it!" Barbara said through clenched teeth. Then she sprinted for the back porch.

"What's the matter?" Eileen asked when she saw Barbara's face. She had been putting away the breakfast dishes which she and Barbara had done together earlier.

"Somebody hashed my car," Barbara said.

"Hashed your car?" Eileen asked, uncomprehending.

"Opened the trunk and ripped things out of the motor," Barbara explained. "Sometime during the night. Now Paul Gillis will have to admit that I'm being targeted, because none of the other cars were touched."

"Why are you being targeted, Barbara?" Eileen said, looking frightened and even a little angry. "Where did you really go yesterday afternoon?"

Barbara stared at her mother, brought down from her outrage by this sharp observation.

"I know you've been trying to humbug me about going shopping," Eileen went on. "You've been investigating again. Who did you offend this time?"

"Offend?" Barbara said. "What makes you think I've been offending people?"

"Oh, please stop," Eileen said. "I ran into Mary Wenner at the post office, and she told me it's all over town that you've been playing detective. George Heim was apparently pretty upset about it."

"Well, George Heim knows more than he's willing to tell about Uncle Tony," Barbara protested. "Maybe he's upset because I've sensed that about him."

"My guess would be that you went to see the Novaks yesterday," Eileen went on in a steady voice, "because we saw Charlie in the morning and you asked me why I put his name on the list for the sheriff."

"Well, well, Mum," Barbara said, smiling ruefully in spite of herself. "You're quite a detective yourself. Yes, I saw the Novaks for a few minutes, and they were about as uncooperative as they could be. And Billy Novak came close to threatening me. Now my car has been vandalized. I see a connection there, don't you?"

"Oh, Barbara!" Eileen said, shocked. "How could that be? He can't even walk."

"Doesn't he drive?" Barbara asked. "You told me years ago he went to a special class to learn to drive modified vehicles."

"That's what Mary told me," Eileen said. "And he does drive a car, but even if he could drive here, how could he have damaged your car?"

"We would never have noticed the sound of a car driving into the lot, and neither would the other tenants; we don't even wake up to that sound anymore. He could have wrecked my motor without leaving his car. You should see the muscles in his upper body, Mother. And you should see the meanness in his eyes."

"He's had a lot to bear in his life," Eileen said softly.

"I know that," Barbara said, "but I can't accept that as an excuse to be vicious to me or to destroy my property. I'm going to call Paul."

Sheriff Gillis stood in the parking lot, shaking his head back and forth, his sandy hair flopping from side to side as he did so.

"You haven't touched anything?" he asked.

"Nothing," Barbara said. She'd changed from her running clothes into slacks and knit top. "You can't say this is just coincidence."

"No, I can't," he said, squatting to peer at those engine parts lying on the ground. "Somebody is mad at you specifically. And anybody who would do this to a bug must be pretty darned mad."

"I think it's Billy Novak," Barbara said, her voice a little tentative. "I was visiting out there yesterday with his parents, one of the couples my mother thought you should interview. Billy is their son and—."

"I know Billy," he said straightening up. "We played

162

basketball against each other in high school; he was a starting guard for Casson. I also know he's in a wheelchair now."

"He's pretty agile with that chair," Barbara protested.

"I don't suppose you were just paying a little social call on the Novaks," Paul said, raising his eyebrows. "You were being a cop again, and I thought we had an agreement about that."

"I'm just trying to help along," Barbara said lamely. She wanted to tell him about the cemetery, the feet on the other side of the hedge, and then seeing Charlie a few minutes later in his truck, to make him understand the connection. But standing here looking into those calm eyes, that reasonable face, she realized how it would sound, and she felt a horror of seeming foolish in front of him.

"You could be screwing up the whole investigation," he said. "Did you ever think of that?"

"Is there some law against my visiting old neighbors?" Barbara said, drawing herself up.

"There's a law against interfering with the police," he said evenly.

"Interfering with what?" she demanded hotly. "I don't see any police doing anything that I could be interfering *with*."

"You don't know what I've been doing about your uncle's death," he said. "You never asked me." He didn't seem angry. In fact, his eyes looked slightly amused.

"Well?" she said. "What have you been doing then?"

"Interviewing people," he answered. "Following leads that I'm not ready to talk about yet. If I let you in on anything, you're liable to land in the middle of it with both your pretty feet."

"Don't patronize me," Barbara said, her temper flaring again.

"What's patronizing about that?" he demanded, and his own eyes were angry now.

"It sounds just like 'Now don't trouble your pretty little head about grown-up business,' " she answered. "Not everybody thinks that kind of stuff is charming, you know."

"Sorry," he said simply. "You're right. I do that from time to time. Now tell me, what makes you think Bill Novak did this?"

"He threatened me."

"What did he say?"

"He said 'Somebody should teach you better manners.' "

Paul Gillis stared at her for a moment and then chuckled softly.

"That's not a threat," he said. "Sounds like something I might say."

"You didn't hear the tone," she said. "And you didn't see his face. I want you to go find whatever car he drives, and I'll bet you'll find grease on the steering wheel. Whoever did this got plenty of grease on his hands."

"Grease on a steering wheel is not proof," he said. "I would guess that it's fairly common on farms."

"Aren't there fingerprints in all that mess?" Barbara asked, gesturing at the wreck of her engine.

"As a matter of fact, there's a pretty clear hand print here on the fender," he said, pointing with a lean finger at a greasy mark.

"Right," Barbara said, leaning forward to look. "That's good. Now all you have to do is take Billy Novak's fingerprints and match them."

"Not so simple, I'm afraid," he sighed. "If you look

close, you'll see that the impression is kind of stippled. My guess is that whoever trashed your car was wearing work gloves."

"Well, of course," Barbara said, throwing up her hands. "Once again, there's no way to prove anything."

"Look, Barbara," he said, his voice patient. "I believe there's a connection between this mess and your interview sessions. And it *does* seem that the closest link is to the Novaks because you were there yesterday. I'm going to talk to Bill about this, among other things. But you have got to stop expecting the clear clues and the sixty-minute solutions that you see on the TV cop shows. The real world isn't like that."

"All right," Barbara said, folding her arms. "I can see what you're saying. I'm just so mad about all this. And a little scared, too."

"Sure you are," he said with real sympathy. "But I don't think you're in personal danger."

"I'm not so sure of that," she said quietly.

"What do you mean?" he asked, his voice sharp.

"I've been thinking it over while we were waiting for you to get here," she said. "The Novaks were 'ready' for me when I got there yesterday. I mean, they seemed to know why I'd come. Somebody warned them and I think it was George Heim. He could have called Charlie on Monday or even Tuesday, after I talked to him and Mae."

"I'm not following this," Paul said.

"Well, I still don't believe that was just a Peeping Tom outside my window Tuesday night," Barbara said emphatically. "Everybody around here must know how that boy goes about looking into windows, even what he wears when he does it, so anybody could imitate his behavior if they wanted to. I think that by Tuesday night

165

there were at least three able-bodied men who knew I was poking around into my uncle's murder. I mean Charlie Novak and Raymond Heim and George Heim, even though you seem to think he's too feeble to be jumping from ladders. One of them might have been scared I would find out something important, scared enough to come after me and make it look like it was that boy who'd done it."

Paul scowled without speaking.

"If my mother finds me strangled in my bed some morning," Barbara said grimly, "don't blame that poor boy, whoever he is."

"Don't be absurd," he said, but he sounded a little worried. "Nobody's going to strangle anybody in my county."

"Well, I'll do my best to prevent it," she said, laughing a little to dispel the look on his face. She suddenly wanted him to go back to his easy assurance that she was in no danger. But Paul Gillis said nothing, only frowned more deeply. Barbara decided to change the subject.

"What am I going to do about my car?" she asked. "I'm supposed to go back to Chicago in three days. Do you know a good mechanic?"

"Only one I would trust with this beauty," he said, giving the car an affectionate pat.

"Who's that?"

"Me."

"Oh, come on."

"I mean it," he protested. "There's really no garage around here that's set up for Volkswagens. I used to do all the maintenance on my own bug, and she just hummed all the time like the happy beetle she was. There are no mysteries under this lid for me."

"I can't ask you to fix my car," she said, looking up

at him with renewed surprise; she was just never able to predict what this man would say next.

"You didn't ask me," he grinned. "I insist. You'll be doing me a favor, letting me get my hands on this little honey."

"You have the county to take care of," she said wryly.

"Not twenty-four hours a day, seven days a week. Two of my deputies are taking shifts this weekend. I could come over Sunday afternoon, and you could hand me my tools and pour me a beer or two."

"Won't Mrs. Gillis think it's odd for you to be fixing cars on your day off?" Barbara asked, recognizing the flirtatious tone of his last speech.

"There isn't any Mrs. Gillis anymore," he answered. "Except for my mother, that is."

"Anymore?" Barbara asked.

"In 1980, my wife ran off to New York with a man who said he would make her a high-fashion model. I haven't seen her since."

"My, my. You say that very easily."

"I'm glad you think so. I had to practice a lot of years to make it sound that way."

Barbara looked up at him sharply. Behind the bland expression, she could detect the shadow of the old pain, in the eyes mostly.

"She didn't contest the divorce," he went on. "Just signed the papers and sent them back to my lawyer. I've never seen her on any magazine covers, so I guess the man was wrong, or lying to her."

"Was she beautiful enough to be a model?"

"Oh, yes," he said simply. "But she really didn't look it in pictures. Too self-conscious in front of a camera, I guess. Maybe that's why her career didn't work out in New York. I hope she's not too unhappy."

Barbara could see that he meant it. An awkward silence fell.

"I should get going," Paul said finally. "Are you here by yourself? I didn't see your mother."

"She's at Mary Wenner's. We're having lunch there. Mother went on ahead to explain why I would be a little late. I suppose I'd better get over there."

"Do you need a lift?"

"No, no. It's just a few blocks. Mum took her new bicycle, but I'd like to walk. Besides, you have investigating to do."

"Right," he grinned.

They walked in silence to the front of the house, where his car was parked.

"Paul," Barbara said, as he reached for the door handle, "did the medical examiner say whether or not a woman could have struck the blow that killed my uncle?"

"I asked him that," Paul replied. "He said it was quite possible, if the weapon was long enough. The wider the swing, the more force at impact. So even a small person can deliver a harder blow with a golf club, say, than with a short pipe."

"I see," Barbara murmured.

"You're thinking of Caroline Heim Bower?" he said, cocking his head at her.

"So, you *have* been getting some answers," she said with a smile.

"Of course," he said. "Do you think she's able-bodied enough?"

"What does that mean?"

"Well, you said that three able-bodied men might be candidates for the ladder business on Tuesday night," he shrugged. "Wouldn't an able-bodied woman be a possibility, too?"

"But Caroline Bower isn't in New Augsburg," Barbara said.

"Hmmm," he said. "Do we know that for sure?"

"Are you making fun of me?" Barbara asked as he got into his car.

"Maybe just a little," he grinned, closing the door. "But keep your windows closed, huh? Use the air conditioner."

"Right," she said. "Conserving electricity be damned." And she began to walk in the direction of Mary Wenner's house.

Mary's apartment was smaller than Eileen's, all on one floor, with a single bedroom and an eat-in kitchen rather than a dining room, but, of course, it was attached to her son's house, where she spent quite a lot of her time. Barbara remembered Ron Wenner as a big, good-natured man, quiet like his father. Whatever his wife might think of having her mother-in-law so near, Barbara felt sure that Ron himself must think it a fine idea.

The apartment was as cluttered as Mary's farmhouse had always been: rows of photographs on the living room tables, magazines stacked next to an armchair, needle-pointed cushions scattered on the sofa and chairs. Not a dirty house by any means, but a crowded one, and, like Mary herself, a bit disorganized.

Once during lunch, the door at the back of the kitchen burst open and a little girl of about six or seven ran in.

"Gosh," she exclaimed, wide-eyed. "I didn't think you'd still be eating, Grandma. It's kind of late for lunch."

Mary made proud introductions; this was Ron's middle child, Jennifer. James was three years older, and the baby, Melissa, was only two. Barbara caught Eileen looking wistfully at the little girl, following her with her eyes as the child ran back into her parents' house. Hungry for grandchildren, Barbara thought; poor Mum; poor me.

"Just like her mother," Mary said, beaming. "Bubbly, full of the dickens."

"Yes, I can see," Eileen said. "Her dad was always a quiet person, like your Jim."

"Jim *was* a quiet man," Mary said, shaking her head. "Almost, you might say, a sober man. And it's so odd, because he was pretty lively as a boy. When I first met him, he was something of a cutup. My mother said it was marriage that settled him down."

Barbara saw an opening in Mary's chatter for the subject she most wanted to discuss.

"In those early days, when you and Jim were first going together," Barbara said, "I suppose you knew all the local people your own age."

"Oh, sure," Mary said, rising predictably to the bait. "Why we went around in crowds. Sometimes a car was so loaded down on the way to a dance that you'd a thought the axles would break."

"Were Charlie and Geraldine Novak in your circle?" Barbara asked, and then looked away from Eileen's sharp glance and little frown.

"Well, not really," Mary said, looking a bit distracted by this specific reference in the midst of her generalized memories. "They were married, you know, while all the rest of us were still courting. And Charlie was always so grim about everything. He was only interested in that farm. It was a mess when his father died, and I think he had just made up his mind to make a go of it. And it sure is a showplace now. No, the only time we saw Charlie and Gerry was at the horse-pulling contests. They

170

had a gorgeous team in those days, beat out all comers. Why they—."

"Charlie seems to be friends with George Heim," Barbara interrupted, heading off one of Mary's flights. "Were they close in the old days, too?"

"It's hard to say about those Heim boys," Mary said. "They always kept pretty much to themselves, and they were older than most of us, too. But it would make sense that Charlie would like George, somebody so steady and serious. 'Role models' is what they call them these days, isn't it?"

"Yes, that's right," Barbara said. "But Mrs. Novak didn't like Caroline Heim much, I gather."

"Barbara," Eileen said, rather sternly for her, "stop beating about the bush. Mary knows you've been asking questions all over the township trying to find out who killed Tony, so why don't you just ask directly about what you want to know."

"All right, Mother. All right," Barbara said, embarrassed and a little flustered. "Mary, it doesn't seem likely that Tony's friends on the motorcycles had anything to do with his death because they stopped coming to New Augsburg in early August of that summer. So it seems that someone closer to home was responsible. Gerry Novak seems to think that it might even have been Caroline Heim herself, when she found out she was pregnant by Tony and then discovered that he wouldn't marry her. That could be what George is trying to cover up. The coroner says the blow could have been struck by a woman."

"Well, now," Mary said. She had been warming to the topic almost visibly as Barbara was talking. "I know why Gerry would be likely to say such a thing. She's always so dolled up these days, going to beauty shops regular as clockwork, but she was as plain as a post when she was a girl. And Caroline was a looker; didn't need a speck of makeup either. You know, Gerry and Charlie were both in the same class as Tony in the high school, and people said Gerry had a big crush on Tony for a while. But, of course, Tony wouldn't look twice at a stick like Gerry Fliegel. She latched onto poor Charlie after Tony left school, and they got married just as soon as they could manage it after graduation. Charlie was certainly somebody she could handle.''

Barbara was stunned. Was there no end to the web of sexual jealousy and intrigue that seemed to be at the heart of every story that touched on her uncle? People she had always thought of as old, sedate, *dull* people, whose lives seemed so far from any hint of romantic intrigue that she couldn't think of them as sexual beings at all—these people now seemed to have been part of some complex soap opera in their youth. In New Augsburg!

"But do you think Caroline could have killed Tony?" Eileen asked, caught up in the story herself.

"Oh, I don't know," Mary shrugged. "She always seemed so—I don't know how to say it—so passive, I guess. She let things happen to her, went along with whatever was going on. I don't think she could muster up the gumption to *plan* anything like that. But, I suppose if it happened on the spur of the moment, in anger—those Heims all have tempers."

"Yes, tempers," Barbara said, looking away. "You can do things when you're in a rage that other people wouldn't think you capable of, even people who know you really well."

When she turned back to the two older women, she found Eileen looking at her through narrowed eyes, a little frown puckering her wide forehead.

172

That night, Barbara lay awake for a long time, thinking about what Mary had said at lunch, about the troubled youth of so many of the people she knew, associating it all with her own "dating years" in New Augsburg. Eileen had always fussed girlishly over Barbara's dates, but Joseph Hoffman had regarded each new boy with quiet suspicion. Barbara had found this mildly annoying but "normal" because her girlfriends reported much the same behavior and attitude in their own fathers. But once during her sophomore year in high school, she had parked a long time with Jerry Paulson and had been more than a little disheveled and flushed when she crept into the house at 1:15 A.M. When she switched on the light, she found her father sitting at the kitchen table, a coffee cup in his right hand.

"It's pretty late," he had begun, looking her over carefully as he spoke, squinting a little from the brightness of the light.

"I know. I'm sorry. We all went out for pizza after the game." She wasn't good at lying to him, hadn't had much practice at it.

"Pizza places are all closed by midnight."

"Well, we talked for a while, in the car," she said, a little too quickly, and then she looked away from her father's face, for she'd seen there the beginnings of that cold stare he had turned on Earl Mueller in Smeltzer's tavern.

"Just talked?" He had stood up slowly and walked up to her. When she looked back at him, she saw that he was staring at her sweater. A quick glance downward showed her that she'd rebuttoned the sweater wrong— the right side was raised by one button.

"Nothing happened," she said hotly. It was almost true, because Jerry Paulson had never gone beyond fondling her breasts through her bra; unbuttoning the sweater had seemed to her to be a small concession.

"You see too much of that Paulson boy," her father had said, his voice quiet but ominous. "It's not good for a girl your age. I won't have it."

"That's not fair," she cried, tears on her face. "We didn't do anything wrong."

"Go up to bed," he'd said, and she quailed before the look on his face. She'd actually been afraid he might hit her; in all her life, he'd never hit her except for those little smacks on childish fingers when she reached for something that might hurt her. She'd gone upstairs, trembling, and they never spoke of it again. But she learned to be more careful, became a more practiced liar.

Now she found herself wondering whether it was really Jerry Paulson her father didn't trust or whether it was his own daughter. Did he see Tony in her? Were her adolescent restlessness and romantic dreaming painful reminders of another "wild" Hoffman? And that cold rage which had frightened her so much that night? Was it just a flash of the anger he'd once felt toward his lying, sneaking, "sexy" big brother?

And now she had fresh understanding of why her father had been so happy to have her safely married to a "nice boy" like Tom Mullens, a man *almost* as serious and responsible as his father-in-law. And, of course, she understood clearly at last why Joe Hoffman had reacted with vehement hostility when he learned that Tom had been unfaithful to his wife. The specter of Tony's sexual escapades had risen up across the years to blight any warm feelings her father had ever had for Tom.

When she finally fell asleep, Barbara had a disturbing dream. She was usually a person who slept soundly and didn't remember her dreams the next day. But this one stayed in her mind for the rest of the weekend. In the dream, she was in her old room at the farm and the sound of rain was drumming in her ears. She felt a sense of menace, of danger, that brought her up out of bed and sent her down the hall toward her parents' bedroom. Each detail of the hallway—the white clothes hamper, the small door to the attic, the decorative plate over the light switch—was realistic and possessed an almost surreal clarity. She opened the door to the room at the end of the hall and saw her mother, in a white lace nightgown, sitting up in the big bed; she was alone in the room.

"Where's Andrew?" Barbara said. "I can't find him. Do you know where he is? I've looked and looked."

Eileen just shook her head from side to side.

"Why isn't Daddy in bed?" Barbara asked. "It's very late, isn't it? He should be in bed. Milking comes so early."

Again, Eileen shook her head, tears spilling down her face.

"Are they together?" Barbara demanded, feeling angry with her mother for not speaking. "Are they downstairs?" When Eileen didn't answer, Barbara turned in the doorway and started for the stairs.

"Don't go down there!" Eileen cried, her voice high and frightened. "Please don't go down there."

Barbara descended the stairs, her muscles reduced now to the slow motion of dream, her foreboding increasing with each step. When she reached the foot of the stairs, she saw that the door leading to the kitchen was closed, something that was rare in the house where she had grown up. The white paint was smeared with blood; drops and even small pools of blood stained the linoleum at the base of the door. On the frame next to the doorknob, there was a bright-red handprint.

Barbara felt terror closing her throat, wanted to flee back up to her mother, but she sensed that Andrew and her father were beyond the door. She reached out for the knob, felt the sticky surface in her hand, and then pulled with all her might. The door sprang toward her, making her reel backward, clutching at the edges to keep from falling. Beyond the door, there was nothing, only the blackness of the night with the rain blowing horizontally across it. Half the house was gone.

13

When Paul Gillis appeared on Sunday afternoon, he was clearly off duty, dressed in jeans and a T-shirt, his feet covered by battered tennis shoes. Without the trappings of his office, he looked even more boyish than usual. He parried Barbara's questions about the Novaks as he dragged a big tool box from the trunk of his Toyota. It struck Barbara that the car looked too small for him, as if he would literally have to make himself shorter to get into it.

"Looks like it's going to get hot again," he said. "That dress looks nice and cool, though."

Barbara blushed a little, but she *had* chosen to wear the sundress because he was coming over, and she'd noticed him stealing appreciative glances at her ever since she'd walked into the parking lot to greet him.

"Well, if you're going to talk about the weather, I might as well go inside," she said, half bantering, half angry at him for postponing talk about Billy Novak; standing next to her savaged car, Billy was really all she wanted to talk about.

"That's a good idea," he laughed. "You'll have to

go inside to get me that beer you promised me. Give me some time to get all my stuff out.''

Barbara went through the back door into the kitchen where Eileen was reading the Sunday paper, spreading it out in sections all over the table in the way that had always made Barbara smile.

"I'm going for a bike ride in a bit," Eileen said absently. "Do you think the car repairs will take long?"

"I don't know," Barbara said, taking two glasses from the cupboard over the refrigerator. "Depends how much is trashed, I suppose."

"I wouldn't have thought the sheriff was a mechanic," Eileen said. "Doesn't seem to be exactly up his street."

Barbara heard the edge in her mother's voice—any interested man was a threat to the hoped-for reconciliation with Tom—but refused to rise to the bait.

"Anyone can be interested in cars, Mother," she replied lightly, pouring beer into one glass and iced tea into the other. She'd been feeling twitchy all weekend and didn't want to get into a row with her mother. Partly she felt "grounded" by not being able to use her own car, and partly she was haunted by her dream. She was always careful during her waking hours to keep herself from thinking about the baby, about Andrew, always ready to run from the painful memories. But dreams couldn't be defended against. Whenever she had a dream about Andrew—and these dreams were always fraught with anxiety or a terrible sense of loss and guilt—she was a wreck for days afterward.

"Have a good read, Mum," Barbara said a bit archly, balancing the glasses and heading for the door.

Paul was already hunkered down over the Volkswagen's engine, his long legs so folded up that his knees came almost to his ears.

"Here's your beer as ordered," Barbara said, handing it over.

"Thanks," he said, reaching up with a grin. "I don't think this job's going to be as bad as I first thought. Looks like I won't need new parts, just do some splicing and tidying. I guess you'll be able to leave on schedule for Chicago."

"I'm not going back just yet," she said, looking away quickly as she saw the pleased smile spreading across Paul's face. "I called my downstairs neighbor this morning to tell her she'd have to water my plants a little bit longer."

"I guess I don't have to wonder what's keeping you in New Augsburg," he said, shrugging and taking a sip of beer. "I don't think it's my charms."

"Well, you know what this vandalism means," she said, gesturing at the car. "Someone doesn't want me poking around in my uncle's murder, but I don't scare so easily."

"Well, ma'am," he said, chuckling. "*I* don't want you poking around in your uncle's murder, but I wouldn't say we can be so sure why your car was trashed."

Barbara looked back at him, eyeing him speculatively for a moment.

"Are you or are you not going to tell me what happened when you talked to Billy Novak on Friday?" she said at last.

"I saw all of the Novaks on Friday," he said, turning back to the engine.

Barbara drew a deep breath, waited, but Paul said nothing else. She wanted to ask if Charlie Novak had told the "young smart aleck of a sheriff" about her father's relationship with Caroline Heim, if Charlie had repeated his suggestion that Barbara Hoffman should look

179

a little closer to home for suspects. Was this laconic, seemingly relaxed man, working quietly on her car, already investigating her father as the prime suspect in the murder of Tony Hoffman? Paul Gillis was giving nothing away.

"Okay," Barbara said, struggling to keep the concern out of her voice. "And what, if anything, did you learn about who wrecked my car?"

"Well, she's not really wrecked that much," he said, reaching into the motor to lift a wire. "But all right, all right. I asked Billy about it."

"And he denied it, of course."

"Yes, he did. But it didn't take me very long to find out that he *is* pretty mad at you. Said something about 'big city chick with too much time on her hands.' "

"Hmp!" Barbara snorted. "I'm no more 'big city' than he is, and he knows it. Do you believe him about my car?"

"I don't know," he said, picking up a screwdriver from among the tools arranged in a neat row on the pavement. "I suppose he could have done it, but I don't think I'm going to be able to prove anything if he doesn't admit it. He's a pretty tough guy."

"He's mad at me because I'm investigating Tony's murder, and he did this to my car to scare me off," she said, jiggling the ice in her glass. "I just know the two things are connected." If the Novaks could direct suspicion at her father, well she could turn the tables on them.

"You don't know anything of the kind," Paul said without looking up. "Why would Billy care about a murder that happened before he was born?"

"Because he's trying to protect somebody," she said quickly, eager to explain her theory. "The Heims,

180

maybe. They're old friends of the Novaks, and I could tell that they had already let the Novaks know that I was asking questions. The telephone lines must have been humming. Or Billy could be concerned about somebody in his own family, one of his parents maybe.''

"And what motive would either of them have had for killing Anton Hoffman?" he asked, looking up sharply at her face.

"Mary Wenner told me that Geraldine Novak was sweet on Tony when they were all in high school together." Even she realized how lame it sounded as soon as she heard herself saying it.

"Oh, come on," he sighed, going back to his work. "The Novaks were long married and had two children by the time your uncle disappeared. They didn't like him much, I gathered from what they told me, but I don't think they had much to do with him in the last few years of his life. You'll have to do much better than a high school crush, I'm afraid."

"All right, all right. But Billy Novak isn't off the hook about my car, at least not as far as *I'm* concerned. He was already angry with me when I first saw him on Thursday, and I didn't do anything to him or his family. I haven't set eyes on him in over fifteen years. So how do you explain that spite?"

"I think maybe Billy's angry most of the time," Paul said softly. "He's got a lot to be angry about."

"Maybe that's true," she said, recognizing the sympathy in his voice. "But why focus it on me when all I did was walk around the corner of the porch?"

"You caught him at a bad moment. He told me that you heard him yelling at his dog. And then, he said, you looked at him as if he were a bug."

"I did no such thing!" Barbara was indignant.

"Probably not, but he thought you did." He got down onto the ground to reach under the Volkswagen's bumper.

"Try to put yourself in his place," he went on while he worked, as if he didn't want to see her face as he said this. "He's in that chair and he's just screamed at a dumb animal, and then you appear in front of him. A beautiful woman his own age, somebody who knew him before, when he was a high school basketball star. He feels like a jerk, humiliated, and so he lashes out. It's not you so much as it's his whole life."

"I don't know how you can do your job if you keep making excuses for suspects," she said, exasperated by his attitude. "You did the same for that Peeping Tom kid."

He sat up now, draped his hands over his bony knees, and looked straight at her.

"I don't know how I could be good at police work if I *stopped* trying to figure out what's going on in people's heads," he said gently. "And that's not the same thing as 'making excuses.' "

"I'm sorry," she said, feeling oddly as if she might cry. "But you seem to be taking Billy's side, as if you believe his version instead of mine."

"It's got nothing to do with whether I believe him or not. But I can't help feeling bad for him. And I can't help remembering that I was safe at the University of Wisconsin, marching on picket lines where the worst I had to worry about was a little tear gas, while he was walking through mine fields that finally cut his spine in two."

Barbara remembered what Mary had said about Dick Schneider's feelings during the Second World War, how he felt they all owed something to Joe Hoffman because he was fighting while they were safe at home. Perhaps men on the home front always felt that combination of guilt and awe for soldiers, whether the war involved was a popular one or not.

"I see," she said softly. "I see what you're saying, but *you* didn't hurt him and neither did I. We don't deserve to get whipped for his pain."

"No, we don't," he said, getting to his knees now to give further attention to the engine, his fine hands, covered with grease, carefully pulling up the piece he had pushed up from underneath. "But we can still see that he's hurting."

There was a long pause and Barbara sipped the last of her tea, feeling the sun against her back, an uncomfortable sensation on the exposed skin above the sundress.

"Maybe your picketing helped to save other Billys," Barbara ventured at last. "By bringing the war to a stop sooner, I mean."

"Maybe," he answered shortly. "I don't know. I gave all that up in 1970. Didn't take any part at all for my last two years of college."

"Why?"

"Do you remember the spring and summer of 1970?"

"Sure. I was a senior in high school. That was the spring of the bombing of Cambodia as I recall."

"Yes. And Kent State and the biggest student demonstrations. I came home from school that summer all fired up still, ready to bust heads if anyone criticized the antiwar movement. But that August, protestors blew up Sterling Hall on the Madison campus—my school, you see—and Robert Fassnacht died in the blast. He wasn't supposed to be there. The building was supposed to be empty, but he was there working on his research in the middle of the night, and he died. Do you remember that?"

"Sure. Not details like that, but the main events. Did you know this Robert Fassnacht?"

"No. And I didn't know the protestors who blew up the building either, but I remember the details, all right. Fassnacht was opposed to the war, too. He was thirty-three years old, and he died on his son's third birthday. We were supposed to be against the killing, but now somebody had been killed right here. And I realized that I'd been ready to punch out people who disagreed with me. It all made me feel like such a hypocrite. I went back to school that fall soured on all things political. And now look at me. Now I'm a cop."

"But a very different kind of cop," Barbara said, looking at the back of his well-shaped head. "Mother told me how you talked Alvin Dart out of his house when he went berserk with his gun."

"That's just standard police procedure," he shrugged. "No charging in unless somebody's in imminent danger. Alvin was just taking potshots out of the windows. He let his wife and kids go right at the beginning. He's in a treatment program now for his alcoholism. Coming along pretty well, I think."

"Everybody thinks you did a good job, though," she said, eager to make it up to him for having criticized him.

"It's not a big deal," he said. "Most of what I do is pretty ordinary stuff. My biggest job for the summer is coming up this week with the opening of the county fair. That always brings a few incidents, so we have to patrol more, be visible so to speak. My deputies will be on full-time duty for the duration."

"So you won't have time for anything else for almost a week," Barbara said, feeling irritated again. "And a forty-year-old murder will get the back burner."

"Not entirely," he said, "but I'll be pretty busy, sure. To be fair, whatever *can* be known about your uncle's death isn't going to go away in a week."

"You can't be sure of that," Barbara replied. "You'll lose the element of surprise if all of these people have time to use their grapevines. They'll prepare their defenses, clam up all over the county."

"Give it a rest, Barbara," he sighed. "Give yourself a rest. I know this case is important to you, but it's going to sort itself out one way or the other. And maybe there are no answers."

"I *have* to know who killed him." She realized she had spoken too quickly, too urgently, and she hastily backed off when he raised puzzled eyes to meet hers. "He was family to me and I think there are plenty of things that people aren't telling you."

"Well, you have to leave it to me anyway," he said firmly. "Why don't you take a break and come to the fair?"

"I haven't been to the fair since I was in high school," she snorted.

"All the more reason to check it out again. You could go with me, go on the wild rides. It might be fun."

"Aren't you going to be on duty?" she asked playfully.

"Technically, yes. But you could meet me there and be 'visible' along with me as I cruise the midway. I'll win you a teddy bear. What do you say?"

"I don't know," she said, running a cool hand over the warm skin at the back of her neck.

"None of your suspects will be at home anyway," he said, and now he was really laughing at her a bit. "They'll all be taking a break from being suspects to go to the fair."

"Oh, all right," she laughed. "When?"

"Tuesday is opening day, nothing much going on. Wednesday would be good, though, especially if you're interested in hog judging."

"Oh, hog judging has always been high on my list of things to see." She was beginning to enjoy the banter.

"About two o'clock? I'd meet you at the main gate."

"Fine. Do they still have the Scrambler? That was always my favorite ride."

"Oh, I think the Bullet is better."

"Too wild for me."

They looked at each other for a moment.

"I could use another beer," he said at last, blushing a little under his tan. "This is a two-beer job, definitely."

"Of course," she said, moving toward the house. "Is there much left to do?"

"Just a little. I'll have this little sweetheart humming again before suppertime."

"Will you stay for supper?" Barbara said, turning back toward him.

"Thanks, but I can't. My mother is expecting me. You know how mothers are."

"Yes, I sure do," Barbara said, wondering what Eileen would say about her date with Paul Gillis. "We must be mindful of what mothers expect." And she trotted up the three steps to go inside the kitchen, where she knew her own mother was waiting and wondering what was going on in the parking lot.

14

On Monday, Barbara drove her mother into Green Bay for some shopping; she herself needed more light sports clothes now that she was extending her visit into the warmer days of summer. The Volkswagen hummed along nicely; Barbara thought it sounded even better than it had before Paul Gillis had fixed it.

Green Bay had changed dramatically since Barbara's childhood. For one thing, to get there, they had to drive through bustling suburbs which had been dairy farms when she was in grade school. And the downtown area was now entirely unfamiliar to her. The rows of quaint little shops along Washington Street were gone; the hodge-podge of turn-of-the-century buildings which had housed them had simply been demolished to make way for parking lots to serve the huge Port Plaza Mall that now dominated the bay end of the street. Pedestrian overpasses connected the mall to a gleaming new hotel, and even the venerable Prange's Department Store looked different, dwarfed by the new buildings. It wasn't that Barbara hated malls; she was trendy enough to like the convenience and the plenty of these modern institutions.

But she was made slightly uneasy by the materialism and by the fiction of "climate control" which seduced people into forgetting the caution and attentiveness that were the sensible responses to Wisconsin winters. Hurrying from store to store outside, with caps pulled down and scarves wrapped high, at least encouraged shoppers to notice the falling wind chill or the imminence of a blizzard.

Thoughts of winter immediately brought into her mind the Christmas shopping expeditions she had made with her parents when she was growing up. She and her father had always gone off together to find Eileen's presents in the shops along Washington Street, handling scarves and gloves at Nau's, spraying perfume at Prange's cosmetics counter. And every year they would take time out to duck into Kapps, a wonderful old German restaurant full of dark paneling and cosy, leather-padded booths. She always had hot chocolate, and her father had coffee and cake. Kapps, too, was gone now, and a platter her father had bought for her at the auction was all she had left of that treasured place, that magical time.

Stepping across the hot asphalt of the parking lot, remembering Kapps, Barbara felt again the agony of her father's loss, the shame of suspecting him, the helpless fear that something sinister was going to taint his memory forever. She remembered that she had already dreamed about him as separated from her by a door marked with blood. Though she went through the motions of shopping, even bought herself some shorts and a sleeveless tank top, Barbara's mind was busy with other things, with a renewed resolve to prove her father's innocence.

"Where exactly does Peter Heim live now?" Barbara said to her mother over breakfast on Tuesday. They were both still in their nightgowns, taking a certain low-key pleasure in the decadence of a late-starting day.

"Why do you need to know that?" Eileen asked, looking at her skeptically. She had been rather obviously "refraining from comment" ever since Barbara told her on Sunday that she was going to the fair with Paul, but now she seemed dangerously close to voicing all sorts of concern and disapproval.

"I don't 'need' to know it," Barbara answered, picking at her eggs. "I was wondering, that's all."

"Are you planning to interview the rest of the Heims now?"

"Mother, I just asked where Peter lives, that's all!"

"I told you, somewhere near Red Banks. I don't know anymore than that." She took a sip of her coffee. "You *are* going to leave detecting to the sheriff, aren't you?"

"He doesn't have much time for detecting right now, what with the fair opening today."

"That doesn't answer my question, my girl."

"Let's drop it, Mother," Barbara said, standing up. "What do you have on for today?"

Eileen waited for a moment before answering, clearly debating with herself about how much to press her moody daughter. Finally she sighed and stood up to gather her own dishes.

"I've got a 10:30 appointment with Ed Seidl at the hardware store. I'm applying for a job."

"A job!" Barbara turned back toward her mother, mouth agape.

"Just part time," Eileen said, drawing her small frame into an attitude of defiance, as if she expected to be mocked. "I can't just retire, Barbara. It would drive me mad to have nothing to do except play cards and totter back and forth between gossiping friends. I'm too young for that.''

"Well, I think it's marvelous," Barbara said. "It's just that you caught me by surprise, that's all. You're full of surprises."

"Sign of life, that," Eileen chuckled, putting her cup and saucer onto the counter. "What are you plotting for your day?"

"I'm not plotting," Barbara answered, her voice edgy. "I'm going for my run first, and then I might drop in on Cheryl Blahnik's folks, find out how she's doing in California, see some pictures of her kids. And maybe I'll go over to the IGA to see if they have any raspberries. I've been craving raspberries."

"I'll probably be gone when you get in from your run," Eileen said. "Could you remember to pick up some mayonnaise at the store? We're almost out." How easily Eileen had fallen back into saying "we" now that Barbara had been with her more than two weeks!

When Barbara got back from a grueling ten-mile run, it was almost eleven o'clock and the apartment was empty. She showered quickly and changed into her new shorts and top—the day was already very hot. Then she walked the few short blocks to the IGA. Her trip to the grocery store had an ulterior motive she hadn't told Eileen about. She knew that George Heim's youngest daughter worked there as a checker and that it would probably take very little coaxing to make her reveal exactly how to find Peter Heim's farm near Red Banks; local people had the habit of explaining with precision how to find places in the country, citing landmarks along the way in their eagerness to go maps one better. It was, Barbara

190

reflected, a way of showing off what they knew, in the same way that her graduate school classmates would cite obscure reference books.

But Barbara never got the chance to ask Rita Heim Bennick where her Uncle Peter lived. As soon as she mentioned Peter's name, Rita volunteered the information that he and his sister, "Aunt Caroline," were "home for the fair," staying through the weekend at "the home place." Barbara paid for the raspberries and the mayonnaise, wondering if this visit had been planned before the discovery of Tony's body, or if telephone calls from Oshawanee County to Brown County had brought the brother and sister to George Heim's home for a powwow to get the story straight.

How could she talk to Peter and Caroline now? There was no excuse she could make for going back to the Heim farm since George had practically run her off the place. And the more they talked to each other, the less likely it became that Sheriff Paul Gillis would be able to get at the truth of what they were hiding—she was sure they were hiding something. And how was she now going to meet Caroline Heim Bower, the "beauty" her father had loved, over whom he had wept in the Schneiders' kitchen that late-summer night in 1943? What was Caroline like now? Barbara felt almost as much curiosity over that as she did about what Caroline might know concerning Tony Hoffman's death.

As Barbara was unlocking the front door of the apartment, she remembered that the mail usually came before noon, so she balanced the bag of groceries on the narrow porch rail and reached over to lift the lid on the long aluminum mailbox.

"What on earth—?" she said aloud when she saw what was inside.

191

A white, Trim-line phone, its cord piled neatly next to it, almost filled the box. Barbara's hand had begun, almost automatically, to reach for the object, as if to confirm with a touch that her eyes weren't deceiving her. But she stopped herself, her right hand suspended over the box, as a chill of fear swept over her despite the warmth of the sun.

"It looks like Mummy's phone," she said, again speaking out loud as if she were explaining something to an invisible companion.

Indeed, Eileen had such a phone on a small table next to her bed. She'd been almost apologetic about having two phones in such a small apartment, arguing defensively, "Once I'm upstairs for the evening, I'd hate to run back down to the dining room"—arguing to convince only herself, for Barbara had said at once that she thought the second phone was a good idea.

Now Barbara pushed the front door open, peered inside the apartment, and called, "Mother!" Only silence answered her. She picked up the small grocery bag and stepped inside the house, moving cautiously, setting her feet down carefully as if she were afraid to be heard. On a small table inside the front hallway, there was a neat stack of letters atop a catalog. Barbara had used the back door when she came in from her run and hadn't even glanced at this table when she'd hurried through the front hall on her way to the store. Had Eileen brought in the mail? How had a telephone got into the mailbox, and when was it put there?

Barbara's mind was racing, though her body was moving with an almost instinctive caution. Inside the living room, she set down the groceries and her purse on the first available chair, preparing herself for a quick flight if necessary. Her deep sense of foreboding made this gesture seem reasonable.

Yet the downstairs rooms looked completely undisturbed, as tidy and ordered as they had been the last time Barbara had seen them. She walked through the kitchen to the back door and found it locked. The sudden coming on of the central air conditioning made her jump and draw in her breath sharply. She paused for a few seconds to steady herself and then started for the stairs, tiptoeing across the kitchen tiles before reaching the carpeting which would muffle her steps for the rest of the search.

Barbara paused in the upstairs hallway, her heart slamming, perspiration clammy on her forehead and upper lip. One part of her mind was telling her how silly it was to be so afraid in a quiet apartment in the middle of the day. But her physical reaction seemed to have a life of its own. She couldn't shake the feeling that something sinister had happened in the apartment. She glanced quickly into the bathroom and her own bedroom; both of these doors were standing wide open. Finally she turned to face the closed door of her mother's bedroom.

She wanted to call "Mother" again, meant to do it, but she found that her voice wasn't working; her throat was so tight that she couldn't force out a sound. She stood at the door for a moment, her hand on the knob. It struck her that this was very much like the scene in her dream when she'd been torn between a need to open a door and terror about what she might find on the other side. Finally she turned the knob and flung the door open.

The room was in perfect order, the bed made, the dresser top covered with the bottles and boxes that Eileen always lined up in ranks like soldiers. Beyond the bed was the table where the white phone should have been.

Even from the doorway, Barbara could tell that the phone was gone. But something else was in its place, something dark that Barbara couldn't identify. She started forward, peering first around the door to confirm her impression that she was alone in the room.

When she rounded the big double bed, she could finally tell what was on the little table. It was a crumpled piece of blue fabric, sodden and matted with a dark liquid that had run through to the tabletop and trickled down the front of the single drawer. Both the color and the smell, faintly sweet in the still air, convinced Barbara that the liquid was blood. And the stained embroidery along one edge of the blue fabric made it instantly familiar, too. It was the nightgown Eileen had been wearing when Barbara last saw her at 9:30 that morning.

15

"Mummy," Barbara breathed, her knees almost giving way under her. "Oh God, Mummy."

It came to her all at once that the door to Eileen's bedroom had been closed when she came upstairs to shower and change after her run. She had simply assumed that her mother was off on her job interview, hadn't believed there was any need to check on her. This blood-stained nightgown had already been here; the phone had already been in the mailbox.

Barbara forced her legs to move, raced downstairs to the telephone in the dining room. She had already dialed "0," to ask the operator to contact the sheriff's office, when she thought of something else. She hung up again and grabbed for the phone book. When she found the number for Seidl's Hardware, she dialed with a shaking finger, listening to the sounds of the connection finding its way across five blocks. The lazy buzz of the ring sounded over and over again—five times, six times.

"Come on, come on," Barbara said out loud. "Answer the goddamned phone."

Just as she heard the cracking sound of a lifted receiver

and a voice saying, "Seidl's Hardware," Barbara distinctly heard another sound—a key turning in the front door.

She hung up the phone at once and darted around the half-wall that separated the dining room from the kitchen. Crouching behind the counter, she heard the door open and close, waited for footsteps with the breath held inside her lungs. They were a long time coming, for the new arrival had apparently paused inside the short hallway. Finally, there were footsteps, advancing slowly into the living room. Barbara measured with a glance the distance to the back door, but then fought the impulse to flee. She rocked forward on her haunches and stole a peek around the counter where an unobstructed path through the dining room and into the living room was visible.

Standing in the middle of the living room, holding the white phone in both hands and looking dazed, was Eileen. Her navy blue purse hung from the shoulder of the crisp dress she had obviously thought proper attire for a job interview.

"Mummy!" Barbara cried, springing up from behind the counter and running toward the living room.

Eileen screamed and dropped the phone, her little hands flying up to her face in bewilderment as Barbara bore down on her and folded her in a tight hug.

"What on earth—?" Eileen gasped. "What is going on here? Why are there groceries in the living room?"

This fixing on the most insignificant of the details in the scene struck Barbara as wildly funny. She burst into laughter, a long peal of laughter whose hysterical edge she was aware of even as she struggled to control it.

* * *

Paul Gillis arrived a little before two o'clock to find the women huddled over tea in the kitchen. After one trip upstairs to show Eileen what was on the bed table, neither of them had felt any impulse to investigate further on their own. The phone was still lying on the living room carpet where Eileen had dropped it.

"You're sure you locked both doors when you went out?" Paul said to Eileen after he'd made a careful circuit of the apartment, listening to breathless explanations from both women who followed behind as he went.

"Oh, quite sure," Eileen said.

"I let myself in the back door when I got back from running," Barbara said, "and the front door when I got back from the store, so I know they were both locked. And the windows are all closed because of the air conditioning. There was no forced entry. Whoever did this had a key."

"But there are only two keys," Eileen protested. "I have one and, Barbara, you have the other."

"The trouble with small towns is that no one has the locks changed when an apartment changes hands," Paul said, pacing a little in the living room as the two women sat down next to each other on the sofa. "There could be any number of keys floating around—former tenants, friends of former tenants. People have extra keys cut to leave with neighbors when they go on vacation and then never bother to get them back. I'll have to do a lot of checking."

"Judy Wenner used to live in this apartment," Eileen said suddenly, and Barbara looked hard at her.

"Who?" Paul asked.

"Mary and Jim Wenner's daughter," Eileen answered. "Our old neighbors at the farm. Judy lived here for a few months after she got married—she's Judy Gordon now. But, of course, that was a few years ago, and several people have lived here since. These flats are never advertised that I know of. People just sort of pass them along to relatives and friends. I heard about this opening here when Mrs. DeGroot moved into the nursing home, and I remembered Mary saying it was a nice little place."

"Do you know all of the tenants who've lived here?" Paul asked.

"No, no," Eileen said with a firm shake of her head. "These buildings went up in 1975, and the turnover is quite brisk, I think."

"Of course, it doesn't even have to be a key from someone who once lived in this apartment," Paul said. "As I said, some former tenant could have given a spare key to a neighbor who doesn't even live here anymore. We could use more big-city paranoia around here, I guess."

There was a little silence now. Barbara's forehead was puckered into a thoughtful frown.

"That *is* blood upstairs, isn't it?" Eileen asked, a little shudder in her voice.

"Yes, I think so," he answered. "And it looks as if it was poured over the night dress; there are no other signs of blood, no hand prints. The lab boys will be able to tell us more. I'll take the gown with me if you can find me a plastic bag."

"What kind of a sick person would do such a thing?" Eileen asked as she stood up and started for the kitchen.

Paul looked hard at Barbara before answering.

"Well, I think it's some sort of a message," he said at last.

"Message?" Eileen called from the kitchen.

"Yes, Mum," Barbara said. She'd been thinking exactly the same thing while they were waiting for Paul to arrive. "Someone is saying, 'I can get at you.' It's a warning."

"A warning about what?" Eileen demanded, coming back into the room with a plastic bag. "A warning to whom?"

"To me, I think," Barbara said, watching Paul's face to see if he would concur. "Somebody is telling me that he can get at my mother if I don't quit asking questions about Uncle Tony. That's it, isn't it?"

"Looks like it might be," Paul said quietly.

"But I haven't done anything," Barbara cried, her nerves near the breaking point. "Since I went out to see the Novaks last week, I haven't been trying to find out anything. I haven't gone anywhere; I haven't interviewed anyone."

"But I have," Paul said, looking at her intently. "I was here on Sunday to fix your car. We talked for a long time. That might appear suspicious or threatening to somebody."

"But that would mean that somebody is watching us," Barbara said. "Spying on us."

"Sure," he shrugged. "Somebody had to be watching the house this morning to see that both of you were out for a predictable period of time—long enough for it to be safe to do all this."

Barbara and Eileen exchanged a wordless glance. Someone watching them, keeping track of their comings and goings! Barbara shuddered as she remembered the watcher in the cemetery. Obviously someone knew all their movements. Again, she felt the impulse to tell Paul about that incident. This would be the right time for it. But she hesitated, realizing that he would be angry with her for withholding the information. And she wondered, too, if it could really add anything to what they already knew.

"This incident is making me rethink the Peeping Tom business from last week, too," Paul went on. "You might be right about that, Barbara. Maybe all of this is connected somehow. Trouble is, we've got problems with most of our suspects, haven't we? It might have been Billy Novak who trashed your car, but he couldn't have been on a ladder outside your room, and he couldn't have got up and down the stairs to pull this stunt today. And old George Heim might have wrecked the car and switched the phone, but I still don't see him creeping up to a second-story bedroom."

"Of course, that's absurd," Eileen said, sitting down again. "I've told Barbara it's daft to think George has anything to do with any of this, including what happened to Tony forty years ago."

"But somebody could have delegated the job," Barbara argued. "Or at least some of the jobs."

"You mean the Heims' son, Raymond," Paul said.

"Yes," Barbara answered. "Why not?"

"Oh, Barbara," Eileen interrupted. "Raymond seems so inoffensive. I don't think he's very bright, either."

"It doesn't take brains, Mother," Barbara said. "It only takes somebody telling him what to do."

Then she looked up at Paul again, watching him pace.

"You can take the phone away and have it checked for fingerprints," Barbara said. "That should tell us something at least about *this* little terrorist incident."

"Think that over," he said, pausing to stand before her. "That phone was installed, what, two or three weeks ago? And it's not a brand new phone, is it? So, it has the installer's fingerprints on it, prints from whoever packed it to bring it here, your prints. And Mrs. Hoffman handled it again when she brought it back into the house today. How is that going to help us?''

''But the unfamiliar ones don't count if it has the ones that matter,'' Barbara said, her voice intense.

''And how do we make a match?'' he went on. ''Most people in America don't have their fingerprints on file. You don't, do you?''

''Well, *take* fingerprints from—.'' She broke off because she had almost said a name. ''From potential suspects,'' she finished.

''That's not how the law works, Barbara,'' he said gently. ''I can't just go up to people and say, 'Hello, I'm here to take your fingerprints.' I have to have grounds for an arrest, and only then do we routinely fingerprint those arrested people.''

''Then you're trying to say that nothing can be done about this,'' she said, sinking back onto the sofa.

''No, I'm not. There are other ways to proceed. Ways which you are to leave to me, understand? Meanwhile, get somebody to change your locks, Mrs. Hoffman.''

''I certainly will,'' Eileen said, getting up as Paul started upstairs to collect the nightgown.

''I'll walk Paul to his car,'' Barbara said, her voice still tense. Eileen took this as her cue to stay behind, though she looked a bit dubious over Barbara's obvious desire to talk to the sheriff alone.

''I'm sorry I can't get you the results you think I should be getting,'' Paul said without looking at her as they walked down the porch steps together. ''But I'm going to do everything the law allows me to do.''

''I'm trying to accept that,'' Barbara replied. ''And I'm trying to believe that you will, as you say, 'proceed.' ''

He stopped now to look down at her.

"Just because I don't make a lot of noise about it doesn't mean I don't know my job," he said, and his voice was a bit angry now.

"All right," she said, blushing a little under his direct gaze. "I wanted to tell you that Peter Heim and his sister Caroline are in town for the fair, staying with George and Mae."

"Yes, I know," he said. "George told me last week they were coming. Saves me a trip to Brown County."

"You *do* know your job, don't you? Why didn't you tell me on Sunday that you'd interviewed the Heims?"

"Part of my job is keeping things to myself until I'm ready to draw some conclusions."

"I'm sorry I've been so impatient, Paul. I guess my mother is right about my being obsessive. But when I saw that blood—well, I can't tell you how it frightened me. I can handle anything that's aimed at me, but this is my mother. If anything happened to her—."

"Nothing's going to happen to her," he said, taking her elbows into his long hands. "This is a warning, as you said. So be it. Take the warning and leave detective work to me from now on. Whoever did this will notice and back off."

"Sure," she said. "That's what I'll do."

"Are we still on for tomorrow?" he asked, not yet letting her go. "For the fair, I mean."

"Yes, of course," she said. "About two o'clock."

"By that time, I'll know something about this blood," he said, tossing the bag into the car before climbing inside after it.

* * *

Barbara spent the afternoon in a daze. Eileen seemed to recover more quickly. She began describing her job interview, reporting happily that she would begin work with a training session on Friday morning.

"It'll be just fifteen hours a week," she said, busily tidying the kitchen after lunch. "No weekends and no evenings. It'll make for a nice bit of extra lolly." Eileen frequently produced British slang words when she meant to be diverting. It was obvious that she could see Barbara's abstraction.

"That's nice, Mother," Barbara murmured, but she was thinking about Paul's many duties, duties that would keep him from spending much time on Hoffman family business for the next few days while the fair was on. He'd already indicated that finding out who might have extra keys to this apartment was a pretty big job all by itself. Maybe she could help with that at least. Checking with the landlord about past tenants could hardly be construed as investigating a murder. Besides, who would know?

When the locksmith arrived from Green Bay at 3:30, Barbara pleaded restlessness and announced that she was going for a walk. She actually went looking for Matthew Krieger, who owned both the bowling alley and the feed mill. The bowling alley was closer, so Barbara decided to begin there, a short walk up Main Street.

Only when she'd reached the end of the long block leading away from the apartment building did she remember what Paul had said about someone watching them. She began to glance around furtively, examining parked cars to see if someone was sitting inside, looking at upstairs windows to see if any neighboring building afforded a clear view of her mother's apartment. The creepy feeling of danger lurking nearby was one she'd often had in Chicago, but it was wholly new in these surroundings, a feeling so unwelcome here that she almost felt like crying. She circled the block with the Blahniks' house on it, a diversionary tactic, and glanced behind her often before she felt confident that no one was following.

Mid-Town Bowl was a long, narrow building with a barroom just inside the front door and, behind that, four alleys stretching away almost as far as Oak Street. Barbara stepped out of the blazing afternoon sun into the darkened bar and was met by a blast of icy air that made her shudder in her new shorts and top. The room was empty except for a young woman lounging behind the long bar. She stood up slowly and turned her face from the alleys toward Barbara. The sound of scattering pins came from the left-side alley, the one Barbara couldn't see.

"Hello," Barbara called to the young woman.

"Hiya," was the laconic answer. "What can I do ya?" As she walked along the bar, Barbara could see that she was wearing a tube top over tight jeans. Her heels made a sharp tapping sound on the tiled floor.

"I'm looking for Mr. Krieger," Barbara said, wrapping her arms against the air-conditioning, amazed that this girl didn't seem cold.

The girl stopped and leaned against the bar, her face gone cold as she looked Barbara over from head to toe. Barbara didn't know the girl, but she recognized the type because she had grown up with girls like this, the sort of girl who always wore a brightly colored nylon jacket with the name of a bar embroidered across the back— wore it even to church.

"Which Mr. Krieger," the girl said, "the old one or the young one?" Her voice had taken on a challenging air, her jaw had stopped working the gum she was chewing. Barbara was at a loss to explain this apparent hostility.

"I'm looking for Mr. Matthew Krieger," Barbara said evenly. "He's my mother's landlord. Are you a relative?"

"Nah," the girl said, her jaws beginning to punish the gum again. "I tend bar afternoons."

There had been a sudden stop to the sounds of bowling a moment earlier, and now Barbara heard another sound. She looked up to see Billy Novak rolling his wheelchair into the barroom. The sight of his scowling face struck instant fear into Barbara. That he should be here in the village when she pictured him as attached somehow to his parents' farm made her think immediately of the blood-stained nightgown and the phone in the mailbox. Billy rolled his chair along the bar and came to a stop with a slight sideways lurch in front of Barbara, as if he had stopped himself just in time from running her down. Under the red mustache, his mouth was pulled into a sneer and his eyes were focused, not on Barbara's face, but on her bare legs, his glance traveling up and down from her sandals to her shorts.

"Well, well, well," he drawled. "Look who's here. I didn't know you were a bowler, Barbie. Come out back with me and I'll show you some balls."

The girl behind the bar snickered, a snuffling, unpleasant sound. Barbara looked at her sharply, saw the snicker fade into an insolent smile.

"Is Matthew Krieger here?" Barbara asked, hearing the tremor in her own voice.

"I'll handle this, Heather," Billy snapped when the girl started to answer. "You aren't being very polite, Barbie. Don't you say hello to old neighbors?"

"I don't think I owe a greeting to anyone as vulgar and hostile as you are," Barbara said, flaring into anger at last.

"Vulgar and hostile!" Billy's voice was a mocking imitation of her own. "Just listen to that when all we want is to make nice. What do you want with Matt Krieger?"

"I need to speak with him about my mother's apartment," Barbara said tonelessly, avoiding Billy Novak's leering glance.

"Something going on over there?" Billy asked.

"I need to see Mr. Krieger," Barbara said even more quietly.

"The sheriff was in here about 1:30 and he's looking for Matt, too," Heather said. "What's the problem?"

Barbara was taken aback by the information that Paul had apparently also thought of beginning the investigation in this way. It occurred to her that she might have been underestimating the sheriff all along.

"Our little Barbie likes to sic the law on people," Billy said, his powerful hands rocking the wheels of his chair back and forth in front of Barbara's feet. "You wanna be more careful about that, sweetheart," and he looked up intently at her face. "You can't hide forever behind that sheriff. He's not such hot stuff as you think he is."

"Why don't you just knock it off?" Barbara said, anger finally overcoming her caution. "For reasons best known to yourself, you've been trying to scare me, to run me out of town. But I'm not going to budge. You don't frighten me, do you hear me, Billy Novak? You don't frighten me.''

"Don't I?" he said, his hard eyes narrowing. "Don't I?"

Barbara looked at Heather, who was leaning on the bar, her breasts pushed forward into the skimpy tube top. Then she looked back at Billy. Were these two a couple? They seemed to know each other well. Their suspicion and hostility hung in the chill air, forming a wall she knew she wouldn't be able to scale. What was it? Was it that her education and her life in Chicago seemed like a betrayal of some sort to them? Or was it that they, tied so irrevocably to New Augsburg, resented her escape? Or both? Or was it something more sinister? What was behind Billy Novak's insulting sneer?

"Never mind," Barbara said, her voice expressionless again. "If the sheriff is taking care of it, I don't need to see Mr. Krieger."

She turned her back on them and walked to the door. Just as she was pulling it open, she heard Heather's voice, raised just enough to carry across the room: "Snob!" But Barbara didn't turn around. She stepped outside, feeling the shock of the hot air against her chilled flesh.

16

Barbara stood just inside the main gate of the Oshawanee
County Fairgrounds waiting for Paul Gillis. She had
driven the fifteen miles from New Augsburg with all the
windows down in her car, an effort to combat the hot,
muggy air which had dominated the weather for the past
three days. The breeze had done little more than mess
her short hair and turn her makeup slightly damp. As she
was approaching Oshawanee, she had felt a moment's
concern that, after all these years, she might not be able
to find the turnoff to the fairgrounds, but this was not a
place given to change, and she recognized familiar landmarks almost at once: the same Shell station, the same
Red Owl store, even the same color paint on the
houses—all unchanged since her girlhood. She had
parked her dusty bug in the familiar lot at the top of the
hill and walked down to the two men sitting at a card
table at the narrow entrance. Both were wearing caps
with wide bills and adjustable snaps across the back; one
cap said "Corn King" and the other, darker one said
"VFW" in gold letters.

"Are you Barbara Hoffman?" the Corn King man said when she asked for a ticket.

"Yes, that's right," she said, too surprised to correct him, to give her married name.

"Sheriff Gillis already paid for you," he said. "Just go right on in."

"How did you recognize me?" she asked, snapping her purse shut.

"Young Gillis described you," the VFW man said, his bland face studiedly without expression as he looked her over again. "And he said to look for you just about two. Figured you'd be on time, he said."

"Oh, did he?" Barbara had replied, feeling irritated that a man she'd just met seemed to think he knew her so well.

She saw Paul working his way through the crowd toward her, in his uniform, towering over most of the people who both greeted him and made way for him. She also watched the women and the way they looked at Paul Gillis. He was that rare breed, a really good-looking man who seemed wholly unaware of his looks. Even his walk seemed self-deprecating, Barbara thought, with a slight slouch in the shoulders—none of the strutting or swaggering that seemed the almost unconscious gait of most men who knew that women were looking at them.

"Hullo," he said as he came up to her. "You look nice."

"Thanks," she said, brushing her hand through the top of her hair in yet another effort to undo the work of the hot wind. She had worn red cotton slacks, a bright print blouse, and her white sandals with the little heels. "You look nice yourself."

"Oh, this old thing," he laughed, pulling on the front of his brown shirt.

"What do the 'lab boys' say about my mother's nightgown?" she asked as they began to walk toward the midway.

"Chicken blood," he said abruptly.

"Chicken blood?" she gasped, stopping short to look up at him.

"Yup. Lots of farmers around here still butcher their own chickens, you know. It wouldn't be hard to collect about a cup of blood if you planned some stupid stunt like that. Doesn't help us figure out *who*. I'm afraid your mother's nightgown is ruined."

"Oh, I don't think she wants it back, anyway," Barbara said. "Did you find out from Matt Krieger who lived in Mum's apartment, who might still have keys?"

"I talked to Mr. Krieger, yes," he said, frowning sideways at her. "I was right about the locks never having been changed. There were seven former tenants, including your friend's daughter and her husband, all connected to each other in some way. Your mother was right about Krieger's never having to advertise the apartments."

"So, does that help us zero in on who pulled this chicken blood stunt?" Barbara asked.

"No, I'm afraid not," he said with a slow shake of his head. "Makes it even more complicated when we start considering the tenants in the neighboring apartments. George Heim's second daughter lived in the building next to your mother's building for seven months in 1982 when she was separated from her husband. Recommended to her by her good friends, the John Petersons, who were living in your mother's apartment at the time."

"And they might have left a key with her while they were on vacation or something," Barbara sighed. "And who knows if they ever got it back? I see what you mean. Any number of people could have access to old keys. We really *are* far too trusting of each other around here.''

"I'm going to keep following leads," he said firmly. "Don't worry about it. There, now. That's the last we're going to say about police business today. Okay?"

She wanted to tell him about seeing Billy Novak at the bowling alleys, about Heather's attitude. She'd been thinking about it ever since, reflecting that Heather could have been Billy's legs for him in the business of the nightgown. Just bright enough to do what she was told, as Raymond Heim was. Maybe Heather knew some former tenants of the apartment. She wanted to tell Paul how scared she was when Billy had rolled in on her the second she went back to "investigating." But she'd half-promised Paul Gillis that she would give up all further efforts to "help" him, and now she didn't want to spoil the day by announcing that she'd broken that promise three hours after giving it. Besides, Paul had that odd sympathy for Billy, might not think her fears justified. It was best to keep quiet.

"Whatever you say," she said, smiling up at him.

"Would you like to take the whole midway tour first," he asked, "before we decide what we'd like to try out?"

"Yes," she said with a delighted laugh, for this had always been her own way of approaching the fair, walking the whole length of the midway to see what might be new. But perhaps it wasn't such a coincidence, she thought, falling into step beside him; perhaps everyone made the midway tour first.

In just a few yards, they were enclosed by the crowd, the noise, the colors, the smells of the fair. Wood shavings, hauled in by the truckload to keep the ground from turning into mud in case of rain, crunched and rustled under their toes. The smells of cotton candy, caramel corn, and cheap hot dogs mingled into the slightly sickening medley so exciting to children. Flashing lights, a whirl of faces, and stagey screams marked the faster rides, while the carousel and ladybug ride offered the more leisurely circling of three- and four-year-old faces, rounded cheeks flushed with excitement or exhaustion or both. At the sight of these faces, Barbara couldn't wholly fight off the thought, "Andrew would look like this now." She turned her face sharply away and focused instead on the gaudy brilliance of the gaming tents which crowded toward passersby every few feet.

"Win that pretty lady a genuine pearl necklace," shouted a shirtless man whose bronzed skin looked uniformly grimy as if he waited until the end of each town's engagement before he bothered to bathe.

"Show that gorgeous creature that a lawman knows how to shoot straight," yelled a fat man behind a counter of air guns, each gun chained to a ring. Barbara didn't look to see either the targets or the prizes. A thin teenage girl in filthy jeans and a tight tank top leaned against the corner post of a striped tent, calling in a bored voice, "Place your bets. Which hole will the mouse go down? Winner every time." Behind her, rows of plastic dolls, pink stuffed bears, and toy penguins looked balefully down on a big roulette wheel whose numbered wedges ended in holes large enough to provide escape for the terrified mouse the girl would dump onto the wheel every time three or more people were willing to place fifty cents on a number.

"Nothing changes here," Barbara said. "Nothing at all. This is exactly the way the fair was when Cheryl Blahnik and I used to strut up and down the midway in our wheat jeans, hoping some of the boys from high

212

school would take us on a ride. I'll bet some of the carnies are the same ones who came here then."

"Boy, I remember wheat jeans," Paul said, stooping a little toward her ear so she could hear him above the racket. "You girls all looked mighty inviting in those."

"When I washed mine, I used to put them on while they were still damp because it was the only way I could get them closed," Barbara laughed. "Then they would dry to the shape of me. After all that, we used to wear huge shirts borrowed from our dads to cover up the most obviously tight places. Talk about mixed signals."

"Hello, Mr. Schneider. Mrs. Schneider," she heard Paul say, and she turned to see Dick and Rosa standing before a booth where a man was blowing glass ornaments. Dick's pale face and enormous eyes were even more obvious in the outdoor light where everything around him was so vivid, so full of color.

"Well, hello," Barbara said, taking Rosa's hand. "Enjoying the fair, I see."

"Dick has to get some daily exercise," Rosa said, as if she felt the need to explain why she would bring a man who looked like this to a county fair.

"We're going to take in the tractor-pulling this evening, if I don't poop out first," Dick said, his bluish lips pulling away from the false teeth in what was meant to be a smile, but looked more like a grimace.

"You know Sheriff Gillis?" Barbara asked, turning awkwardly toward Paul.

"Yes," Dick said more quietly. "He paid us a short visit last week."

"We told him all we know about poor Tony," Rosa said, her eyes behind the thick glasses swimming out of focus whenever she moved them. "And, of course, we also told him he wouldn't find any murderers in New

Augsburg. It wasn't anyone local who hurt Tony. It couldn't be one of us."

"Rosa," Dick said, putting his emaciated hand on her arm, "the sheriff is having a holiday today. He doesn't want to talk about business."

"We might see you on the grandstand later," Paul said smoothly, taking Barbara's elbow and piloting her into the crowd again.

Barbara walked along in silence. She knew, of course, what Rosa meant by saying "It couldn't be one of us." People who had lived for generations in a close, and closed, community had a deep sense of network, of fundamental identity with each other, even when they didn't see or speak to each other more than four or five times a year—and then the conversation was purposely general. They simply *understood* that the values, beliefs, spirit of the community were shared by each member of the group. Outsiders were treated politely, but with profound suspicion. Insiders were, simply, "us." And loyalty to us was automatic, almost a reflex. Barbara had always felt herself just enough different from New Augsburg solidarity to substitute reason for reflex, but she had always seen the strength of the communal impulse as well as its weaknesses. And a side of her still envied its absolutes.

"What ride do you want to try first?" Paul said abruptly as they reached the last few tents of the midway.

"Are we actually going on the rides?" Barbara said, startled and a little embarrassed. "I thought you had to patrol."

"No, no," he laughed. "I said I had to be visible, and we can be seen on rides as well as walking around."

"Well, I noticed the Tilt-O-Whirl back there a bit," she said. "That's a pretty tame place to start, I guess."

The Tilt-O-Whirl was a series of eight high-backed

buckets, each fitted by rollers onto its own small, circular track; the tracks were built into a moving floor which made a much bigger circle of its own, undulating up and down over a series of shallow hills. Most of the time, the buckets would just swing back and forth on the "downhill" phase of the ride's movement, but if they were beginning just the right momentum at the crest of the hill, they would whirl in tight circles, faster and faster as the next hill gave them another firm thrust. When a bucket was working in this way, the screams of its occupants were quite genuine. When Paul and Barbara were seated in one of the buckets with the bar closed across their laps, he stretched his long arm across the wire mesh back, just behind her neck.

"As I remember," he said, "this ride is hard on the neck. Just put your head back against the mesh and don't fight the centrifugal force. My arm will cushion your neck."

"I know how this ride works," she said with a little edge in her voice, but she did slide closer to him and rested her neck against the crook of his elbow. As the ride launched into motion, she breathed in the smell of Paul's spicy aftershave and found herself thinking how nice it was to be on a ride at the fair with a nice-looking man. If only she could go back to the days before life got so complicated, or if only she could forget all the pain between then and now. As the bucket began to swing, it occurred to her that she really was out of practice at the art of dating. Since her divorce, she had kept men at arm's length with her sharp distrust, and her graduate studies kept her very busy.

Friends at the university would periodically "fix her up" with somebody they thought might be "right" for her. But most of her friends were much younger than she was, and the men they found for her were twenty-four and twenty-five years old. She looked young for her age and her running regimen had kept her figure very trim, so her dates were initially quite pleased to be fixed up. But most of them confidently expected sex on the first date and seemed to believe that a divorced woman had no excuse for saying no. Barbara began to resent these insulting assumptions, the barely veiled suggestion that she should be *grateful* for offers of a tumble in the hay. She found these boys very easy to resist and soon lapsed into her powerful impulse to stay free of emotional entanglements. And the loneliness? Well, she had begun to believe that nothing could touch the loneliness anyway.

Now she was thinking what a relief it would be to let herself trust again, to let go of the fear, the nervous terror of being hurt or betrayed, to take some time to get acquainted with a man, a man who was old enough to remember wheat jeans and cars without air conditioning. Yet the emotional risks of letting her guard down still seemed almost overwhelming. The bucket had begun to whirl in earnest now, and in one blurred pass, Barbara thought she saw the ride's operator deliberately slowing and speeding the movement of the platform in order to make their bucket get the most action. Probably his way of getting a bit of his own back against the law—a safe way to "beat up on" the sheriff. Barbara resolutely refused to scream, but she did sink against Paul's side and bury her head in his shoulder. He closed his long arm around her and put his chin on the top of her head, the side of his own head braced against the mesh back.

When the whirling finally slowed, Barbara sat up, feeling the faint nausea brought on by dizziness. Paul seemed utterly unfazed, jumping nimbly out of the bucket as the ride stopped and pulling her up by both hands. She let herself be led to the short flight of stairs that would get them back to the steady earth and had reached the second step before she looked up and found herself focusing rather unsteadily on George Heim's craggy profile. The old man was standing about four or five feet away from her and was looking out toward the grandstand. Behind him, Barbara could make out Mae's plump but half-obscured figure. Mae was clutching a white purse in both hands as if she feared one of the noisy children crowding past her would snatch it away.

Barbara lowered her own face, hurried down the rest of the steps, and darted off to the right. The Heims hadn't seen her, she was sure. When Paul caught up to her, she bent over slightly and hung on to the chain-link fence used to keep potential riders in line.

"Just let me catch my breath and stop being dizzy for a minute," she said. She wasn't really very dizzy, but she wanted to look back at the Heims from behind Paul's sheltering presence.

"Sure thing," Paul said with a little laugh and then turned his own gaze out over the crowd, becoming once again the professional lawman, watchful, observant.

Barbara noticed that George Heim was talking to someone, and when she moved her glance in that direction, she saw at once that the other man must be Peter Heim; the family resemblance was unmistakable. The younger brother was even bigger than George, a towering bear of a man with wide shoulders, big hands, forearms still firm with muscles developed by a half century of hard work. His thick hair was still dark with only a few traces of gray over the ears. Like George, he assumed, apparently unconsciously, an aggressive stance, elbows tipped out, shoulders and head thrust forward, as if he were saying "Come on! Take a swing if you dare" to anyone approaching him.

The woman next to Peter Heim made an impatient movement with her upper body and therefore drew Barbara's attention to her for the first time. Barbara stared, blinked for a few seconds, and finally comprehended. Peter Heim had never married. This woman was his sister, Caroline Heim Bower. What was simply bigness in the brothers had run to fat in the sister. She was tall, an impression exaggerated by the spike-heeled sandals which looked absurdly small and precarious as a foundation for such a large woman. She was wearing white knit slacks and a black and white zebra-striped knit top, both a size too small for her, so that horizontal rolls of fat were sharply emphasized at breasts, midriff, and lower abdomen. A second chin rested between her jaw and the place where her collarbone would have been visible if not obscured by flesh. Her hair, teased into the bouffant style of the early seventies, was not so much blonde as yellow, the color achieved by years of home dying with no professional stripping or toning. Even at this distance, Barbara could see the turquoise-colored eyeshadow and the overly rouged cheeks.

Paul had noticed Barbara's stare, followed it with a glance of his own, and now turned back to her with a little smile.

"Feeling any better?" he asked, his voice bantering.

"What?" Barbara said, forgetting for a moment that she had pretended dizziness. "Oh, yes. I'm fine. Let's go."

They started back down the midway, pausing at some of the game tents, trying a few more of the rides. Paul won a small stuffed dog by knocking over a pyramid of milk bottles with a baseball.

"I used to play baseball in high school, too," he said, as he handed the toy to Barbara. "The secret to that milk bottle game is to hit the lower bottles at the base of the pyramid. They use weighted bottles, so if you aim high, you'll just knock off the top bottles and the bottom ones won't budge."

"What a lot you know," Barbara said, sincerely impressed. She took his arm and tried to enjoy the rest of the day, but every now and then, she found herself scanning the crowd, looking for the Heims, looking for the "beauty" her father had once been in love with.

Dinner was chili dogs and beer at a stand behind the Ferris wheel. Barbara and Paul stood among other diners crowding the stand, for the few stools were already occupied by some old-timers who were discussing the weather, as they probably did every day of their lives.

"Radio says there's a temperature inversion," one man was saying, or rather shouting. "Cold air just sliding up on top of this hot stuff, holding it down."

"Clouding up already," another man said, gesturing at the horizon.

"Gonna be a fog before dark," the first man said. "Radio says bad fog."

"You have quite a drive back," Paul said to Barbara as he finished his beer. "Do you want to leave now and beat the fog?"

"Nonsense," Barbara said briskly. "I'm not afraid of a little fog. The fair is always more exciting at night, don't you think? All the lights make you forget how shabby it really is."

"Okay," he grinned. "Let's get dessert at that ice cream tent and then go up on the grandstand for a while. The mini-tractors are kind of fun to watch if you don't mind the noise."

"I can't remember the last time I saw a tractor-pulling contest," Barbara said. "I used to go with my dad when I was a kid."

On the way to the ice cream tent, they were brought to a stop by part of the throng simply backing up into them, lots of people obviously making way for something. Paul led Barbara to the outer edge of the row of people, intending to circle them, but then he stopped again, his height having allowed him to see, a few seconds before Barbara saw it, the reason for the pause in the crowd's movement. Billy Novak was rolling toward them, the wheels of his chair crunching over the wood shavings, the chrome rails reflecting the colored lights of the game tents. Beside him walked the bartender, Heather, dressed in yet another spectacularly garish outfit—skintight, purple sweat pants topped by a peasant blouse which would have been grounds for an indecent exposure arrest if it had been one more inch "off the shoulder." Barbara glanced at Paul to see if he had noticed Heather, had made the connection. When she looked back at Heather, she saw that a tall, dark-haired young man had slipped his arm over her bare shoulders and was nuzzling her neck as they walked. He had been there all along, of course, but Barbara hadn't noticed him until now, so sure had she been that Heather was Billy's girlfriend. When Billy caught sight of Paul, he came to that abrupt stop that seemed so practiced.

"Evening, Sheriff," Billy drawled, swinging the chair toward them so that Barbara could see the big teddy bear stuck next to his withered legs.

"Hello, Bill," Paul said mildly.

"Did you win that little dog for our Barbie here?" Billy asked. He had pointedly not greeted Barbara or even looked up at her face, so she guessed that Billy had seen them together earlier in the day.

"How would you like something bigger, Barb?" Billy said as he turned his sneering face to look directly at her. "I could part with this teddy if you asked me real nice."

"No, thank you," Barbara said coldly, looking away from him into the crowd.

"I was gonna let Heather here have it," Billy said without looking at the girl, "but now I guess Danny'll have to win something for her after all. You remember Danny Krieger, don't you, Barb? You musta went to school with him."

Barbara looked hard at the dark-haired man who was cuddling Heather. He had narrow, sharp features; even his teeth looked sharp, narrow and pointed. This was Matt Krieger's youngest son. She remembered him vaguely as a scrawny little boy in the lower grades when she was in the eighth grade, but he hadn't started high school when she graduated and left New Augsburg. Odd how the tyranny of age operated among children: the younger kids always cultivated the acquaintance of the older kids, but eighth graders barely spoke to sixth graders, and third graders were outside of notice. So it was, Barbara thought, that she could have, in some senses, grown up with Danny Krieger without ever knowing him at all. And she saw now the source of Heather's initial hostility in the bowling alleys, saw the significance of her asking whether Barbara wanted "the old Mr. Krieger or the young one." Heather considered the young Mr. Krieger her personal property, was jealous of any attractive woman asking for him.

221

"You don't mind if I give an old neighbor a little present, do you, Sheriff?" Billy asked, and Danny and Heather snickered at the sound of the drawling singsong Billy adopted whenever he addressed Paul.

"The lady seems happy with her dog," Paul said, bristling just a little. "You've been to the beer tent a few times, haven't you, Bill? Better take it easy."

"Hey, taking it easy is what I do best," Billy said. "I'm always sitting down, as you can plainly see." The last phrase was in the tone and rhythm of a nursery rhyme.

"Just take care," Paul said evenly, his tone conveying more than the words. He took Barbara's arm as they moved away, and she leaned gratefully against him.

"Can you see now why I'm afraid of him?" she asked when they were out of earshot.

"He's a bitter man," Paul answered. "But it's mostly bluff, I think."

"I hope you're right," she said, glancing over her shoulder. But the crowd had closed again around the wheelchair, and she couldn't see Billy or Danny or Heather.

17

The sun had gone down and the floodlights were turned on to the track by the time Barbara and Paul got up to the grandstand.

"Barbara!" someone called. "Here, Barbara. Sit here with me."

It was Mary Wenner with her grandchildren and her quiet son sitting in a row off to her left. But sure enough, there was room for two on her right. Barbara rolled her eyes at Paul, sighed, and walked over to Mary.

"You haven't missed the mini-tractors," Mary said happily as they sat down. "They're up next."

"Are mini-tractors *good* for anything?" Barbara asked, puzzled by this phenomenon which had grown up since she'd moved away from Oshawanee County.

"Just for the contests," Mary said, as if that were more than sufficient justification. "The young guys build them themselves. It's very popular now. Betty's boy has one here tonight." Betty was Mary's niece, something Barbara fortunately knew because it was Mary's habit to talk about people as if, of course, everyone knew who she meant.

Barbara settled herself and looked around. The stands were filling fast now, and just before Barbara's gaze turned from her right view, somebody in her line of vision sat down, revealing the Heims, all seated in a line three rows in front of Barbara. They'd been joined by Raymond Heim, George and Mae's big, silent son, the dutiful one who lived with his parents and worked the home farm. It struck Barbara that he was heavier now than he had been when he was younger; as he approached middle age, he was beginning to take on the bear-like conformation of his father and uncle. She suddenly remembered that the man on the ladder outside her window had moved with the clumsiness of a heavy person. But even as this thought crossed her mind, Barbara's attention was drawn to Caroline Bower, to the broad back, the yellow head, which kept swaying from side to side as she spoke first to Mae and then to Peter.

"Tractor pulling is all right," Mary was saying to Paul. "But it doesn't really come up to the horse-pulling contests we used to have. Of course, you young folks don't remember that, don't even remember when farmers *had* horses."

"My uncle kept a team until the late fifties," Paul answered, as usual polite, attentive. "I remember those horses very well. Used to ride around on one."

"We had some fine teams in the old days," Mary went on as if he hadn't spoken. "And Charlie Novak had the finest of them all. He's sitting right over there, see?" And she pointed off to her left. Barbara turned at this mention of the name Novak and saw Charlie and Geraldine craning their necks for the first glimpse of the mini-tractors which were being pushed into the center of the track. "He had a matched pair of Belgians, big brutes they were. And they licked every team in the county when we had pulling contests. One summer, Jim's dad thought he might have found the team to take them on, but it was no use. It was over at Davister's track, in New Augsburg, you know. And when Dad's team got beat, Tony Hoffman steps forward and says his horses will whip those Belgians any day; he'll go home and get them right now. He was drinking all day and everyone tried to talk him out of it, but he *would* go and get those horses."

Mary was in full flight and neither Paul nor Barbara seemed to know how to stop her.

"Well, by this time most of the neighborhood was alerted to come see Tony get beat. He comes back with his horses, a nice team, too, the last one they had before the war, but it's just no contest. Charlie even holds his horses in at first to let Tony think he might have a chance, but then he just flicks them up into their top form, and they leave Tony's horses in the dust. Charlie is usually such a quiet guy, but he had a big laugh at Tony, really sorta gloated. I'm sorry to say it, Barbara, in front of you, but the men said that Tony beat those horses of his afterwards, because they lost, you know. Funny I should think of that now, but I guess I just been talking and thinking about Tony so much lately that lots of things are coming back to me. Let's see now, when was that? It was late summer, I remember, and Jim and I weren't engaged yet. But the men were already talking about the war, about how Albert Zimmer had joined the army and might fight in Germany, and wouldn't it be a shame if he had to kill some of his own relatives, because, of course, his father was born in Germany and they still had people there."

Mary had the true spirit of an oral-tradition storyteller, a passion for accurate details, for coming up with the right name and the correct date, even when these details had no particular relevance to the story she was telling.

"So it must have been 1942, definitely, the late summer of 1942." And she fell silent, a look of profound satisfaction on her big, mild face. Both Barbara and Paul were at a loss as to what response, if any, they were expected to make to this monologue, but they were almost immediately saved from trying by the beginning of the first mini-tractor pull. The little machine exploded into motion, and its custom-built engine soon reached such a pitch of screaming noise that conversation was impossible. Red dust went spewing straight up some fifteen feet into the air, and the little tractor was soon engulfed in the cloud. Just as the engine reached a frantic tone and stalled, a man came running up to Paul.

"Sheriff," he panted, "I'm glad I found you. There's a fistfight behind one of the tents on the midway. Looks like there's drinking involved. The usual crazies."

Paul stood up at once.

"I'll be back when I can," he said to Barbara.

But Barbara had noticed Caroline Bower stand up and begin to pick her way around spectators toward an aisle. The other Heims were, apparently, staying put.

"Why don't I just meet you at the Ferris wheel a little later," Barbara said to Paul. "I'm not going to stay here much longer."

A little frown formed between Paul's clear eyes, but he obviously had no time to argue.

"Okay, but this probably won't take more than about half an hour," he said and then hurried to follow the man who had come to find him.

Barbara watched Caroline carefully and, when it was clear that she was heading toward the exit, said to Mary,

"I'm too restless to watch this, Mary. I'm going to get back to the midway."

"Sure, sure," Mary said, but she clearly couldn't understand why anyone would prefer the midway over the dust and noise of the mini-tractor pull.

Barbara hurried toward the exit chute, catching a glimpse of the yellow hair as it disappeared down the stairs. She quickened her pace and reached the top of the stairs just in time to see Caroline turn left at the bottom of the flight, odd since the direction to the main gate was to the right. Then Barbara remembered the old bathrooms at the far end of the lower level of the grandstand. By the time Barbara was in high school, portable toilets had been brought in every year for the fair, conveniently located in rows alongside the center part of the midway. But Caroline Heim might not know that, would remember only the old facilities under the grandstand. Sure enough, Barbara saw the large figure receding into the gloom— the county no longer even lit the area. During the fair, it housed the rabbit cages where every variety of domestic rabbit was brought into the shade for the judging and display, using only the light of day pouring through the gates at either end. At night, the rabbits, presumably, went to sleep, and human fairgoers went upstairs for their excitement. The noise of feet overhead mixed with the now dimmer sounds of the mini-tractors.

Barbara followed Caroline down the long corridor of rabbit cages until she heard the opening and closing of a door. Then a faint halo of light along the floor showed that the county was still investing in electricity for the bathrooms themselves. She was beginning to feel rather foolish. What was she doing here? Did she think it would be appropriate to sneak up on Caroline Heim in a public toilet and say, "I need to talk to you"? And then even if the woman agreed to speak to her, how would she begin in such a setting? What would she ask? She slowed her steps and stopped about three-quarters of the way to the bathrooms, changed her purse from her left shoulder to her right, turned around and then back again—all symptoms of her uncertainty.

Behind her, Barbara heard something, a rustling and another sound that might have been footsteps. She whirled, peering into the growing darkness that stretched away a hundred and twenty feet in the direction from which she had come. The outlines of the rabbit cages were dimly discernible. Was it just the rabbits moving around, disturbing their cage lining, bumping into cage walls? Or was some other human in here, following the follower? There were so many places to hide along the walls, all those cages to duck down behind. She turned back toward the bathrooms; the halo of light on the floor was the same; the door was still closed. Now there was another rustling sound, closer this time, and Barbara simply lost her nerve. She turned and ran toward the pool of light that surrounded the main entrance.

At the stairwell leading up to the seats, she stopped, panting, and peered back into the darkened corridor. For a long time she saw nothing. Then a white figure glimmered into view and finally became Caroline Heim Bower returning from the bathroom, tottering at an unhurried pace on her high heels. Nothing else in the cavernous darkness seemed to be moving at all, and Barbara's eyes were burning from the strain of staring.

"Mrs. Bower?" Barbara said as the big woman approached her. Caroline stopped short and looked Barbara over carefully, her eyes blinking fast as the only sign that she was startled, but she didn't speak.

"I'm Barbara Hoffman, Joe Hoffman's daughter. I'd like to talk to you about my Uncle Tony, if I could." Barbara knew that George would have told his sister all about the snoopy Hoffman girl, so subterfuge would be useless.

The big woman took two more steps closer to her and squinted, examining Barbara as if she were a doll on display.

"You don't look a bit like Joe Hoffman," she said at last in a husky voice.

"I believe that I resemble my mother," Barbara said evenly, "but I have my father's coloring."

"Yes, yes you do," Caroline said, "only more like Tony than Joe. It was Tony who had the gold in his hair."

"You must know that my uncle was murdered," Barbara said. "Would you please talk to me about him? There's so much about him I don't know." Barbara couldn't interpret the older woman's face in the gloom.

"The boys wouldn't like me talking to you," Caroline said, putting her hand onto the stair rail, ready to start up; the "boys" were, presumably, her brothers.

"I know that," Barbara said quickly. "But you can decide for yourself, can't you?"

Apparently, it was just the right thing to say. Caroline Bower drew herself up, puffed visibly larger with an intake of breath, and let go of the railing.

"I wouldn't mind a beer, if you're buying," she said, and then she glanced up the stairs. "They won't miss me for a while."

The beer tent was crowded as usual, but two middle-aged men stood up from their stools and motioned the

229

women to a seat. Barbara ordered two beers and then took a long look at the face next to her, illuminated by the harsh lights inside the tent. It was a face whose present condition couldn't wholly obscure what it had once been. Under the slabs of flesh on forehead, cheeks, and jaw, there were traces of the bone structure whose regularity and proportion would in youth have been arresting. The hairline had a dramatic widow's peak, and the ''hawk's wing'' shape of the eyebrows seemed natural. The eyes themselves, when she finally lifted them to look at Barbara, were obviously her best feature—widely spaced, dark brown, fringed by thick lashes that probably didn't need the mascara that was caked onto them. They would have been beautiful eyes if it hadn't been for their opacity, as if their color and expression were all on the surface. In a young woman, this expression might have passed for a look of innocence; in a woman of sixty-three or sixty-four, it looked more like stupidity.

''I was sure Tony had just run off,'' she was saying now, her husky voice raised to be heard above the noise of the other drinkers. ''Imagine my surprise when George told us he'd been here all along.'' It sounded rehearsed.

''From all the information he's been able to gather, the sheriff thinks Tony was killed in early September of 1943.'' Barbara thought it best to ascribe theories to other people, to minimize her own investigation.

''That was very long ago,'' Caroline said, and again Barbara heard a stagey quality in the voice, as if she'd been coached in a series of responses which would add up to ''At this distance of years, I just can't remember clearly.'' Barbara decided to cut through the preliminaries, to try for a shock.

''It must have been soon after you found out you were pregnant,'' she said and watched the effect: a little jump of the brown eyes and then a slow blurring of the features into an expression of stupid blankness.

"Yes, yes," she said vaguely. "About that time."

There was a long pause, and then Caroline's eyes took on a focus again.

"Say, you went to college, didn't you?" she asked.

"Yes, I did." It was Barbara's turn to be startled.

"Well, maybe then you can tell me about something I heard just the other day." Now Caroline Heim's voice was chatty, pleasant. "My friend Hilda was telling me about something they discovered that'll strip the cholesterol right out of your arteries, she says. I have to think about that sort of thing, you know, especially because I like this sort of thing." And she raised the glass of beer to take another swallow. Barbara was too much at a loss to speak.

"Hilda says it's something called Kayenny," Caroline went on, putting her hand to her hair which was sprayed so stiff that all of it moved when one side was touched. "She says it's some strange spice that you can get in bulk at the Co-op. Only trouble is, she don't know how you're supposed to take the stuff, dissolve it in something or just put a teaspoonful in your mouth, or what." She paused, her face thrust toward Barbara, her earnestness obviously sincere.

"What did you say it was?" Barbara asked.

"She spelt it for me," Caroline said. "C-a-y-e-n-n-e."

"Oh, cayenne. Cayenne pepper. It's red pepper."

"Well, you've heard of it then. Do you think it's true, about it stripping out the cholesterol?"

"Well, I don't know about that," Barbara said with a little smile. "But it would clear up your sinuses if you put a teaspoonful in your mouth."

"Really?" the older woman said, her face all interest. "I got that problem, too."

Barbara stared. Was this an act? Was she being put on because she'd asked an embarrassing question? The broad face opposite her showed not a trace of irony, not a flicker of humor.

"Mrs. Bower," Barbara said at last. "Cayenne is a very hot ground pepper. It would probably be dangerous to put even a small amount of it into your mouth. I use only a tiny pinch to season a pot of chili."

"Oh, I see," Caroline said, and her face took on the blank look again.

"I know it must be painful for you to discuss your relationship with my uncle," Barbara said, feeling embarrassed at having to raise her voice to say this, but the noisy patrons nearby didn't seem to take any notice, engrossed as they were in loud conversations of their own. "But you must have known that some people in New Augsburg figured out long ago that your first child was Tony's."

For a few seconds, Barbara didn't think the other woman was going to respond. Then her face took on a dreamy expression, as if she were staring at something Barbara couldn't see.

"He looks like him, you know," she said. "My Glenn. Of course, he's twice as old now as Tony ever got to be, but when he was in his twenties, he was the image of Tony. My husband didn't like that, the fact that Glenn didn't look like the other kids. I got five kids, you know, three boys and two girls. Your pa, he never had any boys, did he? Just you?"

Barbara thought she saw a glimmer of malice in the bland face.

"Just me," she said simply.

"Well, it's none of my business, I suppose," Caroline said. "Maybe your mother didn't want a lot of kids. She's some kind of foreigner, isn't she? But I always think a man wants boys, don't you?"

Barbara thought of her mother's miscarriages, the difficulty of bringing even one pregnancy to term, the near-fatal illness Eileen had suffered afterwards, and the mental image of her mother's upright little figure made Barbara want to slap the smug expression off Caroline Heim Bower's face.

"We were talking about Tony and 1943," she said coldly.

"Did you know I was dating your dad then?" Caroline seemed determined to avoid a straight answer.

"Yes, of course I knew that," Barbara said, reluctant to let this woman know how recent her knowledge was. "But you were seeing Tony, too, all that summer and keeping it a secret from my father and from your brothers."

"Your dad was such a nice boy," Caroline said musingly, looking again into that middle distance where she seemed to see her own past. "Too nice for me, I guess. I was kinda wild in those days, and Tony was—well, Tony was different from your dad."

"Didn't you and Tony ever talk about the way you were deceiving my father?" Barbara asked, not because it would help to solve her uncle's murder, but because she, personally, wanted to know.

"Well, we didn't talk much," Caroline said with a sly smile. "But sometimes we talked about Joe, sure. You know Tony kinda resented Joe because their ma—your grandma—always favored Joe, always depended on him even though he was younger, just a kid. But I think, too, that Joe was the only person on earth Tony had any respect for, after their ma died. It's funny that he could have both those feelings at the same time, but I think he did. He would say that it served Joe right that he had his girl, but then he would tell me not to let on, not to break it off with Joe over him, almost like he was afraid to hurt him."

"Afraid?" Barbara said, startled by the word.

"Well, you know what I mean. Didn't like the idea of hurting his feelings." And she took another sip of beer.

"Did you know you were pregnant that night when your brother caught you with Tony and ran him off the place?" Barbara asked.

"No, not for sure," Caroline said, leaning forward to be more comfortable. She seemed to have entirely forgotten that she hadn't intended to be confidential. "I didn't want to say nothing about it to the boys. Peter was already like a wild man. But a few days later, Mae guessed, and then it started up all over again, the yelling and the cursing."

"When was that?" Barbara tried not to sound too eager. If Peter Heim had learned of his sister's pregnancy in early September, right after Joe Hoffman enlisted—.

"Oh, just a few days after Peter run Tony off," Caroline said. "It was August, I remember, because the Rendezvous kermiss was still coming up and George wouldn't let me go. They wouldn't let me out of the house to go anywhere at all, except to church and then only to 5:30 mass when hardly anybody else was there. When Peter found out about the baby, he said I could just make up my mind to stay home for nine months."

"Did Tony know about the baby?" Barbara asked, covering her disappointment and searching for another possible cause of confrontation. If Tony had learned about the baby and tried to see Caroline, if he had defied those big, angry brothers—.

"I don't know," Caroline said, shrugging her plump shoulders. "I thought he would do the right thing if he knew, but the boys wouldn't let me see him. They said even if he *would* marry me, which they doubted, they wouldn't allow it. So I wrote to Tony. Twice. But I never heard anything back."

"You wrote to him?" Barbara was very interested now. "How? How did you manage it if your brothers wouldn't let you off the farm?"

"Well, I told Mae I was going for a little walk outside, and then I put the letters in the mailbox for the mailman to take away. That's how we always mailed letters. But I didn't put the flag up, either time, for fear one of the boys would see it and know I was sending letters."

"So you can't be certain that the mailman actually took your letters away?" Barbara asked. "One of your brothers might have intercepted them."

Caroline's opaque eyes widened.

"Oh, I don't think they would have thought of that." Then she mused a little. "But they wouldn't let me go out to get the mail during that time. Mae did that. I guess they were afraid Tony would try to write to me. But I always thought he would get my letters and just come riding into the yard on that motorcycle and take me away, rescue me like those princesses in the stories. But he never came, and I just gave up hoping. Then I got married to Frank and moved away."

"You don't know if your brothers ever went to see Tony after they learned about your pregnancy? Tried to make him 'do the right thing'?"

Now the dull face took on a look of suspicion, a slow dawning.

"No, I already told you," she said. "They wouldn't a let me marry Tony even if he'd begged on his knees to have me. You're trying to make it sound like one of my brothers killed Tony, but that just isn't the truth. We *all* believed that Tony run off to keep from facing the mess he made. We never knew he was dead under his house all the while."

It was odd for Barbara to hear her home referred to as Tony's house, but, of course, that was how people had once regarded it. Now, she sensed a need to placate Caroline, to keep her talking even though her beer was almost gone.

"I don't mean to imply such a thing," she said soothingly. "I'm just trying to figure out what happened during those two or three weeks in the fall of 1943."

"Well, don't you try to hang it on us, that's all," Caroline said, gulping the last of her beer, and again Barbara understood the whole meaning of "us." "We none of us Heims saw Tony again after that night Peter caught him in our yard."

"Did you see my father again after that?" Barbara finally brought herself to the question she had been postponing, dreading to ask.

"He kept coming over, but the boys wouldn't let him in the house," Caroline answered, her voice returning to an easy, conversational tone. "Wouldn't explain why, either, they were so mad at Hoffmans in general, I guess. I could hear from the front room."

"Then you didn't speak to him before he went into the army?" Barbara said, a leading question spurred by her feelings of relief.

"Oh, sure I did," Caroline said blandly, looking around and then down at Barbara's hands. "Aren't you gonna have that beer? You hardly touched it."

236

"I guess I wasn't very thirsty," Barbara said numbly, afraid to ask her next question.

"Well, can I have it then? Shame to waste good beer."

"Sure, sure," and Barbara pushed the beer over toward Caroline's fat hands. She watched as the older woman lifted the sweating glass and gulped several times.

"You *did* speak to my father before he left for the army?" Barbara prompted, her throat dry and tense.

"He came to the house one night, during the Rendezvous kermiss it was. I remember because I was so disappointed I couldn't go." Caroline didn't seem, even now, to find it inappropriate that an eighteen-year-old pregnant girl whose lover had been driven off by her enraged brothers should have wanted to go to a public dance. "Peter sent Joe away but he came back later, and George finally gave in when Joe said he only wanted to talk to me for a few minutes, there on the porch, and then he would go away and not bother us again."

"Did your brother listen to the conversation?" Barbara asked, her breathing more labored now.

"No, no," Caroline said, waving a hand in an expansive gesture. "George wasn't like that. He just said, 'Five minutes,' and went on in the house. Joe was so sweet, so quiet. He asked me was it true about me and Tony, about my seeing Tony on the Q.T., I mean. When I said yes, he cried, just stood there with tears pouring down his face. Isn't that something?"

"Yes, that's something," Barbara said in a choked voice.

"Then he asked me if I wanted Tony for keeps. He actually said 'for keeps,' I remember, like you say if you're trading marbles or something. If I really wanted Tony instead of him, he said, he would go away."

"And what did you say?"

237

"Well, I was thinking maybe he could take a message to Tony for me, you know, so I told him that, yes, it was Tony I wanted and would he please tell him that for me. Would he tell Tony I was waiting for him."

Barbara was imagining this scene, her father's tear-streaked face, and this last callous effort to use him, and she wanted to strangle Caroline Heim Bower, to bury her hands in the layers of fat and just choke the life out of her.

"Did you tell him you were pregnant?" Barbara was at last able to say after watching Caroline's throat swallowing three more gulps of beer.

"Oh, no," Caroline said, wiping the side of her mouth with the fingers of her left hand. "Poor Joe didn't need to know that. I wanted that to be between Tony and me, you see, because I still thought then that I was going to marry Tony, and then we could just tell folks that our first kid was premature. People did that in those days, you know, though I don't suppose many were fooled."

"Did you and my father say anything else?" Barbara asked.

"No, not much. I wished him luck and then he said goodbye."

"He wasn't angry, with you or with—with anyone else?"

"No, not at all. Just sad. Real sad." Caroline said this as a scientist might report on an observation, not with any regret or sense of remorse.

Barbara's mind was racing. Her father didn't know about the pregnancy. He was sad but not angry. He said goodbye and went straight off to enlist as he'd told the Schneiders he would do if Caroline rejected him. He hadn't killed his own brother, hadn't branded himself for life with the mark of Cain over this bloated, self-regarding, vulgar woman.

"What the hell are you doing here?" The voice was directly behind Barbara's right ear, a snarling voice that made her jump and turn around. Peter Heim's hulking form actually cast a shadow along the bar.

"I'm just having a beer," Caroline said, in a mincing tone, half defiant and half placating. "I don't like all that noise on the grandstand."

"And who is this?" Peter said, scowling down at Barbara with his black eyes snapping as he walked around her to stand between the two women. "Let me guess. This would be the Hoffman girl. Didn't I tell you not to talk to her?" And now his fierce gaze was trained on his sister.

"I got no say about who sits next to me at a beer tent," Caroline flared. "I'm a grown woman, aren't I? I don't have to account for every move to you." Yet her eyes were supplicating—even, Barbara thought, flirtatious. She guessed that this was an old pattern between brother and sister: possessiveness and rebellion on the surface; fierce and permanent attachment at the base.

"We got nothing to say to you," Peter Heim said, swinging his water buffalo's head back at Barbara. "You take that long nose of yours back to Chicago and let well enough alone if you know what's good for you."

"It does you no good to threaten me," Barbara said, as calmly as she could manage with the old man leaning so close to her. "I have a right to find out what happened to my own uncle."

"You don't know nothing about him," he said grimly, standing up to his full height. "You been protected all your life from knowing what he was."

"Protected?" Barbara said wonderingly.

"Yeah, protected," he said. "Your whole family. Everybody in New Augsburg has kept quiet for fifty years so Hoffmans could hold their heads up."

"Kept quiet about what?" Barbara said, her own eyes flaring. "Do you think my uncle was the only young man in the history of the world who got a girl pregnant and then didn't marry her? Families don't have to hang their heads for fifty years for that."

Barbara saw at once that the reference to Caroline's pregnancy had stung the big man into a fury. She cowered away from the sudden way he thrust his enraged face at her.

"You're an ignorant girl," he hissed. "Anton Hoffman wasn't just some wild kid who made a few mistakes. He was a burner!" He spat the word at her, spraying her face with saliva.

"Peter!" Caroline said warningly, and Barbara could see a fat hand on Peter Heim's shoulder, tugging ineffectually at the big man.

"What do you mean by that?" Barbara gasped, wiping her face with a trembling hand. "What is a burner? Do you mean because he got kicked out of high school for setting a prank fire in a closet?"

"Hah!" the old man said, standing straight again and shrugging off his sister's hand as if it were a fly. "You don't know nothing. Ask your friend Mary Wenner. She's so eager to tell you everything about Heim family business. Ask her what happened to Wenners' corn cribs. Ask her if she knows about that!"

Barbara looked up into the fierce eyes.

"Why don't *you* tell me about it?" she said, struggling to control her voice.

"No," he said, obviously having a struggle of his own

240

to keep from saying more. "I told you we got nothing to say to you. Come along, Carrie. Right now."

The fat woman stood up, unsteady for a moment on her spike heels, but she seemed, temporarily at least, reluctant to further defy her brother. Barbara watched them walking away together, the hulking, slightly stooped man turning his head every now and then to say something to his sister. Just before the crowd swallowed them up, Barbara saw Caroline stop, raise her arms in the air, and say something up into the dark face above her. Then she turned unsteadily and marched back toward Barbara, wobbling perceptibly—two quick beers seemed enough to make her a little tipsy.

"It occurs to me," she said with a blurry smile as she came up to Barbara. "It occurs to me," repeating the phrase as if she liked its sound, "that my Glenn is actually your cousin. I know you don't have a lot of kinfolk, so I thought you might like to get to know him someday. He knows, of course, that Frank wasn't his dad—Frank let him know it lots of times—but I don't think he knows about you. He lives in Colorado now. You give me a call sometime, and I'll give you his address."

She glanced over her shoulder, smirking at her brother who looked ready to charge at her.

"You just pick up the phone and give me a call," she said, and sauntered back toward Peter Heim, her wide hips swinging back and forth as she walked.

241

18

Barbara paced up and down in front of the Ferris wheel waiting for Paul. A thick mist had formed on the horizon and had even invaded the midway; the colored lights at the far end had the blurred look that Barbara had been able to produce as a child with her birthday candles by slightly crossing her eyes. She was so lost in thought, going over in her mind every detail of her conversation with Caroline, that she several times nearly collided with people. One man mumbled, "Hey, it's not that foggy."

"Here you are," Paul said from behind her, and she turned to see his nice smiling face. "Well, we had to take the pugilists to opposite ends of the fairgrounds and give each one a talking to, but they finally settled down. I got some sober friends to drive them home. How was the tractor pulling?" And he took her elbow in his hand as they began to walk together.

"Oh, I didn't stay to see too much of it," she answered. She found that she wanted to tell him all about seeing Caroline Heim Bower, about thinking someone was among the rabbit cages, about what she'd learned. She wanted to tell him everything and end by saying,

"Wasn't it silly of me to suspect my own father?" just so she could hear his kind, reasonable voice saying, "Of course, I knew all along that he couldn't have been the one." But she still felt a reserve about actually saying that she had thought her father capable of fratricide, and now there was this new worry—Peter Heim calling Tony a burner, saying "Ask Mary Wenner." What might that mean, and where might it lead the sheriff if she told him about it?

"What would you like to do?" he said when they'd walked along in silence for a while.

She couldn't tell him that what she really wanted to do was to go back onto the grandstand, find Mary Wenner, and ask her what happened to Wenners' corn cribs, so she just shrugged and said, "I don't know. Nothing much, I guess. Maybe I should be heading home."

He stopped short and looked down at her.

"It's not even 9:30," he said in a hurt voice. "Are you that bored?"

"Of course not," she said, bristling a little. "But the fog seems to be getting worse, and I don't think I should wait for it to thicken up anymore."

"Sure, I see," he said, immediately himself again. "I should have thought of that earlier. Guess I didn't want anything to cut this evening short, especially after I had to 'go on duty' and spoil things."

"You didn't spoil things," she said. "You couldn't help it. I'm just not a very good date, that's all. You'd have been better off skipping the preliminaries and saying right out that you wanted to head straight for the nearest bed."

He let go of her arm and stepped back.

"What the hell kind of a thing is that to say?" he asked quietly, but she could hear the anger in his voice. "What

243

do you think of yourself that you would say such a thing? What do you think of me?''

"Lighten up," she said, angry at feeling herself scolded. "I was making a joke."

"It didn't sound like a joke to me," he said. "Don't you think you're somebody a man might like to get to know? Don't you think there might be one or two men left in the world who are interested in something besides a quick hump?''

Suddenly Barbara felt exhausted and dangerously close to tears. He was right; he had put his finger directly on her feelings of inadequacy, her self-loathing. *If I were a worthy person, my husband wouldn't have turned from me to another woman. If I were a worthy person, I wouldn't have let my baby die.* But she couldn't admit it, couldn't let this stranger into her pain, couldn't take the risk. So she pulled herself further away from him.

"I'm tired," she said, sounding drained. "I'm just going to leave now."

"I'll walk you to your car," he said with a resigned sigh.

"No, that's all right," she said. "You just make yourself visible down here. I can find my own car, thank you.'' And she strode away from him before he could say anything else.

She wanted to run, to just sprint through the crowd and up the hill to the parking lot. It took an act of will to make herself walk normally. What on earth was the matter with her? How could she have tumbled so quickly from the euphoria of thinking that her father had not, after all, killed her only uncle to this anger and depression? Was it that the scene with Peter Heim had frightened her more than she'd at first admitted to herself? Or was it that she couldn't control her impulse to fight Paul Gillis away from herself emotionally? Her muscles itched to explode into action; if she were running, she wouldn't have to think.

In the darkened parking lot, the fog was more obvious than it had been on the midway. Barbara felt a surge of alarm when she realized that she couldn't see the lights of Oshawanee. But she climbed into the little white car anyway and started the engine into its familiar chugging rhythm. After all, the only tricky part would be the first few miles until she got back to County Trunk L; then it would be a straight line to New Augsburg, good road, and not much traffic at this time of night. She would take it easy, drive very slowly, keep the headlights on dim all the way. She pulled out of the lot onto the street and noted that her headlights would penetrate the drifting fog for only about three car lengths. That would mean no more than thirty miles an hour, she reminded herself as she almost missed the first turn.

After one or two more near misses, Barbara found herself out of the Oshawanee city limits on a road that would eventually connect her with County Trunk L. Now the fog seemed to close in even more, hugging close around the little car, so that Barbara could see forward very little more than the length of her car. Reflectors along the tops of the roadside fence winked dimly as her lights found them, reassuring her that she was going to be able to follow the line of the road. To the sides of the car, the fog was simply a blank wall, permeated with darkness as if night had been poured down it like paint. Barbara reflected that city people, used to street lights and traffic, to the glow of buildings lit up all night long, couldn't really appreciate how profound the darkness of

245

country roads could be, even without fog. She was no longer used to it herself after the years in Columbus and Chicago. The Volkswagen crept along.

Just as Barbara was beginning to wonder how close she might be to her final turn—she had forgotten to look at the odometer when she left—headlights appeared behind her, looming suddenly out of the fog and approaching her rear bumper fast. The lights were on bright, haloing straight out into the fog. Barbara accelerated quickly, fearing the car behind her would simply ram the back of her car. Indeed, the lights came so close that they disappeared below the line of the back window, but there was no collision. Barbara let out her breath in relief. Now that the driver had seen her car, he would drop back, dim his lights, allow her to return to a safe speed. Sure enough, the headlights reappeared in the rear window, but they were not dimmed, and after about thirty seconds, it was clear that they were not dropping back to a safe distance. The car behind her was staying no more than ten feet from her back bumper.

Barbara let up on the accelerator. If she slowed to her original speed, this driver might get the idea that efforts to speed her up weren't going to work. The other car slowed, too, just enough to maintain the dangerously close distance. Barbara speeded up again slightly, listening to the chugging of the Volkswagen engine as it began to rise in pitch. The headlights behind her never moved. She slowed again, this time taking her foot off the accelerator altogether until her car had slowed to fifteen miles an hour. Again the lights behind her stayed in the same position, fixed in the center of her rearview mirror as if they were on a platform attached to the bumper of her own car.

Barbara's heart began to beat faster. Was this someone who wanted to pass but was afraid to try it in the fog? Did the driver think she could be frightened into driving at his speed? She set her jaw and took the car back up to thirty miles an hour, the speed she'd judged safe for conditions, and then she tried to concentrate on the road ahead of her. She knew that her turn onto County L was coming up fairly soon. Perhaps that would solve the problem and her tailgater would just race away into the fog after she was out of his way. She realized now that she had no idea how close to the intersection she actually was—less than a mile because she'd noticed the last intersection before L just as she slowed down the last time. She no longer lifted her eyes to the mirror because she could tell by the shroud of light around her car that the lights behind her hadn't changed position; she just kept her head down and thrust forward, straining to see the sign that would announce the imminence of County Trunk L.

At last, the white rectangle appeared, looming alarmingly close to the car; Barbara realized she must be almost on the shoulder of the road. She flipped on the right turn signal and began to slow down, a gradual process until she felt she was only crawling along. Would that intersection never come! Just then the headlights behind her disappeared again under the line of the window—the other car was very close again—and she saw the break in the dark line of the ditch. She turned, feeling the right side wheels bump off the pavement onto the graveled shoulder; she adjusted the steering quickly and knew herself to be safely on the road from which she wouldn't have to turn again until she was in New Augsburg. Her relief was very short-lived, though, because she saw almost at once that the other car had turned with her and was now in its accustomed place some ten feet behind her.

No, sir! Not for another ten miles! If this guy wanted to pass, Barbara would let him. She knew that L had wide, level shoulders where she could pull off safely, so she signaled right, slowed down again to a crawl, and eased off onto the gravel. The lights followed her, coming to a stop as she came to a stop. Barbara sat there for a few seconds, stunned. Then she began to feel a prickly sensation at the back of her scalp.

It was another beat before her muscles reacted, and then she punched down the door lock next to her, and flung her body against the seatbelt to reach the lock on the passenger side. She sat there panting, straining her ears to listen for the slamming of a car door behind her. But fog muffled sound, too, didn't it? Somebody might already be sneaking up on her car. He wouldn't have to close the door on his car after he got out, would he? She twisted around inside the shoulder strap, staring back into the lights. Nothing seemed to be moving. Under her feet, she could feel the floor vibrating to the idle of the engine.

A movement, just the drift of fog, caught Barbara's eye off to the left and she whirled back to her own windshield, punched in the clutch, and shoved the gear shift into low. She pulled out onto the road much more quickly than she meant to, lurching over the yellow line into the other lane. By the time she had corrected her error and steadied the swerving, the other car had pulled out behind her.

"Fine," she said out loud through gritted teeth. "That's just fine. You stay right there. I'm driving straight to my mother's house, and then I'm going to call the cops. If you follow me into the village, I'll have enough light to see your license plate.'' Her voice sounded unnaturally loud in her ears, as if it filled up the little car. She fell silent again, willing herself to watch the road, to concentrate on that center line that led straight to safety.

Suddenly the glow around her changed, shifted to the left. She flicked her eyes up to the mirror and saw the headlights positioning themselves for a pass. Thank God, she thought. He's going around me. He's tired of this foolishness. The lights moved slowly forward, far in the other lane, and came up even with her own headlights. And then they stopped moving. The car was running parallel with her, not speeding up, not dropping back. Barbara's breathing was becoming more shallow now, the tingling in her scalp more widespread. Did he mean to just stay there? She hazarded a look to the left, a hard look. The car was larger than her own so she saw only the front fender and part of the passenger-side door. Was it red? Or maroon or rust? She couldn't tell, for the fog drifted between the cars, visible and thick as jet stream. The other car didn't edge closer to the side of her car but stayed as far to the left as it could without going off onto the shoulder.

Maniac! Barbara thought as she accelerated and the car next to her kept pace with her. *He* was the one in most danger if he stayed there. If there were another car coming toward them, it would smash head-on into him. But, of course, she reminded herself, she would never be able to avoid the collision herself, and it would be a three-car pileup. She slowed and the other car slowed, speeded up again and it speeded up exactly as much. She was going faster now than she judged safe, but she couldn't shake the panic that was closing her throat and making her pant. Slowing down seemed impossible. She lost track of distance, of time. It seemed to go on for hours, this double illumination of the center line. Out of the corner of her eye she noticed a mailbox at the side of the road. There had been mailboxes all along, of course, but she noticed this one, recognized it because it was shaped like a red hip-roofed barn. Leo Borchard's farm was there in the fog behind that mailbox, and the driveway was very near. She could turn in, go to the house, and get help. Any of these farms could be a refuge. But what if no one was home? There was no way of telling whether any or all of these people were at the fair. And if she found the house dark, she could be trapped in the farmyard by anyone crazy enough to follow her in.

But she knew where she was now and knew that the unmarked intersection with Drossart's Road was less than a hundred yards ahead of her. Barbara's mind was racing. She would turn right, no warning, so she couldn't slow down much, and the other car would go past the intersection, have to stop and turn around if it were to follow her. After a mile, Drossart's Road intersected with County Trunk M, where a left turn would take her to the highway three miles later; then a second left turn would point straight at New Augsburg from the south. She would get away from him.

Eyes straining, foot backing off the accelerator only slightly, Barbara watched the right shoulder of the road. When the intersection appeared, she turned too soon, cutting the corner and bouncing through a shallow ditch at thirty miles an hour. The car shot up onto Drossart's Road, heading straight for the left-side ditch and the trees beyond. Barbara fought the wheel, heard the tires screaming against the pavement, and finally righted her course. There was no center line here, but the fence posts along the road were metal and reflected her head-lights in a nice straight line. Barbara knew how straight the road was, appreciated as never before the perfect geometric squares laid out as a result of the Homestead Act. She looked down now at the odometer, mentally recorded the number 4 on the moving roller. Then she threw the shift lever into high gear and punched the accelerator to the floor.

The little car wound itself up, the engine's tone rising to an almost hysterical pitch. Fifty-five, sixty, sixty-five. Barbara was driving blind. The white wall before her never moved more than ten or twelve feet from the front of her car. But there were no lights behind her, nothing but the night. Let there be nothing in this lane, she prayed, no vehicle, no animal, no pothole. Periodically, her glance flicked down to the odometer. The 8 passed, and then the 9. When she saw the 3 moving past, she began to brake sharply, feeling the rear end of the car trying to pass up the front bumper. But sure enough, there was the intersection with County M. She swung the car left, making a true diagonal across the intersection and was already shifting up to high gear by the time she was straightened out on the other road. Again she raced up to sixty-five, now using the center line to guide herself. Only after she saw the odometer roll past 8 again with no sign of lights behind her did she begin to relax.

"All right, you son of a bitch," she said out loud. "I lost you. I lost you."

She slowed down a little and checked the odometer again. Seidl's Road was coming up and she would have to be careful of this intersection. There were no stop signs either way and cross-traffic could be fatal. She was looking up from the rolling disk which had just turned the 3 when she saw headlights just ahead and off to her left. She hit the clutch and brake simultaneously before she realized that the headlights weren't moving. They were just sitting there, waiting, at the intersection of Seidl's Road and County Trunk M.

It couldn't be, Barbara told herself; it was another car, somebody else, being extra cautious in the fog. She lifted her feet and felt the car shake itself back into gear. Her car was moving only about thirty-five when it passed the enormous halos of light—just headlights, on bright, the car behind them swallowed in the gloom. Barbara held her breath, not daring to glance behind her, accelerating as fast as the little car could manage. But the glow swung into position behind her before she had gone a tenth of a mile further, moved off to the left, came up alongside, and then stayed there.

No, oh no, Barbara's mind was screaming at her. It could mean only one thing. The other driver knew where she was going, had known all along who she was. He'd never stopped at Drossart's Road, but had just speeded up, turned right on Seidl's Road, and was waiting for her when she passed, as he knew she must, on M. Somebody had watched her leave the fairgrounds, had deliberately followed her to terrorize her in this senseless way. Who? Why? It wasn't like the movies, where a pursuing car was trying to ram her car, to force her off the road. This car was carefully maintaining a distance, just staying with her, yet the sense of menace was almost overwhelming.

Barbara was back up to sixty-five again, and the red car—maroon?—kept the pace exactly. Idiot! He couldn't care much whether he lived or died. There were shallow hills along here and no way at all to tell whether another car was coming toward them. Twice Barbara thought she saw an oncoming glow of light, but it was only the reflection of the other car's headlights off a slowly drifting bank of fog. It was still more than a mile to the highway, and Barbara suddenly knew that her nerves wouldn't stand the rest of the trip at this speed. It occurred to her that if she hit the brakes suddenly, without warning, the other car would shoot past her—he wouldn't be able to react in time—and she might be able to get a good look at the car, maybe even see the rear license plate.

She braced herself and stomped on both pedals, fighting the wheel to steady her car. The other car seemed to leap past her, the door handle and rear fender coming suddenly into view. Barbara had just registered that it was a two-door car when it began to fishtail wildly, the glow of its headlights swinging first right and then left. The driver had just then hit his own brakes. Barbara had to steer for the ditch to avoid the wildly careering vehicle next to her. The Volkswagen bounced down off the road, jarring her feet up off the pedals, and restoring her ability to control it as soon as the brakes were disengaged. The sounds of sliding tires, the other car's tires, were still in her ears as she drove back up out of the ditch, crossing in front of the bouncing headlights to her left. She was braced for the collision which, miraculously, didn't come. Relief was flooding along her nerves until her headlights picked up the side of a station wagon crossing the road directly in front of her—some innocent motorist coming out of Orchard Road, the last intersection before the highway.

On sheer reflex, Barbara swerved hard left and cleared the rear bumper of the station wagon by half an inch. She found the center line again only by noticing that it was on her right and that she was heading toward a row of mailboxes. Another swerve put her back onto the right side of the road, and she found herself able to breathe again. Her breath was coming in sobs now, not loud, but little moaning sobs, as if she were afraid someone would hear and find her. She stayed at twenty-five miles an hour now; the risk of an accident was surely worse than her fear of the headlights. But she saw now that they were gone. There was no light behind her at all. It took most of the last mile to the highway to convince her that they wouldn't reappear. Had he fishtailed himself into the ditch? Had he given up? She didn't care which, just so that there was only darkness behind her.

The highway was wide and marked with a reflecting rail. The last mile into New Augsburg was without incident. Barbara met one car, going as slowly as she was, and then she turned into the parking lot of her mother's apartment building. The only light in the row of buildings was coming from Eileen's upstairs bedroom; she must be reading. Only when Barbara had stopped the engine and taken her hands from the wheel did she begin to shake, an uncontrollable trembling that made it very hard for her to breathe. She wrapped her arms around herself and rocked for a moment. When she was finally able to move again, to steady her breathing, she reached down for her purse but came up with the little stuffed dog instead. She stared at it almost as if she didn't know what it was; it seemed months ago that Paul Gillis had won it for her by knocking over milk bottles. Finally, she moved it into her left hand, scooped up her purse, and opened the car door.

Just as Barbara was pulling herself unsteadily to her feet, she heard a sound off to her right, on the other side of her car, a faint grating noise as if something were being dragged along the gravel near the utility shed. She froze, her heart slamming against her ribs. God! He had beaten her home. He wasn't in a ditch after all, but had turned left on Orchard Road, gone back to County L, and got ahead of her a second time; was waiting for her again. The adrenaline rush was urging Barbara to run, to sprint across the parking lot to the back door of her mother's apartment. Would he chase her, catch her before she could get the door open, grab her mouth before she could scream? In those frozen seconds before her paralyzed muscles could begin to function, Barbara had reconsidered running. The car was safer. She would get back in, lock the door, and then just blast away on the horn until someone came out of one of the buildings.

As she started to duck back into the car, she heard another sound, the unmistakable sound of running footsteps. She glanced through the windshield of her car and saw the running figure, crouched over, but it wasn't moving toward her. It was heading for the garbage dumpsters along the fence at the edge of the parking lot. She watched until it came to a stop and ducked down between the dumpsters. Why would the reckless fool who had driven next to her in the wrong lane at sixty-five miles an hour in a blind fog run away now and then hide like that? What kind of a lunatic was this? Barbara mused for a moment and then leaned over to take her flashlight out of the glove compartment; she did this by feel alone, because she wasn't taking her eyes off the blurred shadows near the dumpster.

She got back out of the car quickly now and slammed the door, not hard, but not cautiously either. She walked steadily, telling herself repeatedly not to rush, toward her mother's back porch. Whoever was at the fence over there wouldn't be able to tell if she actually went into the apartment or not; the angle meant that the corner of the house would block his line of vision to the porch. When Barbara reached the shelter of that blind spot, she darted off to her left, running now in the soft grass, circling the building so that she would come out at the front and could cross to the other driveway entrance, the one where the fence started—the shortest escape route for anyone who wanted to get out of the parking lot and back to the street. At the front corner of the house, she stopped, hidden by the building, the flashlight poised with her thumb on the switch, and she listened, holding her breath. Fog drifted under the street light a block away.

At first Barbara heard only the slamming of her own heart, but soon she was able to discern another sound approaching along the fence across the driveway from her, the sound of stealthy footsteps, not hurrying, pausing every now and then, advancing again. Only when the crouching figure was parallel with her did Barbara move, aiming the flashlight and snapping the switch all in one motion. The beam of light seemed to leap across the driveway and land on the dark-clad figure opposite, like a live thing, like a pouncing cat. The circle of light framed and froze the figure, which twitched upright and made a low whimpering sound, not even a human sound, but a noise that a frightened animal might make. Barbara was already registering the sound when the face seemed to leap into focus, white and round above the dark shirt, dilated eyes staring blind into the sudden light. Then she saw the face crumble into abject terror, a horrible transformation, just before the whole form lurched and then burst into motion, whirling past her to the street before she could move the light. In three more seconds, the fog had swallowed up the running figure. Then there was the sound of a slamming car door and the sudden screech of tires.

Barbara stood with the light in her hand, her brain numb. It had been the face of a young man—moon-shaped, fat, an almost featureless face. She had never seen it before in her life.

19

Deputy Sheriff Donald Erickson sat with Barbara and
Eileen at the kitchen counter. It was almost midnight,
and the women had been waiting a long time for the
deputy to arrive.

"I can't reach Sheriff Gillis," a woman's voice had
said when Barbara phoned the sheriff's office. "He and
two deputies are working the fairgrounds. Deputy Erickson is on a call in Portersville at the moment. Are you
out of danger right now, ma'am?" When Barbara answered that she was inside a locked apartment, the woman
had calmly assured her that "someone will be there as
soon as possible."

"It wasn't very wise to try to apprehend the intruder
by yourself," Deputy Erickson was saying now as he
tapped the eraser of his pencil against a notebook. He
was fiftyish, a bit pretentious, and obviously took his
part-time job very seriously; his uniform was starched
and pressed into knife pleats, he wore a narrow tie, and
he had a big, shiny gun strapped to his hip. Seeing this
weapon had made Barbara realize for the first time that
Paul Gillis did *not* wear a gun.

"I wasn't trying to apprehend him," Barbara said, her hands wrapped around a steaming cup of tea. "I was trying to get a look at him."

"But the deputy is right, Barbara," Eileen said. She hadn't bothered to put her hair back again and now sat looking pale and girlish in her ruffled bathrobe with her dark hair falling around her face. "Suppose he had attacked you instead of running? What made you do it?"

"I don't know," Barbara sighed. "I guess I was finally more angry than I was scared. I wanted to know who would terrorize me, follow me and endanger lives all over the county by driving next to me like that."

"About the car, ma'am," Deputy Erickson said. "Describe it for me in as much detail as you can remember."

"Well, it was some shade of red, maybe maroon or even brownish orange; it's so hard to tell in that unnatural light. A big car, bigger than mine, and a two-door. I saw that much when he went past me for a second there, before the fishtailing I was telling you about. I remember a dark line down the middle of the door, maybe a stripe or some kind of trim; it didn't look like chrome, but I can't be sure about that."

"Did you notice the make or model of the car?"

"No. No, I didn't, but it was newish, not an old car. The shape looked new."

Deputy Erickson rolled his eyes at the ceiling, his expression clearly saying, "Women! Don't ask them about cars."

"Look," Barbara said, bristling at once. "I was driving sixty-five miles an hour in a dead fog with a maniac beside me. I was afraid to take my eyes off the road for more than half a second at a time. So, no, I wasn't taking notes about the make and model of the car."

The deputy recomposed his face, now affecting seriousness, concern.

"Of course not, ma'am," he said. "And you didn't see the car here in town when the intruder ran away from the house?"

"I couldn't see much beyond thirty feet in that fog," Barbara answered, relaxing a bit. "I heard the door slam, the engine start, and the tires squeal when he pulled away, but I didn't actually see the car."

"If you didn't recognize this man," Erickson said, glancing over his notes, "why do you think he would follow you from the fair, and how would he know where you were going, where you live?"

"I don't know," Barbara sighed again, taking a quick sip of tea. Her hands had finally stopped shaking. "I've been wondering that for a couple of hours now. I was so sure it would be somebody I knew, somebody I saw at the fair."

"Why somebody you'd seen?" he asked. "Somebody in particular? Did you have a suspect in mind?"

Barbara looked back and forth between the deputy's quizzical look and her mother's worried frown.

"Well," she said lamely, "Sheriff Gillis would understand. I thought this chase might be connected to my uncle's murder. You know about that, I guess. The sheriff was at the fair and we saw—we saw several people who are involved in the investigation of that murder. So I made the connection, that's all."

"Well, ma'am," the deputy said, flipping the notebook so it closed, a one-handed gesture he must have learned from a television cop show. "It seems we've got as much as we're going to get tonight. I checked out back, and the door to the utility shed is standing open. I think the scraping sound you heard was somebody opening that door. This guy was probably hiding in there when you pulled into the parking lot and made a move too soon, alerting you. I'll pass all of this along to the sheriff in the morning, and he'll decide about how to proceed.''

"Will you tell him to get in touch with me tomorrow?" Barbara said, standing as the deputy rose to leave. ''I'd like to know what's going on about this.''

"I'll surely convey that message, ma'am," he said, straightening his belt and moving toward the back door.

When Barbara rejoined Eileen at the counter, she could see that her mother had passed into the stage of suspicious curiosity. She'd spent a long time just comforting her trembling daughter when Barbara had first come inside the apartment. She'd moved on to outrage and pale terror as Barbara told her the details in a shaking voice. But now that everyone was calm and had consumed the requisite two cups of tea, Eileen's blue eyes had taken on a shrewd look, the expression she had used when Barbara used to come home from a date and would say only "Nothing much," when asked, "What did you young people do tonight?"

"And who *did* you see at the fair, Barbara?" she asked as her daughter sat down again.

"Just about everybody we know," Barbara answered. "Some new sort of tractor-pulling contest seems to be immensely popular."

"Oh, the mini-tractors," Eileen said. "I read about it in the fair schedule. Daddy used to get quite a kick out of them. Called them 'expensive toys.' "

"That's what they seem to be. I sat with Mary Wenner for a while on the grandstand. Charlie and Geraldine Novak were there, too, Gerry dressed to kill as usual. Do you think she wears a wig?"

Eileen sipped her tea without comment. She recognized this as a diversionary tactic.

"That's hardly 'everybody we know,' " she said at last.

"Well, I saw Billy Novak, too. The Schneiders were there. And the Heims."

"How many Heims did you see?" Eileen's voice was slightly playful.

"So you know Peter and Caroline are in town," Barbara said with a resigned sigh. "Who told you?"

"Mary, of course. That woman is better than hiring a private detective. And one never even has to ask. She just pours it out."

"Yes, I saw all the Heims," Barbara said, "and I talked to two of them."

"Was Caroline one of them?" Eileen said softly after a little pause.

"Yes."

"What do you think of her?"

Barbara stood up and walked into the dining room.

"Not what you expected, is she?" Eileen called after her.

"How do you know what I expected?" Barbara said coming back into the kitchen.

"Because I know you, my girl," Eileen said with a little laugh. "You just found out that your father had a 'first love,' and you immediately began creating a whole person in your imagination. An idealized beauty, a girl of mystery, who must certainly have aged gracefully into a striking and faintly tragic woman. So much more romantic than your ordinary old mum."

Barbara glared at her.

"You think you're so damned smart," she said. Because, of course, it was all quite true.

"Oh, Barbara," Eileen said. "You've done that all your life. When you just make people up like that, in your head, you're bound to be disappointed by the genuine article. And then you just can't forgive them for not being like the people in your mind."

"Are we still talking about Caroline Heim here?" Barbara asked, suspecting a veiled reference to Tom Mullens in her mother's speech, and resenting, as usual, Eileen's advocacy for Tom.

"So, what did you find to say to each other?" Eileen asked. "How did you start a conversation?"

Here, Barbara was more cautious, thinking through her reply before answering and covering her hesitation by pretending to swallow tea, even though her cup was empty. She didn't want to let on to her mother what she had really discussed with Caroline.

"I bought her a beer," Barbara said, setting down the cup. "Two beers, as a matter of fact. Paul had to go break up a fight, and she was leaving the grandstand just as I was, so I introduced myself."

"Just like that?" Eileen's fine eyebrows rose toward her hairline.

"Just like that. She said I didn't look a bit like Daddy, and she bragged about having five kids. Made it pretty clear that Daddy had been cheated by having only me."

"You should have remembered the fable of the lion and the fox," Eileen said. "That would have made you smile about her bragging."

"What fable is that?"

"Oh, you must remember," Eileen said, reaching out to cover Barbara's hand with her own smaller one. "Actually it's about a lioness and a vixen. The vixen mocks at the lioness because she, the vixen, has seven kits, and the lioness has only one cub. 'Only one,' says the lioness proudly, 'but a lion.' ''

Barbara felt tears stinging her eyes.

"Thanks, Mum," she whispered, giving Eileen's hand a squeeze. "She's just generally pretty awful. Do you think Daddy knew? I mean, how she turned out?"

"Of course," Eileen said. "He saw her a few times over the years, when she came to visit George and Mae. Once, about six years ago it was, we talked to her for a few minutes in the drugstore. On the way home, Dad said, 'Isn't it lucky you don't always get what you think you want?' ''

"*Did* he?" Barbara said, relieved in some profound way. "Did he really say that?"

"Yes, he did," Eileen answered. "Let me tell you something about your father. He didn't always get what he wanted, but he always wanted what he got. More than wanted it—loved it dearly. He was devoted to me all our lives together, and he was simply mad for you. When you were about two and I was feeling really well again, I suggested to him that we should try for another baby, for a boy, because I believed that he wanted sons. He wouldn't hear of it, refused to let me risk my health with another pregnancy. 'Besides,' he said. 'How could we ever do better than our little Bubbles.' Do you remember when he used to call you Bubbles?"

Tears were sliding down Barbara's face now.

"Thank you for telling me that," she said. "I needed to hear it right now. But why didn't he tell *me*? Why did he never talk about his feelings to me?"

"Oh, Barbara," Eileen sighed. "Some men just can't express themselves about what's most important to them. He didn't always express himself to me in words either, you know. But some things are more important than words. Daddy was a man who showed his love by adding safety devices to the farm machines, so we wouldn't get hurt.''

"Yes, I know that,'' Barbara said, remembering the care her father had always taken to teach her about safety around the farm. He knew better than anyone how quickly machines could maim and kill. "It's just that everything I've been learning the past few weeks makes me feel as if I never knew Daddy at all.''

Eileen drew herself up, her blue eyes snapping.

"Stuff and nonsense!'' she said. "Of course, you knew him. You knew what he *was*, what he made of his life. And there was never a finer man.'' Her voice broke now, and tears spilled from her eyes.

"I know, Mummy, I know,'' Barbara said, patting her mother's arm. "I'm sorry to upset you. I guess I'm just a wreck after everything that's happened tonight.''

"Well, then,'' Eileen said briskly, embarrassed as usual by open displays of emotion. "We needn't go on about that. Now what made you tell that deputy that you thought that man chasing you was connected to Tony's death? And why would you think it involved people you saw at the fair?''

"I don't know, Mum. It's hard to explain. It's just that I think all those people are holding something back. They know more than they're telling, about Tony I mean. I think they're protecting somebody.''

"Even if that were true,'' Eileen said thoughtfully, "why would one of them chase you in the fog? It would hardly make you *less* suspicious.''

"I know that,'' Barbara said, standing up again restlessly. "It doesn't make much sense, does it? And now it seems that my intuition about that was dead wrong. I never saw that young man in the parking lot before. There

doesn't seem to be any connection between any of the things that have been happening: my car being wrecked, the phone in the mailbox, this crazy chase. It just seems that this guy is very angry at me for some reason, but I don't even recognize him. Random violence is not something I associate with places like New Augsburg, so I guess I just keep thinking there must be a connection to finding Tony's body. That's when all of this started.''
She was pacing now, to the dining room and back.

"I see what you mean," Eileen said, her forehead puckering into a frown again. "Of course, this can't be just a series of coincidences. But don't you think it's just a bit silly to think that people like George Heim or Charlie Novak would be creeping about trying to scare people?''

"Yes, that's part of the problem," Barbara admitted. "And now my tailgater turns out to be a stranger, and I don't know what connection he could have to the other incidents. Or why.''

"Well, we can't do anything about it just now," Eileen said, standing up at last and clearing teacups. "Perhaps the sheriff can come up with some theories. I haven't much confidence in that deputy person.''

"Me either," Barbara agreed. "I don't suppose he *closed* that door on the utility shed.''

"Probably not," Eileen said, turning from the sink. "But we aren't either of us going out to check on it tonight. Why don't you just crawl in with me again, so neither of us is at the back of the house. I'll put up my book and we'll try to get some sleep.''

They switched off lights and started up the stairs in silence. Halfway up, Barbara said to her mother's narrow back, "Caroline said that since her son Glenn is my cousin, I might want to contact him. She said she'd give me his address in Colorado if I called her.''

Eileen stopped and turned around.

"And how do you feel about that?" she said.

"I don't know," Barbara said. "He might turn out to be like her."

"Yes," Eileen said, turning and going up again. "Or like Tony."

20

Barbara stayed in the apartment all the next morning waiting for Paul Gillis to either call or appear at the door. It was a clear, windy morning, much cooler than the day before, and she longed to go running, to pound out of her system the anxieties of the day before, to banish the memory of the fog from her mind as decisively as the wind had banished it from the sky. But lunchtime came without any contact; the phone didn't ring even once all morning.

"He's busy with the fair," Barbara told herself. "I'm not the only case in Oshawanee County." But she felt hurt, resentful, certain that the quarrel of the evening before had caused the handsome sheriff to move Barbara Mullens to a back burner permanently. This conviction made her more and more restless, more and more eager to run. She picked at her lunch, drank too much coffee. When the phone finally rang at 1:30, she fairly exploded out of her chair in the living room.

"I guess you'll get that," Eileen said good-humoredly, looking up from her book.

"Barbara?" someone said in answer to her eager

"Hello." In those three syllables of her name, Barbara was able to recognize the voice. It was Tom Mullens.

"Yes, Tom," she said, cool, polite. "How are you?"

"Worried," he said. "Weren't you supposed to be home Monday night?"

It struck Barbara as odd to hear Tom refer to her Chicago apartment as "home."

"I decided to stay on a bit longer," she answered. "I don't start my research job until after the middle of July."

"Do you plan to stay up there until then?" His voice sounded surprised and disappointed. No doubt he remembered the remarks Barbara had often made about visits to the farm, her complaints that after five days, she found herself sliding back into the same relationship with her mother that she'd known as a teenager.

"I don't really have any definite plans about it," Barbara said, struggling to keep her own voice neutral. "I'm playing it by ear."

"Well, I suppose it *is* vacation," he said. "Is something going on up there? Is Eileen all right? Does she hate the new place?"

The concerned questions, the comfortable way he could still first-name her mother, the fact that, of course, he remembered the "old place" very well, the assumptions of a shared past—all these factors worked together with the soothing and familiar voice to unsettle Barbara's planned aloofness toward her former husband. She found that she wanted very much to confide in him; it would seem so natural to say, "There's been a murder. Do you remember that old cistern?" In the early years of the marriage, she would even have been able to tell him what she was most afraid of, that her father had killed his brother. And he would have laughed at her—that hearty, reassuring laugh of his—and said something like, "Better

269

not let your mother find out that you've been having such idiotic suspicions. I wouldn't put it past Eileen to spank you."

"It just isn't as easy as we thought it would be," she said at last, the habit of shutting him out overcoming her impulse to confide in him.

"I could come up there," he said quickly. "I'm on vacation, too, you know."

"Don't be silly, Tom," Barbara said, the edge coming back into her voice. "We're not exactly helpless. We'll be just fine."

"Okay," he said, after a little pause. "Will you let me know when you get back though? I thought you'd had an accident or something when I kept calling your apartment and you didn't answer."

Barbara almost started to say, "You're not part of my life anymore, Tom, so I don't have to check in with you," the speech she would have made three weeks ago, but instead she murmured, "We'll see. I don't know."

"Take care of yourself," he said softly.

"Yes, yes I will," she said, feeling tears in her eyes and angry with herself that they should be there.

Eileen looked up over the edge of her book when Barbara came back into the living room. Of course, the size of the apartment made it impossible for her not to have heard.

"Nice of Tom to worry," she said, aiming her own voice at a neutral tone.

"Hmp!" Barbara snorted, sinking onto the sofa. "He should have worried about me a bit more a few years ago."

Eileen stood up and closed her book with a little more force than usual, Barbara thought.

"I've got to get ready for my card club," she an-

270

nounced, moving toward the stairs. "We're meeting at Laura Robson's today. Don't you stir from this house until I get back, either. I want to know what the sheriff has found out about last night."

"Well, it doesn't look as if he's going to get in touch with me at all," Barbara snapped. "I hate being stuck inside waiting for anybody."

"Don't pout, dear," Eileen said from the stairs. "It looks so sour, and it's bad for the skin, I'm sure."

By the time Paul Gillis appeared on the front porch at 4:15, Barbara was almost twitching with repressed energy; at the sight of his face, she found herself torn almost equally between outrage at his having kept her waiting all day and acute embarrassment over their last meeting. She mumbled a perfunctory greeting and then walked in silence in front of him into the living room. Behind her, he had already begun to explain the day-long silence.

"I've been playing law officer all day long, and on your case alone. I have some answers for you and some questions, too."

When Barbara turned back to look at him, she could see that he, too, felt some awkwardness; this was an official call, yet this was the man to whom she had said, "You should have taken me straight to bed."

"Won't you sit down?" she said, hearing the stiff formality in her own voice and feeling silly about it.

"Is your mother at home?" he asked, hesitating before moving toward the place on the sofa she indicated; Eileen had sat in that place whenever he'd been here on official business.

"She's at her card club," Barbara said. "Why? Do you need to see her?"

271

"No, no," he said, blushing. "I just wondered, that's all." He sat down, his long legs as usual forming a pair of upswept number sevens in front of him.

Barbara's impulse was to take the chair opposite him, but she stopped, gave herself a quick mental lecture about overreacting, and then sat down at the other end of the sofa.

"So," she said, assuming a more hearty tone, "can you tell me who that was in the flashlight beam last night?"

"Yes, I can," he said, relaxing against the back of the sofa. "I knew who it was as soon as Erickson gave me the description, and I confirmed it this morning in a long interview with my suspect. I guess you could say I've obtained a confession."

"Well," she said impatiently. "Who?"

"His name is Alan Nelson. You don't know him, but you've seen him several times before last night. You just didn't know who he was. Alan Nelson is our Peeping Tom."

Barbara stared, incredulous, suspicious that, once again, the sheriff was going to insist that there was no connection between her being terrorized and her uncle's death. Paul held up his hand when he saw that she was about to speak.

"Now this is what I know for sure," he said calmly. "Listen and, as they say at awards banquets, hold your applause until the end."

He waited for her to nod before he went on.

"Nelson knew when he saw me that the game was up. He knew you could identify him, so he broke down right away, admitted that he was the one on the ladder outside your window last Tuesday. He'd seen you on one of your runs and then again at the IGA just as I thought he might have, found out you were staying here, and cased the house. He'd started that before Tony Hoffman's bones were found. When you almost caught him on the ladder that first time, it scared him, made him think he'd go somewhere else.''

"But that doesn't—,'' Barbara started to say.

"Wait for it,'' he said with a grin. "Wait for it.''

She fell silent but returned the smile with a little one of her own.

"These night visits of Nelson's are a compulsion,'' he went on. "He can't control very well where the compulsion will take him, he says. Gets interested in one girl—that's his word, not mine, so don't raise your eyebrows at me—and can't forget her until he's seen her—well, seen her through a bedroom window. He saw you again by accident last Thursday at the church—you were there to bury your uncle's remains—and he was driving by. He says he followed you and your mother on foot into the cemetery, hid behind a hedge—. What? What is it?'' He had seen the change in her expression.

"That was *him*,'' Barbara said, her face flushing now in earnest. "I saw him. Well, I saw his shoes and his trouser cuffs. But I thought it was—well, I thought it was someone else.''

"Who?'' he demanded; his eyes had narrowed, and his long back had stiffened. "Who did you think it was?''

"I thought it was Charlie Novak,'' she said feebly, "because I saw him in his truck a few minutes later, coming from the other side of the cemetery. It seemed to make sense at the time.''

"Let me get this straight,'' he said. "You thought one of your 'suspects' had sneaked up on your uncle's burial

273

without wanting to be seen there, and you didn't tell me about it. And then you went straight to his house to play free-lance detective.''

''I suppose I should have told you,'' she murmured, ''but I couldn't be sure. I wanted to get a look at Charlie's shoes, but he wasn't wearing the same kind when I got to his house. If they'd been the same shoes, I would have told you about it.''

''I wonder,'' he said, sinking back again. ''But never mind that for the moment. It was Alan Nelson in the cemetery, and after that he began to get obsessive about you again. He came around here a few nights in a row, and last night he thought he might have his chance. Most of the other tenants were at the fair, it was foggy enough to cover a quick escape if he needed to make one, and there were lights on here in your mother's apartment.''

''So he went to the fair to find me and follow me home?'' Barbara asked, too amazed to keep quiet.

''Oh, he didn't do *that*,'' Paul said simply, his face indicating that he thought this so self-evident that he was surprized she would need to ask. ''He just watched here all evening, hiding in the utility shed. Krieger still hasn't got around to locking it, blast him. Nelson saw your car come in; he'd guessed that you heard him when he pushed the door open to watch you, so he ran.''

''I heard a car,'' Barbara said, still unable to give up the connection she had made between the red car and the prowler. ''He had a car.''

''Sure,'' Paul said. ''His mother's car. It's a silver Chevette.''

''He wasn't following me?'' Barbara asked, shaking her head as if she were trying physically to dislodge the idea that the terrorist had followed her *all* the way back.

''No, he wasn't. And he didn't vandalize your car or

exchange your mother's phone for a bloody nightgown, either. He could never pull stunts like those; much too overt, too aggressive for him. He's really just a scared rabbit.''

Barbara remembered the animal cry, the round face disintegrating into that shocking look of fear.

"Yes,'' she said thoughtfully. "I saw that but I couldn't make it connect, so I just pushed it to the back of my mind. I should have thought of the Peeping Tom, I guess. It seems so obvious, now. You told me he was young, a kid. I was so *sure* though that whoever had followed me in the fog had got ahead of me and into the parking lot that I just blocked out everything else. I even convinced Mum.''

It crossed her mind that she had made a mistake about Billy and Heather, too, had allowed her presuppositions about Billy's guilt to carry her to the hasty conclusion that Heather must be his accomplice. Wrong again. Blindly wrong.

"What's going to happen to this boy?'' she asked finally after a little pause.

"Well, that's up to him—and to you. I told him that I'd try to talk you and your mother out of pressing charges if he gets the counseling he needs. He's terrified of jail.'' Paul's face had a pleading look.

"What happened to your reservations about court-ordered counseling?'' Barbara asked.

"I talked with him for a long time,'' Paul said. "I think he sees now that he needs help. He's ashamed of himself, frightened that this compulsion of his could have got him into this much trouble. I think it's worth a shot. Jail can't help him.''

"I agree,'' Barbara said briskly. "Mum will, too. I'm sure of that.''

"Thank you," he said simply.

"That takes care of your morning," she said, dismissing his thanks with a wave of her hand. "How did you spend your afternoon?"

"Looking for red cars," he answered.

"Or maroon cars," she said, mimicking Deputy Erickson. "Or rust-colored cars. Which is it, ma'am?"

"Okay," he chuckled. "Maybe I should arrange some sensitivity training for my deputies. But I'm sure it won't surprise you to learn that shades of red make up the most popular color choices for car owners in this county."

"But it can't be just anybody's red car," Barbara said, mollified a little by his quick appreciation of her anger. "Whoever was in that car last night knew I was coming here; otherwise he couldn't have found me so easily again after I turned onto Drossart's Road."

"You say 'he,'" Paul said musingly. "Erickson told me you said 'he' last night. Did you ever get a look at the driver? Are you sure it was a man?"

"Well, I thought I saw him in the parking lot when I got back here," Barbara said, looking up at him shrewdly. "But, of course, it was two different people, and I never saw the driver of the red car at all. Why do you ask? What have you found out?"

"I ask because I'm a good lawman," he said, smiling in a noncommittal way. "And this is what I've found out. The Novaks have two red cars, and both of them were at the fairgrounds yesterday. One is the father's car, and one is Bill's. It's been modified so he can drive using only his hands. Caroline Bower has a reddish orange car, but she came to the fair in George Heim's black station wagon. At least that's what she says and what her brother and sister-in-law say."

Barbara was impressed by the distinction, relieved to

276

know that he didn't automatically accept as fact something the Heims had told him, even when all of them agreed.

"The Schneiders have a wine-colored hatchback," Paul went on, "but they say they left the fairgrounds at about seven and were home before eight."

"Oh, it wasn't a hatchback," Barbara said quickly.

"You're positive?" he asked, poising a pencil above his notebook, where he had been glancing on and off as he listed the cars.

"I don't think it was," she said at last, "but I guess I'm not positive. I'm positive that it had two doors, not four."

"All the cars I've mentioned have two doors, unless we count the hatchback as a three-door. But there were probably lots and lots of two-door reddish cars at the fairgrounds yesterday, and one of them might have been driven by some drunken prankster who came up on you in the fog, thought it would be fun to scare you, and guessed right about your general destination; there's not much out here except New Augsburg, after all."

"No way," Barbara said emphatically, standing up abruptly. "We can eliminate three incidents that belong to that Nelson kid, but we're left with too much for it all to be coincidence. And you know it, too. There's my car engine, there's the phone in the mailbox, and now this reign of terror in the fog—all hostile and all aimed at me. Somebody wants to scare me off, maybe even scare me back to Chicago, and there's only one explanation I can find for that—I'm asking uncomfortable questions about a murder."

"Well, so am I," Paul said, watching her pace. "And nobody is harassing me."

"That's different," Barbara said, stopping to give him

277

an exasperated look. "Somebody's afraid that things will be said to me that would never be said to you." And instantly she thought of Peter Heim telling her that Tony was a "burner." Again she felt the impulse to tell Paul all about her encounter with the sister and brother at the beer tent, but warring with that impulse was a nameless anxiety; the more she learned about Anton Hoffman, the more she feared that his life and death were inextricably bound to some deep secret whose unraveling would bring disaster on someone she cared about. She remained torn between the desire to speed this unraveling and the desire to stop it. The impasse kept her silent and made her sit down again.

"You don't really think that was a drunken prankster who guessed right, do you?" she asked, looking straight into Paul's eyes.

"No, I don't," he said, leaning toward her. "And that's why I'm worried about you. You've got to promise me that you're going to stop provoking this kind of attention. Peter Heim told me that you were talking to his sister."

"Did he tell you what we were talking about?" she asked, a little too quickly.

"He said he didn't know," Paul answered, frowning. "Are *you* going to tell me?"

"We talked about her son, her oldest son, Glenn," Barbara said, deciding on a partial disclosure. "She confirmed that he's Tony's son, offered to give me his address in case I wanted to look him up. She claimed she didn't see Tony again after her brothers ran him off the place in August of 1943."

He waited, but she offered nothing more.

"Do you think one of her brothers chased me in the

fog because I talked to Caroline?" she asked finally. "Or maybe her nephew?"

"Anybody could have seen you with her," he said. "And it's not much of a secret what you wanted to talk to her about, is it?"

"You're right, of course," she said, thinking of the crowd around the beer tent, of the stealthy noises among the rabbit cages under the grandstand.

"Now are you going to promise me or not?" he said, taking hold of her shoulders and giving her a little shake.

"You really are worried about me, aren't you?" she said wonderingly.

"Of course I am. Aren't you?"

Tears came to her eyes, so suddenly that she was surprised to find herself crying.

"Yes," she whispered. "Yes, I'm scared. I was so terrified last night that I'd never get off those roads alive." Now she began to shake with sobs, the crying she hadn't allowed herself the night before when she felt she had to be brave for her mother.

"Come on," he said, pulling her against his chest and folding his long arms around her. "Have a good cry. I always find it does wonders for me."

Barbara gave a little snort of laughter at this last remark and found that, oddly, it made her cry even harder. She relaxed against Paul's chest and noticed that his uniform smelled as if it had been dried in the sunshine. Then her crying stopped up her nose so she couldn't smell anything at all.

"I bet you don't cry enough," he murmured against her hair. "I bet you don't let yourself cry." And he rocked her back and forth as if he were comforting a frightened child.

Barbara enjoyed the relief of crying for a few minutes more and then she sat up, but she didn't feel embarrassed as she had the night before; it was as if she had finally realized that she could trust Paul Gillis with her less attractive emotions. He was not a user, and he wouldn't save up points to use against her later.

"I've made your shirt all damp," Barbara said, touching the wet place with her index finger.

"Never mind," he said, covering her hand with his big right hand and holding it there against his chest. "It's a windy day, so it'll dry in a hurry. I haven't heard a promise yet."

"Okay," she said, smiling wanly. "I promise. No more hunting up suspects for interviews. I quit the force as of now."

"Good girl," he grinned and touched her cheek with his free left hand. "And I promise you in return that I won't give up on this case unless I'm convinced that there's nothing useful left to learn about it. How's that?"

He stood up and pulled her up, too. She didn't feel at all uncomfortable about it when he put his arm around her shoulders to walk toward the door. In fact, she slipped her own arm around his waist, a little surprised at the firm muscles she could feel through the loose shirt; he was a thin man, but he obviously kept himself in good shape. Just before she opened the door, he bent and kissed her forehead—not a quick little peck, but a soft, lingering kiss. When the door opened, he let go of her and assumed his public role.

It was almost eight o'clock that evening when Barbara went running. Over a cold supper, she had answered Eileen's questions about the sheriff's visit, but felt too

280

restless to spend an evening reading or watching television. To her mother's protests—"It'll be dark soon. I don't like you running in the dark. Why can't you just skip today?"—she had pointed out that it was not fully dark until after nine, and promised that this would be a "short workout" so there was no need to fuss.

She ran north of the village and then west, straight into the still-brisk wind. For a change, she was not using the run as a way to keep from thinking; at a steady non-pushing pace, she could use it as a chance to review the events of the past twenty-four hours. The discovery of Alan Nelson's role in her recent life simplified the puzzle in some ways and complicated it in others. Three incidents of harassment could now be connected to her interest in Anton Hoffman's death and not one of them required agility or strength, so there was no need to eliminate a suspect on the grounds of age or sex. Only the nightgown incident would have been impossible for Billy Novak because he couldn't climb stairs, but it didn't rule him out for the other two.

It embarrassed her that she had "gone after" Charlie Novak after mistakenly believing that he was the listener in the cemetery, but surely she hadn't just imagined Charlie's reserve that afternoon when he'd parried her questions about Tony. He'd been warned to tell her as little as possible, and he was hiding something; of that she was certain. And the Heims were guarding secrets, too, giving her glimpses only by accident or in anger. A solution seemed as elusive as ever, but the harassment, the secrets, the stonewalling all added up to a bottom line that gave Barbara great emotional comfort: a conspiracy to protect a still-living murderer. Joseph Hoffman could be eliminated as a suspect.

This happy conclusion of her sorting out was repeating

itself to the sounds of her own feet pounding against the grassy shoulder of the road when it occurred to Barbara that she had run further from New Augsburg than she'd intended; because she hadn't been concentrating on her running, habit had simply taken over. If she were going to keep her promise to her mother, she would have to think of a shortcut back to town. Slowing to a jog, she projected her attention out onto the landscape over which dusk had spread like a gray blanket; she found that she was on the northwest corner of the Schneider farm. A diagonal line across this land would considerably shorten her run back to New Augsburg and Barbara knew there was such a line, a lane that her father and Dick Schneider had shared and maintained jointly so they would have easy access to their back fields with big farm machines.

The Schneider and Hoffman farms were back to back, splitting the northwest 320 acres of the section. The property line was a rough diagonal following a twenty-acre strip of woods that acted as a windbreak and a natural protection against erosion. The woods had been trimmed back but never wholly cleared, and the lane went through it, opening on one end on the road near Schneiders' barn, and on the other end on the road just east of the Hoffmans' garden. Without any hesitation, Barbara ducked under the wire gate and ran behind the Schneiders' barn. The path was beaten clay, an ideal running surface in dry conditions, and she was soon up to optimum speed, sailing along through the twilight with the wind at her back.

In just a few minutes the path entered the woods, territory so familiar to Barbara that she was able to identify and anticipate individual trees, the rock pile where they had always brought the stones picked up by hand out of the fields and tossed onto a slow-moving wagon, the clump of thorn apple trees that grew so close together that they made a little fort where Barbara had imagined herself fighting off Indian attacks. When she saw the old water pump looming out of the gloom on her right, she came to a stop. It was here she had come so often in her childhood during the long summers because it was her job to fill the watering tanks for the cattle turned out to graze in the back meadow. The tanks were gone now—that meadow had been growing cash crops for years—and the pump was badly rusted. Would it still work, she wondered, grasping the handle and lifting it two or three times. But she gave it up before any water could have risen from the deep springs under her feet.

There had been another reason to stop in this spot, for here, she knew, there was a gap in the woods that allowed a full view of the Hoffman land, sloping downhill toward the buildings at the opposite end of the farm. Barbara lifted her eyes from the pump and looked out over her old home. Darkness was falling now, but she didn't need much light to make out the fences and lanes she knew so well. The outlines of the barn and sheds stood out against the fading light, but the silhouette was wrong, of course, because there was no shape at all where the house should have been; there was only the little knoll to the east of the barn.

Barbara felt an overwhelming sense of nostalgia, a grief almost as sharp as a pain, and she suddenly remembered a line of poetry that had struck her when she was in college and had stayed in the back of her mind, waiting, apparently, for this moment: "All he would ever know on earth again of home." Something in the line, its rhythms perhaps, or its odd syntax, made its sentiment even more poignant. Why, she wondered, did she feel such a fierce attachment to this chunk of geography? Why did the word "home" always summon it up whole inside her mind's eye no matter where she was? She didn't want to live in New Augsburg; she had no desire to take up farm life again. Why this pain, then? Perhaps, she thought now, it was because she'd reached an age when most women have established and developed "homes" of their own—that sense of rootedness that comes with a mortgage and church dues and a membership in the PTA. She had no such home. She'd reacted with a moment of genuine puzzlement when Tom had asked, "Weren't you supposed to be home Monday night?" She had almost said, "But I *am* home."

She was just about to turn back to the lane when a movement caught her eye. She peered into the darkness toward the farm buildings, scanning from right to left. On the knoll where the house had been, there was now a silhouette, and it was moving, a tall, narrow shape— a human shape. Barbara drew her breath in sharply. Someone was walking near, or even on, the floors of the ruined house, on the western side where the kitchen had been. There was no sign of a car in the yard, though it was hard to tell for sure, since the bulldozer had apparently knocked over the yard light along with the house and trees. Was this shape a curiosity seeker with a general interest in crime scenes? Or was it someone revisiting the scene of his own crime?

Barbara didn't think for more than five seconds before deciding what to do. She crawled swiftly under the bottom strand of barbed wire on the fence separating the lane from the farm and ran straight across the field toward the buildings. First-crop hay had been recently harvested, so the surface was close-shorn, fairly smooth. Angling for the corner of the barn, Barbara kept watching the slow-moving figure, which seemed to grow larger as she shortened the distance between it and her straining eyes.

When she was about thirty yards away, she ran to her right for a few seconds so that the barn would completely shield her near approach if the prowling figure should happen to look around. At the northeast corner of the barn, she came to a stop, panting from excitement rather than from exertion. Leaning forward, she peered around the corner. There was still enough light to show the outline of the knoll and the foundation that rose slightly above it. The tall figure was gone.

Barbara felt the familiar prickling at the back of her scalp, the taste of panic in her mouth. Her eyes flicked to the road, first east and then west as far as the barn permitted her to see. Nothing. She edged forward along the east wall of the barn, past the double doors which were standing open, and peered at last around the southeast corner. No one was on the road heading west. Whoever had been at the house couldn't have got away so fast on foot, must be circling the outbuildings to pass behind the barn on the west, to keep out of sight. Perhaps she'd been seen or heard, and the prowler was trying to get away unseen or to hide. But, Barbara thought, her mind flying at a lightning pace, she knew these buildings better than any prowler. She turned and moved noiselessly through the east doors of the barn and down the center alley. It was almost totally dark inside the barn, but Barbara had no fear of colliding with anything; she knew every square inch of this building and tiptoed without incident to the west doors, Dutch doors whose top halves were open—Barbara had seen that slightly brighter rectangle as soon as she'd entered the barn.

She moved to the right side of the doors where she knew there were two light switches, one above the other. The bottom one turned on the barn's interior lights, and the top one turned on a big outside light that was attached to the wall halfway up to the hayloft. During harvests, when work often went on into the darkness if bad weather were expected the next day, this light shone out toward the fields on the side of the buildings where the yard light didn't reach. Pankratz had probably maintained the electricity in the outbuildings; the people who harvested his crops would need lights. In fact, they had already put first-crop hay into the loft overhead. If there was no electricity, she would be safely hidden in a darkened building where she could move about and reach escape even if she'd been struck blind. If Pankratz had kept the lights as she suspected—well, she could see over the locked lower half of the Dutch doors in three directions, and the light could reach a long way. She found the upper switch with her right hand and stood there holding it, listening intently to the night outside the doors.

The wind, still brisk, was blowing across the young corn rows in the field outside, making that sound like rustling paper which she remembered so well. In stronger gusts, the wind made a low, moaning sound under the wide overhang of the barn roof. Barbara soon realized that these sounds would mask any noises that an approaching person might make, especially if that person were trying to move quietly. And she was afraid to put her head over the doors to look around; there was just enough light left here on the west side of the barn to produce a silhouette, and then she would be exposed. Her idea was that she would see the prowler, identify him, and then run back out the other side of the barn. She was confident that she could outrun anyone who would have to either unlock the doors or circle the buildings to follow her. The sound of the wind was becoming unnerving.

Finally Barbara decided to risk the light. She moved

a little to her left so that she could see over the doors enough to command a view twenty or thirty feet in either direction. She drew a deep breath and lifted the switch. Instantly, the light flooded into a broad semicircle around the barn, and what it showed Barbara made the blood drain from her face and forced her mouth open into a soundless scream. Suspended outside the barn, less than five feet from her face, was a human skull.

21

For ten seconds, everything seemed frozen; even the sound of the wind seemed to have disappeared, as if the blood leaving Barbara's head were taking with it her sense of hearing. Then the skull moved, seeming to float toward her, and she staggered backwards. The pupils of her eyes had contracted sharply with the coming on of the light, but they had recovered now and she was able at last to see that the moving object was really Dick Schneider's ravaged face. Pale and hairless above his dark shirt, with the eyes even wider than usual, his head had seemed for a few seconds like a disembodied skull.

"Dick!" Barbara gasped. "You scared me half to death."

"Who is it?" he said, coming closer, and only then did she realize that she was still partially hidden inside the darkness of the barn.

"It's me, Barbara," she said, stepping up to the door.

"You gave me a turn when that light came on," he said, and indeed, he was shaking as if from cold. "I thought I heard somebody sneaking around behind the barn, and I was intending to take a peek from this side."

"That was me, all right," Barbara said, noticing now how much she was still hyperventilating. "I saw you from the woods, and I thought I'd better find out who was prowling around the place."

"What on earth were you doing in the woods?" he asked, and now that he was recovering from his fright, he sounded a bit exasperated.

"I was taking a shortcut back to New Augsburg," she answered, feeling along the doors for the bolt that would unlock them. "I was running and it was getting dark, so I thought I'd use the lane through the woods. What are *you* doing here?" She had unlocked the doors now to let him inside.

"I take a walk every day now," he said, pulling one of the doors toward himself so he could get around it. "Sitting around the house with nothing to do is driving me crazy. So this is my second walk today. I haven't been over here since Christmas. And, of course, I was curious about where they found the bones. I suppose it seems creepy to you, my wanting to see the place."

"No, no, Dick," she said, fighting an urge to offer him her arm, so slow and unsteady was his progress into the barn; he was holding onto the door for support. "It's natural to be curious. But should you be walking all this way by yourself, and in the dark?"

"Rosa would scold me something fierce if she knew," he said, and his chuckle made a wheezing sound. "She's not home this evening. Some of the grandkids are having a birthday party. We have those two born only a week apart, you know. And I said I didn't feel up to going. But I got restless and—well, here I am."

Barbara locked the doors again and put on the inside light.

"I guess we're both out after curfew," she laughed.

"We'd better head home right now. I'll keep the light on until you get to the other side of the barn."

"Why?" he said, turning his hollowed eyes to look at her in surprise. "I'll get the light for you."

She could see that he was hurt at being treated as old and infirm. This once robust man still had his pride.

"It's just that I know the barn so well," Barbara said hastily.

"You forget that I know it pretty well myself," he grunted. "I ran this farm for a while after your pa died and before I got sick."

"Of course you did," she said. "And years ago, too, when Daddy was in the army. I'll just cut the lights and we'll go out together."

She pushed down on both switches and a profound darkness fell over them. They began to walk side by side, Barbara slowing her pace to stay even with Dick. In the blackness, she could hear his unsteady breathing, as if something hurt him and he was keeping himself from crying out. At the east side doors, Dick paused and leaned against the building for a few seconds. Barbara's decision was now firm.

"I'm going to walk with you to your house, if you don't mind," she said and then hurried on when she heard him starting to object. "It's too dark now for me to go on into the village alone. I can call Mum from your place and she'll come for me in her car. Would that be all right?"

"Of course, of course," he said, straightening. "I've got my wind back now. It's just that you gave me such a turn, like I said. We can cross the field and then take the lane back to the house. There's a gate in the fence over there," and he lifted his arm to point to the north-west. Now that they were in the open air and their eyes had readjusted to the night, they could see each other fairly clearly.

As they began to walk, Barbara wondered if she should ask to take his arm, pretend that she needed support so that she could help him. But she remembered his shrewdness, realized that he would see through the ruse. Didn't he know quite well how independent she'd always been? She decided to respect his pride and just stay close in case he stumbled. He started at a normal pace, as if to convince her that he had, indeed, recovered his wind, but he soon slowed to a shambling gait. Barbara had to take short steps to remain at his side.

"Of course you must know this farm almost as well as your own," she said, trying to make up for her earlier gaffe. "You farmed it during the war when Daddy was in Europe. He was always grateful for the way you kept it up, rotated the crops, took care of the fences."

"The food was needed for the war effort," Dick said. "It would've been a crime to just let it lay here."

"I know," Barbara said. "But you could have bought the place for a song at auction if the taxes had stayed delinquent. But you paid the taxes so it wouldn't be auctioned."

"And your pa paid me back for those taxes over the years." It was too long a sentence for one breath and he had to pause halfway through.

"Still, it was a generous and neighborly thing to do," she replied. "My father always appreciated it, too. He would sometimes say that not many people would have been able to resist the temptation."

"Well, I wouldn't have done it for just anybody either," he said, and he was almost panting now. "Your dad was like a kid brother to me, and I always hoped he'd come back. I'd have farmed the land and took care of it, because that's the way I am about waste. But I wouldn't have paid the taxes for anybody else. I can tell you I wouldn't have done it for that brother of his, for Tony."

Suddenly Dick stopped and bent almost double, breathing in a loud wheeze. The effort of walking and making such a long speech seemed almost too much for him.

"Dick!" Barbara gasped in alarm. "What is it? What can I do for you?"

"Nothing," he panted. "Just rest a minute. Have to."

Barbara put her hand onto his withered shoulders and patted him gently, the universal gesture of concern.

"I could go on ahead and come back for you with a truck or a tractor," she said, bending to bring her face close to his ear, "if you tell me where to find the keys."

"No, no," he said, straightening up again. "I'll make it fine if we stop every once in a while and if you do most of the talking." And he started off again at his shuffling pace.

They walked in silence for a few minutes. Barbara could see the dark outline of the woods drawing closer, but the painfully slow pace made it seem miles away.

"I met Caroline Heim at the fair yesterday," she said, talking both to fill time and to air her chief concern before a sympathetic audience. "She's nothing like what I imagined. Mum says I romanticize everything, and I suppose she's right, but it's hard to believe that Dad could ever have cared for her. He was just so young, I guess."

"Mmmm," Dick murmured, a noncommittal sound.

"I talked with her," Barbara went on. "Even bought her a beer. She didn't have much to say about that last summer in 1943. I mean not much that I didn't already know. Peter saw us together at the beer tent. He didn't like it much, I can tell you."

"I bet," Dick said shortly.

"But he said something very strange," Barbara said. "He called Uncle Tony a 'burner.' And he told me to ask Mary Wenner what happened to Wenners' corn cribs. What could he have meant by that, Dick? Do you know?"

"Bah!" he grunted. "Old gossip. Just old gossip."

"But old gossip is all we have to go on," Barbara insisted. "If we're ever going to find out who killed Tony, we have to find out everything that can still be known about him."

"The gate," Dick said, lifting his arm to point.

Barbara sprinted forward to open the gate and waited for Dick to shuffle through it before she swung it back and latched it again. In a few more steps, they had reached the first trees of the woods.

"There's a few stumps over here," Dick said, gesturing with his head. "We'll sit for a while."

They found the stumps and Dick lowered himself carefully onto one of them. Barbara paced for a bit while he caught his breath.

"I'll just find out from Mary if you don't tell me," she said at last. "You know Mary. She'll spill everything she knows."

"She won't be able to tell you much about this," he grunted. "Peter meant the old Wenners, Jim's folks. It was *their* corn cribs that burned and it happened before Jim and Mary got married."

"And what would that have to do with my uncle?" Barbara asked, sitting now on the stump next to Dick. "What is the old gossip you were talking about?"

"There were rumors that Tony started the fire," he said. "Nothing could be proved. There was nothing much left in the cribs, mind you. It was spring and the corn was almost gone."

293

"Why would Tony do such a thing?" Barbara asked, horrified, even angry. "Fires happen all the time and people never know what started them. So when they want to fix blame, they pick on somebody like Tony. Somebody they don't like anyway."

"Sure, sure," Dick said soothingly. "That's probably what happened. Just because there was a little trouble between Jim and Tony at a dance."

Barbara sat up straight, remembering.

"Mary told me," she said slowly. "Jim hit Tony, punched him over something he'd said, and Tony didn't fight back, just smiled." She paused now, her mouth dry. "Did the fire happen after that?"

"Yep," Dick said. "Not too long after, either."

"Well, it still doesn't mean that Tony did it," Barbara said, flaring up.

"Of course it doesn't," he said, his voice gruff, raspy. "I *told* you it was just old gossip, but you had to ask about it anyway. Now you're mad because I told you."

"I'm sorry," she said softly. "You're right. I'm behaving badly, but I'm just getting so tired of all this innuendo about Tony when there don't seem to be any hard facts."

"Well, let it alone, Barbie," he said more gently. "Why do you want to go digging around in the past where 'hard facts' are not so easy to come by? Why is it so important to you?"

Instead of answering, Barbara stood up and began to pace again, the thickly matted floor of the woods crunching and crackling under her running shoes.

"Did Daddy know?" she asked at last, stopping before Dick's huddled figure. "About the rumors, I mean?"

"You grew up here, girl," he said, standing up slowly.

"You know how everybody felt about your father. Nobody wanted to hurt him, so nobody would talk about such things in front of him."

Barbara remembered Peter Heim's words: "Everybody in New Augsburg has kept quiet for fifty-odd years so that Hoffmans could hold their heads up." And there was something else, too, that she almost remembered, some buried image from her early childhood that was struggling to come forward into consciousness, called forth by the night and by Dick's words. But something else in her mind veered away from the memory, fought it off. She focused instead on Dick's movements as he began to walk again.

"Do *you* believe Tony was a burner?" she asked.

"It doesn't matter what I believe," he sighed. "It doesn't matter after all these years."

Barbara started after him, preparing her next question, determined not to let it alone; then she saw Dick double over again, heard a sharp cry, though he'd apparently tried to muffle it. She ran toward him and took his arm.

"Goddamn it!" he snarled through gritted teeth, and he struck his side feebly with his left fist. "Goddamn this cancer!"

Barbara was struck dumb for a second. When she spoke again, it was almost in a whisper.

"Let me go for help. You can't make it back."

"No," he said quickly. "It'll pass. It always passes after a while. I can make it home. Don't you worry yourself."

She slipped her arm around his shoulders, shocked at the sharpness of the bones she could feel through his shirt, and bent forward, trying to look into his averted face. Finally, he straightened a little and turned to look at her. Even in the darkness, she could see the half-guilty look in his eyes, as if he had uttered some obscenity in front of her instead of the word "cancer."

"Oh, Dick," she whispered. "You're not getting any better, are you?"

"No, Barbie," he said, and she heard the ominous wheeze again. "No, I'm not. They couldn't do anything else for me in that hospital, so I just left. I'm not going out with my body all stuck full of needles and tubes. I want to be here, on my own land, at home."

"Does Rosa know?" she said, her face and mouth numb.

"She suspects," he said, standing up all the way now. "I can't hide too much from that one, but I wanted to keep her hopeful as long as I could so I wouldn't let the doctors tell her. She takes things so hard you know. But I know I can't keep it much longer. We had this couple of weeks at home now, and it was a good time for us, but I'm planning to tell her sometime this weekend. Otherwise it'll scare her something awful if I just keel over on her."

"Yes," Barbara murmured. "It's better to prepare her." But she was just making sounds; she couldn't make her mind work, couldn't find appropriate words.

"I think we should get along," he said after a pause.

"Yes," she said. "Will you please lean on me now, let me help you?"

"Sure," he said, as if he were doing her a favor, and he slipped his right arm around her shoulders. She passed her arm around the thin waist, afraid to clasp him, afraid she would touch the place that gave him pain, the place he had struck with his fist. But he *did* lean on her now and they walked together that way down the lane, through the sweet-smelling night, sheltered by the woods from the wind that still stirred the leaves above their heads.

It wasn't until they'd reached the Schneiders' lighted back porch that Dick spoke again.

"I gotta rest a minute," he panted, "before we do the steps." And he released his grip on Barbara to grasp the railing that flanked the shallow flight of stairs.

Barbara took a few paces backward and turned to look at him. He lifted his head and she could see his face clearly in the light that poured from the single bulb above and behind her. He looked inexpressibly tired, the skin over his sunken cheeks almost gray from pain and exhaustion.

"Will you take a little advice from an old friend?" he said, and a crooked smile turned up one side of his mouth.

"Of course," she said, hearing the crack in her own voice.

"Life is real short," he said, his eyes taking on an intense light. "Shorter than you think. Go forward with your life, honey. Don't get stuck in the past, in regrets, in rehashing old mistakes. You've got so much going for you, but you don't seem to know it. Be happy, won't you? For old Dick?"

"I'll try," she whispered. "I promise you I'll try."

"You can help me inside now, if you will," he said and reached his thin arm out for her.

She supported him on the steps, walked him through the kitchen and into his room. When he insisted that he could put himself to bed and assured her that Rosa would be home soon, she went back into the kitchen and called Eileen, whose worried scolding Barbara cut short with a few sharp words. Then she sat down at the big oak table, buried her face in her hands, and wept: for Dick, for her father, for Andrew, for all the lost times, all the old bonds that seemed to be fading even while she looked at them. She cried without noise, stifling the sobs with her hands, because she didn't want Dick to hear her. She knew that if he heard, lying there in his darkened room, alone with his knowledge and his pain, he would think he should come out to comfort her. Dick Schneider was like that.

22

The next morning, Eileen Thompson Hoffman left the apartment at 8:45 to begin her first half-day of work at Seidl's Hardware store, and Barbara did the breakfast dishes, so deep in thought that she was hardly watching what she was doing. She and her mother had cried together a long time the night before—the Wenners and the Schneiders were the closest thing to brothers and sisters that Eileen had in America—and then each had retired to her room to lie awake with memories and sorrows. Barbara couldn't speak for her mother, but she'd slept very little. The past two days had given her two new pieces to the puzzle that was Tony Hoffman and these pieces didn't seem to fit into the picture she'd been constructing so carefully ever since the bones were uncovered. Now she was turning these pieces over again in her mind as she rinsed cereal bowls and coffee cups.

Peter Heim had called Tony a burner, hinting that all of New Augsburg had been protecting Hoffmans from this knowledge for a long time. Dick Schneider had confirmed for her that New Augsburg believed Tony had burned Wenners' corn cribs in retaliation for a public fight with Jim. She put these two puzzle pieces next to the earlier information that Tony had been kicked out of high school for starting a fire in a closet; until now, that information had seemed, at the least, inconsequential and, at the most, part of the pattern of wild-young-man-with-a-chip-on-his-shoulder—the picture she'd *thought* would solve the murder if she could just find all the missing pieces. A school fire and a rumored act of revenge. Were those two things, occurring some ten years apart, enough to fix the label, enough to make Peter Heim suggest that Hoffmans wouldn't have been able to hold up their heads in the community if they'd known? Or was there more, more puzzle pieces of this new variety that were yet in hiding?

Well, fires weren't like broken romances and hushed-up pregnancies and smoldering jealousies; fires, Barbara knew, were part of the public record. And the trained history student, the practiced researcher, knew how to uncover such records. She rinsed out the dish cloth, wiped the empty sink, and sprinted up the stairs to change out of her running clothes—a run could wait until afternoon—and into a skirt and blouse. Downstairs again, she scooped up her purse on her way to the back door.

The local newspaper office was within easy walking distance. When Barbara turned onto Main Street, she came to an abrupt stop as she recognized the figure of the man apparently waiting to cross New Augsburg's only busy street. Standing at the corner opposite the drug store was Raymond Heim, his burly shoulders held in that same attitude of belligerence Barbara had noticed in both his father and his uncle. He wasn't looking in her direction but was staring off into traffic.

Barbara started walking again, conscious of the clicking sound her sandals made on the sidewalk, uncertain whether or not she wanted Ray to notice her. He turned his big head toward her just as she was about to pass behind him. The puffy face registered surprise, even more color flooding his sun-reddened cheeks. Then his eyes hardened, showing for the few seconds it took Barbara to pass him a sharp resemblance to his father's flinty glare. She'd meant to nod, to greet him in some way, but the hostility in his expression made her hurry on, her own face flushed.

Only when she'd turned onto Elm Street did Barbara begin to wonder what Raymond Heim was doing in the village so early on a weekday morning. Surely there were plenty of things to do on the farm. But then she gave her head a quick shake. Paranoia must be pretty far advanced if she couldn't see an old neighbor without becoming instantly suspicious. She knew now, of course, that Raymond hadn't been the man on the ladder outside her window, knew that she should recast her fears about him. That look of his reflected his family's attitude toward her at the moment, but could hardly be called menacing. She would just put it out of her mind.

The office of the *New Augsburg Post* was in a rectangular addition built onto the back of Olga Tempe's house. For fifty-seven years, Olga had edited the weekly and acted as its chief reporter as well. Often she would gather news by simply calling people up and asking, "What's new?" Still alert and spry at seventy-eight, Olga's only concession to age had been to hire two assistants, one to staff the office and the other to do on-site reporting; the editorial role she had kept firmly in her own hands.

Olga wasn't there when Barbara came into the office. The paper came out in the village on Friday and arrived in rural mailboxes on Saturday, so Thursdays were long ones for her; she always took Friday mornings off. The young woman who greeted Barbara from behind the desk was a stranger to her.

"Are back issues of the *Post* kept here on the premises?" Barbara asked.

"Yes, in the basement," the young woman replied.

"On microfilm?"

At this, the girl rolled her blue eyes up at the ceiling.

"Oh, no," she sighed. "I think it'll be a while yet before microfilm comes to the *New Augsburg Post*. They're all down there in bundles."

"Could I look at them?" Barbara said, flashing her most ingratiating smile.

"Gee, I don't know," the young woman said. "I've never had that request before."

"I'm at Northwestern now, but I'm originally from New Augsburg," Barbara said smoothly. "I have a research project due next month on rural America during World War II. This would be such a help, and I'm sure Miss Tempe wouldn't mind."

"Oh, okay," the girl said. "I'm sure you'll be careful."

"Oh, yes," Barbara replied. "Very careful."

The basement was surprisingly dry and warm, and the air had no odor of damp, though it smelled definitely of newsprint. Olga Tempe had clearly taken her role as archivist seriously and had installed dehumidifiers to preserve the newspapers which were stacked on wide shelves near the center of the room. Even a cursory investigation revealed that the papers were carefully arranged, each bundle containing fifty-two issues and labeled on the top with a sheet of paper listing the year. The newspaper was tabloid size and frequently no longer than eight or ten pages, so the bundles weren't heavy. It took no time at all for Barbara and the young assistant to find 1942 and 1943.

"There's a table with a light behind the stairs there," the young woman said. "I don't suppose anybody'll bother you. Tie everything back up again when you're finished."

Barbara thanked her and settled down to her research, using her usual method of first laying out note paper and pen. Then she carefully untied the twine on the bundle labeled 1942. She had debated on the way over about whether or not she was breaking her promise to Paul by doing this. She'd promised to stop interviewing people and, by implication, to avoid any behavior that would further aggravate whoever had followed her in the fog. But, she reasoned, reading through old newspapers could hardly be considered "covered" by that promise; nobody would even know she was doing it.

The papers were remarkably well preserved and so small that it took very little time to skim the headlines in each issue. In the next two-and-a-half hours, Barbara looked through all the 1942 issues of the *Post* and the 1943 issues through the end of August, reasoning that news items after that date would have no bearing on the death of Anton Hoffman. Whenever she found a story about a fire, she paused and took notes: more notes if the case seemed even remotely connected, by proximity or acquaintance, to her uncle; fewer notes if the case seemed to have no family link. Right from the start, she was struck by how many fires there had been in and around New Augsburg during those twenty months back in the forties. The primitive state of electrical wiring in rural areas—barns were often wired by their owners without professional help—combined with the volatile conditions under which crops were stored in those days, produced an alarming number of barn fires; when the newspaper bothered to list a cause for a fire, it was frequently characterized as "spontaneous combustion in a hay mow" or "overheated wiring."

In April of 1942, Barbara found the headline "Fire Destroys Corn Cribs"; the article gave the location of the Herbert Wenner farm, mentioned that the cribs were almost empty, and ventured no guess as to cause. In an early September issue from 1942, she found a surprise —under a headline reading "Blaze Destroys Abandoned Chicken Coop," she discovered the name Charles Novak as the owner of the burned building; the article explained that the Novaks weren't keeping chickens at the time and speculated that a lightning strike had started the fire, since there had been a storm the night the fire was discovered; a subsequent downpour had saved a nearby machine shed from catching fire, too. Barbara took her notes carefully and was about to set the paper aside when her eyes caught a square advertising in bold type "Horse Auction Saturday." Horses, horses—what had she heard recently about horses that was crowding forward into her attention? Of course! Mary Wenner had been babbling about horse-pulling contests and she had remembered a contest in which Charlie Novak's team had beaten the team that Tony Hoffman had insisted on pitting against it. And Charlie had "gloated" about it; that was the very word Mary had used. And Mary had remembered the time it happened—late summer of 1942.

Barbara felt her stomach beginning to knot. Jim Wenner had publicly hit Tony at an Easter dance in 1942 and his parents' corn cribs had burned on April 15th. Charlie Novak had made much of Tony's defeat in late summer of 1942 and one of his buildings had gone up in flames on September 2nd. This couldn't be coincidence. This was what the old people knew and were keeping secret; this was what Peter Heim meant by calling Tony a burner: not a high school prank, but a pattern of revenge, a cowardly and despicable way to get back at people he thought had humiliated him. This was the real reason the Heims considered a marriage between their sister and Anton Hoffman "out of the question." Barbara had grown up on a farm, and she knew that nothing was more dreaded than fire, not even bad weather. What a louse Tony must have been! It was, for Barbara, the final and permanent blow to the image of him she had nurtured in her girlhood.

She sat back in the chair, her mind racing. Here was a motive for murder she'd never considered. Because Tony had always been such a romantic figure to her, she'd instantly latched onto the details of sexual intrigue, jealousy, and betrayal as soon as she learned he'd been murdered. And, she had to admit to herself, it was also a case of personal projection: *she* had been betrayed by the man she loved; *she* had wanted to kill him as a result. Therefore, Tony the lady's man must have been killed by either a jealous man or a betrayed woman. And the most likely jealous man, of course, was Joseph Hoffman. But if Tony had died because someone knew he'd set a fire—couldn't prove it but knew it anyway—then there was no connection at all to her father. All the efforts to scare her off the investigation made sense in this new context.

Barbara sat forward again, looking intently at her notes. The problem with her new theory was immediately obvious. The dates were wrong. If Tony had set fires in 1942, why would either the Wenners or Charlie Novak wait until the autumn of 1943 to kill him? There had to be something else, something later. She began scanning papers again, noting that the number of fires, predictably, went down in the winter months. The rate picked up again in the early summer of 1943. Barbara was just about to put one granary fire under her "unlikely" column when she read, "Rataychek, who is a part-time policeman in Gale, says he had no chance to save the building because the blaze was already out of control when his son was awakened by the sounds of the fire about 4 a.m." Again, Barbara found herself struggling to remember something she had heard; it was the mention of Gale that seemed to trigger the connection. She went over her recent conversations in her mind—the Novaks, the Schneiders, the Heims. No, earlier than those interviews, before the start of her anxiety over her father. She began suddenly to think the memory had something to do with kiwi fruit and then she knew. Mary Wenner had come to lunch, so long ago it seemed now, and had told about Tony roaring around all summer on his motorcycle, about the speeding ticket he'd got in Gale; and Mary had remembered that Tony was very angry about the ticket. Barbara moved her pen over to the column labeled "likely," and wrote "Revenge for speeding ticket!" next to it.

In the July 16th issue, the second page yielded unexpected paydirt. The headline said, "Disaster Averted at Heim Farm." Barbara eagerly read every word of the story, which wasn't very long. The item reported a fire in the brooder house attached to the barn, a fire which had killed fifty newly hatched chicks, but which had been prevented from spreading because Peter Heim, making a late-night check of the buildings, had discovered the blaze and was able to put it out with a water hose he had earlier run through a window in order to have a good supply of fresh water for the chicks. "The brooder lights were too close to the straw bedding," George Heim was quoted as saying. "You can see pretty easy where the fire started."

Barbara wrote hastily, copying almost all of the item, and then sat back to think. What if the Heims had later come to believe that they were wrong about the cause of the blaze? What if Charlie Novak, their very good friend, had made them see a connection to Tony because *he* believed Tony had burned his chicken coop? Then when they learned that Tony had been sneaking around with their sister, it could have driven them over the edge into violence. Much as Barbara favored this theory, the objective scholar in her had to admit that it had some problems, too. As far as she knew, Tony would have had no reason to set a fire at the Heim farm—not in July. He was at that time having a secret affair with George and Peter's sister, but was not discovered in this affair and run off the Heim farm until late August. And, once again, there was the problem of timing. Tony Hoffman hadn't died in July, and he hadn't died in August; he'd been seen in public during the first weekend of September. Could one or both of the Heim brothers have kept a smoldering anger going for more than two weeks and then planned the murder for revenge? Well, she thought with relief, it was at least more likely than imagining that someone as mild as Jim Wenner would wait more than a year after being provoked to do the same thing.

By the time Barbara got to the August 27, 1943, issue of the *New Augsburg Post*, she had recorded seventeen fires, six of which she had labeled "likely"; two of these were on the list only because they'd happened fairly near the Hoffman farm, not because the farmers involved seemed to have any connection to Tony Hoffman. She was just about to close this last issue when a name under a seemingly irrelevant headline on page 6 seemed to jump out at her; the headline was "Land Dispute Settled" and the name was Anton Hoffman. The item read in full:

Judge Cecil Hannon this week disallowed Anton Hoffman's claim to a strip of wooded land that stands between his farm and the Richard Schneider farm in the corner of section 30 west of the village. A surveyor's report, ordered by Judge Hannon, showed that the area lies mostly inside the land originally homesteaded by Schneider's grandfather. A 1912 drawing of the section on which Hoffman had based his claim was inaccurate, Hannon ruled.

Odd, Barbara thought, that she'd never been told that the woods she had known so well as a child, and through which both Hoffman and Schneider vehicles rolled without question on either side, really belonged to Dick. But perhaps not so odd. Dick and her father were such old friends that they would naturally avoid any reference to such an ancient dispute, especially as Dick apparently had no intention of using the woods for farming purposes; he could easily have had the fence line moved while Joe Hoffman was gone from New Augsburg for six years if he'd wished to insist on his claim to the land. But it was like both men simply to pretend the issue had never been raised; good relations meant more to them than a twenty-acre strip of trees.

At the thought of Dick Schneider, Barbara again felt tears welling into the corners of her eyes. She looked up quickly and then glanced at her watch. It was almost noon and that meant her mother would be returning to the apartment soon. She knew that questions could be best avoided if she were there when Eileen got home, so she tied up the bundles of papers, replaced them on the shelves, and hurried up the stairs.

Olga Tempe was now occupying the desk chair, and the young assistant who had admitted Barbara was gone. Olga was a lean, erect old woman with wildly frizzy white hair and keen eyes.

"Laura tells me you're a local girl," she said, peering intently at Barbara from behind her glasses.

"Yes," Barbara said. "I was Barbara Hoffman before my marriage. I've just helped my mother move here to the village from our farm. I told Laura about my research paper."

"Seems to be a lot of interest in those old papers lately," Olga said, turning away to pick up her coffee cup.

"Really?" Barbara said, feeling her breath catch slightly. "Someone else doing research?"

"That new young sheriff was in here on Monday afternoon," Olga said, swinging her gaze back to Barbara's face. "Interested in 1940 through 1943. I thought it might have something to do with that old skeleton they found out at your farm, but he wouldn't say. What do you think?"

Barbara fought hard to keep her face expressionless. Nothing was lost on this old woman, she realized. A lifetime as a reporter had made her razor sharp.

"I'm sure I wouldn't try to second-guess the sheriff," she said evenly. "I've got to run now. Meeting somebody for lunch." And she fled from the office into the quiet street outside.

* * *

309

Back at the apartment, Barbara was relieved to see that Eileen was not yet home. Tucking away her purse and slipping out of her sandals, she crossed to the front door to bring in the mail. There were two bills for Eileen, three pieces of junk mail, and one sealed business-size envelope on which was printed one word: "Barbara." No stamp, no postmark, no return address. The lettering of her name was peculiarly tall and spiky, as if someone had deliberately chosen an exaggerated style. In the apartment again, Barbara dropped her mother's mail onto the little hall table and carried the strange envelope into the living room, her heart beating fast, for once again it seemed that someone had been watching the house, waiting for everyone to be gone before leaving something in the mailbox.

And Raymond Heim had been in the village this morning. Was there a connection? There was no way to tell where he'd come from to that corner on Main Street where she'd seen him standing. He might have been waiting to cross to the drug store. But he might have been watching the corner, waiting for the moment when both Eileen and Barbara would be out of the apartment. You could see the building quite easily from that corner, she now realized.

Barbara sat down and considered how to handle the envelope, but then she remembered what Paul had said about fingerprints and simply ripped open the flap. She pulled out a piece of typing paper and opened it up. The sheet of paper had two blocks of printing on it, one in the center and one near the bottom; this printing, too, was absurdly tall and narrow, as if it had been slowly sketched rather than just printed. The block in the center of the page said:

Caroline Heim wrote two letters to Tony Hoffman. Why did Joe Hoffman have them and why did he hide them in his house all his life?

The bottom block, which looked darker, as if it had been printed with a different pencil or with more force, said:

Letters for sale at Tomchek's Machine Shop
Midnite tonite

Barbara sat there feeling her fingers tingling, her mouth filling with the bitter taste of fear. She'd spent the morning learning definitely, she thought, that Tony's death had no connection to her father, and now the old specter of her suspicions was being raised again. Her next response was one of complete disbelief. Somebody was fabricating this business of the letters. It was absurd to imagine that her father would have those letters and would have hidden them. Even if he had, who would *know* that he had; who could have recovered them now? Of course, it was a lie. But who knew that there were letters to lie about? Caroline, of course, and probably her brothers; they might have intercepted the letters before they could actually be mailed. And since Wednesday, Peter had probably browbeaten Caroline into telling him what she'd discussed with Tony's niece at the beer tent. If she'd told him that she mentioned the letters, he could have sent Raymond to town with this note. Or might he have told someone else? Perhaps his good friend Charlie Novak? Whoever left the note, it was just another effort to intimidate her, perhaps even to terrorize her, and she would just ignore it.

But there was still the sick feeling in her stomach, the

agony of hearing the "other voice" which spoke in her mind despite the efforts of her will to silence it. The voice was relentlessly reminding her that if the mailman had found Caroline's letters, he would have taken them to the Hoffman farm; it whispered that Tony Hoffman was not the only one living there at the time; it raised a series of disturbing questions. What if Joe Hoffman had found those letters sometime after his last meeting with Caroline Heim? He would have learned that she was pregnant and was appealing to her lover for help. What if he had confronted Tony with the letters and learned that Tony had no intention of marrying Caroline? Would sudden rage have blinded him to consequences, made him grab a poker there in the big kitchen?

No, it was nonsense. Even if he had done such a thing, he would have destroyed the letters, wouldn't he? Just burned them up? Why would he hide them? So this ridiculous note was pure fiction. She stood up and paced a few steps before reading it over again. She should just give it to Paul, she thought; that would be the right thing to do. Then he could keep the appointment at midnight and grab whoever would resort to this sort of trickery, and he would have his arrest, would be able to take fingerprints at last. Barbara walked briskly to the phone, picked it up, and then put it down again.

Did she really want Paul to know that there was some strong suspicion that Joseph Hoffman had killed his brother? Paul was obviously more on top of this case than she'd realized. He had found out from someone that Tony was suspected of setting fires, or why would he have been checking old issues of the *Post*? He'd known that as long ago as Monday and hadn't said a word about it to her. What else wasn't he telling her? If he saw this note, would it confirm something he already believed?

And what if the letters did still exist and the note writer could show that Joe Hoffman had hidden them for forty years? There was just that slight possibility, silly as it seemed. Besides, she thought, looking at the note again, there was something familiar about the name Tomchek. Where had she heard it before?

The directory was on the shelf next to the phone, and Barbara took it down to begin searching. There was no Tomchek Machine Shop in New Augsburg. She opened the drawer where she'd seen her mother put the regional Yellow Pages, and here she had better luck. Tomchek's was in Casson township and its address was a trunk road, so it had to be out in the country. What connection could any of her New Augsburg suspects have with this place?

Just then, Barbara heard her mother's key in the lock and she sprinted upstairs. She felt she couldn't face Eileen just then, not with this awful note in her hands. She answered, ''In the bathroom,'' to Eileen's shouted ''Where are you?'' and thus bought a few more minutes to compose herself. Over lunch, she was grateful that Eileen was so full of chatty details about her first day in the hardware business that she was unlikely to notice how quiet her daughter was.

By 2:30, when Eileen went outside to pull weeds out of the flower beds and snip the last faded blooms off the peony bushes, Barbara had decided on a course of action. She dialed Tomchek's Machine Shop, waiting through seven rings before she heard the lifting of a receiver and a man's voice say abruptly, ''Tomchek's.''

''Yes, hello,'' she said. ''This is Barbara Pankratz. My husband and I recently bought the Joseph Hoffman farm here in New Augsburg, and we're looking around for someone who will take good care of our machines for us. I found you in the Yellow Pages.''

"Well, you've come to the right place, ma'am," he said, much more animated now.

"You understand, of course, that we have a big investment in our machinery," she went on smoothly; she'd rehearsed this all ahead of time. "And we want to be careful to pick a good mechanic right from the start. Are there any of our new neighbors who could tell us about your work, any nearby farmers who've trusted you with their machines?"

"Did you say the Hoffman place?" he asked.

"That's right."

"Well, sure," the voice said happily. "I've done work for some of the folks out there. As a matter of fact, I'm just finishing a job for the Novaks right now, and they're just west of you. I'm modifying a haybine so their son can drive it. Maybe you haven't met them yet, but he's a paraplegic and he can only use his hands to drive. And I service tractors for Roman Weinfurter and George Heim; they're pretty close neighbors around there, too."

"I see," Barbara murmured. "Any other references?"

"Well, you could talk to either one of the Wenner boys about me," he said. "They used to live on the farm right across the road from you there. I'm married to their sister Janet."

Of course, that was it! Eileen had written Barbara in Ohio years ago about Janet's wedding, and Barbara had sent a gift, had written "Mr. and Mrs. Tomchek" on the card inside.

"Thank you for being so helpful," Barbara said. "We'll find out what we can and get back to you."

"Oh, thank you, ma'am," he said. "Let me know if you need more information."

So, Barbara thought as she hung up the phone, that wasn't as much help as she'd hoped it would be for zeroing in on whoever had left the note in the mailbox. She'd hoped that this shop in another township would be linked to only one possible suspect, but she ought to have known better. If one farmer was satisfied with the service he got from any merchant, especially where his machinery was concerned, his neighbors, relatives, and friends would soon be patronizing that merchant, too. It was the chief reason why so few businesses of this sort bothered with advertising; those who *had* to advertise didn't last very long.

That Novaks or Heims might be responsible for the note didn't surprise Barbara, but the connection of Tomcheks to Wenners was disturbing. This was the second time the name had been raised in connection with an attempt to frighten her. Judy Wenner Gordon had once lived in Eileen's apartment and now Janet Wenner Tomchek was connected to this maddening note. And only this morning, Barbara had confirmed that Jim Wenner once had a motive for killing Tony Hoffman. Was someone trying to protect Jim's memory? But who? Surely not the quiet and gentle Ron Wenner. Mary? Could it be possible that Mary's "gossip" wasn't random, but purposeful? Could that scattered, warm, oversized woman be capable of terrorizing old friends? Impossible! Still— her devotion to Jim was almost legendary and her fear that he might be suspected was obvious from the first moment she heard about Tony's murder.

For the rest of the afternoon, Barbara vacillated between two positions. Half the time she was convinced that the note was a fraud and that it would be foolishly dangerous for her to respond to it in any way. If the note came from the same person who had chased her in the fog, she could be in real danger of being killed at that remote shop in the middle of the night, because that

315

person was clearly crazy; and *she* would be crazy to go there without an army to back her up. The other half of the time she was sick with fear that the note was genuine—that her father had kept Caroline's letters and that his keeping them could mean only one thing. Someone knew that he'd killed his brother and was now hoping to get a little blackmail money for this evidence. Could she afford to ignore the note? Would the next note go to Paul Gillis?

By evening, Barbara was worn out from the conflict, hardly touched her dinner, and used the excuse of a headache to go up to her room early. But she didn't go to bed; in fact, she changed into jeans, a work shirt, and her running shoes. Then she stretched out on top of the spread, waiting in the dark for her mother to go to bed, waiting still longer to be sure that Eileen had fallen asleep. Only then did she get up, turn on the desk lamp, and spread out her Wisconsin map.

23

The Volkswagen made good time along the roads leading to Casson township. It was a quieter night than the night before because the wind had died down to an almost imperceptible breeze, but Friday night is party night everywhere, so there were quite a few other cars out on the country roads. Barbara drove attentively, with her window rolled down a few inches. On the passenger seat next to her was the jack handle from her mother's car— a long, straight, formidable-looking piece of metal. She had no intention of leaving the protection of her car without some form of self-defense. Next to the jack handle was her flashlight.

Tomchek's Machine Shop turned out to be easy to find, a huge building with its name emblazoned all along the side facing the trunk road, exactly where Barbara's map had suggested it should be. A high fence surrounded about an acre of land that included the building, but there was no gate, only a large open space in the fence facing the road. Barbara drove in and then slowly all around the building. There were three tractors parked in the back, the two bigger ones looking like the parents of the smaller one between them. But there was no car. Barbara brought her car to a stop and turned the flashlight onto her watch. It was 12:15. She'd deliberately timed the trip so she would be a little late, intending to make the note writer wait for her rather than the other way around.

She put the car in low gear and drove around the building again to the main doors which faced the rear of the building. These doors, big enough to admit even the largest of farm machinery, were firmly closed, but on this pass, Barbara noticed a smaller door next to the main doors. She stopped the car so that the headlights were trained on this door; it appeared to be slightly ajar. She sat there for a moment longer, considering again that the smartest thing she could do would be to drive straight back to New Augsburg. Then she switched off her engine, turned out the lights, and got out of the car, slipping her keys into the pocket of her jeans.

Flashlight in one hand and jack handle in the other, Barbara approached the building across the crushed rock surface of the parking lot. She knew stealth was probably useless, but found herself on tiptoe anyway. Around her, the night air was very still, so that the crunching of the stones sounded preternaturally loud. She found that the small door was, indeed, standing open about eight inches. She pushed it wider with the jack handle and pointed the flashlight beam ahead of her as she stepped inside.

The interior was cavernous and very dark, at least sixty feet wide and more than a hundred and thirty feet long; the flashlight beam didn't reach the other side. Hulking shapes loomed to left and right.

"Hello," Barbara called firmly, but jumped a little at the echo her voice made. "Is anyone here?"

There was no answer. Barbara made a resolution to make sure no one got between her and her car, trusting as usual to her swiftness of foot to get her back there if she needed to flee, so she began methodically training her light on everything to either side of her each time she took a step forward. A corn cultivator on the right got a thorough search before she was sure no one was hiding behind it; the same treatment was accorded the tractor to her left—she even circled this machine before going further into the gloom. The machine directly in front of her, some twenty feet into the building, was a John Deere haybine, and Barbara recognized it as soon as her flashlight beam fell on it. It had been one of her father's favorite new toys during the last few years of his life. She remembered now that her mother had told her that the Novaks had bought it at the auction. So this was the haybine Charlie was having modified so Billy could drive it.

The haybine was a big machine and needed careful inspection before Barbara would go beyond it. It was shaped like a very big tractor, but she remembered that, in motion, it always looked as if it were backing up, for the front wheels were the big ones and the body of the machine sloped away from a high, forward-thrusting, glass-enclosed cab toward the small back wheels. Below the cab and jutting out before the front wheels was a big, spike-studded cylinder. When this cylinder was rolling, it combed an eight-foot-wide swath of hay into the slashing blades under and behind it and, when the hay was cut, into an auger that funneled the hay into a neat row on the ground. Barbara circled this machine, shining her light behind the big wheels, even stooping to pass the light under the haybine's body and rear wheels. Satisfied, she moved past the machine and began sweeping the light back and forth before herself. There were no more machines for as far as the light could travel.

Barbara was beginning to hyperventilate now. The silence and the dark were menacing. She came to a stop when her light picked up the back wall of the huge room, and searched this wall from corner to corner with the probing light. In its center was another regular-sized door, a screen door, leading she guessed to the office which was built onto the front of the building facing the road. No one was here, not in this room anyway, so she would have to drive around to the front and knock on the outside door of the office; crossing the rest of this big empty room did not appeal to her. Probably, she thought with disgust, there was no one in the office either. This had been a wild goose chase, after all. What an idiot she'd been to respond to that stupid note!

Behind her, the silence was suddenly shattered by the roaring cough of a big engine coming to life. Barbara whirled just as the headlights of the haybine came on, flooding the building with a brilliant light and spotlighting her as if she'd just stepped onto the stage of a big, empty theater. She was frozen in shock, her mind failing at first to comprehend. She'd heard no sounds; no one could have come into the building behind her and climbed up into this machine. Then her mind moved, formed a chilling insight: someone had been in the cab all along. While she searched all around the wheels and even under the body, some silent watcher had been there, behind the tinted glass, waiting. The throbbing of the engine seemed deafening, a deep guttural noise, like the snoring of an oversized bear.

Barbara stood with the flashlight beam feebly shining at her shoes, the jack handle hanging loosely at her side. For some twenty seconds, it was like a strange face-off in a western movie, each antagonist appraising the other without making a move. Then the absurd one-sidedness of the contest struck Barbara with keen force and she made a dash to her right, angling for the side wall in a race to get past the haybine. But the machine lurched into motion, and the headlights swung with incredible speed. Barbara found her path blocked. She stopped and backed off; the haybine came to a stop. Again there was the pause. Then Barbara turned and sprinted for the other side of the building. The haybine was astonishingly swift and agile, pivoting like a basketball player; it spun and ran parallel with her, blocking her and crowding closer to her as she ran.

Barbara came to a stop again, retreated toward the back wall, and spun to the right again. But the haybine stayed with her, wheeling and turning, crowding her further away from her escape, like some gigantic cat playing with a mouse. The jack handle banged against her leg as she turned, so she finally dropped it. When only twenty feet remained between her and the back wall, Barbara stopped and faced the headlights, which came to a sudden stop, too, eyeing her.

"Cut it out!" Barbara screamed. "I know that's you, Billy Novak, so you can just stop it. I know that machine was fixed so you can drive it. You've hidden your chair someplace in here and pulled yourself up there into that cab." She was panting, half sobbing, but angry, too, humiliated by what she believed was an effort to scare her rather than to really hurt her.

Now the tone of the machine changed, a sound of moving levers followed by a deepening of the growl. Barbara could see that the cylinder was lifting up into the air, could hear the soft "squoosh" of the hydraulic pistons. When it had reached a chest-high level, it stopped, and other noises were followed by a whirring sound. She stood as if hypnotized and saw the cylinder begin to spin, its spikes flashing in the light from the powerful lamps above it. Barbara stared at the glinting wall of glass above the headlights, but there was no way her eyes could penetrate that tinted surface in the dark. Now she heard the gear change, and the haybine began to move forward.

She sprinted to the side and raced for the back wall, hoping to give the appearance of circling in panic. Maybe she could do a quick feint at the center of the wall and dash past the haybine as it came close to her. In the first run past the screen door to the office, she grabbed for the knob; it turned, and she stopped to pull on the door. It rattled but wouldn't open. Hooked, she thought as she heard the haybine, which had overshot her a bit, spinning back toward her. She dashed in the direction from which she'd come, luring the driver into thinking she would at last head for a corner where she could be pinned. But her mind was racing at full speed now, too, remembering how they used to open the hooked screen door on the back porch of the farmhouse when someone would forget to unhook the door from the inside, thereby locking out some member of the family.

Fifteen feet from the corner, with the haybine bearing down on her, Barbara wheeled around, her ankles aching from the sudden turn, and raced for the small door. She could hear the screaming protest of big tires as the haybine began its spin behind her, but she reached the door, flashed her own light through the screen and, finding the hook, gave the door frame a smart rap with her right fist. The hook jumped once, but didn't come out. Lights were pouring at her now so she didn't need her flashlight any more. She pounded as hard as she could and the hook jumped out of its ring. She didn't look around at the roaring monster she knew was bearing down on her fast, but snatched open the door and jumped through the doorway. The haybine caught the door and snapped it off its hinges before it could swing shut.

Barbara ran through the office, slamming her hip into a chair and stumbling against the far wall. But she reached the outer door and opened it easily—it wasn't chained or locked with a dead bolt. By this time she was talking aloud to herself.

"Got you! Got you. You can't get that monster out of there and you can't chase me on foot."

She was running now on reflex, not even thinking which way around the building would get her to her car faster, already flying ahead in her mind to what she would say to Paul Gillis: "This time he tried to kill me." Suddenly, she heard a pounding behind her, a thumping in a sort of syncopation to the sound of her own feet against the ground. She looked over her shoulder and what she saw almost knocked her to her knees. Someone was chasing her on foot, a dark figure running in a straining crouch. It was impossible! Billy Novak was crippled; he couldn't run. For a split second, she was sure he'd been fooling everyone all along, only pretending to need that wheelchair, just so he could spring into a run here at this moment. Then thinking stopped and adrenaline kicked in. Barbara turned on her racing speed, rounded the corner of the building and dashed for her car, glimmering white at the far end of the one hundred and fifty feet of parking lot. Barbara was running flat out now, all her conditioning working to push her body to its limits. But she could tell that whoever was behind her was gaining. This was no paraplegic; no seventy-year-old man, either. She realized she wouldn't have time to stop at her car, open the door, get inside, and lock the door before she was caught, so she dashed past the Volkswagen and made for the road. Her brain had now clicked into overdrive and she was thinking that her endurance might make up for her disadvantage in the sprint; she could, after all, run for ten miles if she had to, so she would have to hope she could stay in front of her pursuer long enough for him to get winded, to play out.

At the road, she turned right and raced up the grassy ditch to the smooth surface of the pavement. Behind her, she could still hear the pounding of the other feet, closer now than they'd been in the parking lot, but she didn't dare to slow herself the fraction of a second it would take to look over her shoulder. And now she began to think her ears were playing tricks on her, for she thought she heard many running footsteps, as if other people had joined in the chase. She was looking desperately forward for car headlights, hoping for some help from a passing motorist, when she heard behind her, close behind her, a muffled groan and then a thud. He's fallen! she thought. I can get ahead now.

When she'd run a few seconds more, she heard, not footsteps, but curses and shouts. Someone distinctly said, "Give it up!" She risked a glance over her shoulder and saw the outlines of a moiling bundle about fifty feet behind her, as if the contents of a laundry truck had been dumped beside the road and had suddenly come to life —angry, snarling life. Barbara stopped, her body teetering as if this sudden halt in her forward motion threatened to tip her over. She stood panting, her brain slowly absorbing what she was seeing. Two people were fighting in the ditch behind her. She saw two heads rise up as one combatant tried to pull the other to a standing position, and then both went down again into a heap. She trotted toward them and then stopped again.

Only now did she realize that she was still carrying

her flashlight in her left hand. She shifted it to her right hand, made a few more tentative steps toward the struggling shapes, and pointed the beam of light at them. It seemed to freeze them momentarily and she could see that one, the taller one, was Paul Gillis, and that the other one didn't have a human face. The shock of that grotesque cross between an ape and a clown almost made Barbara drop the flashlight. The frozen moment was enough for Paul to land one roundhouse punch, and the other fighter slumped onto the grass.

"Barbara," Paul called toward her. "It's all right. Come here. Bring the light."

She ran now in sheer relief, her feet seeming to fly over the road as if she'd never been exerting herself at all. Paul caught her in his arms and held her for a moment before taking the flashlight out of her hands and training it down at the groaning bundle at his feet. The fallen man was wearing a Halloween mask, one of those rubber ones that fit over the entire head. Paul squatted and Barbara kept her hands on his shoulders, reluctant to let go of him. He slipped his fingers under the mask and lifted it up and out, revealing a narrow, feral face underneath.

"Danny Krieger!" Barbara gasped.

"Yes, Danny Krieger," Paul said, looking up at her, and he didn't sound a bit surprised.

24

Paul stood up from Danny Krieger's prostrate form and slipped one arm around Barbara's shoulders.

"Are you all right?" he said. "Did this bozo hurt you?"

"I'm fine," she breathed. "A little winded, but not hurt."

"What are you doing here, anyway?" Paul asked.

"Were you following me?" Barbara asked almost at the same time.

"No, I was following him," he said, gesturing at the inert form on the ground. "I've had Ed Granger watching him for a while now. Tonight Ed followed him out of New Augsburg and radioed me from his squad car. I picked up the tail at the township line and sent Ed home. I lost Danny for a while because I was afraid to get too close, and I wound up following the wrong car for almost three miles. When I backtracked, I couldn't find him for quite a while. His car is parked about a quarter mile over that hill. I kept cruising around until I spotted your bug back there, and then I heard some sort of a tractor."

"Haybine," she corrected. "He was chasing me in a haybine. But why were you following him?"

"Later," he said, rather severely. "Right now, I'm asking the questions. What on earth are you doing out here?"

"I got a note," she answered, looking down at her feet. "A note suggesting I should come here at midnight to find out something about my Uncle Tony."

"What kind of a note would make you do such a fool thing as to come out here in the middle of the night without telling me about it?" he demanded. "Wasn't your chase in the fog enough to make you use your brains about something like this?"

Danny Krieger groaned and rolled over onto his back.

"You stay down there," Paul said to him sharply, "or I'll step on you." Then he turned back to Barbara. "What kind of a note?"

She pulled the folded paper out of her back pocket and handed it to him. He opened it and trained the light on it for a minute or so.

"I see," he said quietly. Nothing else, just the two words of complete understanding.

"Billy Novak wrote that note," Danny said very clearly from the ground; he hadn't been so unconscious as they'd believed. "This was all his idea. All of it."

"You shut up, Krieger," Paul snapped. "I haven't read you your rights yet."

"I know what my goddamned rights are," Danny snarled. "Can I get up?"

"You can sit up," Paul said, "and put your hands behind your back."

"I'm hurt," Danny said.

"The hell you are," Paul said mildly. "Now you can

stand up with cuffs on, or you can stay there on your back.''

Danny sat up and put his hands behind his back. When Paul had snapped on the handcuffs, he helped the prisoner to his feet.

"I'm telling you, this wasn't my idea," Danny growled. "Billy done it all. He wrecked her car and he chased her home from the fair. He was a drunken maniac that night." Danny hadn't looked at Barbara once she'd joined the odd little group in the ditch.

"You can tell me all about it at the jail," Paul said, giving him a little push in the direction of the squad car, which, Barbara noticed for the first time, was parked with its lights on near the front office of Tomchek's Machine Shop.

"Are you feeling up to driving home by yourself?" Paul said to Barbara, his voice softening noticeably whenever he talked to her. "I'll tell you all about it in the morning. Get some sleep."

"I'm coming with you," Barbara said firmly. "I couldn't sleep anyway. I want to know what he says about Billy."

"Now, look," Paul said. "I'll radio from here for one of my deputies to bring Billy in. They should get to Oshawanee just about the time I do. The questioning will probably go on for quite a while. You can't sit in on any of that anyway. Just go home and I'll call you as soon as it's all over."

"Is there some law saying I can't sit inside the county jail waiting for you to get finished?" Barbara said, drawing herself up.

"Your mother will worry if she wakes up and finds you gone," he said shrewdly.

"I'll call her from Oshawanee to tell her to ignore the

note on my pillow," Barbara replied. "She'll know I'm safe if I'm with you."

"It's a free country," he said with a sigh, but he didn't seem very angry; in fact, he seemed a bit pleased.

Barbara paced up and down the small office at the front of the county jail, glancing at her watch from time to time. It was 2:30 in the morning by now, and she had leafed through every magazine she could find. Billy had already been taken to a holding cell when Barbara followed Paul and Danny into the jail. When she'd pulled her Volkswagen up behind Paul's squad car, she'd noticed that another police car was already there. Inside, a sleepy-looking deputy (not Erickson, but a younger man) was waiting for them. Since that time, both Paul and the deputy had been back in the cells taking turns interrogating the two prisoners.

Barbara called Eileen immediately, saying that she was all right and didn't know when she'd be home. Paul came out once to show her how to work the ancient coffee maker on a shelf near the door, but was completely noncommittal about what, if anything, he was learning inside.

At quarter to three, Paul came into the office and sank wearily into the desk chair. His shirt was rumpled and grass-stained, and there was a distinct swelling on his left cheekbone.

"Well," Barbara asked. "Is it over?"

"For now," he sighed. "We file charges tomorrow."

"Why don't you start by telling me why you were following Danny," Barbara said, perching on the edge of the desk next to where he'd put his feet up.

"He was with Billy at the alleys the other day when

I went to look for his dad,'' Paul said. ''He left with me to find Matt, but I'd already begun to put things together. He would have access to his father's passkeys, so he could get in and out of your mother's place, and even if somebody saw him, who would wonder what business the landlord's son had there? So he could be Billy's legs for him. And he's a bad egg in general, is our Danny Boy in there. Trouble with the law before, but we couldn't make anything stick.''

''What kind of trouble?''

''Assaulting women. One just a kid, and he hurt her, too. But her father wouldn't let the D.A. press charges.''

Barbara gaped at him.

''Do you mean that he—?'' She couldn't finish the sentence.

''Yes,'' he said quietly. ''He meant to rape you. Of course he denies it, says he was only trying to scare you, for his friend, but I know better. With that mask, you couldn't have identified him afterwards. Terror first, then rape. That's his style.''

''God,'' Barbara breathed. ''And Billy Novak set that up?''

''No, he didn't,'' Paul said, easing his head back against the cushioned chair. ''Billy wrote only the first part of the note and told Dan to put it in your mailbox. Danny added the last part on his own before making the delivery.''

''Says Billy Novak,'' Barbara snorted.

''And says Danny Krieger,'' Paul replied. ''He finally admitted that Tomchek's was a bit of free-lancing on his own that Billy didn't know about.''

''But what did Billy hope to gain by the note,'' she asked, still incredulous, ''if he didn't mean for me to be terrorized like that? There aren't any letters, are there?''

"No, they made it up after they heard you and Mrs. Bower. It might help if I could just go back to the beginning and lay it all out for you in order."

"Good idea," she said. "I'd like nothing better than to have this mystery cleared up in detail."

"When Billy first saw you at his parents' house last week, all the bitterness of the last fifteen years of his life came to a head. He thought you were beautiful, and he wanted you almost as soon as he saw you—don't start to object, because you *are* pretty spectacular, you know. But you caught him at his worst, before he had any chance to impress you, to make you see something besides a freak in a wheelchair—those are his words, now. And his father had heard that you were questioning people about your uncle's murder, trying to pin it on George Heim, he said. So the attraction turned to rage, I think. He started drinking that same afternoon, after you left, and then went over to your mother's apartment at night. Just to look, he said, but then he saw your car and—well, you know what he did."

"Yes, I do," she said. "Where does Danny come in?"

"Well, he and Billy are sometime drinking buddies," Paul said. "Danny helped Billy to learn how to bowl from his chair a few years ago. So Bill made a confidant out of Danny, just drunk talk at first about how stuck-up he thought you were, how high-toned and interfering, how you wanted to make trouble for decent folks who'd never done you any harm."

"Well, don't I sound charming!" Barbara said, reddening with anger.

"Billy had to see it that way, I figure," Paul said quietly. "He thought you were way out of his league, even though you grew up next door, especially with him in that chair. But he couldn't turn it on himself, so he turned it on you. Then Danny suggested a 'practical joke' to get back at you, to 'bring you down a peg or two,' as he put it. That was the phone trick, and Billy thought it would have the added bonus of scaring you away from 'trying to pin the rap' on his father's friends.''

"But it wasn't Danny who chased me in the fog, was it?" she said.

"No, that was Billy," Paul answered. "He saw us together at the fair, and it just made him wild. It seemed you *would* go out with a local boy, he said to me, if the boy could walk. So he sent Danny to follow us around to see if we would leave together. When Danny saw you heading for the parking lot alone, he got back to Bill, who went straight for his own car. He must have been driving seventy miles an hour to catch up to you when he did.''

"What was he trying to do?" Barbara said, standing up in exasperation. "Did he think he could get a date with me if he crippled me, too?"

"I don't think he knew what he was doing," Paul said, standing up, too. "He'd been drinking when we saw him, and he drank almost nonstop after that. Just blind with frustration and anger. I think he was as much intent on killing himself as on hurting you. Maybe more.''

"Yes," Barbara murmured, "I thought that even at the time. But we still haven't got to the note.''

"Well, now we have to pick up Danny's narrative," Paul said, crossing to the coffeepot to pour himself another cup of the strong brew. "He was tailing us at the fair and when I left you to break up that fight, he stuck with you. Says he followed you under the grandstand, hid behind the rabbit cages until you and Mrs. Bower went out together. He stood behind you at the beer tent, in the crowd, and you never knew he was there. Says Mrs. Bower looked straight at him, but, of course, *she* didn't recognize him. He heard everything you two said to each other and reported it all to Billy, but not until the next day. That night, he just told Billy you were leaving and Billy followed before Danny could say anything else.''

"So Danny was Billy's ears as well as his legs," Barbara said.

"That's right. And Billy was outraged again when he heard what you'd been saying to Mrs. Bower because it showed that you were still aiming to implicate George Heim or his brother, or both, in your uncle's death. He latched onto the details about Mrs. Bower's letters to Tony because he remembered how angry you were at his parents' house when his father suggested that you might 'look closer to home' to find a suspect. If you could point fingers at his friends, Billy said, he could point some fingers at your father and see how you liked it. It would scare the hell out of you, he told Danny, and you deserved it. So he wrote his part of the note. That was his intention—to make you scared, to get back at you for going to the fair with me, for hating him.''

"I don't hate him," Barbara said lamely. "Where did he get that idea?"

"Oh, I guess because he sort of hates himself," Paul sighed, pausing to take another sip of coffee. "So he makes himself hateful to other people. It's like a self-fulfilling prophecy.''

Barbara was silent, thinking.

"Billy didn't have any idea that Danny was after you for his own reasons," Paul went on. "He's really appalled by it. Danny chose Tomchek's because Bill told him the haybine was being converted for him there, and Dan knew it was remote, out of the way. He broke in and waited for you."

"And you believe all this?" Barbara said, looking hard at him.

"Got the same story from each of them separately," he answered. "Eventually, at least, when Dan decided to come clean. All the details are the same, so I've got to believe it."

"So you don't think any of this has anything to do with my uncle's murder?" she demanded.

"Only very indirectly," he said. "Your little investigation was one of the things that made Billy so mad at you."

"I want to see him," she said abruptly. "Billy, I mean. I want to ask him myself."

"These are not visiting hours," he said softly.

"Are you going to let me see him?" she said.

"All right, maybe you should," he answered. "Maybe it will help you to understand a few things."

Billy's chair was facing the corner of his cell, as if he'd been sent there as a punishment. He wheeled slowly around when he heard the footsteps and then looked quickly away from Barbara, his haggard face coloring. Paul opened the cell door and ushered Barbara inside.

"Barbara wants to ask you something," Paul said calmly.

Billy kept his head averted, said nothing in reply.

"Billy," Barbara said, finding her own voice shaking. "I want to know why you did all these things to me. I want you to tell me if any of this was intended to scare

334

me off because I was getting too close to finding out who killed my uncle."

"No," he said at once, his voice thick, muffled.

"Please look at me and tell me," she said. "If you're really sorry for what Danny Krieger did to me, if you really didn't plan that, look at me and tell me the truth."

He turned his face toward her and met her eyes with his own gaze. His eyes had lost their meanness. They looked wounded, as if he were in pain.

"I didn't think you were getting close to anything," he said. "I was just mad at you, that's all. And I didn't know Danny would try to hurt you. I didn't." All the sneer was gone out of his voice now. She could hear the ring of sincerity in what he said about Danny.

"And you don't know who killed Tony Hoffman?" she said, hearing that her own voice had become gentler, less challenging.

"How would I know that?" he said, looking up at her from red-rimmed eyes.

"Then why?" she asked, because now she really wanted to know, to hear it from him.

"I can't make you understand," he said slowly. "You can't know what it's like. Do you think everything else stops when a man gets put in a chair like this? Do you think he stops thinking about women, stops wanting them? Do you think he's some kind of a gelding? He isn't. Believe me, he isn't. But no woman can look at him anymore like a man. Oh, some can pity him. I've been with a few girls over the years who let me have them out of pity, but I could see how disgusted they were. One or two even got it on with me because they thought it was kinda kinky, but I don't care for girls like that—not in the morning, at least. Nice girls, pretty girls like you, just look through me like I wasn't there—not there like a man, I mean. They just see a 'case,' something to feel sorry for. Sometimes I get so, so—. I don't know who I want to kill, them or me."

Tears were spilling down his cheeks, running into his beard. He seemed ashamed to be crying, but uncertain whether wiping his face would be even more humiliating. Barbara looked away.

"I'm sorry, Billy," she whispered, in danger of weeping herself. "I never meant to make you feel that way."

"And I never meant for Danny to hurt you," he said.

"I believe you," she said. "I believe you." And she turned around so Paul could let her out of the cell.

In the office again, Barbara sank down onto the wooden bench next to the outside door.

"Will he have to stay in jail?" she asked as Paul came up to sit beside her.

"Do you think he should?" he said by way of answer.

"I don't know," she sighed. "He's got a lot of problems, but I don't think he's a criminal."

"That's what I think, too," Paul said, smiling at her. "You don't have to press charges. I think he'll cooperate in the charges against Danny in any case, but we could say we would trade for his testimony. That would save his pride."

"But what's to stop him from going berserk with some other woman?" she said, thinking again how nice Paul's eyes were up close like this.

"There are some good programs now for Vietnam vets," he said. "Some of them right here in Oshawanee. I think his father's been overprotecting him, keeping him tied too close to home. I could insist that he get into a good program, some group therapy."

"For a man who doesn't believe in court-ordered therapy, you're sure a walking encyclopedia on how to get people into it," she laughed.

"I just don't think some people belong in jail, that's all," he said. "Krieger's another story. I'd like to throw away the key on that one. As it is, we won't get him for much more than about eight months. But one of these days, I'm going to nail that son of a bitch, send him away for a long time."

Barbara sighed, a long weary sigh. It occurred to her that she must be close to the edge of exhaustion; she had slept only fitfully the night before, and most of this night was already gone, too. Yet the excitement and the coffee were keeping her in a twitchy, pumped-up state that was unfamiliar to someone as regular in her habits as she normally was.

"I think I could use a drink," she said at last.

"Well," Paul chuckled. "All the bars are closed, but I could give you a gin and tonic at my place. It's just a block and a half down the street, above Goltz's drug store."

"Can you just walk out of here?" she asked.

"Sure," he said. "Rollie's in the back, and he knows he can just pick up the phone if he needs me."

25

Barbara found Paul Gillis's apartment something of a surprise. She'd expected a poky little place with lots of bachelor clutter, but this was a spacious, bright, tastefully furnished apartment with lots of books and some interesting abstract paintings—big pieces—on the walls. And it was spotlessly clean.

"Boy," Barbara breathed when he put on the lights. "You must have to accept lots of bribes to afford a place like this."

"It's really pretty cheap," he laughed. "The rent, I mean. Nobody wants to live this close to the jail. And Oshawanee County pays its public servants a living wage."

She sat down on the six-foot-long sofa while Paul went into his kitchen to make the drinks. Only now was she absorbing the full significance of what she'd learned on this wild night. The harassment was over and, apparently, explained away, but she felt no relief—only a strange feeling of emptiness and foreboding. Now, sitting here in Paul's surprising apartment, safe and protected, she was beginning to realize how much she'd counted on the evidence of harassment to quiet her fears about her father. As long as she could believe that someone was trying to scare her off the case, she could believe in a still-living murderer—someone who might *be* the actual harasser or someone who might be protected by another person. But here she was, back almost to square one. Everything she'd learned about Anton Hoffman in the past two-and-a-half weeks suggested that lots of people had good reasons to want him dead. Now she had to put her own father's name back near the top of the list of suspects, for he'd had better reasons than most. And it was certainly suspicious that he'd been so secretive about his life before the war.

If, on the other hand, Tony's killer had been one of his arson victims, the murderer might be dead now, too, or never discovered. The harassment had made her confident that there *was* something to learn, if only she were brave enough to stick to the search. But now she couldn't be sure that a solution was possible. She examined her numbed feelings, trying objectively to decide which would be worse—*never* finding out who had smashed in Uncle Tony's head or learning with unequivocal certainty that Joseph Hoffman had been, at one moment in his buried past, a killer. In her present state, she couldn't give an answer. It crossed her mind, vaguely, that knowing for sure might be a sort of relief to the obsessive agitation she'd been feeling ever since she learned about her father's first love.

"You're a long way off," Paul said, sitting next to her and handing her the gin and tonic. He'd made one for himself, too, had even found a lime for garnish.

"I guess I'm still a bit in shock over everything that happened tonight," she said and then took a long swallow of the sparkling drink. "I'm trying to absorb it all."

"Yes, you've had a bad couple of weeks," he said, real sympathy in his voice.

"Oh, Paul," she sighed. "I've had a bad couple of years."

"I know," he said, patting her hand. "I know. Lost a lot of people all at once."

She saw the subject of Andrew looming on the near horizon and dodged it deftly.

"Yes, but lately I've also lost my childhood home. I don't just mean the house. I mean the farm, New Augsburg, my family—all the ways I used to look at them, to think of them. Now I know that a lot of that was a dream. The truth is that it's like every other place—it has murder and betrayal and sexual deviance. Whatever makes us think in the first place that small-town life is immune from all that stuff?"

"I don't know," he sighed. "But seeing the underbelly at last shouldn't make you think that all the good stuff was a facade. It isn't that one version is true and one is false. They could both be true, couldn't they?"

"I think maybe you're a wise man, Paul Gillis," she said and found that she had tears in her eyes. "How the hell did that happen, I wonder?"

He stretched out his right arm along the back of the sofa, in a gesture remarkably like the one he had used to protect her neck on the Tilt-O-Whirl, and put his fingertips against her cheek.

"I know why that note scared you enough to send you out alone to that godforsaken shop," he said softly. "But maybe—."

"Well, we know now it was a fiction created just to hurt my feelings, don't we?" she said quickly. "It was silly of me to worry in the first place, so we don't have to go into it. I'm ashamed that I was foolish enough to bite on such ridiculous bait. I really don't want to talk about it right now.''

She looked a direct appeal into the warm hazel eyes. Paul tipped his head to one side and raised his eyebrows, as if he couldn't quite accept so easy a dismissal. Barbara turned her face into his palm and pressed her lips against his wrist, just at the point where the pulse can be found.

"Couldn't we find more interesting things to give our attention to?'' she asked softly, turning her eyes up to his without lifting her face from his touch. She saw the change in his face at once, a second of confusion and then the first flicker of desire. Barbara lifted her own hand to the swollen place on his left cheekbone, touching it gently.

"Does it hurt?'' she asked.

"No,'' he said hoarsely. "Not much.'' And then he pulled her face to his own and began kissing her greedily, on her mouth, her eyes, her throat. Without being much aware of moving, Barbara erased the space between their bodies and slid her arm up around his neck. She could feel the slight rasp of his whiskers against her neck, the delicious softness of his open mouth. The buttons of her work shirt pulled open easily as his jaw plowed through them on its way to her breasts. His left hand was already against the bare flesh of her back, sliding swiftly upward. Barbara bowed her face against the sandy hair, a little surprised at this urgency, this hunger; he had seemed to her, in everything else, so calm, so patient.

But finally she, too, lost the capacity to think much about what was happening. Her own hands became eager to have the coarse brown uniform out of her way. Getting out of their clothes became an erotic dance that started on the sofa and ended with them standing up in the center of the room, a dance in which the pauses were more

341

delicious than the movements. Then he lifted her straight up until her shoulders were above his own, and she wrapped her legs around his lean hips as he carried her into the bedroom. After the first eager coupling, the second was more leisurely, more playful. In the joy of rediscovering the pleasures of her own body, Barbara realized how much she had missed this abandon, so luxurious, so sweet when it was with someone you liked and trusted. Resting against Paul's shoulder, she knew with a great sense of relief that she didn't have to be afraid of this man, not physically and not emotionally either.

"I'm sorry about what I said to you at the fair," she whispered. "With you, the preliminaries have a lot to recommend them."

"And the getting straight to bed is pretty good, too," he laughed, running his fingers up and down her arm.

"I don't even know why I thought I was mad at you," she sighed, snuggling her face into his throat.

"Well, I think it's always a strain when you're trying to hide things from somebody," he said softly.

"So what about you then?" she said, slapping his stomach lightly. "You were hiding things from me, too."

"Such as?"

"Such as, you knew all along that Danny Krieger moved my mother's telephone."

"I didn't *know* that. I just suspected." His fingers had left her arm now to slowly trace a vein along her right breast.

"And such as," she went on, "what were you doing looking through all those old newspapers on Monday?"

He lifted his head off the pillows to look down at her.

"How did you find out about that?"

"I saw Olga Tempe this morning—or is it yesterday morning by now?—and she told me."

"Just happened to run into her, did you?" he said and put his forehead down against hers.

"Okay," she said with a slow smile, "I was looking at old newspapers, too. Did you find out about those old rumors that my uncle started fires?"

"Yup," he said, stretching his long body with a luxurious sigh. "A farmer named Weinfurther said he heard the rumor when he first moved to New Augsburg after the war and was asking around if your place was for sale."

"So, what do you think?" she asked, lifting herself up on one elbow to look down into his face.

"Oh, no," he groaned. "Not now! There's only one way to shut you up about this." And he pulled her mouth down to his, ending the kiss with a gentle bite on her lower lip.

"Come on, now," she said. "Confession is good for the soul. Just tell me what you think about the fire at Heims' barn."

"Oh, that one checks out with the fire department records," he said, resigning himself. "It really was started by incubator lights being too close to some straw. But the others—well, I don't know what to make of it. I don't see much of a pattern."

"Did Mary Wenner tell you about the fight Tony had with her late husband?" Barbara found that she finally wanted to share what she knew with this man.

"Oh, I got that connection already," he said. "Corn cribs burned up on his father's farm. And I made the connection to the Novak fire when Mrs. Wenner was telling us about that horse-pulling stuff. But after that, I

343

have unrelated fires, fires without motives, motives without fires.'' He was getting into the subject in spite of himself, the professional puzzle solver taking over for the moment.

"What are the motives without fires?" Barbara said, resting her chin against his sternum.

"One particular motive," he answered. "George and Peter Heim caught Tony with their sister, ran him off the place, even roughed him up a little they say, and just generally let it be known that he was forbidden to see their sister again. But apparently Tony didn't try to burn anything on their place. Maybe he was just afraid of the Heims. I'll tell you, I've met Peter Heim and *I'm* scared of him. He must have been something forty-five years ago."

"And what about the fires without motives?" she said.

"Well, it could be any number of them, couldn't it?" he sighed. "If we knew enough about each case, we might find a motive. So who can tell? Did Tony torch Grassels' pig barn, Rataycheks' granary, Schneiders' barn?"

"Schneiders'?" Barbara said, lifting her head sharply.

"Yes," he said, stifling a yawn. "Didn't you read about Schneiders' barn?"

"No," she said, keeping her eyes on his collarbone, trying to keep her breathing quiet. "I only looked at 1942 and 1943."

"Well, this one did happen in 1943, September 9th, to be exact," he said. "And it was a doozy. Lost a lot of livestock, all of the harvest. Paper said it was probably caused by a short in some lights that were left on by mistake, but the fire department records don't list a cause."

Barbara's mind was racing. She remembered that Rosa Schneider would occasionally refer to their barn as "the new barn," but she'd never made anything of that because farm people called any building new that wasn't the original structure, so that a granary built in 1920 would be "the new granary" forever after if the first granary on the homestead had been torn down, or blown over in a high wind, in 1919. But people talked about big fires, rehearsed them in detail, as cautionary tales or, perhaps, in an unconscious effort to exorcise their deep dread. Why had she never heard that the Schneiders' barn had burned? Why had her father never mentioned it? Why had she never heard Dick describe it, or listened to the two men clucking over it the way they did over a hailstorm that had once battered their corn crop? It could only mean that they had some secret understanding about it, some unspoken agreement not to bring it up.

"You don't know any reason why Tony might have started that one, do you?" Paul said, ruffling her hair.

"No, no, of course not," she said, seeing in her mind's eye "Land Dispute Settled," grateful that Paul had clearly missed that small item in his own search through the *New Augsburg Post*. "Dick Schneider was always a good friend to our family, almost *like* family."

And now she remembered something Dick had said to her last night during their walk together back to his house—something that made her blood freeze, something that had made one of her own memories come almost to the surface there in the woods. She remembered it now, and everything she'd learned in the past weeks fell into a coherent pattern; clues she hadn't even recognized as clues suddenly made sense—terrible sense. She fought an impulse to jump up from the bed, worked hard to concentrate on keeping Paul from knowing what she was thinking. She put her cheek down onto his chest, but her eyes were darting nervously around the room.

"That looks like dawn coming through the window," she said at last, keeping her words slow and affecting a yawn. "I'd better be going."

"No, no," he said and folded both of his arms around her. "You should at least try to get a little sleep before you drive home. And then I'll find a nice way to wake you up."

"What will my mother think?" she said, hoping that her laugh didn't sound forced. "I'm already going to have a tough time making her believe that it took this long for you to question Billy and Danny."

"Well, just *tell* her where you were," he said. "Aren't you a big girl now?"

"Not that big," she said, pushing herself gently away from him. "Would you tell your mother?"

"You're right," he sighed. "I'll walk you to your car."

"No," she said. "That's not necessary. Nobody's going to jump me at dawn in front of the jail. You get some sleep." And she kissed the middle of his forehead.

"Can I call you later today?" he said, holding on to her wrists as she stood up. "Much later so you can sleep a long time, that is?"

"Of course," she said, surprised that he would feel it necessary to ask. "Call me, of course."

"Good," he said, grinning sleepily. "Because I think you ought to know that I consider casual sex much overrated—and even old-fashioned these days."

By the time Barbara got to her car, her hands were shaking so hard that she could hardly unlock the door. Inside, she put her head down onto the steering wheel, breathing, "No, no, no." Finally, she fitted the key into the ignition and put the little car into motion, driving east into the rising sun, fiery against the horizon.

What she'd almost remembered in the woods stood before her eyes with horrible clarity now. She'd been only five years old at the time. She and her parents were coming back from the Milwaukee Zoo in the old Chevy, late at night, when traffic had slowed to a crawl and then finally came to a standstill. A glow in the sky off to the right made clear why everyone was stopped. They all got out of the Chevy in answer to Barbara's repeated insistence, "I want to see. I want to see." After scrambling up the steep embankment next to the road, they were at last able to see the fire, a barn about two hundred yards ahead.

Barbara had, by that age, seen a barn being built, and her immediate impression was that the fire was unbuilding the barn, stripping off the "skin" of outer boards and devouring the crosspieces and timbers which stood out clearly against the lurid red light. And as they watched, the timbers began to collapse inward, knocking against each other and sending a dazzling burst of fire even higher into the sky. Finally the whole structure rushed downward, leaving a glowing heap on the foundation.

When she turned excitedly to her father, ready to say, "The fire unbuilded the barn," she found him staring, his face lit to an eerie redness by the glow. The expression on his face was one she had never seen before. It was a look of such horror, such pain, that it cowed her into watchful silence. He looked, she thought in her childish fear, as if the fire were burning him up.

26

At 10 a.m. on Saturday, Barbara was sitting on a bench in Dick Schneider's small apple orchard beside the "new barn." She'd been sitting there for more than half an hour waiting for Dick to come out.

"He's still asleep," Rosa had explained when Barbara appeared on the back porch asking to see Dick. Rosa's eyes behind her thick glasses were sunken and red-rimmed from weeping or sleeplessness or both, so Barbara guessed that Dick had told her at last how much future he really had.

"Don't wake him," Barbara had said, taking Rosa's hands. "But when he does get up, I'd like to talk to him for a while."

"I can't have anything tiring or upsetting him," Rosa said, her usual mildness set aside by this fierce protectiveness.

"I know, I know," Barbara replied. "I understand, Rosa. But I have to talk to him. It's very important. I'll wait in the orchard. Will you ask him to come out to me?"

"I'll see what he thinks about it when he wakes up,"

Rosa had said abruptly, but then her good nature prevailed again. "Here. You take a cup of coffee with you."

So Barbara sat now with the cup in her hand, remembering how her mother's face had looked that morning. When Eileen got up at eight, she had found Barbara sitting at the kitchen counter with her head in her hands.

"You look awful," Eileen had exclaimed at once. "What's the matter with you?"

"I've had a hell of a night, Mum," she had replied, her voice husky.

"Why didn't you wake me when you came in?" Eileen scolded. "I would have the whole story, and you could be fast asleep."

"I don't know," Barbara answered, her mind so numb that she could barely remember the fiction she'd created on the phone at 1 a.m., a tale of an ambush she and Paul had planned together after she received a note saying, "Come to Tomchek's to find out who killed Tony." She had decided that her mother must never know the real contents of the note or why she'd responded to it as she did. She'd convinced Paul to agree to the ambush story if the subject ever came up in front of Eileen. "I guess I thought I'd disturbed your rest once already last night," Barbara finished lamely.

"But why did *you* stay up?" Eileen said, her blue eyes full of suspicion.

"To tell you what happened," Barbara said. "And then I'm going out again."

"You're balmy!" Eileen snorted. "Where are you off to this time?"

"To see Dick Schneider." She was too numb to think up a lie. "I have to ask him something." And then she managed a feeble lie: "About something Billy Novak told me."

349

"You're not going to worry that poor man now," Eileen snapped. "And that's all there is to it."

"I have to ask him one thing, that's all," Barbara said doggedly. "It won't take long. Now do you want to hear about Billy Novak and Danny Krieger, or not?"

Eileen had listened quietly to the slightly edited story while she made a pot of tea, clicking her tongue from time to time. When Barbara finally fell silent, her mother said, "And what did Billy say that you have to ask Dick about?"

Again Barbara couldn't make her brain work fast enough to fabricate a lie. She just stared at Eileen for a moment.

"I can't tell you until I know the answer," she said finally.

"What do you mean, you can't tell me?" Eileen said, and her voice was shrill. "Is it about Tony, something you think Dick knows about Tony?"

"Please, Mummy," Barbara said, half weeping and looking away. "Please don't push me. I'm too exhausted to take it. Please."

"All right," Eileen said in a changed voice. "All right then."

When Barbara looked back at her, she saw in her mother's face something she was not used to seeing there—fear.

Now Barbara glanced up from the empty cup to see Dick Schneider making his way across the yard, moving in that deliberate shuffle she had first seen at the barn Thursday night. She stood up to wait for him, her head grazing the hard little apples on the tree behind her. When Dick got to the bench, he was breathing hard despite his snail's pace. He looked at Barbara without speaking as he sat down. She sat again next to him, setting the cup on the bench behind her.

"I found out last night about your barn fire," she said. Neither of them seemed in a mood for the pretense of normal conversation.

He blinked but didn't seem surprised.

"I figured it must be something big to bring you out here like this," he said, still panting a little from the effort of walking. "Wanting to see just me, and out here, too."

"Tony set that fire, didn't he, Dick?" she asked, her haggard eyes fixed fiercely on his face. "He lost the woods to you in court, and then he came over here and burned your barn to the ground."

"You've been very busy at your detecting, haven't you?" he said, and the wheeze turned into a cough for a moment. "Is this something the sheriff told you?"

"Paul doesn't know about Tony losing the woods," she said, not moving her gaze. "I found it in an old paper, just a little item."

"I remember," he said, looking out over the orchard. "But it wasn't little enough."

"Did Tony set the fire?" she demanded, reaching out to squeeze his thin forearm.

"Yes, Barbara, he did," Dick said, looking back at her with his glittering eyes. "He burned my barn like he burned other people's barns."

"And that's when Daddy found out, isn't it?" she asked, taking his other arm into her grasp as if she felt he would turn away from her if she didn't hold him. "You all tried to keep it from him that Tony was a burner, to protect him, but he couldn't help seeing the connection when your barn caught fire right after Tony lost in court. Daddy must have seen the fire that night. How could he miss it? Did he come over? Did you tell him then, while your crops were still blazing up into the sky?''

"Why do you think your dad knew about Tony?" he asked, not trying to release his arms, not moving at all.

"It all makes sense to me now," she said. "I was such a dope thinking it was about Caroline, but it was about the fires all along. The clues were there, but I just wouldn't look at them."

"What clues are you talking about?" Dick said, pulling his arms away from Barbara's grip as if he were in pain.

"My father never, ever talked about anything that happened to him before the war," Barbara said. "It was as if he just closed himself off from that experience. Mum thinks it was the war that did it, but I think the real trauma came just before he left for the army. And Charlie Novak let something slip when he was angry with me. He said that nobody around here had ever seen Tony again after Daddy enlisted. Charlie must know that Daddy found out about the fires—he must have believed all along that Daddy killed Tony, and that's why he was always so cool to Daddy. Even though he'd had a fire, too, the year before, he couldn't reconcile himself to the idea of fratricide."

"That's all just wild guessing," Dick said, but he was looking away from her.

"Is it?" Barbara asked. "Mary told me that you and Jim always said you owed something to Daddy, and she thought you meant because he went off to fight in the war. But you meant something else, didn't you? At least *you* did. Did Jim know, too? Did Jim know that Daddy had stopped Tony for all of you?''

352

"Give this up, Barbara," Dick said wearily. He still hadn't met her gaze.

"No, I can't," she said, and her voice caught on the beginning of a sob. "There's more. Peter Heim told me that all of New Augsburg tried to protect my father from knowing what Tony really was. So everybody knew, or at least suspected, that Tony had been setting those fires. At the end of that summer, Daddy found out about Tony and Caroline, and that hit him hard. But it couldn't have been a big shock to him because he knew how his brother was with women. But your barn fire made him see all at once that Tony was really evil. That must have been a terrible shock, especially since it was *you* who'd been victimized. So that became part of Daddy's buried past, too. How could it be that I grew up right over there and never once heard about that fire? You and Daddy never talked about it, never. I don't even think my mother knows about it. It can only mean that you two men had some secret about the fire, a secret you didn't ever want brought up again."

She paused to wipe the tears from her eyes.

"You were more like Daddy's big brother than Tony ever was, and Tony did that to you—cattle, harvest, everything destroyed. Daddy couldn't let that go on. I bet he felt responsible—he was like that. So he waited to get Tony alone at home, and he smashed his head with a poker. And then he told you, didn't he, to make sure you would know that he'd tried to make it right before he went away? He thought he was going away forever then, didn't he, because it would be impossible for him to live here after that?" She was beginning to weep now.

"Barbara," Dick said firmly, "I want you to tell me

why you would think such a thing. Why do you think *I* would know these answers?''

"Because you knew all along Tony was dead," she said, tears spilling down her face. "You told people that you thought he'd run off, but you knew he was dead."

"Why do you say that?" he asked, his voice almost toneless now.

"Because of what you said Thursday night. You said you paid the taxes and kept up the farm for Daddy, because you hoped he would come back someday. And you said you would never have done it for Tony. But Daddy was the younger son. He wouldn't have inherited the farm by himself if Tony had come back, too. But you knew Tony wasn't coming back, couldn't come back, so you *could* do it for Daddy alone. He killed Tony because of the fire, because of you, so you saved everything for him, told him to come back when he wrote you in 1949.''

"Barbara," he said softly. "Oh, Barbie."

"Just tell me, Dick," she said, and she was sobbing. "I thought I didn't want to know for sure, but I do. You've got to tell me."

He lifted his frail arms to her shoulders, patting her clumsily.

"Yes, I knew," he said tenderly. "I knew Tony was dead. You've found most of the right clues. You're a better detective than you wanted to be. But clues and guesses can't tell you what it was like then. Facts maybe aren't the same thing as truth."

"Then you tell me," Barbara whispered. "Tell me what it was really like."

He shifted his weight on the hard bench, a gingerly movement as if he were afraid of awakening some pain.

"I never told this to anybody in forty-five years,

but now I'm gonna tell you, tell all of it, right from the start. I suppose I should do it at least once while my brain is still clear enough to get it all right. Pretty soon, the pain killers are gonna be fuzzing my brain, you know.''

"Dick," she whispered, "I'm so sorry." It was all she could find to say.

"Now you wanted to know this, Barbie," he said, lifting his jaw to a determined angle. "You moved heaven and earth to find it out. I might have known you would find the scent; you were always such a bright little thing. Well, now you're gonna hear it, the way it really was, and then maybe you won't judge so harshly. Okay?''

"Okay," she agreed, her voice barely audible, as if she feared talking out loud would make her sob.

"Something let go inside of Tony when his ma died. Oh, he'd been wild before that, sure, but she could always keep him on a leash, sorta. Your pa told me once that Tony got drunk after her funeral, kept blubbering over and over, 'I can't ever make it up to her now. I can't make it up to her.' After that, he seemed to just love picking fights, goading people to scrap with him. He got in lots of fistfights, mostly over girls, because he was so damn handsome that girls would go for him when they first saw him. But later he stopped hitting back. He would just smile and walk away, a kinda crazy smile."

"The way he did with Jim," she said softly.

"Yeah, that's right. And then he would burn something, like Wenners' corn cribs, to get back at the guy. He *told* Jim he did it. Found him alone and just said, 'I put my cigarette lighter to them cribs.' Gloating like that.''

"Why didn't Jim go to the sheriff?" Barbara asked quickly.

"He did. Something that serious, of course he went to the law. Didn't do a speck of good. Sheriff said there were no witnesses to the conversation or to the fire either. It was just Jim's word against Tony's and the sheriff couldn't make no arrest on that. But Jim told me about it. He had an idea I might have some influence over Tony, but that was a sad mistake. Old Jim was sick about it because he thought it was his fault Tony was mad, but it was his dad took the kick for it. He never breathed a word about it to Mary because the fight was over her and he didn't want her feeling guilty like he was feeling."

"And Tony burned Charlie's chicken coop after Charlie's team won in that pulling contest," Barbara prompted.

"That's right," Dick said, his face lighting briefly with an appreciation for her skills as an investigator. Now that he'd been sitting quietly for a while, his voice was stronger. "And Jim figured out real fast that it was Tony who done it and why, because Jim was at that contest. We both went to Charlie to tell him, because we thought the sheriff would have to do something now, because it was two men against Tony. Charlie was just wild; you wouldn't think it, because he seems such a quiet type, but he was working like a slave to get that farm on its feet, had some kids to support by then, and here was Tony trying to burn it up. Sure enough, Tony got Charlie alone, followed him out of the mill one day, and told him. 'Maybe next time, I'll just burn up them fine horses of yours,' he says."

"Did they go back to the sheriff?" Barbara asked.

"Sure did. But he said it still couldn't be proved. They were both 'known to dislike the man,' he said, so a lawyer could just say they were making it up about Tony telling he started the fires. He used some such word as 'collusion.' But it still looked like Tony had some little bit of control left in his burning, because he seemed to pick things to burn that wouldn't be great big losses. The corn cribs were empty, and Charlie had no chickens in that coop, so I told them to just wait and see.''

''They wanted to do something?''

''Charlie did. He wanted to beat Tony up, teach him a lesson. But I said it would just make him crazier and who could tell what he might do next time. That next summer, Tony was raising hell all over the county, but we didn't think he was setting fires. Then he got it into his head that the woods were on his land—'my pa's land,' he says to me. Somebody showed him an old map. And he took it into his head to cut the woods down, all of it, and farm the land. It was crazy, a piece of spite, to pick a fight, because that strip is too narrow to be much good. I couldn't let him do that, Barbara. That woods is needed where it is. You know the land slants downhill all the way from my buildings to your pa's buildings. Without those trees, my topsoil would wash away all the way to County Trunk H in five years. But Tony wanted to go to court, so I had to fight it. When the surveyor found the mistake was in the other direction, I hoped it could be kept real quiet. I figured Tony lost his mind if he felt somebody had made a fool out of him in a big, public sort of way. So I tried to play it down that I'd won. There was just that little item in the paper, the one you saw.''

''But it wasn't little enough. I see now.''

''I thought of telling Joe then, to get him to help watch Tony, but I saw what was coming for him over Caroline Heim, and I didn't have the heart. I tried following Tony for a whole week. I thought if he tried something and I could catch him in the act, the sheriff would have his proof. That's why I remember that Rendezvous kermiss

357

so well. Rosa went there in the car, but I followed Tony there in my pickup. But he didn't make a move for my buildings, and I was played out trying to keep up with him. So starting on that Sunday, Jim and Charlie and me took turns keeping watch at night, sitting up behind the garage there. By Wednesday morning, I was starting to think maybe Tony wasn't gonna try anything, so I told Jim and Charlie to stay home. I left all the lights on in the barn so it would look like somebody was there, but then I fell asleep on the back porch; I musta been sleeping like a stone, I was so wore out, because when Rosa woke me up about three in the morning, it was too late.''

His eyes shone with the horror of his memory. He was staring past Barbara at the new barn.

"I got some of the heifers out of the north side doors, but that was all. It was too hot for me to go back. I had to stand over there in the yard, right over there, and listen to my horses scream.''

He fell silent, and Barbara's tears started again. For a long time, she thought he might not speak again, but finally he shook himself a little, as if he were trying to wake up.

"And that's when Daddy came over?'' Barbara prompted, thinking the pause was meant to spare her feelings. "He saw the fire and came to help.''

"Yes,'' Dick sighed. "Poor Joe. There was nothing any of us could do, except stand there. Pretty soon the other neighbors started showing up—the Heims, Charlie, then Jim. Charlie just went wild when he saw Joe. I couldn't stop him from talking. 'Your crazy brother done this,' he screams at Joe. 'We been trying to stop him, but he sneaked over here and burned Dick's barn just like he burned my chicken coop. The bastard won't stop 'til he burns everything in the county.' Other stuff like that. Joe was stunned. He kept looking at me, waiting for me to say it wasn't so, but I couldn't do it. With my barn going up right in front of me, I just couldn't help him.''

"What did he do?'' Barbara was whispering again.

"He finally just screamed at Charlie, 'You're a liar, a damned liar.' And then he ran off down the lane there.''

"Did he go looking for Tony?''

"I guess so. I couldn't think much about it just then. Fire trucks was coming in. Other cars, too. The whole road was full of lights. The barn burned all the next day. The fire engines from two townships couldn't put all that smoldering hay out until afternoon on Thursday. I took Charlie and Jim aside, and we slipped away to find Tony. When we got to your place, we found Joe sitting on the porch, just hunched over with his head in his hands. He was waiting, too. He told us he hadn't seen Tony since the Saturday night, after that dance, said they'd had some hard words that night when Tony got home. I guess Joe had talked to Caroline that same night, too.''

"Yes,'' Barbara murmured. "Caroline told me. She told him she wanted Tony, not him. Said he should carry that message to Tony for her.''

"Well, Joe didn't look at us when we sat down, just kept saying that Tony hadn't been around since the weekend and so he couldn't have started the fire. It was getting dark by then, and all of a sudden, Tony comes roaring in on that damned motorcycle, trying to look surprised to see us there, but I could see he was scared. He kept looking at Joe, quick little looks to see what was in Joe's face. Charlie screamed for a while, but finally let me ask Tony some questions. Tony said he didn't know what I was talking about. He just got back from Green Bay, he said, and he was sorry to hear about my barn. What a shame. He was almost convincing.''

"Maybe it was true," Barbara ventured. "Maybe one of those lights did short out."

"That's what Joe kept saying. He wanted so bad to believe that Tony was telling the truth, I could tell. After a while, I could see we was getting nowhere, so I made Jim and Charlie come away with me. We left them there, Joe sitting on the steps and Tony standing next to that bike."

He fell silent and the constriction in Barbara's throat made it impossible for her to speak for a long time. At last, she swallowed and managed to whisper.

"And you never saw Tony again?"

"What?" Dick said, focusing on her with a confused look. "Sure I saw Tony again. The next day. I was by myself, raking through some of the mess early in the morning, and Tony just comes sauntering down the lane over there, all alone and looking like he hasn't slept or changed his clothes in about five years. Comes right up to me and says, real quiet, 'I put a torch in the haymow. That back door slides real easy.' And then he walks away. Just like that."

"He must have been insane," Barbara said.

"I thought about it a lot over the years, and the way I got it figured is that Joe's finding out about Caroline was sorta the breaking point for Tony, especially when Joe got so mad at him. It snapped the last hold the place had on him. You know, I think Tony had a kinda respect for Joe, even though Joe was younger. But when Joe was finally so disgusted with him like that, Tony didn't care anymore if what he burned was empty or not. I think even now that he mighta someday burned a house, killed somebody."

"Where was Daddy when Tony came to see you that morning?"

"I don't know," Dick replied. "But he came over himself that morning about ten, I think. Drove in with that old black 1940 Ford he had then. I was still so mad about what Tony had told me, about his lying in front of other men and his own brother like he done the night before and then sneaking over to tell me when he had me alone with no witnesses—well, I just couldn't help myself. I told Joe all about it. I could see he believed me. He knew I wouldn't lie to him about something like that. He was pale as a ghost, just suffering over what Tony done. God help me, I couldn't be much comfort to him. I almost hated him for having such a brother. I guess it was the last straw for him. First Caroline, and now this."

"The last straw," Barbara whispered, her face numb and tingling as if from novocaine.

"Yes," Dick said. "I guess it made up his mind for him once and for all."

He was looking out over the fields now, the glittering eyes abstracted, as if he were seeing the past instead of fences and hay stubble. Barbara's control broke at last. Her head sank forward and sobs shook her entire body. Dick lifted his hand toward her without looking at her, but let it fall again.

"How did he do it?" Barbara was at last able to gasp out a question. "How did he kill him?"

Dick's gaze swung back toward her, the sunken face even more gray than usual. Some struggle was going on in the huge eyes. Even through her tears, Barbara could see him vacillating between pity for her and something else, some other emotion she couldn't identify. Finally he gave a shuddering sigh and spoke.

"I can't let you believe that. Your pa didn't kill his brother. Joe packed a bag that day and left for Milwaukee to enlist. He came over in the late afternoon to say goodbye to Rosa and me. Said he was never coming back to New Augsburg again. Said he couldn't after what Tony done. Rosa cried. Joe cried. Then he just drove off in that old Ford and we didn't see him again until 1949."

Barbara had been staring at him, her eyes wide, distrustful.

"But Tony could have been dead by then," she said at last. "Daddy could have killed him before he came over here to say goodbye."

"He could have, but he didn't," Dick said softly. "It was on the Friday that Joe went away, and Tony didn't die until Monday. So you see, your father was long gone by then."

"How—?" Barbara gasped, pulling back from him sharply, sliding herself away along the bench.

"How do I know that?" he asked and smiled a wry, bitter smile. "Same way I knew Tony was dead all along. Because I'm the one who killed him."

27

Barbara sat staring at Dick Schneider for a long time.

"You didn't," she said at last, and her voice was almost indignant. "You're just saying that."

"No, it's the truth," he sighed, and his voice sounded as tired as if he'd been awake for days. "Jim Wenner and Charlie Novak helped me plan it and they were there at the time, but I'm the one who hit him."

"Jim and Charlie?" She was dumbfounded, unable to speak except in monosyllables. Her mind was reeling, trying to make the change in direction that his words demanded, trying to realize that, once again, she had let her obsessions take her to the wrong conclusions.

"If you let me get on with this story, all your questions will be answered, okay?" he said, and he looked so tired that she feared he might not be able to finish. She nodded wordlessly.

"Jim and Charlie and me, we talked about it most of the weekend. We decided Tony had to be stopped, that it was sorta like our duty to make it stop because we knew and the law couldn't do a thing. We decided to go looking for Tony on Monday night. Charlie didn't want

to do it then because Monday was the 13th. He's got a
real strong superstitious streak, Charlie has. But it had
to be then because the women had a bridal shower that
night for Angeline Kollross, so they wouldn't know what
we was up to. Rosa didn't want to go, but I made her
go, told her it would take her mind off things.''

Now Dick's face had taken on the faraway look again,
as if Barbara had ceased to exist for him, as if he were
actually reliving the experience he was narrating.

''We met here first, after the women was gone. We
took bars from one of the stanchions. They was charred
from the fire but still sturdy enough. I guess I figured it
was fitting, made it seem like a ceremony or something,
where the things you use have to be picked out with some
thought. We walked over there from here. Tony was in
the kitchen, drinking alone at the table. I think he musta
been drinking for a long time. We didn't really talk ahead
of time about just what we was gonna do. I don't think
I knew too clearly what we intended, just that we were
agreed we had to make Tony stop. When I saw him
through the screen door looking so worn out, even miserable, there by himself in that empty house with all of
his family gone from him forever, I almost felt sorry for
him. And when he saw us, he looked so scared. He
jumped up from the table, spilled a whole bottle of whiskey.

'' 'What do you want?' he says. 'Stay away from me.
You better not. You'll be sorry.' And it come to me then
what we should do. We should make him even more
scared, really make him believe we was gonna kill him.
Then we could kinda back off, tell him to leave New
Augsburg forever, go off into the army like Joe done. If
we ever saw his face again, we would kill him, just
execute him like the criminal he was, with no warning,

364

even. So I started swinging the bar, started backing him around the kitchen, telling him he was in for it now. Charlie done the same thing, crowding him from the other side. Jim hung back, didn't say a word, but cut off the door so Tony couldn't get out. Tony was looking pretty green by this time, that good-looking face of his all puckered with worry.

"Then Charlie actually cut Tony with one swing against his legs. I don't think Charlie even meant to do it. Tony went down screaming, rolled over, and then jumped up again, really cornered now against the sideboard. But he'd become like a lunatic now, yelling at Charlie. 'You son of a bitch!' he screams. 'You'll pay for that! Did you forget so fast what it sounds like when hay and straw are burning up? It makes a noise, don't it? And all your cattle. They'll go up, too. And your horses. They'll scream just like Dick's horses done.'

"So then I knew. I realized that he'd been there all along, watching my barn burn—hiding somewhere and watching. I almost lost my mind in that minute, I think. He had his back to me, just sorta spitting at Charlie, who was so bowled over and surprised that he was backing off from Tony. I swung that stanchion bar with all my might, caught Tony right on the back of his head. It made a sound—an awful sound."

He paused now, as if listening to that sound across the years.

"He went down like a sack of feed. I didn't expect all that blood either. I remember being surprised by the blood. We all just stood there, not talking, waiting for him to move. We waited a long time without touching him. But he was dead all right. Jim threw up when I checked for a heartbeat and couldn't find one. Charlie and me talked for a while, in whispers like we was afraid

Tony might hear or something. Finally we decided on the cistern and pushed Tony's body down there. Charlie and me, I mean, because Jim wouldn't touch him. We cleaned up the kitchen so it would look like nothing happened there. Later I burned the rags we used, burned them up in the ashes of my barn. We took a oath that night, Jim and Charlie and me, never to tell any living soul about what we did—not wives, not friends, nobody. Only Charlie broke that oath, but that was later, much later. I'm getting ahead of myself."

He stopped again, breathless, as if remembering the events of that night were hard work, exhausting work.

"I still don't understand something," Barbara said at last.

"What?"

"If Daddy didn't know about Tony's murder, what did he make of his disappearance for all those years? Didn't he ever ask?"

"I didn't hear from Joe until 1947," Dick said slowly, as if he were just becoming aware again that Barbara was there. "Then it was just a note from England to tell me he was all right, still alive, and that he was gonna get married. But I could tell from some of the things he said in the letter that things was not so good in England, financially, I mean. So I wrote back, told him the farm was waiting for him and his bride if he would come back. I said that Tony had gone away, that he musta realized he'd finally gone too far and couldn't face people around here. We hadn't seen him in four years, I said, and didn't think he would ever come back. We didn't hold no grudge against him—Joe, that is—on account of his brother and would be glad to have him home again. Joe waited two more years and then wrote me again, saying things was pretty bad over there. Was Tony still gone? I wrote again along the same lines, and Joe and your ma finally came home. We none of us ever mentioned Tony to him again, and nobody ever talked about the fires—it was sorta like an understanding everybody had. Joe never said a word about it to us either.''

There was a long silence now.

''What about after Tony—after he died?'' Barbara asked. ''How did you all react?''

''Jim seemed to take it the hardest right at the beginning,'' Dick answered. ''For almost a year, he would throw up whenever anybody mentioned Tony's name. And it changed him. He got real quiet, serious, kinda brooding, like. He never went back to his old self either. Killing Tony changed his whole life, and I even believe it shortened his life. Doctors say that bad things in your mind can do bad things to your body, weaken it. Jim's people lived into their eighties, on both sides of the family, but he died at sixty-three.

''Charlie was the one that seemed strong. Just going about his business in the usual way. Threw himself into work more than before, maybe, but he seemed real calm. When your pa came home after the war, though, I could see the signs of what the killing might be doing to Charlie. He wouldn't look Joe in the eye, not ever; he stayed away from him as much as he decently could. He told me he thought Joe would be able to see it in his eyes, just look at him and know he had killed his brother. Crazy notion, but I couldn't talk him out of it. Then Billy got hurt in Vietnam, came home in that chair, and Charlie almost lost his mind. He told me it was the judgment of God on him for helping to kill Tony; it was his fault the boy would be crippled for life. There was nothing I could do with him and he couldn't talk to Gerry about it.

''Finally after a few months of that, he tried to kill

himself, ran a hose from the tailpipe of his car to the inside and started it up one night. Gerry found him in time. In the hospital, I made him see that he had to stay alive for his family. I *used* his superstition that time, told him that if God crippled Billy to punish him, then it was his job to take care of Billy, to make up to the boy for losing the use of his legs. That seemed to work. After that, he did everything for that kid. Maybe too much. Built a gym in the new house, bought him expensive cars, all kinds of stuff. But somewhere along the way, he told Billy about Tony. I just found that out when the bones were uncovered. I guess Charlie just couldn't carry it around by himself anymore.''

"So, Billy was protecting somebody, after all," Barbara said quietly.

"Yes, but he was doing it all wrong," Dick sighed. "I told him that stuff wouldn't work with you. That the best way to put a stop to the investigation would be to keep very quiet. Of course, Billy don't buy that malarky about God trading his legs for Tony's killing, but he knows Charlie believes it, and so it eats at him now, too. They're close, those two, though they don't either of them show it much to outsiders.''

"Billy's in jail," Barbara said, her eyes dry at last.

"I know," he said. "Charlie called me last night after the deputy came to take Billy away. He's beside himself with worry and guilt. Says that if Billy has to stay in jail, he'll shoot himself.''

"Billy won't have to stay in jail," Barbara said, her voice flat, as if all emotion had finally been drained out of her. "Paul's going to get him together with other veterans for therapy.''

"Good," Dick said musingly. "Probably what the boy needs.''

"And what about you, Dick," Barbara said finally. "How did you react to killing Tony?"

"How do you think?" he said, looking at her with his enormous eyes. "How many times would you say I was a guest in that house after your pa moved back home? How many times did I have to walk the floor over the place where we put him?"

"Why *did* you put him there?" Barbara interrupted. "Why didn't you just bury him someplace?"

"Lots of reasons," he shrugged. "It's dangerous to bury something on a farm if you want to hide it. Somebody might plow it up, or dig it up making a new fence someday. Then, Jim wouldn't touch the body. And we didn't have time, either. The women wouldn't stay very late at that shower, and we wanted to be home waiting for them when they got back. Didn't want them in it at all."

"Do you think they suspect now?" she asked.

"I really don't think so," he said. "Trusting is an old habit."

"Yes, I know. It takes a lot to shake our faith in people we've loved all our lives."

He looked away from her intent gaze, through the trees, out over the farm.

"You know," he said after a moment, "we told ourselves—and each other—that we done the right thing, that it was a duty, like an execution. But all along, we really did it out of anger, out of revenge, even out of jealousy. Charlie couldn't forget that Gerry had sorta settled for him when Tony wouldn't look at her."

Now he looked straight into Barbara's eyes with the fierce stare that seemed to come from deep inside himself.

"There has not been a day of my life since that night that I haven't regretted doing it, not a day when I wasn't scared. Nothing is worth that, Barbara. Nothing."

"I believe it," she whispered, tears welling up in her eyes again just when she had begun to think she had none left. "I can imagine how you felt when you heard that the house was going to be torn down."

"Charlie got almost paralyzed with fear," Dick said. "I told him they would just bury the foundation and that would be the end of it, but he was sure they would find him. And he was right, as it turns out. I called a lot of the neighbors after the bones were identified and asked them, as a personal favor to me, to keep quiet about Tony starting fires. I said that your ma and you had enough grief, with Joe's death and losing the farm, without having old rumors like that to deal with. George Heim said he didn't like the idea of protecting Tony's memory, but they would do it for me, if I really wanted them to. The Heims don't know a thing about how Tony died, by the way. I thought it might all blow over if the stories about the fires could be kept quiet."

"And then *I* started nosing around," Barbara put in.

"Yup, that's what you did," he said ruefully. "George told Charlie about you dropping in there and Charlie called me right away. I was just done talking to him on the phone when you came here that day. I hope you'll forgive me for it, Barbie, but I'm the one who suggested to Charlie that you might stop asking questions if you thought Joe might be a suspect, that you'd back off, and maybe even persuade young Gillis to go easier on the case. But I never meant for you to really *believe* Joe was guilty, and I never thought Billy would turn so mean about it. When I heard about Billy chasing you in his car, I told Charlie if that boy did one more thing to devil you, I was gonna tell the sheriff everything. He promised to put Billy on a tight rein."

"Billy, it seems, had his own reasons for being mad

at me," Barbara sighed. "But I don't think he meant to hurt me, and I don't think you did, either."

How could she tell him that all she could really feel right now was relief, immense relief? She could never make him understand how grateful she was to him for telling her the truth when he could so easily have protected himself by letting her go on thinking her own father was a murderer.

"You've got to decide now," Dick said. "Decide what you're gonna do with what you know. It don't matter much about me. I'll be gone before a trial could get started. But there's Rosa. And the Novaks. And the Wenners."

"The law is an imperfect thing," Barbara said slowly. "I've been finding that out this summer, I guess. What could the law do to you and Charlie that you haven't already done to yourselves? And Jim—well, Jim has already been before the judge, hasn't he?"

"Yes," he said, and now the glitter in his eyes was partly caused by tears. "And I'm going there pretty soon myself. Thank you, Barbie. For Rosa, I mean. The woman takes things so hard."

"I know," Barbara said, standing up. "She's probably wondering what's taking you so long."

"Would you tell her to come out here?" he said, rising slowly himself. "When you go by the house, I mean."

"Of course," Barbara said. Then just as she began to turn from him, she thought of something. "You know, Dick, Caroline wrote to Tony twice, telling him she was pregnant and asking him to come for her. I wonder if he ever got those letters."

Dick lifted his emaciated face to look at her for a moment.

"George told me something about that once," he said

at last. "About the time Carrie married Bower. He said she put letters in the mailbox without putting up the flag. He found them and burned them, but he didn't let on because he knew Peter would be so mad at her for trying. But he wasn't gonna let her get in touch with Tony, never again.''

"So," Barbara said, "Tony died without knowing that he was going to be a father."

"It wouldn't a made any difference to him," Dick said, his voice almost angry.

"Probably not," she sighed. "His course was set long before that, I guess."

"It's such a shame, too," Dick said almost dreamily. "Everybody thought so well of his folks, and of your pa. Tony was the only one who didn't seem to fit in anywhere."

He looked back at her with a supplicating expression.

"We *tried* to put up with it," he said. "We tried a long time."

"I know, Dick," she said softly. "I know."

Barbara turned away from him now, walked out of the orchard and across the yard. Just before the new barn would have hidden Dick from her view, she turned to see him still standing where she'd left him, one hand lifted to examine one of the apples he would not live to see ripen, the shirt that had once fit him hanging from his shoulders like the clothes on a scarecrow.

28

Barbara stood quietly looking down at her father's grave and the newly sodded strip next to it. It was Monday morning, a breezy, cloudy day with the faint smell of rain on the wind. Barbara had come to the cemetery out of an odd feeling that she ought to tell her father something, that she owed him an explanation of some sort, but now she just stood here with a series of impressions passing seemingly at random through her mind.

When she'd returned to her mother's apartment on Saturday morning, she had simply taken Eileen's shoulders in her hands and said to her, "Dick Schneider killed Tony, Mum, because Tony burned his barn and killed his livestock. Dick won't live until the end of the summer, the way it looks, so there doesn't seem to be much point in telling Paul, or anyone else, about it. We can spare Rosa that pain, I think, with a clear conscience."

She saw Eileen's face register, not shock or horror, but relief, and in that moment Barbara knew that, at least for a while, she and her mother had shared the same fear, the same suspicion. The two women looked at each other for a long time, each realizing what the other knew, but neither saying a word. With their eyes alone, almost identical eyes, they made a silent pact never to speak of it at all.

"I'll give you details later," Barbara sighed. She'd already decided that Eileen shouldn't have to know about the involvement of Jim Wenner and Charlie Novak, shouldn't be burdened with that moral choice, so she would have to give some thought to how she must edit Dick's account. "But I'm so exhausted right now that I'm just going to fall into bed."

And she had done that, sleeping soundly for twelve hours, so soundly that she didn't hear the phone when Paul called. Eileen had reported her asleep and suggested that she would call him back. But she still hadn't called him, had spent most of Sunday thinking—not just about Dick's story, but about her own life, about those aspects of her life that the shocks of the past few weeks had suddenly put into a new perspective for her.

She understood now why there had been so many blanks in her father's life, why he'd responded as he had to certain things in his relationship with her. Joe Hoffman had lived all his adult life with the knowledge that his only brother was not just a drunk and a womanizer, but a criminal. That brother had gone beyond personal betrayal; he had become a dangerous lunatic who seemed to have no restraints on his hostility and aggression. So Joe Hoffman had made himself into Tony's opposite, had become the man who never lost his temper, the man who never took a drink, the man who never let his feelings to the surface—not even his best feelings.

When he saw in his daughter any reminder of Tony— her adolescent rebellion or her wild fantasizing—it must have frightened him badly. So he'd unwittingly used her devotion to him to pressure her into conformity, un-

374

knowingly taught her to bottle up her own feelings, to deny them, even to run away from them, as he had run from his terrible knowledge about Tony.

Was it any wonder that she'd begun in childhood to prefer fantasy, where dashing and adventurous people openly lived their feelings and always included her in their emotional lives—included her without expecting her to respond in kind? The trouble with living in a fantasy world, of course, was that it didn't prepare her very well to deal with the harsher realities of the real world.

Most of her life, she now saw, she'd projected onto the world her own versions of reality. Excessive romanticism had given way to cynicism in the face of her child's death and her husband's infidelity. But the cynicism was just as excessive and just as unrealistic. When she got an idea, she always pursued it blindly, ignoring whatever didn't fit her theory. And so her conclusions were hopelessly wrong. Recent weeks had shown her some glaring examples of her own bumbling, but none so appalling as the *idée fixe* that her father had killed his own brother. So now she had come here with this need to begin atoning for at least some of her mistakes.

Behind her, she heard footsteps in the closely cropped grass and turned to see Paul Gillis walking slowly toward her.

"Your mother told me I could find you here," he said as he got closer. "I decided to come around when you didn't call."

"I'm sorry about that," she said, smiling guiltily up at him. "I had a lot of thinking to do."

"Some of it about me?" he asked, his eyes crinkling a little with worry.

"Yes," she said simply. "Some of it."

"And some of it about the murder case," he said, and

it wasn't a question. "I called your mother's apartment twice on Saturday. Once about noon and then once about four. When I called at noon, she told me you were out at Dick Schneider's farm."

"I know," she said. "Mum told me."

Now she looked up in silence at his kind face, weighing what she should say to him next.

"Do you remember," she began slowly, "that you once promised me you would stick with my uncle's case until you were satisfied that there was nothing useful left to learn about it?"

"Yes, I do," he said.

"And can you accept it if I tell you that there *is* nothing useful left for you to learn?" She knew that her face was more pleading than her words.

"You know that for sure?" he asked, dropping his head to look at her even more intently.

"I know that for sure," she said and found that the tears had come back into her eyes.

Paul looked at her for a long moment, and she could see him contemplating the possibilities.

"No good," he said, walking away from her a few paces. "First-degree murder is first-degree murder, even if it happened before the Flood. If there's anything *at all* left to learn, I've got to keep on."

"Paul," she said, "what if I assured you that the law can't exact the penalty, even if the murder is solved?"

He looked back at her with a penetrating stare. Then his gaze dropped to the headstone behind her.

"If I could believe that the perpetrator is really beyond the law," he said carefully. "If the perpetrator were dead, for instance. . . ." He left the sentence unfinished.

Barbara understood at once what he was implying. If she could let him believe that her visit to Dick Schneider

376

had *confirmed* her worst fears, fears Paul knew about, then he would drop it, would spare her and Eileen the pain of further investigation. It wasn't hard for Barbara to make a decision. Now that she knew her father was innocent, she could sacrifice this one little corner of his earthly reputation.

"That's what you can believe," she said earnestly. And, after all, she thought, it wasn't really a lie—not completely. Jim Wenner was buried there across the narrow road. She blinked away fresh tears.

Paul looked hard at her and then walked back to stand beside her.

"Okay," he said. "I guess I'll put it into my 'unsolved' file drawer."

"You are a good man," she said, wiping her palms under her eyes.

"Shhh," he said, and then he blushed and looked away.

"I'm going back to Chicago tomorrow," she said after a moment.

His head snapped back, his forehead furrowed in a deep frown.

"Why?" he asked. "Can't you stay at least through the 4th?"

"I have a lot of unfinished business back there, Paul," she said, eager to make him understand. "For one thing, I don't think I've ever really faced my baby's death. I just ran away from it. And I see now that I've spent a lot of my life being wrong about people, making bad mistakes because I expected too much from them, or expected the wrong things, pushing them away when they didn't turn out exactly the way I wanted them to be. I've got a lot of growing up to do."

"And you can't do it here?" he asked, his eyes looking

hurt. "I could help. I'm so damned mature, I'm practically old."

"I know you are." She laughed in spite of herself. "But one of the people I was most unfair to is my ex-husband, Tom. I ran away from him, too, when he needed me, and then I dropped him because he wouldn't just keep on running after me. The prince had to keep right on being charming, every minute, or I would have none of him. If he turned out to be just a human being, I would treat him as if he'd turned into a toad right before my eyes."

"Are you trying to tell me that you're going back to him?" he said, his eyes filled with pain.

"No, that's not what I mean," Barbara said, wanting to touch him, but holding back, struggling for clarity in her own feelings. "I don't think I can ever regain completely the trust I lost there. But I know I have to resolve things with him in some way, make my peace with him before I can go on with my life. At least I've got to find a way to stop being so mad at him."

"What about me?" he asked. "Was the other night another one of your mistakes?"

"No, of course it wasn't a mistake," Barbara said, putting her hand onto his arm at last. "The other night was wonderful. You're the first man I've let myself really care about since my divorce, and I'm not a bit sorry it happened. But some of the reasons I went to bed with you were the wrong reasons. I needed reassurance; I wanted to forget the things that were scaring me; there were things I didn't want you to ask me. You're too nice a man for me to just use you. I've got to get my life straightened out before I can have a healthy relationship with anyone."

Paul was looking up at the clouds now, his lips pursed and his eyes moist.

"Okay," he said finally. "I can see what you mean. You have to get the past straightened out so it doesn't hang around your neck like a stone. The future doesn't seem so inviting if you're looking at it from that stooped-over position. I know. I spent a few years looking at the future that way myself. But could you give me a hint or two about what sort of healthy relationship you're looking for once your life is straightened out?"

"That's an easy one," she said, smiling up at him. "I'll probably be looking for a man who collects abstract art and doesn't believe in casual sex."

"And you won't forget that Oshawanee County has a wonderful historical society? Maybe they can use you when you finish that degree."

Barbara took two steps forward and put her arms around his waist and her face against his clean uniform.

"I've got a good memory," she whispered.

He hugged her so hard that her ribs hurt, and then he walked away without another word. She watched him all the way to the squad car, but he didn't turn around. Only when he'd driven away did she turn back to the headstone behind her.

"Oh, Daddy," she said out loud. "How could I have been such a dope? I don't know how I could have misjudged even you. You had such a rotten beginning, there before the war—stuff bad enough to wreck a life—but you overcame most of it and you never deliberately hurt anyone. Your life, the way you lived it, more than made up the balance for Tony's. If the universe has such scales, I don't know. But if it does, your side wins."

The breeze had picked up, the sky was darker, and the

smell of rain was clearer now, coming from the south-west. Barbara turned away and began to walk toward her car. Behind her, the wind swept under the hedge, blowing first over the brown-edged squares of sod and then over the older grass of the grave next to them. The coming rain would begin to blur the line between the two sites. By the time Dick Schneider came to rest in this field, there would be one seamless sweep of green over the Hoffman brothers' bones.

PINNACLE'S FINEST IN SUSPENSE
AND ESPIONAGE

OPIUM   (17-077, $4.50)
by Tony Cohan

Opium! The most alluring and dangerous substance known to man. The ultimate addiction, ensnaring all in its lethal web. A nerve-shattering odyssey into the perilous heart of the international narcotics trade, racing from the beaches of Miami to the treacherous twisting alleyways of the Casbah, from the slums of Paris to the teeming Hong Kong streets to the war-torn jungles of Vietnam.

LAST JUDGMENT   (17-114, $4.50)
by Richard Hugo

Seeking vengeance for the senseless murders of his brother, sister-in-law, and their three children, former S.A.S. agent James Ross plunges into the perilous world of fanatical terrorism to prevent a centuries-old vision of the Apocalypse from becoming reality, as the approaching New Year threatens to usher in mankind's dreaded Last Judgment.

THE JASMINE SLOOP   (17-113, $3.95)
by Frank J. Kenmore

A man of rare and lethal talents, Colin Smallpiece has crammed ten lifetimes into his twenty-seven years. Now, drawn from his peaceful academic life into a perilous web of intrigue and assassination, the ex-intelligence operative has set off to locate a U.S. senator who has vanished mysteriously from the face of the Earth.

Available wherever paperbacks are sold, or order direct from the Publisher. Send cover price plus 50¢ per copy for mailing and handling to Pinnacle Books, Dept. 17-386, 475 Park Avenue South, New York, N.Y. 10016. Residents of New York, New Jersey and Pennsylvania must include sales tax. DO NOT SEND CASH.